FIRES OF RAPIVESHTA

BOOK THREE: A FAMILIAR'S TALE

Verna McKinnon

WolfSinger Publications ❦ Brackettville, Texas

Dedication

This book is dedicated to my husband,
Rick Hipps, for his love and support.
And for the chocolate and coffee he supplied
while I was writing my epics.

CHAPTER 1

The seven dragon clans slept deep underground on Rapiveshta Island. A natural cathedral hewn from stone and nature, the mountain's vast and seemingly endless caverns snaked underground into the mysterious and private haven of the dragons. Clusters of light crystals sparkled alongside the stone walls. Great chambers deep within these catacombs housed the sleeping dragons. Blue mist dragons curled together, their breath bringing heavenly dreams…or frightful nightmares. Sleek green earth dragons slumbered in a chamber abundant with tall rich grasses. Silver ice dragons rested in an alcove frosted with ice, their chilly breath blending with the hot breath of the red fire dragons in the adjacent chamber, creating a pale mist that drifted through the tunnels. Small black shadow dragons coiled in their deep tunnels, content. Sun dragons, their golden skin bright in the shadows, slept deeply. Pale moon dragons huddled near the Drajina's private lair, luminous in their rest.

Sandhya was the Drajina of the seven dragon clans. A moon dragon with iridescent white skin; her forehead bore the mark of the ruler of the seven clans—the silvery star brand. She stirred and opened her eyes, the natural sleep of her hibernation cycle suddenly broken. Her mate, Akash, a crimson fire dragon with skin that sparkled like stardust, slept nearby. The comfort of her mate's presence did not soothe her concerns. She closed her eyes taking a deep breath, but a strange darkness intruded on her peaceful return to slumber.

Perhaps it was her concern for the rookery. Sandhya had been Drajina for nearly a thousand years. Even dragons feel the discomfort of age; and she was old, the longest reigning Drajina in the dragon's history. A seer dragon, Sandhya knew her death would come soon. Before the Eternals summoned her to the Other World, she must be sure the next Drajina would hatch with this breeding cycle else her clans would be without a ruler to guide them.

Even with this time of the long sleep, each clan assigned protectors to the rookery for a given time to share the duties of protecting it during the hibernation. During this moon time, the shadow dragons took their duty as guardians of the rookery. Dragon eggs from each of the clans lay in the rookery, which contained thirty-two eggs, the fruits of the next generation. Large goose-sized eggs, gleaming like pearls, their beauty scored with vibrant colors: blue, scarlet, gold, silver, ebony, and more. They would hatch soon. Sandhya sensed that. The eggs, protected by ancient enchantments cast by each dragon clan, glowed with the aura of magic.

Talon and Fallon watched over the eggs and would often tussle together to break the boredom. Sandhya was often amused by their playful antics, as her lair was across from the precious nursery. Fallon and Talon were unique even among the dragons, for these rookery brothers hatched from the same egg. The smallest of the dragon clans, shadow dragons were only five feet in length, but clever with their tunnel digging, their luminous skin black as deepest night.

Sandhya's amusement disintegrated into a nightmare as visions of Obsydia emerged in her mind, free of her prison of Light. She imagined the crystal shattering and Obsydia taking refuge in her black tower, which no mortal had ever found. Shaken, it brought back memories of Sandhya as a young hatchling when she witnessed the Bloodstone Wars that threatened all creatures, both mortal and magic. The dragons almost became extinct when Obsydia unleashed a mystical plague during the conflict of Light and Dark. Obsydia's ruthless desire to eradicate magic from the world was a terrible time. For a thousand years she had been Light's captive, so why this terrible vision now?

If Obsydia escaped, she knew it would mean chaos. Dark gods do not forgive or forget, even ones that are half mortal like Obsydia. She glanced across the chamber to the rookery again. The dragon eggs shimmered, protected by their lithe shadow dragons guardians. All looked so peaceful until a subtle but disturbing touch, fleeting and elusive, chilled her to the bone. Anxious, she raised her head and glimpsed a strand of intangible darkness in the corner of her eye. An image of a demon man cloaked with sheer mystical fabric illuminated with strange runic symbols formed in her mind. Then it vanished. She had seen this evil before as a young hatchling. She then remembered how she was saved from the threat of these demon men by the boy sorcerer, Cathal.

Talon and Fallon also sensed something was wrong and growled. Then the enchantments on the eggs rang, confirming the danger.

Talon slithered along the ground near the eggs, swishing his tail, angry. Fallon climbed up a pillar and cried out an alarm.

Sandhya frantically nosed Akash's head. "Wake up! There is danger."

Akash woke instantly, uncoiling from his rest. "What is it?"

Sandhya raised her head, searching for the wisp of darkness and the intruder. How could it be a man? It was odd, because she did not smell human. Humans do not live on Rapiveshta, and few are ever invited. But demon men lose their natural scent, she remembered. The harsh sensation of evil and her concern for the rookery prompted action.

"We're not alone. There's an intruder in the rookery! I saw a shadow, in the shape of a man. A man in a cloak enchanted with runic symbols—*the dark kind*. It looked like an Obsydian warrior."

Akash shouted the warning cry, his roar echoing through the tunnels. Soon the sound of dragons rumbled through the tunnels. "There have been no Obsydian warriors in a thousand years, so how could it be? Are you sure? Perhaps you had a bad dream. Even seers have those."

Sandhya shuddered, the aura of evil now palpable. She snapped her head over to where the eggs rested and saw footprints in the dirt—man-shaped footprints walking away from the rookery and a wisp of unnatural shade. "Look there on the ground!"

Fallon snarled and somehow managed to catch an edge of a fragment of darkness in his teeth and clamped down. A faint dark mist sparked and Talon's nimble claws seized the spectral magic like a trail of black light and ripped a rune cloak from the invader. The cloak's concealing magic vanished like shadows in sunlight. The stranger materialized.

Sandhya surveyed the enemy. It was a human, or at least it had been human, for the face had lost its soul to darkness. Red eyes stared at her coolly. The last time she saw such an abomination was a thousand years ago during the Bloodstone Wars.

"Kill it," Akash shouted.

"No wait," Sandhya cried. "We must learn why this evil is here, and why it even exists after so long a time. It's a threat to us all. We have seen this mark before, Akash. You too lived during the Bloodstone time. Many of our clans now have no such memory to warn them of its dangers."

Talon and Fallon surrounded the stranger, growling and clawing at the ground.

"It does smells of demon, Drajina," Fallon said. "But not like trolls. It was near our young. He must have wanted to hurt our eggs, or even steal one. Let us kill it for you."

"Not yet, but soon, my little guardians," Sandhya promised.

Akash sniffed the air. "You were right. He is demon touched."

Sandhya leaned closer to the spy. "Yes, I smell bloodstone magic. Why have you trespassed? Who are you? Speak carefully, thief. The manner of your death depends on it."

The prisoner was void of emotion and looked directly at Sandhya. "Obsydia commanded I come here."

"She is a prisoner of Light," the Drajina countered, though she knew this was no longer true.

"Foul light no longer imprisons our dark queen. Obsydia is free. Darkness shall rise. Light will be destroyed."

Her terrible vision confirmed as truth, she turned to Akash. "Send someone to check the crystal chamber. If Obsydia is indeed free as I saw in my vision, Cathal would have tried to leave us a message. He knows our times of hibernation." She turned back to the warrior. "Why did you come? One lone assassin is not enough to kill seven clans of dragons. You planned to harm our eggs."

"Obsydia longs for a dragon to control. The next Drajina is within your rookery. To turn a dragon evil would be a great victory. I was ordered take it and then destroy what remained of the rookery too, but alas I have failed. My rune cloak was conjured to conceal me, but dragon magic is different, I think. I was told your hibernation was deep, and did not suspect you could sense me. I would have killed you too, Sandhya, if I could have done so and escaped. Obsydia would enjoy a cloak made from dragon skin."

"I have been a fool," Akash moaned. "This monster came too close to harming our rookery, and you, my mate. Forgive me."

"No Akash," Sandhya said. "We have lived alone and in peace for centuries. The solitude of this island has been our sanctuary. We have all grown lax with the bounty of peace. The diabolism of Obsydia is not easy to detect. Many have been deceived by her tricks in the past. Now we will kill this villain, though it is strange he speaks so freely of his plans."

"Perhaps the wicked welcome death," Fallon remarked, keeping his gaze on the prisoner. "Let us give it to him."

The Obsydian warrior pulled off his glove, revealing a ring of obsidian stone set in ebonite. He kissed the ring. "Forgive me, Queen Obsydia. I have failed."

A deep feminine voice echoed through the chamber, full of dark beauty and frightening promise. "I forgive you."

The ring on his finger flared black and fiery, swiftly spreading through the warrior's body, consuming the demon with a flame burning hotter than a fire dragon's. Fallon and Talon leapt to the stone pillars to evade the burst of flame. A brief wail of agony would have earned pity, if the demon man had not been Obsydia's assassin. When the burning ceased, only a brief flash of his skeleton shimmered before it crumbled into a pile of smoking black ashes.

"What the hell was that?" one of the shadow dragons cried.

Sandhya circled the smoldering ashes. "That was Obsydia's forgiveness."

The dragon clans were awake now and would not return to hibernation, not as long as Obsydia was free to walk the world.

One of the earth dragons entered the chamber and bowed his head. "Drajina, we checked the crystal chamber and Cathal did leave us a message that Obsydia has escaped. He could not come to us now, as his family is in peril."

Sandhya proclaimed, "This is only the beginning. We must protect our children." She closed her eyes, for her visions now opened to her to reveal the path she must take. She knew her egg with the white and red shell was the future of her race. She knew the next ruler of her clans was in peril. "Rapiveshta Island is no longer safe. The Obsidian War is coming. The Topaz Age is gone. All nations will war in this conflict of Light and Dark."

Akash flicked his tail. "Let the humans war, as they do that often enough."

"This is different, for the fate of the world is at stake, Akash. If it were only humans, we would never interfere. There can be only one victor in this war—Light or Dark. If Darkness wins, the world will be doomed to shadow and chaos, magic will go extinct, and everyone will die."

"What must we do?" Akash asked.

"Each clan must act now to protect the next generation. We will scatter the eggs and hide them around the world. It is not safe for them to be in one place. The demon tried to take our egg, Akash, and Obsydia will not stop until she succeeds. We were her first target in the Bloodstone Wars. Now she is free to wreak havoc. There will be no rest for us now."

"We must protect our egg," Akash affirmed. "Our offspring is precious, be she the next ruler or not."

"We must find Cathal. He saved our race once. His sorcery provided an antidote to Obsydia's poison. Now I will ask him to safeguard the future of the dragons again."

CHAPTER 2

Mellypip patiently sat next to Runa, turning the pages as she read and making sure she drank her tea. "You should get some sleep. You've been watching over Rualla almost every night."

"I'm fine, Melly." Runa curled up in an overstuffed chair next to Rualla's bed, holding her mother's hand and balancing a book on her knees.

A tall vase filled with sunflowers sat by Rualla's bedside. Liat brought her sunflowers because they were her favorite. He wished Rualla could enjoy their bright colors, but she still remained in her strange sleep. It was near morning and the hearth embers burned low, casting a soft glow in the room. Runa's staff rested against the wall. Mellypip was ever watchful of her staff which sometimes glowed in a mysterious fashion.

"Does the new magic book say anything helpful?" Mellypip asked.

Runa closed the book and rubbed her eyes. "No. Nothing new so far, though I can't focus much right now."

"You've been scouring over every book or scroll you could find in the sorcery chamber. I think you should give your eyes a rest. They're all red and puffy. You know what Opaline says about puffy eyes."

"It tarnishes a girl's youthful glow? I know. Damn it Melly, Grandmother woke up. She seems even fully recovered, so why doesn't my mother come out of this? It's been nearly four weeks since she was rescued from the tree of bones. Raghnall is stumped too."

"You need sleep," Mellypip suggested, stirring her tea and dropping an extra sugar cube in the cup. "If you don't, you'll end up with even puffier eyes. You'll be cranky and we have enough cranky in this house already. He's called Belwyn."

Runa managed a thin smile and scratched his ears. "You better hope Belwyn doesn't hear you."

"I'm a cautious wampu. I tread carefully when crabby owls are present."

"I just wish I could find a way to help my mother. The tree of bones curse Koll cast on her and my poor grandmother trapped them for years. Now the spell has finally been broken and they are free. Why does my mother remain in a deep sleep which no sorcery can break. Why does she still suffer?"

Mellypip was perplexed and just as lost. He did not want to upset Runa, yet when she was like this it was best to just engage. "Dark curses are strange and wicked things. Cathal and Raghnall both warned there could be odd side effects. Drink your tea. I think you need to warm it up. It's cold."

Runa casually waved her hand over the cup and it steamed with fresh heat. She picked up and cup and sipped, opening her book again.

The flash of lightning and a heavy crack of thunder unnerved Mellypip. The darn weather had grown cold and wet since Obsydia escaped. It was still summer, and he was miffed to be denied precious sunshine. All it did lately was rain, rain, rain. He looked out the window at the dawn, which was grim and grey as stone. No sunshine today either.

"Why aren't you two in bed?" Belwyn's unexpected voice disturbed Mellypip. He looked around to find Belwyn perched on the bedpost, staring at them.

Mellypip flicked his tail. "I know owls are stealthy, but you should really announce yourself when you fly into a room. Maybe you could hum or wear a bell?"

"I'm not a cow. As your teacher I prefer to keep you on your paw tips," Belwyn replied. "At any rate, we owls are known for our surreptitiousness."

Exasperated, Mellypip's fuzzy brow wrinkled in confusion. "What does that even mean?"

"It's a long word for *crafty*," Belwyn replied dryly.

Mellypip's nose twitched and he carefully walked across the end of the bed. "How do you know Runa didn't just get up early?"

"Because I'm Belwyn. I've helped raise several sorcerers and their familiars. I checked your room a few hours ago, and Runa's bed has not been slept in. Opaline was sleeping and snoring like a congested harpy, with Grimm curled up on the floor next to her bed on a rose patterned quilt. How does he tolerate the noise?"

Mellypip shrugged, scratching his belly. "Poor Grimm's been so alone all of his life, he doesn't mind her snoring so much."

"I'm watching over Mother," Runa replied smoothly.

"You should rest. Cathal would not let you stay up all night if he were here," Belwyn pointed out.

"Grandpa and Neelam are away in Ironia on secret business."

Belwyn's golden eyes looked at Runa sharply. "When Cathal's not here, I'm in charge, Missy."

"I'm not five, Belwyn. You don't intimidate me anymore. I can't take any chances. There's too much darkness lurking about. Obsydia is free, along with Koll and his damned snake. Doesn't evil ever die?"

Mellypip shivered. "No one has seen them since they went through the mirror in Skarros."

Belwyn walked along the bedpost. "I'd like to think they are in a hellish underworld, but I think Obsydia and her minions are building up their strength in her dark tower in the sea."

"Have you ever seen it?" Mellypip asked.

Belwyn shook his head. "No, and I don't want to. I've read Obsydia's *Gospels of Shadows* when we first fought her a thousand years ago. Her black tower is from Ahridum's own hand, surrounded by storm clouds in the middle of a violent ocean. It is not a place for mortals."

"Has there been any word about Darcus?" Runa asked.

"No, but I don't expect to hear anything anytime soon. Darcus went to the Ivory Kingdoms to find his sister. It's a dangerous place now since Levandius has openly declared himself a follower of Obsydia. Now, enough talk about wicked immortals. Go to bed. Where is Raghnall anyway?"

"He had an idea about a cure. All night he's been cooped up in his makeshift mystical laboratory, but at least he recruited poor Liat to assist him. It helps keep him distracted. I did not want to wake Grandmother. She may be recovered, but she is not well enough. Caliste is exhausted. I don't think she's slept much either. She was my mother's foster sister and they were very close. I know everyone is working so hard to find a way to cure my mother, but I want to help too. She's my mother and I don't even know her. I can't sleep, so I might as well be productive."

"We will find a solution," Belwyn assured her. "But wearing yourself down won't help."

"Why can't magic fix this?" Mellypip asked Belwyn pointedly.

"Do you mean Rualla's mystical coma, Jadon running off like a petulant child, or Obsydia running amuck?"

Runa's angry flinch alarmed Mellypip.

"I don't want to talk about him," Runa snapped.

"Now you've done it!" Mellypip said with a moan. "You had to bring up the *J* word."

Belwyn cocked his head. "Why? What did I say?"

Runa fumed, angrily flipping through the pages of the book. "I do hope Jadon lives long enough to come back so I can kill him."

Mellypip burrowed his face in his paws and moaned. Whenever the subject of Jadon came up, Runa flew into a tizzy fit. She refused to discuss Jadon even though she wore the beautiful wooden ring he carved. Runa doted on Darkleaf, who remained with them because he would not go home without Jadon. Rono helped keep Darkleaf company while they looked for Jadon. The sweet gryphon was happy to distract the peryton from his grief.

Belwyn winged over to Runa and settled next to her. "Remember what your grandfather said about keeping your hope alive? Magic will find a way. Jadon will be fine."

"We'd have to find Jadon first," Runa grumbled. "He's alone out there. He's been missing for weeks. I have no idea if he's alive or dead. And people won't be too friendly with someone who looks like a demon from Ahridum's Underworld."

"Jadon may be suffering from the cursed effects of Chimera's damned demon bite, but he's also a ranger. The boy can look after himself until he comes to his senses. Iona confirmed he still has his soul and is just changed on the outside."

"At least Grandpa killed the demon," Runa said. "I hope Chimera is roasting in hell."

Mellypip pondered this, confused. "Is hell a good or bad thing for a demon?"

Runa flipped the pages of the book. "Why did Jadon run away? He's making all of us suffer. How could he do this to me? To his father? Ryen is worried sick about his son and has been hunting for him for weeks. Dealing with a depressed peryton is not easy Ryen insisted Darkleaf remain here with us in case Jadon returns. Poor Darkleaf. He's so distraught. He won't eat or sleep."

"Sounds familiar," Mellypip remarked pointedly and urgently nudged Runa's teacup toward her. "Please calm down and drink your tea. Jadon will come back when he realizes he's been an idiot. Everything will be fine."

"Do boys ever think clearly?" Runa asked sharply.

"Never in my thousand years of life experience have they ever." Belwyn confirmed. "Now rest. Stay here if you must, but get some sleep."

"How can I possibly sleep?" Runa asked.

"Close your eyes," Belwyn suggested. "It works wonders."

Opaline's tired voice interrupted them. "I'm glad to see you're all so wide awake."

Opaline stood sleepy-eyed in her pink robe, Grimm at her side. "I'm going to start breakfast. Runa, the dark circles under your eyes are big as moons." She looked at Mellypip. "After breakfast, make sure Runa gets some sleep."

Mellypip nodded eagerly. "Yes, Opaline."

Runa slammed her book closed. "How can I rest? We have curses and dark immortals to contend with. Normal life ceased to exist when Obsydia escaped her crystal prison and fled through a dark mirror dragging Koll and Xabral behind her. Who knows what chaos they have caused by now! I've been reading the gospels too. Obsydia is a revulsive abomination who ruined kingdoms and slaughtered thousands. How can I sleep?"

Opaline's ominous look silenced her.

"Very well," Runa agreed quietly. "I'll try to rest, after we eat, but I can't promise anything."

"Nice work," Belwyn remarked to Opaline.

Opaline coolly glanced at Belwyn. "Indeed. Not bad for someone who snores like a congested harpy." She and Grimm turned away to go downstairs.

Mellypip sighed and straightened Rualla's quilt. "I think we made Opaline cranky. I hope Sirah makes pancakes today, with maple syrup and butter. Maybe Runa will eat more than two bites."

"She is wearing herself thin, but food does not solve problems," Belwyn warned.

"Life would be so much simpler if it did," Mellypip replied. He looked at poor Rualla and stroked her dark hair. "Especially drobba. It's a wonder food. Have we tried to wake her with drobba?" Mellypip jumped over to the window, frosted over with cold, searching for the semblance of light resembling morning. "Belwyn, do you think Darcus made it safely to the west?"

"I hope so. The west isn't safe now," Belwyn grumbled. "They've already begun to call the Ivory Kingdoms the Red Empire now. Still, Darcus is the toughest human I know." Belwyn shook his beak in despair. "He had to search for his sister, Eshra. I just hoped she and the nuns survived the scourge on the abbeys and holy houses and escaped. I liked Eshra and would not deal kindly if anything harmed her or the sisters."

Worried, Mellypip chewed on his furry tail, because he liked Abbess Eshra too and all the kind sisters who protected them when Runa was injured. Belwyn was right. Darcus was shrewd and tough. The scent of magic flooded the room again, but this was an unusual scent.

"Do you smell that?" Mellypip exclaimed. "I smell magic of some kind...piping hot magic. It's so strong!" There was always an undercurrent of mystical scent in the Sorcerer House, but it was subtle. This strong odor perked Mellypip's keen sense of smell. He bounded over to the windowsill and looked outside. "Belwyn, look! Lots of white ravens are flying toward the house."

Belwyn joined him on the windowsill. His golden eyes narrowed. "Necromancers."

"Why are there so many?" Runa asked, joining them.

"They are usually very solitary. This is strange." Belwyn flew out of the room. "Stay here. I'll gather the others. Something's afoot."

Runa kissed Rualla on the cheek and squeezed her hand. Mellypip sensed something and glanced over to where Runa's staff was propped against the wall. The image of Striker's eyes glowed on the wood. Something other than magic, something more primal and raw filled Mellypip. The panther's spirit essence had become part of Runa's staff from the willow oak bough which grew from his grave, and a pair of panther eyes had marked her staff ever since. Lately, he felt the presence of Striker keenly, especially since they found the tree of bones and rescued Yllia and Rualla.

"Striker?" Mellypip whispered. "Are you in there?" He touched the staff.

Suddenly, Mellypip was in a wintry forest. It all felt so real and frightening. In a clearing of dead grass lay Rualla in a shallow grave on a stone bed. Clothed in a white shroud and covered with dead flowers, vines and thorns. Striker stood over Rualla's grave, his crimson fur contrasting against the grim white.

"Grief and death holds Rualla captive," Striker warned. *"Save her."*

Then it all vanished. Mellypip was back in the bedroom again, shivering in front of the hearth fire. He moaned, woozy as he backed away from the staff. Runa scooped him up. "Come on, Melly. Pointessa is awake and will watch over mother for a bit. Belwyn is calling us downstairs. I wonder why the necromancers are here."

Caliste and Pointessa entered the room.

Pointessa yawned and curled up on the rug by Caliste's feet. "You go on, children. We'll look after Rualla. Liat should wake soon to relieve us."

"Thank you," Runa said. "Where's Sanura?"

"Sleeping soundly on her favorite pillow. I was reluctant to wake her. You need to get some sleep too," Caliste said. "Mellypip, I task you with making sure Runa gets some rest."

Mellypip nodded, but doubted he would succeed. "I promise to try, if my sorceress will listen to her familiar's wisdom." Mellypip clung to Runa, looking over her shoulder at the staff as she carried him out. "Sleep is hard when dreams are bad. But what I saw was not a dream. I saw a vision of mama Rualla in the forest. Striker came out of the staff and spoke to me. He told me grief is holding her captive. He wants us to help her. It scared me."

"You saw this? You didn't fall asleep and have a nightmare?" Runa whispered.

Grimm walked up to them in the hallway. "It was not a nightmare. Mellypip saw Striker's ghost. I've seen it too, many times."

CHAPTER 3

Darcus surveyed the ruins. Nothing remained of the Abbey of Araema but charred earth and ruined heaps of fire-blackened stone. Everything had been razed to the ground. Darcus recalled his last visit here, born of desperate urgency when Runa had been injured. Still, he always enjoyed coming here, even though he rarely had the time to enjoy its serene beauty. Now the main house, barn, stable, guest cottages, and the beautiful chapel—all destroyed. This once tranquil abbey of ancient and sacred stone surrounded by colorful gardens, lush trees, and pastured land had been consumed by the deliberate burning by soulless men. The stench of seared ash still clung to the cold wind, though the flames were long dead.

A sleek chestnut horse trotted up to Darcus. He absently stroked the horse's neck, frowning at the devastation.

The horse gazed at the damage and then at Darcus' stark expression. "Your sister isn't here. We have not found any bodies either. I know you're worried, but it's a good sign."

Darcus grimaced, surveying the scorched earth of the ruined abbey. "Good signs can be misleading. I've heard Levandius openly practices sacrifice now. If they were taken prisoner for the blood rituals, it's not exactly comforting."

"From what you told me, your sister is clever. Now take the damn amulet off. It's bothering me."

"It's not safe," Darcus replied firmly.

"You know I can't fly while I'm wearing it."

Darcus relented and unclasped the silver chain from the horse's neck. An amulet of silver stamped with the image of a horse sparkled even in this grim place. When Darcus removed the chain from the horse's neck, the animal shimmered into a crimson peryton. He spread his wings wide and flapped them several times, reveling in the freedom.

"Thank you!" Redstorm said with relief, happily shaking his sharp antlers, "I feel so common when I'm wearing the damn thing."

"Stop complaining. As long as no one suspects you're a peryton, we'll both live longer. And it's only an illusion, even though the magic has some quirks."

"Yes, like not letting me fly."

"Cathal made the amulet for your protection, on rather short notice. If you prefer your head mounted on Emperor Levandius' wall, let me know."

"That's pretty damn blunt."

"My words may be blunt, but the swords of our enemies are sharp," Darcus snapped back.

"You can put it back on later. Let's get back to the issue at hand. Your sister and her nuns probably fled before the enemy even arrived. You told me about the underground tunnels here." Redstorm tread the burnt ground carefully, disgusted by the sacrilege. "You're not alone in this Darcus. You're Raven Wing now—the oldest alliance of rangers sworn to fight the darkness. When we get return, we must go to your new home is Ilyrra, if only to get little Raven settled. You can arrange for folk to look after her when you're called to duty. I still need to teach you Raven Wing customs."

"I've got a lot to learn about many things. I've no idea about being a father."

"Bachelors never do," Redstorm snickered. "What about your parents?"

"I never knew them. They died during a plague outbreak when I was two. My older sister Eshra cared for me best she could. She was only nine, but begging brought little food scraps or coin to our hovel. The nuns took us in and gave us a home. We even got an education and for those who were not adopted, apprenticeships were found when we were older. My sister stayed with them and took her holy vows. I was not so holy. I had a wild streak. It drove the sisters crazy."

"You? Wild? Unimaginable," Redstorm commented dryly.

"I was apprenticed to a blacksmith. The first time I picked up a sword, it felt natural. I decided to become a solider. Eshra was always there for me. I won't leave until I have an answer to her fate."

"We'll find your sister," Redstorm said softly.

"I just hope we find her alive."

"From what you've told me, Eshra is smart."

Darcus mulled Redstorm's words for a moment. "Eshra knew this area better than anyone. They may have taken the old tunnels leading to the river. Let's go." Darcus wrapped the silver amulet around Redstorm's neck.

Redstorm's head jerked back. "Must I?"

Darcus glowered and faced his peryton eye to eye. "Do you really want to argue about this? We're in enemy territory. Perytons are not exactly indigenous here."

"We can cover more ground quickly if we fly," Redstorm said. "This country makes me jumpy and not in a good way. We can pick up their trail between my keen sense of smell and your scouting skills."

Darcus reluctantly pocketed the amulet in his vest pocket and relented. "Very well. I can't stomach the sight of this place anymore."

They flew across the charred holy ground toward the river. When they landed on the banks of the broad river, they were further dismayed by the abandoned way station nearby.

"This was a stopover for a lot of boats. It's always busy—yet everything looks abandoned," Darcus observed.

"Trade and travel are disrupted when there is a fear of death."

Darcus studied the ground and followed a trail leading them deeper into the woods. "These tracks are recent."

"There are several footprints. I smell people too," Redstorm added. "Lots of them."

"Let's just hope they're not soldiers."

Darcus and Redstorm moved deeper into the forest, following the trail until it disappeared.

"Perhaps we should move on," Redstorm suggested. "We have been going in circles for hours. I smell humans, but I can't see them. It makes my antlers itch. Let's find safe shelter before sunfall. We don't want to be caught in the open by the enemy."

"Not yet," Darcus replied.

"You're being stubborn again," Redstorm challenged.

"Something is not right here," Darcus retorted and took a step. "Look, why would the tracks suddenly vanish when–"

The ground shimmered beneath Darcus' feet. He froze, but he sensed trouble too late. A glowing yellow cord sprouted from the soil and tangled around his feet.

"Redstorm fly away!" Darcus shouted as he struggled with the shimmering rope. An invisible force hoisted Darcus several feet in the air. Darcus cursed as he swung upside down with his legs lashed with the golden magical rope, but he had the wits to keep hold of his daggers and gripped one in each hand.

"I'm not leaving you!" Redstorm shouted back, striking the ground with his hooves and lowering his antlers for battle.

More than two dozen people silently raced out from the wooded concealment and circled him with crudely made spears and arrows. They were not soldiers or assassins, but a roughly clad band in homespun rags; faces masked with dark scarves and hoods, leaving only their frightened eyes visible. He sensed they were desperate.

Darcus desperately tried to stop spinning upside down and evaluated the band quickly. He tucked his daggers into his belt. "Hold on. I'm not the enemy." He feared a particular archer was too nervous as he pointed an arrow in his direction.

One of the masked warriors stepped forward, placing a hand on the archer's shaking arm, turning the weapon away. She removed the concealing scarf. "Wait! Hold your fire. He's a friend."

"Eshra!" Darcus cried. Eshra's presence stunned him but relief his sister was not dead almost made him burst out laughing.

Eshra smiled. "Sorry brother, but you stepped into one of our traps."

"All is forgiven if you cut me down."

Redstorm could not stop laughing and even Darcus' sharp gaze did not subdue the great peryton's humor. "I'm sorry. You're so rarely caught unaware the results were startling."

"I'll release him," a familiar voice offered.

"Riva? Damn it, is that you?" Darcus shouted.

A stream of colors glimmered around his ankles and Darcus unceremoniously dropped to the hard ground.

"Sorry," Riva cried.

Darcus jumped to his feet, brushing off the twigs and dirt, cursing with such vehemence Eshra smacked the back of his head.

"Do not blaspheme," Eshra chastised.

They stared at each other for a moment then embraced.

Eshra's appearance shocked him. Since Darcus left the Abbey a few months ago, she looked like she had aged twenty years and her short, dark hair had turned almost completely grey. "Thank the gods you're alive. Since the old Emperor's death, horrible tales have been told of the Ivory Kingdoms."

"They're now calling it the Red Empire," Eshra remarked gloomily.

"I saw the Abbey ruins. How did you escape?" Darcus asked. "I feared you were dead."

"I'm sorry. We nearly met death, but Araema watched over us, as did your friends. Most of us managed to flee. A few of my sisters did not escape. If your warriors and Riva had not come, we would have all been lost."

Two warriors lowered their spears and pulled down their concealing masks.

"Hello sir," Korun nodded.

Pol grinned broadly. "We're happy to see you. Eshra thought you might come looking for her."

Darcus roughly hugged the two young men. "I'm glad to see you two boys are safe. I've been thinking about you two since things went dark here in the west."

"We couldn't serve Levandius, sir," Korun said. "He's wicked. After I saw you in the temple, Pol and I did some thinking. We saw Levandius go evil real quick when he became Emperor. He consorts with demons. He orders the death of innocents. So we left. Now we're wanted men, but I'd rather be an outlaw for the Light than help the Dark."

"As would I," Pol agreed. "Being an Imperial Dragon Knight is not so honorable these days."

"I'm proud of you boys," Darcus said solemnly.

Riva joined them, Buzzy the sloth clinging to him. "I apologize about the trap, but evil is running amuck and it needs a tether. Are you injured?"

"No more than usual from sleeping on the ground and riding all day," Darcus replied, stretching his neck and shoulders. "Cathal's been worried sick for weeks. You should let him know you're safe, Riva."

"I will. I've just been so busy these days helping the sisters," Riva grinned.

"We are fighting the darkness," Buzzy said slowly.

"Riva's traps are a great help too," Pol said. "He's been a wonder helping us with security. I never knew magic could be so useful. But still, I prefer the comfort of my sword."

"Come, we're too vulnerable in the open," Eshra said. "Let's get back to camp while it's still light."

Darcus and Redstorm followed the ragtag band deeper into the forest until they reached a massive wall of thorny green bushes. Riva passed his hand over the mass and it parted, revealing a small meadow and a huge cave.

"Clever," Darcus commented.

"Thanks," Riva grinned. "The marvelous thing is this species of thorn bush grows wild all over, especially in the deep woods." After the party passed through the opening, it sealed behind them. "It's a form of protection not detectible since they are real. I just sprouted them in abundance with a bit of magic. The wall of thorny bushes keeps us safe from enemy eyes. The cave is very deep and safe with ample room and underground springs."

Inside the enclosure, they warriors pulled off their hoods and mask. Among the group were many he recognized as nuns from Eshra's order. They too had changed as his sister had.

Form the corner of his eye he glimpsed little faces staring at him from the cave's mouth.

"It's alright, children" Eshra assured them. "They're friends. This is my brother Darcus and his companion is—" She glanced at the peryton. "I'm so sorry, but I don't know your name."

"I'm Redstorm," the peryton said with a nod.

A flock of over twenty children poured from the cave, momentarily happy with the prospect of meeting someone new and a wonderful magical creature to amaze them. Redstorm was tolerant as the children stroked his feathers with grubby fingers and asked to touch his wings and antlers. They crawled all over him like ants and he endured it with enormous patience.

"Where did you get them?" Darcus laughed, picking up one of the young boys.

"They are rescues," Eshra replied softly with a pained look. "We've rescued so many, but not enough." She turned to the Pol. "Please prepare the defenses for the night."

"Yes, Eshra," Pol replied.

The nuns gathered the children and went inside the cave. Eshra wearily sat on a log.

Sensing Darcus wanted to talk to his sister privately, the sorcerer excused himself. Eshra took the boy from Darcus' arms and handed him to Riva.

"I'll go see if I can help," Riva nodded and walked away, carrying a child with one arm and a drowsy Buzzy with the other.

Darcus steeled himself. "What kind of rescue?"

Eshra looked up at Darcus, her eyes hard. "The temples are no longer holy. Sacrifice to Obsydia is the new law. Most of these children lost their families to the sacrificial knife. They were even planning on killing the children. The Eternals and their wars of Light and Dark have spilled into our mortal world. The consequences are grisly. Men are more terrifying than gods when they claim to do their bidding. Obsydia may be immortal and the daughter of the dark god, Ahridum, but she is not forcing them to kill children. They do it freely."

Darcus knelt at his sister's feet and took her hands, marred by burn scars. "Eshra, listen, I cannot change what has happened, but I can offer you hope."

Her eyes flared at the promise of hope and she squeezed his hands. "Yes, you can. Take these children to sanctuary. We have fighting to do and they need to be safe. Take them to Thill or Ilyrra, anywhere away from this horror!"

"If you wish, of course. Of course I'll take them to safety." He looked down, frustrated and helpless with a woman who was as stubborn as he was. "A lot's happened. I've adopted a daughter. I guess you could call her a rescue too. She was intended to be sacrificed and I saved her. Her name is Raven. She's a lovely girl. Half Ilyrran and very bright. You'll adore her."

"Then you understand," Eshra whispered.

"Of course, so let's make plans and leave this place."

Eshra touched Darcus' unshaven cheek. "I cannot leave here. Someone must stay and help the children. People are dying. I must stay and fight."

Pol and Korun were walking toward them carrying firewood.

"What?" Darcus shouted. "Are you crazy? This land is a hell pit. You must leave. I fight, you pray. That's the way it has always been."

The two young warriors stopped in their tracks and turned around when they heard Darcus' fiery tone.

Eshra shook her head. "Not anymore. Everything is different now."

Darcus paced back and forth. "You cannot be serious!"

"I am quite serious," Eshra replied. "I will not let the holy word of Araema be extinguished by an evil emperor or Obsydia. I've killed people, Darcus. I killed to save children and others we've helped to safety, but I killed. I made a vow never to kill when I took the veil! I broke my vow, Brother. I will never be the same. Until the temple floors are washed clean of blood and the evil is purged from this land, my hands will be stained red too."

Darcus paced, frustrated. "You're not equipped for this. You're a small ragtag group of nuns and peasants."

"And one powerful sorcerer," Riva added, joining in.

"Pol and Korun have been very instructive," Eshra added. "You trained those boys. Who better to help us?"

The cold glance of Darcus sent Pol and Korun rushing back into the cave.

"We're already growing in number," Eshra countered. "And we're not alone in this war. We are scattered for safety, so we can do the most good and to keep the enemy guessing. We have a network of rebels spreading across the Empire. We have help from high places too."

"Who?"

"Lord Rhudon," Pol cried from the cave.

Darcus turned and patiently crooked his finger. "Come out and explain, boys."

Korun and Pol both stepped out and sheepishly approached.

Darcus nodded. "I remember Lord Rhudon. He was an advisor to the old Emperor. He was at the Abbey when you boys were promoted to Imperial Dragon Knights."

"He was kind to poor Opaline too when her father banished her," Korun said. "Rhudon was marked for assassination when Levandius took power."

"So we warned Lord Rhudon and he fled with his family," Pol added. "He's raising an army too. We're not the only rebels. We alerted Riva when he learned they were going to burn the Sorcerer House. We all escaped together, just barely."

"Fortunately, a simple invisible spell enabled us to escape through the backdoor," Riva said. "We didn't even need a silence spell or to fight. The imperial thugs just rode up to the house, shouting like maniacs, and stormed in with torches and burned the house down. I still weep when I think about the library in the sorcery chamber, not to mention the crystal tomes, relics, my journal."

"Your diary is not a shattering loss," Buzzy quipped.

"But I may not have gotten out alive if these good young men took a risk to save me. I was too involved with packing my precious scrolls to be aware of much."

"I will vouch for that," Buzzy nodded.

"We also knew Levandius ordered the burning of all the religious houses not aligned with the dark trinity," Pol said. "They started burning the temples in the city the same night. We knew Eshra's Abbey was in danger, so we came to help them. Riva joined us."

"It's true," Eshra smiled. "Their time was fortuitous. The zealots were already at our gates with torches and swords. We escaped thanks to those boys and Riva's magic. They've been with us ever since. We must fight for both body and soul now."

Darcus grimaced and raked his shaggy hair as he paced. "Look, I didn't come all this way to debate philosophy or tactics with you! I came to here to rescue you if I must drag you all the way to Thill!"

"No," Eshra smoothly answered.

"Damn it!"

Redstorm snorted. "You've lost the battle, Darcus. Just accept defeat and move on."

"How can I leave her?" Darcus choked.

Redstorm snorted and whispered. "Because you're both of the same blood and heart, and will not walk away from evil. Your heart and courage are why I was willing to accept you when they made you a ranger. Let her do this. She will never rest in comfort as long as others suffer any more than you would."

"I still don't like it," Darcus grumbled.

"I know," Redstorm sighed. "But you have an answer to her fate now. She's safe and surrounded by many devoted humans. Take comfort in this."

"I'll take comfort when my enemies are dead at my feet."

Pol suddenly pointed at the sky. "Sir, look!"

Darcus spun around, but his irritation changed to amazement when he looked up at the sky. "What the hell? Are those?"

"Dragons," Redstorm confirmed. "Those are dragons flying above us."

"There must be at least a dozen of them sir," Korun shouted. "All different colors too! I heard about dragons as a boy, but never really thought them to be real."

"They are quite real," Redstorm replied. "What troubles me is they've left Rapiveshta. They rarely leave their island."

"They're flying north," Darcus observed. "I wonder where they are headed."

"It is not where; but to whom they're flying," Redstorm replied.

"I don't understand," Eshra gasped, smiling briefly at the wondrous sight.

"Cathal will know," Redstorm answered cryptically.

CHAPTER 4

"Ghost! What do you mean ghost?" Mellypip asked Grimm, wiggling in Runa's arms.

The black wolf sat on his haunches, cocking his head. "I mean I see ghosts. In fact, I've seen Striker's ghost many times watching over Rualla. He lives in Runa's staff. I thought once my father's spirit left for the Otherworld, I wouldn't see such things anymore. Alas, I must be doomed to see spirits."

"I've seen things too," Mellypip said. "We were told a piece of his spirit enchanted her staff when she conjured it in Moonthorne. I think there's more Striker in her staff than we realized."

"You've never told me," Runa said.

"There's been a lot going on," Mellypip sighed.

Caliste picked up Runa's staff and felt along the wood.

"Do you sense anything?" Runa asked.

Caliste shook her head. "No, but it's hard to see through the other magic inside them. Striker's spirit essence could easily mingle in your staff without detection. You told me a piece of his spirit enchanted the wood, because it was from the tree where Striker was buried."

Opaline rushed past them down the stairs. "Runa, quick come see! White ravens are circling the sorcerer house! Belwyn says it's the necromancers and their familiars."

"We will talk about this later," Caliste said, kissing Runa on the cheek.

Runa followed Opaline into the front yard. "I wonder if they're here because of Panthara. I've read they prefer to keep to themselves. Let's go, Melly."

"But, but…I wanted to hear more about Striker's ghost from Grimm," Mellypip protested as Runa carried him away. Belwyn flew ahead on swift wings.

Grimm ran alongside Runa and Mellypip as they went outside to meet the visitors. "I've little else to tell. Ghosts are troublesome, but restricted by their mystical state. Like the living, they're full of opinions, though I've not spoken to Striker."

Panthara and Iona were already waiting outside. Amun was regally perched on Iona's shoulder and Azmadu huddled close to Panthara, grunting.

The white ravens swarmed in a beautiful dance on the snowy air, swirling until they dropped to the earth. Upon touching land, half the ravens shimmered into veiled, black-robed men and women, and the other half of the pale ravens alighted on the shoulders of their necromancers.

I never knew there were male necromancers, Mellypip said.

Belwyn says because there's so few necromancers most people know very little about them. They tend to keep to themselves because people are usually disturbed by their presence.

Mellypip nodded. *Iona and Amun scared me at first too.*

Belwyn also told you scary tales about necromancers when you were baby, so I blame him for that.

Opaline looked on the scene. "It's rare to see so many necromancers in one place. Do you think they've come to judge Panthara's worthiness as a necromancer?"

Runa leaned in and whispered. "They must be here for Panthara. Iona never said anything about them coming here. I wonder if Iona even knew they were coming."

"Panthara looks pretty worried," Opaline replied. "Maybe you should offer to be with her?"

"You're being unusually compassionate about Panthara," Runa remarked.

Opaline smiled softly and lifted her chin. "I'm not totally heartless. Besides, I expect a full report from you about what happens. Seeing one necromancer is eventful, as they live cloistered lives. Seeing a dozen of them at once is cause for alarm and curiosity."

Runa's grandmother, Yllia, joined them in the yard. Nearly as tall as Cathal, she towered over Runa when she put her arm around her shoulder. "Does Panthara understand what is about to happen?"

Runa looked up at Yllia. "No. Do you?"

Yllia nodded and whispered. "They will examine Panthara to determine if she is truly one of them. This is an unusual situation without precedent. Necromancers are a unique mage caste. Even their familiars, white ravens, bond only with necromancers."

Poor Azmadu is no white raven, Mellypip said through the bonding.

I wonder if they will accept them, Runa answered. *It does not change what Panthara is now. She cannot help it.*

"Necromancers touch death and spirits in ways we cannot understand," Grimm said. "It's a heavy burden, as I have dealt with these things when my father's ghost was teaching me. I resented him at the time, but I miss him. His incessant prodding guided me to my new home and Opaline, for which I'm grateful."

Mellypip's tail switched nervously. "Azmadu looks scared."

"Maybe I should offer to be with her," Runa whispered.

Yllia shook her head. "No, my dear, they would never allow an outsider to witness this."

Runa shifted Mellypip in her arms and walked toward the circle. "I'm not an outsider. I'm her sister." She took her place at Panthara's side.

Are you sure you know what you're doing? Mellypip asked.

No, but I know it is the right thing to do, Runa thought back.

But is it the smart thing? Mellypip sighed.

Iona bowed to the necromancers. "Welcome."

The necromancers bowed in unison.

Sirah joined them in the yard and greeted the visitors with a smile. "Welcome to Aybarr. You may meet in the sorcery chamber on the top floor. It will allow you privacy. If you need anything, all you need do is ask."

A necromancer looked directly at Runa. "We're here to examine Panthara and her familiar. No outsiders are permitted."

"I'm Panthara's sister," Runa replied, standing by Panthara as she took her hand. Panthara, whose expression was regal and stoic, softened for an instant when Runa took her hand.

Iona turned to the lead necromancer. "Runa speaks the truth. She is also Cathal's granddaughter. She can be trusted."

Taran rushed out of the house, a drowsy MacTabbish in his arms. "What's going on? What do they want with her?"

Sirah cautioned. "They just want to talk to Panthara. There's no need to worry."

Grimm sat close to Opaline, keeping his distance from the necromancers. The apparent lead necromancer, who was the only one speaking, looked directly at him.

"The black wolf is spirit-touched," the necromancer commented. "A rare thing, being he is not one of the chosen white ravens who bond with us." She looked down at Azmadu. "The crill lizard is not even spirit-touched."

"His name is Azmadu," Panthara added coolly.

"Please, let us speak inside," Iona offered. "We're attracting too many eyes."

Indeed, Mellypip saw many folk pause on the street and stare at the unusual gathering of black-robed necromancers and their pale ravens.

They retreated inside. Runa remained by Panthara's side as they walked up to the top floor and the sorcery chamber. Mellypip heard Taran arguing with his mother downstairs when she would not let him follow Panthara. Grimm's gloomy face watched them from the bottom of the stairs but did not follow.

What do you think is gonna happen to Panthara? Mellypip thought to Runa.

I don't know, Runa replied. *It's not like she can give this ability back to the wraiths!*

They gathered in a circle around Panthara and Azmadu. Runa remained by her side, but was afraid to speak. Mellypip perched on Runa's shoulder. Iona raised her staff and the door closed. The necromancers removed their concealing veils. Most of the necromancers were woman, but to Runa's surprise, a few were men. Now they stared at Panthara, but not with malice. Runa saw curiosity in their eyes.

The lead necromancer, an aged woman with dark eyes, stood before Panthara. "Iona tells us you now have our gift."

Panthara lifted her head, holding Azmadu close. "It is not a gift I would have chosen."

The elderly necromancer nodded and smiled. "None of us would. But some of us believe you have this gift for a reason."

"What do you mean?" Runa dared to ask.

The necromancer's smile chilled Runa. "Nothing important happens in this world unless it is meant to be, even if it means the touch of darkness. Iona was witness to what the wraith guardians did when the gate of souls was opened. Their touch is a side effect, but one ordained by the Eternals. For an outsider to be able to see and touch a soul is unheard of."

Panthara looked at the necromancer, her blue eyes clear and unafraid. "So, I am an oddity, which does not worry you. You're concerned I might use them for evil."

"It is the reason for your new gifts which concern my brothers and sisters," Iona said.

"We do not judge you or your past. We know Koll and your mother tricked you and your magic for evil purposes. Iona assures us you were a pawn in Koll's game."

Panthara nodded, though her expression was neutral. "I do not blame them, Iona. Darkness looms in the world since Obsydia walks free, enjoying the comfort of shadow now. I sense everyone's fear. I sense yours. I know the wraiths touched me in the cave. I know nothing else until I woke up. I have a necromancer's ability to see souls now. I know what kind of soul a person keeps. It frightens me too. I have not called to the Otherworld yet, but Iona will teach me when I am ready."

A male necromancer stepped forward. "No matter the reason for this, she cannot join our circle. She's an aberration. She was born a sorceress and only achieved this magic a short time ago. How is this Panthara suddenly a necromancer? Not because the Eternals gifted her at birth, but because the wraith guardians marked her for daring to trespass into the realms of the sacred Otherworld. Even her familiar is against our tradition. This small flying lizard grunting in her lap is already bonded to her. This is not our way. Perhaps this is not a gift, but a form of curse or punishment for her transgressions."

Panthara's eyes flamed with anger and her voice was imperious. "I know my sins, Necromancer. I have never denied my past. I know my Azmadu is not the traditional white raven of your caste, but he is mine and he's loyal to me. He is my familiar. You of all people should understand the sacred bond of mage and familiar. I will never part from him. Once a sorcerer bonds with a familiar, it is for life."

Runa spoke. "The evil which threatens us all targets my sister too. She rejected Koll, more than once. What happened to her must be for a reason. I don't believe she's cursed, but maybe Panthara is marked to do something your caste cannot achieve. We will not know until it happens. Not even necromancers can see the future."

"Hush, child," the aged necromancer said. "Our brother speaks with passion, but he does not mean to be cruel or accusatory."

Runa did not miss the old woman's eyes flash a warning to the man, who stepped back, bowing his head.

She continued in a gentle voice. "I don't sense any wickedness from Panthara. She may serve a purpose, one we cannot see. We will pass our judgment tomorrow. While we are here, may we speak with Cathal? With the threat of Obsydia, we want to offer our circle to help with the cause."

"He's in Ironia," Belwyn answered, perched on the fence post. "He promised to contact us tonight on the calling crystal. You are welcome as our guests and you may speak with him tonight when he calls."

Mellypip tugged on Runa's hair. *Something tells me Panthara is not going to like their judgment.*

Runa answered through the bonding, keeping a neutral smile on her face. *Panthara may not care. They can judge her only with words. It cannot change what she is now, no matter what they say.*

I wish Grandpa Cathal were here. He would know what to do.

So do I, Melly, so do I. Ironia is so far away, and danger keeps coming closer.

~ * ~

Cathal and Neelam waited in the private chamber, restless and drinking ale. The comfortable room was large and paneled in dark wood, lined with rich colorful carpets easing the chill of stone floors.

Surya perched on a chair as Neelam paced. He paused to refill his drink or look out the window.

Neelam paused and looked at Cathal. "You're awfully quiet. What's bothering you?"

"Belwyn was none too happy being left behind," Cathal said.

"I know. It's hard for a mage to be separated from their familiar. Belwyn looked downright crabby before we flew off, the way you look right now," Neelam said. "We planned this. Let me send for a bigger stool too. We're used to you weedy human folk visiting us."

"I'm fine," Cathal insisted.

"Your knees are practically up around your ears."

Cathal shrugged, shifting in the stool. "It's not a bother. I'm just tired. We flew here practically nonstop from Aybarr."

Surya preened her snowy feathers. "It's best Belwyn is there keeping an eye on things. Someone had to look after the children. Liat is a walking statue of grief. Dabiro causes nothing but mayhem. Yllia is still recovering. Poor Sirah has her hands full with Opaline and Grimm. Myrsalian is busy running the sorcerer house and dealing with King Caladynn. We couldn't leave all this is in poor Caliste's lap, especially with poor Rualla so ill."

Cathal stood up and stretched. "I don't like leaving my girls alone when dangers are everywhere."

"Especially when those dangers are named Obsydia and Koll,' Neelam nodded. "I know, Cathal."

Cathal's stark expression was not softened by the large mug of ale he downed in a single gulp. "I'm here because King Arawn is a friend."

"Runa will be fine," Neelam assured him, refilling his cup. "I know you're concerned about Rualla. It will just take more time to find a cure. Your wife is awake, thank the gods."

"I count my blessings each moment Yllia has been restored to me. I just wish we had time to be alone, but events conspire to keep us apart."

Guards opened the doors and bowed as Dwarven ruler of Ironia, King Arawn and Queen Dagmar, entered the room. Arawn was a stout white-haired man with a long braided white beard. His wife, Dagmar, was deceptively delicate looking matron with dark hair and bright eyes which missed nothing.

"It has been too long, Cathal," Dagmar said to Cathal, stretching her hands out in welcome.

Cathal bowed and kissed her hand. "Thank you, Dagmar."

Neelam bowed to the royal couple. "We are grateful for this meeting."

"No formalities, Cathal," Arawn said, waving his hand. "Thank you for coming. Sit, sit. Let's have more ale."

"Within reason," Dagmar grinned.

Arawn's expression stiffened and he glanced at Neelam. Neelam took out a smooth gold crystal bigger than his fist and placed it on the table. It burst with bright golden light, cloaking the whole chamber with a gentle luminescence.

"Is it safe now?" Arawn asked.

Neelam nodded. "Quite safe. We may all speak openly now. Neither spy nor magic can penetrate this barrier."

Queen Dagmar took Neelam's offered flagon. "We're grateful you came on such short notice, Cathal. I am so pleased Yllia is recovering. We offer prayers each day for Rualla. How is little Runa?"

"Growing up far too fast," Cathal answered. "She has her own familiar now, a wampu named Mellypip."

"Enough chatter about pleasant things," Neelam said. "Let's get down to business."

"This Obsydia is a foul business," King Arawn nodded. "When I read the bloodstone tales as a boy, I wondered if Obsydia were just an exaggeration or a myth, but sadly she is a historical fact. Her reality is quite harsh. Her mark is already upon the Ivory Kingdoms. Levandius openly worships her and practices blood sacrifices."

"Days I never thought I would see again," Neelam added.

"Levandius always had a bad character, even as a boy. Taran or Opaline would have been much more noble heirs. I understand Prince Taran is actually alive and living in Thill with his exiled sister."

Cathal nodded and put his cup down. "Yes, he is. Emperor Tarsicius had a lot of secrets no one knew about."

A palace guard entered and whispered something in Arawn's ear. The old king grinned. "Excellent! Send them in."

To Cathal's surprise, three more people entered, Hinkleburr Crowyn and Lady Helga, and a grey-haired gentleman in leather armor he recognized as Lord Rhudon of the Ivory Kingdoms.

Arawn gestured for his guests to sit around a table. "Cathal, you know these folk, including Hinkleburr Crowyn our Ambassador to Thema, and the lovely Lady Helga, daughter of our Thill Ambassador, Thorgid."

"This is a pleasant surprise." Cathal grinned, shaking Hinkleburr's hand and kissing Lady Helga's hand. "I was not expecting you here, my lady. Your father is well, I hope."

Lady Helga curtsied daintily. "My father is due to retire, thank you. King Arawn has chosen me to take his place not only as the ambassador to Thill, but as your liaison with the Chieftain."

Hinkleburr nodded. "I personally bring Queen Sarabia's bond to join our alliance of light."

Cathal smiled broadly. "Wonderful news, indeed. I bring King Caladynn's bond to join the alliance, as you know, Arawn."

"Excellent news," Arawn said. He gestured to the third visitor. "Along with myself, I bring another friend to our circle. I believe you know Lord Rhudon of the Ivory Kingdoms."

Lord Rhudon bowed stiffly. "Not anymore. They call it the Red Empire now, thanks to Levandius. We may never be able to wash away the blood and sin of what he is doing."

"You must be a rebel," Neelam commented. He poured a glass of ale and handed it to Rhudon. "That makes you doubly welcome."

"I'm a patriot," Lord Rhudon replied, accepting the drink. "One who lives outside the law and fears for his family and his people. I always disliked Levandius, but he has become a fiend not even I expected."

Neelam remarked. "Levandius is just one more to add to the list of evil rulers who deserve assassination."

"You never were one to mince words, Neelam," Arawn commented.

Neelam's grin was chilling. "Evil gets what it deserves. Rank has damn little to do with it."

"Good thing you are loyal to me," Arawn chuckled.

"Enough chit-chat," Queen Dagmar interrupted. "We must decide a line of communication and codes with our allies. We know war is coming. From which side, we don't know yet. She has Levandius in her thrall, but the dark queen will want more. Obsydia is not content to sit in her shadowy tower twiddling her wicked thumbs."

"Obsydia will attempt to recruit more noble and royal idiots to her side," Neelam said. "She did it a thousand years ago too. No matter what age we live in, there are ambitious idiots and religious fanatics who will do her bidding."

"Which is why we need to be watchful now," Cathal added.

"But what can we do against an immortal queen?" Dagmar asked. "She was imprisoned in Light for centuries, true, but it did not hold. How do you kill a god?"

Cathal set down his ale and looked at the circle of desperate faces. "You will lead the armies. Our job will find a way to kill Obsydia. This time, we will destroy Obsydia."

CHAPTER 5

Koll stepped from the pool and struggled to wrap the towel around him with his only hand. Exasperated, he generated a flash of magic which knotted the towel at his waist. The brief use of sorcery drained his reserves and he collapsed on a marble bench. Amid the ethereal spectral blossoms blooming in shadow, he thought about the last time he saw Obsydia. His memory was fragmented since Obsydia pulled him through the mirror during the battle. Xabral coiled at his side. The hooded guardians in the red glass ferry. Sailing across the violent black sea to the tower. He worried, as he had not seen her in weeks, not since they entered this dark tower.

He walked toward his private chambers, guided by the blue-flamed ebonite sconces. A wave of pain gripped him; the strange phantom throbbing of an arm no longer there, but lost forever. He leaned against the wall, breathing deeply until he could resume walking. When he reached his private chambers, the doors opened for him.

Concerned, Xabral unraveled his long body and slid off the bed onto the carpeted floor. "How is your pain today?"

Koll winced. "Tolerable."

"Liar," Xabral accused.

Koll grimaced, disgusted by his deformed body and internal debilitation. He took a robe of black silk from the bed. "You know I can endure great pain, but the source of my agony, this wretched light, does not fade."

Xabral's eyes flashed with rage. "Cathal will pay for this. All of our enemies will pay with body and soul. Cathal for what he did to you and for butchering Chimera with the Scythe of Rygon!" Xabral dropped his head with sorrow. "I miss her so much! Koll, is there an afterlife for demons? Did Chimera go back to the Dark Realm or is she utterly vanquished?"

Koll sat on the bed and patted the silk coverlet. "Come over here." Xabral eagerly slithered over and crawled up onto Koll's lap. Koll stroked his scales and spoke soothingly. "Perhaps her wicked essence dances in the shadowy ether, waiting for you to come and play with her. Now, we must be thankful for this sanctuary. We achieved our dream. Obsydia is free."

Koll forced himself to stand and glimpsed his image in the large oval mirror. The shimmering silver scar on his shoulder, remnants of Cathal's ruthless beam of sorcery, glittered like flecks of diamonds. Cathal's magic evaporated flesh and bone—like a wisp of paper consumed by a flash of flame. He turned away and pulled on a black silk robe. "I never realized just how powerful the old sorcerer truly was until that moment. I will never again take for granted Cathal's magic nor presume it to be weak."

"The day will come when we will destroy Cathal and everyone he loves. Vengeance shall be our rock."

The door opened. A hooded guardian in black robes strode into their chamber, the face concealed by a deep cowl even Koll shuddered to lift. Grave silent, it beckoned them. These strange beings did not deign to speak to mere mortals, even sorcerers, but somehow it communicated its message before turning away from them.

Koll nodded. "Obsydia summons us at last."

"See, she has not forgotten us."

Koll and Xabral followed the guardian through shadowy halls. According to the sacred *Gospels of Shadow*, Ahridum summoned the black tower from the depths of the Dark Realms to this wild sea to be Obsydia's home in the mortal world. A ring of storm clouds cloaked it with a maelstrom.

As they approached, the tall doors of ebonite opened with mystical invitation. Koll stepped inside the chamber with reverence, treading barefoot upon the smooth black marble. The ceiling a mass of swirling storm clouds hovered above. In the center of this austere chamber, Obsydia stood beneath a beam of shadow more beautiful than any light. Her exquisite face upturned as she drank in the dark nectar glistening around her. She bathed in the dark essence, her shadow hair a dusky mist down her back as the inky tendrils danced on her diaphanous red gown.

Koll knelt and touched his head to the floor. Xabral curled at his feet, head bowed.

Obsydia remained in the shadow's embrace. "Welcome to my Father's Temple."

Koll remained prostrate on the floor. "I am unworthy."

"Of course, you're unworthy, but you may look upon me, Koll."

Koll gazed up at her with reverence. "I worship you. Only you."

Her eyes darkened to silver stones. "Yes…worship. Your devotion freed my immortal self from cursed Light, which is why I permitted your solitude and the retention of *your* life. The battle and what occurred surprised me. Even I did not expect the Winged-Fey. They are solitary creatures. They do not live in the world. Even when I was imprisoned within the cursed crystal, they never appeared to fight me. They left the dirty work for mortals. I also forgot how foolishly savage Cathal could be when his loved ones were threatened." She stepped from the shadow's cascade and down the stairs, her immortal beauty devastating. "Light's imprisonment drained me, despite my immortal essence. Since my return, *His Darkness* has been restoring my strength. She circled him, as a raven circles its prey, beautiful and imperious.

Koll glanced at the mysterious beams with longing. "Perhaps a fragment of his shadow could purge the pain I suffer?"

"Beware, for Ahridum's pure blessing, his *touch*, gives only me strength. It would destroy you, for my father's power consumes mortals born of flesh and bone. Think of what Cathal's blade of magic did to your arm. Imagine a devastating power a thousand of times over." Obsydia's hand gently lifted his head. "Soon, we shall begin to claim this world for Ahridum. The final war of this world will soon rise. Chaos and blood will spread as kingdoms will be razed and rulers will fall. In the end, only my throne shall remain triumphant. So you must grow strong again. I have not forgotten my promise to you. The hooded ones are conjuring an arm of black velvet and ebonite for you. But first, there is a special celebration. Follow me." She imperiously walked away, the great doors opening wide as she passed.

Koll rose and followed her, Xabral slithering on the cool smooth floor close behind him. The altar burned with otherworldly fuel. Koll smelled the ether of the Dark Underworld.

Obsydia watched the altar with eager joy, almost childlike in her delight. "A new era arises, Koll. Ahridum wants this world and I will give it to him. He rejoices in my liberty from Light and is sending me gifts to celebrate."

Voices echoed like a thousand sacrifices crying out their anguish in unison, yet they saw no one but the Hooded Guardians enter the room, their mystery was closed around them like their heavy robes which concealed them. Rapt with the mystery of shadows, Koll and Xabral watched the hooded guardians circled the altar as the summoning began. They spoke the true demon language of the Dark Realms, words no human mouth could form. Goblets of blood were poured on the altar. The red life force smoked upon touching the stone.

From scarlet smoke's thriven mist stepped a creature woman shaped—but unmistakably born of the Dark Abyss. Obscured in a voluminous black cloak, she stepped from the altar and marched toward Obsydia with bold strides. Her dusky garments billowed and revealed glimpses of a feral demonic face. Eyes fathomed like black stars gleamed from the folds of her deep cowl. She reached Obsydia and pushed back the hood to expose a gaunt cadaverous face framed by tight narrow braids of blood-red hair twisted into a bone clasp. She flung off her cloak, revealing a tall skeletal frame and grey pallid skin. Her image was corpselike. Clothed in layers of ragged grey gauze and girdled with narrow strips of red leather stamped with intricate runic symbols of the native Abyss.

She dropped to her knees and embraced the pale hand of Obsydia and kissed it. "Your father Ahridum, Eternal of Darkness and Chaos, sends me to serve you, Queen Obsydia."

Obsydia inclined her head in recognition. "I gladly accept my father's gift. What are you called in this world?"

Proud, she rose to her feet. "I am Shroud. Ahridum chose me to be your Chief Handmaiden of the Claw."

"Claw?" Xabral inquired curiously.

She glanced down at Koll and Xabral with narrowed eyes and sniffed, as though offended. "Who is this mortal slave and strange animal? Why does the human reek of Light?

Obsydia raised an eyebrow. "This is Koll the Sorcerer, my new high priest. The charming snake is Xabral, his familiar."

Shroud's expression was inimical. "He's a mage! Magic is our enemy. Its wellspring is filthy Light. His eyes are not even red. Why haven't you turned him demon?"

Obsydia's cold glance stilled Shroud's tongue. "Koll is special. He does not need my blood kiss to make him my demon slave, though I have made a few since my return. They were sent to steal the dragon eggs for my pleasure. They failed. Koll released me from my crystal prison. He did not fail."

Shroud's hostile eyes scrutinizing them, but her tone softened. "Forgive me, My Queen, but how can you trust this mortal if he is not bound by your blood kiss?"

Koll regarded Shroud without fear. "I know the ancient practice you speak of. It is legend. Obsydia's binding her chosen with her blood kiss. A drop of her blood on her lips, and her kiss transforms even her most virulent enemy into a half-demon, soulless and devoted to her. Her first warrior priest, Solem, was such a man, though he began as her enemy. I am beyond mortal man. I am beyond mage. I am Koll the Sorcerer. My soul is black. My heart is black. I was chosen by Darkness to serve Obsydia."

Shroud hovered over Koll, her noble malevolence startling. Her demonic black eyes examined his mortal ones. She wrinkled her nose and shrugged, "Ah, I see his soul now…black as pitch and hard as stone. The light is not his, but from his scars where his arm once was. It makes him *stink*."

"Cathal's work," Obsydia commented. "He is one of the scions of Light whose profane magic imprisoned me. His sorcery evaporated Koll's arm in battle." Obsydia regally turned away and sat upon a throne of ebonite with a velvet pillow for her comfort, the black metal lavishly decorated with rubies. She sat upon her royal chair and smoothed the folds of her red gown. "Now, continue."

Shroud obediently inclined her head, but her dark eyes glittered at Koll with suspicion, and a hint of jealousy. "As you command, my Queen."

"We serve the Dark," Xabral added, rising on his red and black scales with pride.

Shroud turned away and pointed to the altar. "Your pets are willful, but I will tolerate them for your sake. We have better things to speak of. Your father sends thirteen demon handmaidens, including myself, spawned from the Abyss, who will serve you and the holy cause. Behold the Claw Maidens."

Scarlet mist rose upon the bloodstained stone altar, burning bright until it transformed into a swirling pillar of red-hot flames. The flames divided, revealing a sliver of shadow. From this dark gateway the first claw maiden stepped from the fiery tunnel. As each claw maiden was summoned from the Shadow Realms, they would swear fealty to their queen. Each wore the same black garment, a sleeveless leather sheath with square cut neckline. But each was so different.

The first claw maiden to step through was vibrant with dusky red skin and black hair peaked in wild sprays of inky chaos. Eyes of fiery red burned as she knelt at Obsydia's feet and kissed her hand. "I am Fury." She then stepped back and took her place behind Shroud.

Sin was raw and hungry looking, a temptation of liquid grace with pale grey skin patterned with red runic symbols.

Avarice was thin and ravenous, black-haired with long black nails and narrow red eyes.

Phantom glided across the floor toward Obsydia, her ethereal charms as sinister as she was pale.

Wither could have been Shroud's sister. Deathlike and gaunt with desiccated grey skin and black hair bound by yellowed bone hair pins, her voice was barely a whisper when she vowed fealty to Obsydia. Her eye burned with hollow blackness.

Gloom was like the darkest night, her face a mystery wrapped in shadow.

Torment emerged with flame-colored eyes, her burnt red skin contrasted with her black leather dress.

Venom possessed a poisonous image. Her pale, mottled green skin and liquid movements were serpentine in image. Xabral shook his stinger in appreciation of her beauty. She winked at Xabral as she passed.

"A miracle of the dark," Xabral sighed dreamily.

Siren emerged sensual and full of heat, with luminous beauty of black eyes and blood red hair captivating the eye.

Doom was ominous, her sharp features and mottled grey skin contrasted with ruby red eyes.

Necrosis was deadly with ashy green skin and sunken eyes. One felt death's embrace in her presence.

Succuba stepped from the altar with sensual power and strutted toward Obsydia on bare feet. Her vibrant dark beauty oozed wicked-ness and joy.

Assembled, the handmaidens were striking as they formed a half circle behind Obsydia's throne. The hooded guardians stepped forward and chanted once more. A final object appeared on the crimson-stained altar.

A crown of otherworldly beauty glimmered. Fashioned of ebonite with dozens of tiny black gems, black diamonds, set into the precious, rare gold of the shadows. But the glory of the coronet was a red jewel of amazing brilliance the size of a snake egg. One of the guardians carried it to the throne, and silent handed it to Shroud, who stiffly accepted it and bowed.

Shroud turned to Obsydia and raised the crown in her bony hands and proclaimed, "Behold! The Topaz Era is dead. To celebrate this new era of darkness, your Holy Father, Eternal Ahridum, gifts you with a new crown to celebrate your liberation from the cursed light and to toast the new era of coming Darkness."

"Its beauty is beyond even my imagination," Obsydia said as Shroud gently placed it on her head.

"Your father created it only for you. The chief jewel is the rarest of gems in this world—a red diamond. He bestows you with this new crown to usher in the new age of darkness—The Obsidian Era."

All in the mystical chamber knelt as Shroud placed the crown on Obsydia's head. The stones possessed a dark quality despite their shimmer, because they were created in Ahridum's Kingdom.

"I offer thanks to my Father. We will soon begin to recruit new followers to our cause. Wars will descend and the reapers of death shall be glutted. First, we will celebrate with sacrifices like the days of old. My handmaidens, your first task is to bring me worthy sacrifices to offer upon my father's altar. Go into the world and strike fear."

The demon handmaids scattered to do evil. Obsydia watched them go like an indulgent mother watching her children play. She rose and walked toward Koll, who knelt with bowed head. "Stand Koll," she commanded.

Koll obeyed. The hooded guardians approach them. One of them carried an artificial arm fabricated of ebonite and black velvet, clustered with dark jewels, just as Obsydia promised. At the top of the arm were sharp black hooks. It reeked of dark enchantment.

"My servants have fashioned your new arm, Koll. Go with them now. Take your pet with you, for you will need Xabral's comfort."

The hooded beings led Koll away, with Xabral slithering after them.

"The process of binding your new arm is a long ritual. But fear not, it will be worth the agony," Obsydia promised.

Koll submitted to the hands of the hooded guardians. They laid him on cold marble and brought the mystical arm. They opened his robe, baring his deformed shoulder, scarred by Cathal's light magic.

The mystical powers of shadows surged violently as they attached his new arm.

Koll screamed for hours.

CHAPTER 6

The sorcery chamber radiated magic, soothing the strange feeling haunting Mellypip since he woke this morning. When he peeked into Rualla's room, everyone whispered in quiet desperation, and no one told him anything! Runa again did not sleep last night, so Mellypip stayed with her as she studied volumes of medical or mystical lore. She urged Mellypip to rest, but he could not leave her alone in her sad quest. Opaline helped organize her notes and brought countless pots of coffee. Mellypip rubbed his eyes, sick with exhaustion and worry. The whole house occupied with finding a cure for Rualla. Additional fears about Koll and Obsydia occupied his mind. He felt helpless, unable to help anyone, including his own sorceress. Even his usual studies were cancelled today. Belwyn told him to go outside and play, but to not stray beyond the backyard. The owl's usual acerbic tone was missing, which worried Mellypip. Nothing was normal. And he did not want to play. He could not even talk to Rono, who was away with Darkleaf in yet another search for Jadon.

To distract from his worry, Mellypip ventured up to the chamber to explore the mystical treats tucked away here in this magical refuge—books and scrolls full of potent sorcery, spell boxes sparkled with magic, potion bottles filled to the brim with smoky secrets. Mellypip climbed up to the bookshelf with nimble speed.

"What are you doing?" Grimm inquired, hesitating at the doorway.

Startled by the wolf's voice, he nearly jumped out of his fur. "Oh, hi there, Grimm. You're very stealthy you know."

"Thank you," Grimm nodded politely. "It's a talent which kept me alive when I lived alone in the wilderness. Are you looking for something special?"

"I'm looking for my favorite book. Where's Opaline?"

"She is with Runa and Caliste," Grimm replied. "I did not want to intrude. Everyone is so sad today, but no one's talking. I hadn't seen you and was worried about you, so I followed your scent up here."

Mellypip searched the rows of books until he found the book

he was looking for. Too big for him to carry down, he pulled it out and let it drop to the floor.

"What is it about?" Grimm asked, sniffing the large colorful volume suspiciously.

Mellypip jumped down and opened the book, flipping through bright pages with nimble paws. *"The Guide to the Seven Dragon Clans.* I love this book. Belwyn read it to me when I was a kit. I'll read it to you if you like and then show you the words. As a familiar, you need to learn how to read."

"Opaline and Arial have been teaching me written words. It's a strange hobby."

"Belwyn taught me all about dragons and now I'll teach you."

Grimm twitched his ears as he looked at the drawings of the dragons as Mellypip flipped the pages. "Dragons look dangerous."

Felisia flew into the room and alighted on the back of a chair. Felisia stared coolly at them. Grimm whined a little and Mellypip sucked his paw when faced with her icy gaze. For being such a tiny owl, Felisia could instill fear as much as Belwyn. "Mellypip! Grimm! What are you two doing up here unsupervised?"

Arial, Sirah's snowy wolf, walked in after her and sat next to Grimm. "We are only concerned. You should let us know what you are doing, especially with so much danger afoot. And Felisia's right. You two should not be up here alone."

A weary voiced groaned across the room. "They're not alone." Taran's tubby orange tabby, MacTabbish, sprawled on the window's ledge.

"How long have you been here?" Mellypip asked.

"MacTabbish must also be stealthy," Grimm remarked.

Mellypip leaned close to the wolf and whispered, "No, just a lazy puss."

The plump cat slowly stretched in the sunshine, precariously balanced on the narrow ledge. "I needed a bit of rest and privacy since the fuss with those necromancers finally ended last night. They hogged the chamber for three days."

"Iona was very upset they did not accept Panthara," Arial added.

MacTabbish slowly rolled over. "They hogged the sorcery chamber for days, banning all of us from a normal routine without so much as a thank you."

Felisia sniffed. "Your normal routine is sleeping eighteen hours a day."

"I'm a cat," MacTabbish replied, yawning. "What do you expect? I don't know why they fussed about why Panthara suddenly acquired necromancer magic. The Wraith Guardians touched the lass and changed her. A village idiot would understand. They also prattled on about the worthiness of her wee winged reptile with the velvet eye patch which was annoying."

"My name is Azmadu."

The crill lizard sat in the doorway, eye patch crooked. He looked sad and Mellypip knew the past weighed heavily on Azmadu. He felt responsible for him since they rescued Panthara from Koll and Obsydia. Obsydia may have escaped, but at least Runa, Opaline, and Panthara escaped the sacrifice Koll planned. Panthara was Runa's half-sister, which sort of made Azmadu family too. Mellypip waved at Azmadu. "Come on in, Azmadu. You can help me teach Grimm. We were reading about the seven dragon clans."

Azmadu brightened and padded over to them. "Dragons! I love dragons. My Panthara says crill lizards are long-lost cousins to the mighty dragons."

"Of course you are," Arial commented indulgently. "Panthara was very stoic in dealing with the necromancers."

"My Panthara was a queen," Azmadu said, full of pride. "She would never give them the satisfaction of showing them her true feelings."

Runa's terrified plea entered his thoughts. *Melly, I need you.* His large round ears twitched as he ran out of the chamber.

"Where are you going?" Felisia demanded.

"Runa needs me," Mellypip shouted back.

Azmadu and Grimm followed Mellypip downstairs to the second-floor hallway. Raghnall's dismal face invoked Mellypip's haunted feeling again. Opaline and Panthara stood at Runa's side, a sign of trouble when those two didn't argue. Caliste comforted Liat. Sanura and Pointessa flocked Dabiro, who sat mute and morose by Liat's feet. Belwyn quietly listened to Raghnall, perched on Yllia's arm. The owl briefly glanced down at Mellypip, but did not send him away.

"What's happened?' Mellypip asked.

"My mother is dying," Runa wept.

Raghnall patted Runa's hand, his face crumbled with emotion.

"I'm very sorry, my dear. Curses! I don't know what else to do! Her pulse is almost non-existent and her breathing shallow. She won't last long. I wish I could save her. Neither traditional medicine nor magic is doing any good. I'm so sorry."

"Is there nothing we can do?" Yllia asked, her voice choking with grief.

Mellypip moved to Runa's side and she scooped him up and held him close. "She can't die now. Not after everything we did to break the curse."

"Diabolism is the darkest magic. It has strange effects on its victims," Raghnall said. "What Koll did to her was rooted in the most powerful evil."

"But my grandmother is recovered," Runa protested. "Why not my mother too? There must be something we've missed."

"I will stay with her," Liat announced, "But bring me books to research. There must be something we overlooked."

Raghnall leaned against the wall, rubbing his temples, clearly exhausted. "Only a miracle can help Rualla now. Baldur senses a deep grief in her, but even his empathic powers cannot breach the wall in her mind. There is no infection and the damned curse is broken. I have studied all the medical and mystical. I purged her body of dark magic. At this point I am lost."

Runa clenched her jaw, but her thoughts were wild. *She's dying, Melly! We must do something. She's my mother! All this is because of Koll's evil.*

Please don't lose hope. Striker's sprit is trying to help us. Maybe Raghnall needs to look for another way to heal her. Her soul needs healing, not her body. Let's talk to the staff.

The staff?

Your staff, Runa. Striker lives inside. He has been very active since we freed Rualla and Yllia. He's trying to tell us something.

"What should we do now?" Caliste wept. "Say goodbye? No, I cannot. I will continue to try to the end."

"Send for Cathal," Belwyn said grimly.

Opaline nodded and kissed Runa on the cheek. "I'll take care of this, don't worry. He was on his way home from Ironia. I'll see if I can contact him on the calling crystal. I'll be back soon." She patted Grimm on the head. "Stay with Melly. He needs you."

"I'll look after Runa," Panthara offered, "until your return."

Opaline and Panthara nodded in passing, their love of Runa

binding them in a peaceful truce.

Runa went into Rualla's room, followed by Panthara. Baldur hovered by Rualla, his giant paw covering her pale hands. Liat sat on the other side, grim with heartbreak for a lost love. Dabiro was silent. Runa sat on the edge of the bed. "Thank you for sitting with her, Baldur."

"I just wish my empathic touch helped," Baldur groaned.

The air sizzled and prickled Mellypip's fur. Runa's staff, leaning against the bedpost, burned with bright golden light.

Azmadu backed away. "Runa's staff is glowing again."

"There is another soul in this room," Panthara remarked. "Calling for help."

"Runa," Mellypip whispered. "Striker's soul is calling to us. I'm sure of it."

"Yes, I feel Striker too," Runa replied.

Grimm growled low in his throat. "Striker's spirit is sorrowful. Full of grief. I've seen his spirit spring from Runa's staff more than once."

"Has Striker said anything to you?" Mellypip asked.

Grimm shook his head. "No, not to me, but I sense he is as desperate as are all of you."

Runa picked up her staff, ornately carved by her magic from a branch of the willow oak where the Raven Wing had buried Striker. Her staff blazed like the sun, casting an eerie light in the room.

"What's happening Runa?" Mellypip asked, nervous, clinging to her.

Before Runa could speak, a burst of light and a whoosh of magic enveloped them. Mellypip's consciousness tingled as he was propelled with Runa into the abyss. He vaguely heard the cries of their friends in the real world become distant echoes as they were dropped into a dead forest, so much like the one where they found the tree of bones. They were stunned, dizzy from the unexpected forces, and cold in this dismal place.

"Where are we?" Mellypip cried, shaky from the mystical jolt. "You're not dreaming Runa. This isn't dream bonding. How did we get here?"

"I'm not sure. Maybe, somehow, it's my mother's dream state," Runa said fearfully, trying to stand. She scooped Melly into her arms and held him protectively. "How did we get here? What's happening?"

A great red panther emerged from the wintry forest mist before them. Striker looked at them with sorrow. "I brought you here."

~ * ~

Koll entered the new mirror chamber, Xabral slithering at his heels. He knelt and bowed his head when he reached Obsydia. "You summoned me, my Queen."

"Yes, I have been making new plans for my war. As my high priest and general, you will assist me. How is your health now? Does your new arm please you?"

Koll lifted his artificial arm. "I am forever grateful. I am stronger and my pain is less, despite the lingering effects of Cathal's assault. The arm feels so real." The black velvet glittered with designs of ebonite and rubies. He flexed the fingers as though they were his own, and his sorcery surged through the limb crafted of dark sorcery drawn from the mystic hooded guardians.

"A mystical gift mortals rarely deserve," Shroud said, striding into the mirror chamber, her black eyes bright in her grey withered face. A red-eyed warrior in black leather followed her with mute obedience, his soul and will gone.

"Welcome Shroud," Obsydia said.

Shroud bowed, ignoring Koll's existence. "Your new obsidian warrior is ready to serve you." She turned to the warrior and snapped her fingers. "Kneel before your Queen and Goddess, dog!"

The warrior dropped to his knees and bowed his head to the floor. He kissed the hem of her diaphanous crimson gown and gazed up at her with rapturous joy.

Obsydia stroked the hair of her newly made warrior. "They are mine, Koll. I bless them with my mystical kiss and then devour their souls and turn their hearts black. I have turned many while you recovered. Now they serve me. They will be leaders for you to command. The rest of my army will be recruited from men and the demons of this world. You will lead them, Koll."

"A mortal leading your army?" Shroud gasped. "I know he is your pet, but your warlords have always been turned before to ensure their loyalty."

"Koll is special," Obsydia murmured. "And loyal, though I agree he is only human. Still, demon warriors can blunder, as when we sent them to take the dragon rookery."

"Did they manage to take any eggs?" Koll asked.

Obsydia frowned, her silver eyes dark with anger. "No, my thief failed. I did not even want the whole rookery, just the egg of the next Drajina. The rest he was supposed to destroy. A shame. He was my first since I was released. His soul was sweet in my mouth as I turned him into a demon. But I cannot tolerate the slightest flaw if victory is my goal. I wanted to spite the dragons. Denied this, I destroyed the thief for his failure."

"Send me," Koll offered. "Surely my sorcery can me enable to steal a single egg. I will lay the dragon egg at your feet for you to crush."

"The dragon clans fled Rapiveshta when they realized I was free. Their fires have died in the great empty caverns. Their hibernation was broken and now they have fled, taking the rookery with them. I scry for them, but their magic keeps them hidden from me. I will deal with them later. Shroud and I have been making plans. Gathering fresh recruits is very satisfying. My claw maidens have been a great help. They steal men and women from their fields, battle, or homes, and deliver them to me for judgment. If I deem them worthy, I devour their souls and turn them into demon warriors. Those I do not deem worthy I allow my claw maidens to play with."

Koll was unaware, but not surprised by this new fact. "A fascinating morsel to add to the Shadow Gospels. I knew of your power to change a human into a demon, but did not know you took their souls."

Obsydia walked to the largest mirror in the chamber. Over twenty feet tall and half as wide, it shimmered with power. "We will be moving to a new tower today."

"A new tower has arisen in Skarros?"

A shadowed smile curled Obsydia's crimson lips and she turned, waving her hand over the large central mirror of black glass. "No, our enemies would expect me to go back there. I will send some of my legions to Skarros. It will distract prying eyes and they will be needed for the coming battles. A new fortress has risen by my Father's hand. From where we can plan our strategy in the world. This sacred tower is part of Ahridum's realm of shadows. We must play out the Obsidian War in the mortal world." A spectral tower appeared on the mirror. Its sinister presence rising hundreds of feet above a mass of tangled dead woods.

"Follow," Obsydia commanded, and stepped through the shadowy glass.

Koll obeyed her and stepped into a strange forest dark and feral. "Where are we?"

"This is the tower from where you will serve your goddess," Shroud replied.

Koll nodded patiently, but longed to slap the arrogant look off Shroud's ugly face and hang her from one of the twisted branches by her hideous red braids.

Xabral slithered after him, tongue flicking in and out, tasting the air. "Wickedness lives here! Glorious!"

Obsydia smiled indulgently at Xabral. "Yes, it is lovely. It was once the home of the Ilyrrans, then called Elfsharans. Once, this land teemed with lush green forests and wildlife. Rangers flew on the backs of perytons. Blue rivers, rich with life, where giant snowy swans swam, flowed past lofty trees where the Elfsharans built their gentle towns of nature. I destroyed it all. During the Bloodstone Wars, I defeated them at the height of my glory. Now it is a place of darkness. It was one of my greatest victories. My army of men and demon ravaged their entire country until it was a hollowed husk of death. My dark enchantments vanquished all Light from this realm." She touched a twisted trunk of what was an ancient oak, now deformed into a strange misshapen pillar with monstrous boughs bearing gray dried leaves. They broke away on the cold wind, floating over the woodland of death. "Trees once green withered and blackened with my touch, even after a thousand years my mystical touch has continued to transform this place. Their fruit a poisonous harvest. Demons nest here now. The swans and all other forms of nature have been changed by Darkness. Many strange creatures have risen in this dark realm, waiting for my return. All life here became a fragment of what my father desired. I will do to the world what I did here for the Dark. This kingdom is a reminder of what I can do to the world." Obsydia walked toward the new tower looming before them.

I love it here, Xabral exclaimed, sliding among the black plants toward strange crops of giant red toadstools speckled with black dots.

Shroud walked ahead to the giant double doors and with a wave of her skeletal hand they opened and she stood aside and bowed before Obsydia as she entered.

Koll walked toward the tower, his black eyes on Shroud. He did not trust the demon bitch.

"Beware you do not fail Obsydia, Sorcerer." Shroud whispered as he passed her. "Your fate will be worse than hell and more terrifying than oblivion."

"Beware yourself, slave," Koll replied, black eyes flashing with anger. "My path to serve the Dark was chosen by our god, Ahridum. Pray you do not prick my temper too far, Demoness, else you'll suffer a death to compliment your corpselike beauty."

CHAPTER 7

"We must save her," Striker roared. "Follow me."

Runa tugged on Mellypip to follow Striker as he prowled though the haunted forest until they came to the icy clearing where Rualla lay on a stone bed. Striker sprinted ahead of them, and lay at the edge of the grave, sorrowing over his sorceress. "I am long dead, my body long turned to dust and bone, but her soul and body are still bound together. She can still live. You must wake her."

"How?" Runa cried.

"She must know she still lives," Striker replied. "She embraced death in her long dream state of misery and loss. The diabolism of the curse infected her deeply, but it is not the curse binding her, but her own grief. Magic and medicine will not revive her. Your love is her salvation, Runa, the life you have lived because of her sacrifice may be the only thing to revive her from this self-imposed death."

Mellypip tiptoed over the frosty grass until Runa took him in her warm arms. They reached the grave Striker guarded and she looked upon her mother's pale face, so deathlike. Her body was clothed in a snowy shroud, her long dark hair spread out on a bed of grey stone, clinging vines roped around her body. Dead flowers circled Rualla like a tomb.

"She's lost in sorrow," Striker moaned. "My poor Rualla doesn't know she's alive. She's accepted death. Because she's been bound in the death of a diabolistic curse for so long, it has affected her mind. The dark years of being entombed in the bone curse took a harsh toll. Rualla began to fade long before you came to Thill. Her heartbreak was too great. She lost Ashur. She lost you. We had a final moment before the curse struck, when I stole you away from Koll and the false Ashur. My heartbreak was leaving her there, but I had to save you."

"Oh, Striker, I'm so sorry," Runa whispered, embracing the ghostly panther.

Mellypip dared to touch the spirit, which in this strange place felt very real and warm. The fur was soft, and muscles rippled beneath the skin. He dared to come closer as gentle paw drew him in, embracing and loving.

Runa wiped her eyes. "I'm so sorry for your suffering and for your great sacrifice. How do I reach her Striker? What can I do?"

"Take her hand." Striker cautioned, "But beware, for her dreams are of death. Despite her many years of happy life and memories, she thinks only of the tree of bones and what she lost. I know she has thought of me, wondering where I was or if I saved you as the curse's roots bound her to this living death. Her fragile hope was that I delivered you to safety. Despite our many years together, she only recalls our last look as I rescued you. I could not rest knowing she was still there, trapped in the curse. The Otherworld let my soul remain all this time. I was waiting for you, Runa."

"How did you know I would ever find her?"

Striker looked up at the grey sky of Rualla's dark dream world. "There is much I cannot say, but my faith in the mysteries of the Eternals guided me. The sacred unicorn, the Eternal guardian of the familiars, guided me to where I would find you when the time was right. Now we must free her before it is too late."

Runa carefully touched her mother's icy cold hand. "Mother, please come back to us. You're alive, not dead!"

The wind chilled around them. Runa took a deep breath and ripped at the vines and dead flowers, furiously tossing them aside. Mellypip's stomach knotted with fear and he consciously kept his touch and thoughts connected to Runa. She grasped her mother's head and lifted her up. Runa focused all the magic and light within her on her mother. Striker remained close, his paw resting on Rualla's shoulder.

Fragments of her mother's travails flooded her mind. The terror her mother and grandmother suffered bound by a diabolism ritual. The choking sorrow of her mother and Striker when they parted. Striker's bold move to save Runa from the demon Ashur and Koll. Runa relived what her mother alone experienced during those chilling moments before the curse petrified her body into bone, trapping her soul with it. Not dead and not alive, but a tormented limbo. Then the release of hope, so fragile, gave way to her emotional grave. The surrender to the grave, alone and bereft.

Mellypip sensed the pain Runa drew out as she tried to reach her mother. He offered comfort and a touchstone of reality as the misery cloaked Runa's mind.

"You're trying too hard," A soft, vaguely familiar voice warned on the air. "Focus on love. Focus on life."

Mellypip's gasped when he saw Ashur walking from the mist, Urvuz flying overhead on broad black wings. "How is this possible?"

"There are mysteries unfolding, young Mellypip," Ashur smiled.

"How are you here?" Runa cried. "You're supposed to be at peace now in the Otherworld."

"We come to help, with Light's blessing," Urvuz said, landing on the ground.

Mellypip saw Urvuz as healed and whole again, content with his sorcerer. He was glad for them.

"You're not here to take her soul, are you?" Runa cried, beating him back with her fists. "I won't let you!"

Ashur knelt by Rualla and took Runa's hand, softening her stark terror until she calmed down. "No, my daughter. I am here to help. Darkness and Light are moving towards a great battle. Darkness walks the mortal world now, freed by Koll's machinations. There is so much I want to tell you. Listen to your dreams, Runa. Much will happen now, so you must be ready. I am so sorry, dear. You must be strong."

"Father, I don't understand."

"You will. Now, we must save my beloved Rualla, not only for everyone, including poor Striker, but for her own good. Concentrate on the light! Break the darkness she believes still holds her. She has clung to death for so long because she lost her faith. She needs your faith now, Runa. Your life, your memories, to spark her soul's awakening."

Runa nodded, tears washing her cheeks. She used her magic to feed her mother memories from Runa's childhood and touched the locket she always wore, the one with the tiny portraits of Yllia and Rualla she so treasured. She gave Rualla her memories of life—the tree tower where she grew up, swimming in the lake, her beloved aunts and uncles who visited often, Belwyn's incessant lectures and stern love, bonding with Mellypip, and the love she was blessed with in this world. She kept the secret sorrow of Striker's death held back, fearing its effect on her fragile thread of life. She gave her mother the final image she had of her father's soul, how Ashur was free in the Otherworld and Urvuz was with him. Ashur wanted her happiness. Love was all Runa had to offer and love was what she gave her mother.

Mellypip sensed the drain on Runa. He clung to her, giving her strength, his familiar abilities guiding her focus as she struggled.

"Wake, Mother! Wake up!" Runa at last cried.

Runa's tears fell on Rualla's pale cheeks and her flesh warmed with a faint rosy flush of life.

"Look!" Mellypip cried, "it's working!"

"Rualla!" Striker roared. "Wake up."

"Come back to me," Runa begged softly. She kissed her mother on the cheek and whispered, "I love you, Mother."

The thread she shared with her mother's dream world was rupturing. "I feel the world is shifting. Fading away. A force is pulling me back! Melly! Father!"

"It's happening to me too," Mellypip cried out.

A feeling of warmth and love bloomed around her when Ashur's hand stroked her mother's fair cheek. "Go now," Ashur whispered gently. "You can do no more."

"No!" Runa cried, fighting the darkness. "I can't leave her yet."

"You must go."

A flash of brightness stunned Runa and Mellypip. A strange magic swept over them as they were plucked from the nightmare of her mother's tomb back into the waking world.

They woke up next to Rualla's still body, drained and shaking. Everyone talked at once in frantic tones, like bees buzzing in a jar.

"Runa, are you alright?" Yllia shouted, pulling a dazed Runa to her feet. "What in the heavens just happened?"

"Where's Melly?" Runa mumbled, rubbing her temples.

Mellypip rolled over on the bed, dizzy and feeling sick to his tummy. The room crowded with worried faces as Opaline and Panthara helped Runa to a chair near the door. Yllia picked him up and cradled him gently for a moment before placing him in Runa's lap.

"I'm sorry," Runa wept, head in her hands. "I failed her."

Opaline and Panthara knelt by Runa, Mellypip shaking in her lap. Azmadu huddled next to Panthara, unsure. Grimm sat on his haunches and howled briefly.

"Runa look!" Yllia cried. "Everyone!"

From their corners of grief, they looked up.

Rualla's eyes were open. Confused, she bolted upright and cried out hoarsely, "Where am I? Where's Striker? Where's my baby? Where am I? Koll! The curse! Oh Striker, save my baby! Don't let Koll take my baby!"

"Hush dear, you are safe! We will explain everything," Yllia soothed her, stroking her brow as Rualla's eyes darted around the room. "You are free! We are both free, my sweet child."

Liat rushed to her side, edging a stunned Raghnall out of the way. He kissed her hand over and over, crying, "You're safe now, Rualla. I will protect you."

Rualla stopped crying out when her eyes focused on Runa. Everyone fell silent. Rualla whispered, "Who are you?"

Runa's face brightened with hope. "I'm…Runa. I'm your daughter."

"No! You can't be my daughter. She's just a baby. Where's Striker. He saved my baby. Where's Striker." Rualla sobbed harshly into her pillow. "You're not my Runa! Send her away! I can't look at her!"

~ * ~

Darcus and Redstorm stopped mid-morning to give the children a rest. "This cold and snow worries me."

Redstorm folded in his wings. "You're a tough warrior."

Darcus cast a dry look at the peryton. "Not for me, but for the children."

Riva, huddled in his cloak and rubbing his hands together, with a drowsy Buzzy strapped to his back in his special carrier. "A problem I can resolve. Magic can be practical, you know." Riva laughed and gathered the children in a circle. With a bright glow he transformed the light, thinner garments the children war into warm thick woolens. The delight of the children brought a smile to Darcus' craggy face.

"You're thinking of Raven, aren't you?" Redstorm asked.

"I am," Darcus nodded. "When the children are safe with the sister at the Abbey, I'm taking Raven with me."

"Are you going to take her to Ilyrra after you report to Cathal?" Redstorm asked.

"With the war coming, I must set up a proper home and care for Raven. I know my duties will keep me away a good deal. I fear whole kingdoms will fall before this is over. Raven needs to be safe, even if I'm not with her. It's important she know her people too.

Cathal told me they arrange these things for the rangers." He paused and furrowed his brow. "Do you think Raven will remember me? We had so little time and she was in terrible shock after her father died. I wonder if she is speaking yet."

Redstorm shook his antlers. "Oh, she will remember you. Why don't think she can stay in Thill? Isn't the Abbey safe?"

"My sister's Abbey was not safe. Nowhere is safe now. But I want Raven to be as safe as I can make her. I also want Raven to feel like she has a home, not like she's an orphan."

Riva gathered the supplies and repacked put them in the pack after the children finished eating. "Hard bread, cheese, and dried meat is not very appetizing."

"It'll toughen you up," Darcus grinned. "The sisters will happily fatten up the children when we deliver them to their care. We must focus on getting them out of this damned country. Let's get moving. I want to make the border before sundown."

"Taking the riverboat for half the journey was genius," Riva said, adjusting the backpack as his sloth snored, oblivious. "Though Redstorm detested it."

Redstorm gave Darcus a telling sidelong glance. "I was forced to wear the amulet to hide my true form. And I hate water. Give me solid ground to run or the air to fly. Water is for drinking, not floating on some rickety contraption of wood." He snorted loudly. "Though you could stand to take a dip. Humans tend to stink like trolls unless they wash."

Darcus walked ahead toward the road, grinning. "You'll get over it." He paused mid-step and shifted to the left, pushing Redstorm away just as several black crossbow bolts struck the earth, just a hairsbreadth shy of hitting the peryton, who roared and spread his wings. Darcus jumped astride his back and shouted, "Riva! Protect the children!"

Riva gathered the children close and cast a shield around them. The faint blue glow of the magical dome shadowed their worried faces. "Don't fret, little ones. You'll be fine. But stay where you are!" Riva chased after Darcus, Buzzy bouncing on his back.

Black-armored warriors burst around them from the trees above. Redstorm crashed antlers first into one of the enemy before he had time to load another bolt into his crossbow. Riva's staff shot beams of hot red sorcery at a trio of warriors rushing him, forcing them back several feet, their armor smoking as they crashed to the ground. Darcus guided Redstorm over two more, leaving Redstorm's hooves and antlers to inflict damage and draw blood.

"Who the hell are they?" Riva shouted, his staff burning bright with sorcery as he targeted another group advancing toward the children.

"Ask me when they're dead," Darcus snapped, jumping from Redstorm's back to drop on an enemy, knocking his sword out of his hands and forcing him to the ground. Darcus ran him through. Several more advanced, black cloaks floating on the wintry wind, crossbows and swords raised. Darcus stood his ground, his muscles tensing as he tried to think about his next move.

Thin blasts of fire rained down from above, engulfing the combatants with fiery death. A force of powerful wind nearly knocked Darcus off his feet. Their screams did not shock Darcus as much as what he saw when he glanced up to see their savior flying overhead.

"Was that a fire dragon?" Riva gasped.

"A name well earned," Darcus muttered with awe.

An owl and two snow eagles landed near the carnage. The owl shimmered into Cathal. With a wave of his hand, his magic snuffed out the remaining fires, leaving some burned grass and a pile of bodies.

"Burning down the forest is often an issue when dragons are involved," Cathal remarked.

"What the hell is going on?" Darcus asked gruffly, embracing Cathal briefly.

Neelam shape-shifted from his snowy eagle shape and kicked one of the bodies. "These aren't soldiers from the former Ivory Kingdom."

Cathal knelt down and examined one of the bodies. "No, they're Obsydia's demon warriors. See the red eyes?"

Neelam uncorked a flask and drank, then passed it to Darcus. "Hell-bitch wasted no time, I see. Some things never change."

"How did you know we were here?" Riva asked.

"We warned them," said two unfamiliar voices.

Darcus turned and saw two small black shadow dragons sitting side by side. They could not be more than a few feet long and their black skin gleamed in the light.

One of the shadow dragons shyly spoke. "I'm Fallon."

The other sat up on his hind legs, tilting his head. "I'm Talon."

"We are honored," Redstorm said, bowing his head. His heavy hoof gave a stunned Darcus a nudge, who bowed as well.

"We've been scouting for Cathal and Neelam," Talon said. "We burrow underground and hide in shadows. We fly most of the time, but we love to burrow."

"The border ahead is blocked with many enemy soldiers, some of them demon men with nasty red eyes. But Akash, he's the fire dragon, will soon take care of them." Fallon assured him.

"Are you two related?" Riva asked.

"They are rookery twins," Cathal said. "Brothers hatched from the same egg. A rarity, even for dragons. We were rushing back to Aybarr when we feared Rualla would not live. But she is finally awake now. Opaline contacted us with the good news."

"Thank the gods," Darcus sighed.

"Riva, did you forget something?" Buzzy asked dreamily from his pack.

"Oh my," Riva exclaimed, "the children are still inside my shield!" He ran off to check on them.

Darcus scratched his head. "Cathal, what is going on? Even I know dragons keep to themselves. Are the dragons really going to fight with us?"

Cathal grinned. "We share the same enemy—Obsydia. The dragon clans will fight when the time is right, but more importantly, we must help them."

"How can we possibly be of help to dragons?" Darcus asked.

Then Cathal showed him what he carried in his large satchel and Darcus took another long drink of whiskey from Neelam's flask.

CHAPTER 8

Mellypip stared out the window, watching the sun set. Bored, he exhaled on the chilled glass and made foggy paw prints. "It's darker earlier each day. And colder too. Belwyn said it'll snow tonight. How long is winter?" He sighed and glanced at Runa, sitting cross-legged on her bed with a book. "I know you're only pretending to read."

"I am not," Runa coolly replied, turning a page with deliberate slowness.

"It's not your fault. Even Belwyn says so, and Belwyn knows everything." Runa mutely turned a page, ignoring him. Frustrated, Mellypip rocked back and forth on the windowsill until fresh hope sprang in his mind. "I know! We could try a new scrying spell to find Jadon. Opaline found another whole volume of spells in the sorcery chamber full of locating spells and whatnot."

Runa glanced up from her reading. "Whatnot?"

"It's my word for the day. Belwyn got tired of the other one."

Runa put down the book, her eyes narrowed. "Which was?"

"Harrowing! I experienced harrowing when Dabiro chased me up a tree after taking the last muffin this morning. I guess I used it too often, so Belwyn ordered me to change it. But you're changing the subject now. I know you're sad, but moping is a nonproductive endeavor."

"Did Belwyn say that?"

"Yes, but Belwyn's big words must be true." He hopped down and ran over to the bed, jumping up on the soft quilt next to her. "Please come downstairs. Sirah plans to bake cookies and make hot drobba tonight. Opaline promises to watch. Her cooking is still cursed you know. She tried to bake bread yesterday. It was tragic."

"Oh dear, what happened now?"

"Opaline attempted a spell to bake a loaf of bread...with magic."

"Is that what I smelled yesterday? I thought something was odd."

"You'd know if you came out of your room. Poor Opaline. Sadly, the loaf was big as the kitchen table. It seemed fine, but it tasted funny. She threw it out. I think Opaline's magic went wonky again. You should help her practice her sorcery more."

"I think her poor cooking is to blame, rather than her magic. Since she bonded with Grimm, his influence has calmed her sorcerous accidents."

"Let's go downstairs. It's almost supper time."

"I'm not hungry. You go ahead."

Mellypip folded his paw on his tummy and fumed. "You can't hide in your room forever. Opaline says your acting childish."

"Says the princess who hysterically locked herself in an attic and refused to come out when a minor sorcerous accident made my hair grow thirty or forty feet."

"Caliste says you're too young to be cloistered," Mellypip said.

"Do you even know what cloistered means?" Runa inquired with a raised eyebrow.

"No, but it sounds dreadful."

Runa moaned and dropped her head down over her knees. "I shouldn't have told her I was her daughter! I wished I'd kept my mouth shut. My mother just wakes up from a curse and I upset her so much she banishes me from the room. She was awake for only thirty seconds."

Mellypip sighed with relief. At least she was finally talking. "But it was so unexpected. Rualla took you by surprise when she asked who you were."

"I wish I could banish the way she looked at me from my mind."

Mellypip patted her on the head. "You're not a bad daughter."

"I'm despicable."

"Your mother was just really confused and upset. Curses are nasty. She just woke up."

"I should have known telling her I was her daughter would shock her. I didn't mean to blurt it out. I'm surprised my gigantic blunder didn't cause her to die from shock."

"She's not mad at you. A new quest will help you take your mind off your troubles. We need to find Jadon."

"I know I need to find him! But he doesn't want to be found, does he? I've tried countless spells and nothing has worked."

"Darkleaf is frustrated too. He misses his ranger. Chimera's nasty bite changed Jadon's scent too. Darkleaf told me he would have located Jadon by now if her evil curse hadn't made him smell funny."

"For all I know he's dead. We have no idea what kind of side effects he may have suffered. Someone may even have killed him. I mean, he looks like a demon now. He can't exactly explain how he looks to strangers."

"No, don't say such things! Jadon can't be dead!" Mellypip cried.

"I didn't mean it, Melly. I'm so sorry! Come here. Don't cry." She cradled him gently and he snuggled in her arms until he calmed down.

As he rested in her arms, he thought about the lovely wooden ring Jadon carved for Runa, and how shy he was about giving it to her. "You should wear the ring he made for you."

"I can't," Runa whispered. "It makes me sad."

"It may help give you hope too. Darkleaf is sad and I want him to have hope. Rono is trying to help Darkleaf, because he's so lonely without Jadon. Rono tried singing to him yesterday, but I think it annoyed him. Gryphons aren't good singers. It might make Darkleaf feel better if you wore the ring Jadon made. It's so pretty. Maybe wearing it will help your magic find him."

"You're not going to let this go are you?"

"Nope."

He shifted her in her lap, rolling onto his back, looking up at her. "But we're always hungry. You didn't have breakfast or lunch today. Belwyn says you will never finish growing unless you eat your vegetables."

"Odd words from someone who raided the cookie jar last night."

"Drobba chip cookies always make me feel better. It's like medicine."

Opaline and Caliste strode into the room. Mellypip salivated when he saw the tray of scones, jam, clotted cream, and butter Opaline carried! There was no drobba, but the blackberry jam looked yummy.

"We thought you might be hungry since you didn't come down for breakfast or lunch," Caliste said, arranging the cups and plates. "Cathal would be miffed with me if I let you fade away."

Mellypip tugged at her braid. "See! You can't starve yourself because you're sad."

"I'm not sad," Runa said.

Opaline fixed everyone a cup of tea and added three heaping spoons of sugar to her cup and sat down. "You may feel like pining away, but think of what skipping meals does to poor Mellypip. Why he barely had the energy to escape Dabiro this morning."

Caliste drew Runa off the bed and toward the table with the scrumptious looking scones. "Now eat something, young lady!"

Mellypip hopped up to the table and tied a fluffy white napkin around his neck. "Can I have both clotted cream and jam?"

Opaline grinned indulgently. "Of course, Melly." She fixed plates for everyone, including the familiars.

"How is she?" Runa asked softly, nibbling at her scone. "I've only seen her twice since she awakened, but it was from a distance."

"She's stronger every day," Caliste assured her. "Liat and Yllia are constantly at her side helping her recover. Raghnall brewed some tonics to help her regain her strength. She asked about you."

A glimmer of hope brightened Runa's eyes. "She does?"

"Of course she does," Caliste assured her, taking her hand. "She's lost so much. Her husband and all the years you were growing up to be such a wonderful girl. You should be so proud, Runa, not sad. You saved your mother. I'm not sure what happened, but you saved my sister and best friend. It was just a shock for her to see her only child so grown up. You were a baby the last time she saw you. She loves you very much."

Runa's bows furrowed in thought. "I just want to know her. Has anyone seen Striker's spirit since she woke up? My mother still has my staff. It's fine. I want her to keep it. I just wonder if Striker is still with us."

Caliste brushed her hand against Runa's cheek. "Your staff still bears the imprint of his panther eyes, so I believe he is still with us, but you and Mellypip were the only ones to see or speak with him."

"And Grimm," Opaline added, scratching under his chin, much to his delight. "You may have another special familiar ability. You told me about how fast you can run, which was amazing when you described to me how you traveled across several lands until you reached Skarros. Some familiars have two special magics."

Grimm hung his head. "I would rather possess magic which did not involve talking to ghosts. They're very demanding."

Despite his frequent glumness, Mellypip noticed how happy Grimm was when he was with Opaline. The morose wolf finally found a home and friendship, which made Mellypip glad for his friend. He had such a lonely beginning.

"Rualla clings to your staff like a luck charm," Sanura said, lapping clotted cream from her saucer. "She takes it everywhere."

"Because of Striker," Runa nodded sadly.

"Because of you," Caliste said. "I don't think it's just because of Striker. Give her time."

"Can I take a scone to Rono and Darkleaf? Mellypip asked.

"I think you should take two, one for each," Caliste offered and wrapped two scones in a napkin, tying the ends securely. "Now take these to them, but do not stay out long. It's dark and cold outside. Be careful."

"I will." Mellypip promised.

"I'll go with the little wampu to ensure his safety," Grimm offered. "I would like to say goodnight to Rono too."

"You're very sweet, Grimm," Opaline said, stroking his back. "I know Melly will be safe with you."

"Wanna come?" Mellypip asked Runa, hoping she would finally leave her room.

"Not right now, but give Rono and Darkleaf my love."

Mellypip took the wrapped scones in his mouth and left, sad he could not convince Runa to come with him. Grimm followed him, keeping pace as they ran through the door flap for the outside. The snow had begun to fall, very pretty, but he shivered in the cold as he darted toward the stables. Inside, Myrsalian was busy making sure the stable was warn and secure with some magical warming stones and special protection spells.

Mellypip dropped the bundle. "Hi Myrsalian. Where's Felisia?"

"Inside, on her favorite perch near the fire. Damned weather is upside down."

"Belwyn blames Obsydia. During the ancient Bloodstone Era, weather was crazy all the time. He blames the evil. I think it might have made him extra cranky too."

"Don't stay outside too long," Myrsalian cautioned. "The evil lurking about now has affected more than the weather. Look after Melly, Grimm."

"I will guard him," Grimm promised.

"I'll be in soon," Mellypip promised.

"Hi Melly!" Rono cried, happy to see him, eagerly flapping his wings in his large stall, which was next to Darkleaf's.

"Calm down, Rono," Darkleaf gently told him.

"I brought you some goodies," Mellypip offered, unwrapping the scones and tossing one to each. They chewed their treats happily as Mellypip climbed up to sit next to Rono, balancing easily on the gate.

"Is Runa still upset?" Darkleaf asked.

Mellypip plucked at his furry toes, which were damp from running across the yard. "She's a prisoner in her own room, afraid to see her mother for fear of what will happen. Runa refuses to leave her room, except for potty breaks. Then I am her lookout. She doesn't come down for meals. Not even drobba helps."

"I'm sorry," Rono said sadly. "I wish we could do something to cheer her up."

"Nothing works. I tried to convince Runa to find some fresh spells to hunt for Jadon, but she's upset about him too. I know she still loves him. I wish Jadon would just come home. Runa doesn't care if he's cursed or looks funny."

Rono looked away, shaking. Mellypip stroked Rono's beak to soothe him. "Rono, what's wrong? Are you crying?"

Rono's words were broken as he blubbered uncontrollably. "I can't lie. It's wrong. We must tell someone."

Darkleaf stomped his hooves. "Rono, you promised. Stop balling!"

"But it's not fair! I can't keep lying to my best friends. And Runa needs to know!"

"What's happened?" Grimm asked directly. "When Rono is upset it takes hours to calm him down. Tell me what you're both hiding. We cannot keep secrets in such dark times."

Darkleaf hung his head and muttered. "Very well, I'm weary of secrets and young ones making things so damned difficult."

"What is it? Mellypip demanded.

"We found Jadon in the deep woods several miles from here some days ago, but he refused to come home," Rono sniffled.

"He's where?" Runa's cold voice stunned them all.

Shocked into silence, they turned to see Runa, her face a mask of fury.

Darkleaf hung his head. "I'm sorry, Runa. Jadon is sick too and refused any help. I can't reason with him.

"He's living in a cave all alone," Rono added. "He must be sad. I know I was sad when I was all alone until Grimm found me."

"I can't believe you would not tell me!' Runa cried.

Mellypip tried to think of ways to calm her, but, a strong whiff of magic in the air distracted him. He rushed to the door to see. Belwyn flew out into the night sky in the snowfall, dancing on the air toward another grey owl sweeping down, shimmering with sorcery.

"What is it?" Grimm asked Mellypip, standing by him protectively.

"Cathal is back!" Mellypip shouted.

~ * ~

Images of faces blurred before Koll's eyes as he studied the many mirrors in the chamber. Rimmed with twisted dark wood or rich ebonite, the black glass was a mystical window into unsuspecting lives observed by a dark queen. Which would be a sacrifice or demon warrior for her? Which would be discarded? Obsydia walked through the chamber of mirrors, robed in crimson velvet, exploring each potential victim. The scent of dark mystical power radiated throughout the vast chamber in the new tower. Xabral adored this new place, and was currently crawling through each floor to savor each taste of evil it offered.

"Do you plan make more demon warriors?" Koll asked.

"Not at this time," she whispered. "What I am seeking is more important." Obsydia paused before a black-rimmed mirror, and pointed. Koll saw a deformed woman in rich clothes and a sullen face. "See this woman? Her name is Hadrial. She would have been a queen, but a childhood disease crippled her legs. It even marred her beauty, causing the muscles on the left side of her face to droop, making her ugly and lopsided. The standing law of her country requires rulers to be in perfect health without any deformity, so her younger sister took the crown and left her delightfully bitter."

"She is the elder sister of Queen Sarabia, from whom I retrieved the Scythe of Rygon. It would give me pleasure to inflict pain on her for you."

Obsydia's sinister expression alarmed even Koll. "Oh, pain will be only a fraction of Sarabia's punishment. All my enemies will suffer torment that only an Eternal can conceive. Hadrial could be converted to my holy cause. Through me, her beauty and vitality could be restored, and I could punish Sarabia a hundred-fold with the same ailment, making her hideous. Hadrial hates her sister and despises her love and care. Such bitterness can be molded into something new and deadly. She will be easy. Perhaps we could join her with one of our loyal houses."

"Are you thinking of Levandius?"

"It would be so simple. Marriage was denied Hadrial, so she would eagerly wed, especially a handsome Emperor. It's time Levandius took a wife and joined their kingdoms against our enemies. Visit Levandius. Use the mirror of shadows. Inquire about his health and see how he is coping. He is weak and could falter. I want him watched carefully. Inform him to prepare for an imperial journey to Thema and offer his heart to our ugly princess."

"And if he resists?"

Obsydia's chilling voice was frightening. "Inform Levandius royal hearts are sacrificed just as easily as common ones."

"I will ensure his cooperation. The alliance would be advantageous. The Ivory Kingdoms are west of Thill and Thema is south. Thill would be bordered by enemies."

"We must recruit more royals to fight beneath my banner. Thill is a large country, but its ruler Caladynn is staunchly sworn to serve the good. Perhaps we could influence important nobles within Thill itself."

Koll considered this. Many of the powerful temples in smaller realms had taken power. The legions were growing, but the cause needed more influence. Obsydia's plan for the Obsidian Wars was large scale. Intent on world domination, it required the eradication of current ruling houses or conversion. "We are in the early stages of war, my Dark Queen. Most of the royal family would be useless to even try to bring into the fold. Their loyalty to the Light is well established. However, I sense potential in Prince Morydonn. He hates magic and resents his brother. His jealousy of Caladynn is well known."

Obsydia frowned and gazed up at him with silver eyes so beautiful, he had to pause before he spoke. "His brotherly may be the seed we need."

"Morydonn hates me more than he hates magic. Your direct influence may be required to compel him. Your cause is to destroy all magic in this world. If we could tempt him, show him Darkness is the true path, not Light, as we desire above all else to abolish magic in this world."

Obsydia watched Morydonn in the shadowy mirror, sitting alone in a chapel, his expression angry. She closed her eyes as though she could see into his soul, which Koll believed was possible. "See how he does not even kneel to his gods? His faith is weak. Morydonn hates his place in life, resents his brother. He even lusts after his brother's wife, though he has kept this secret for years. Nothing brings him comfort. He despises his wife. I will visit him, first in his tormented dreams, speaking words of enticement to bring him to our side. You are right, Koll. His hatred of his brother is strong and he merely pretends to be loyal. He is ambitious and full of envy. Such men are easy to pick. He will fall."

Obsydia walked to a different small mirror, where a sad woman in rich velvets sat alone in her chamber, weeping as she did her needlepoint. "I have also watched Morydonn's wife, Faustine, and see her unhappiness like a ripe fruit. She has desires hidden in her heart we should coax out. Their marriage was arranged. Morydonn never loved poor Faustine. She is vulnerable. Her life is a shell of duty and false smiles. She does not even have the comfort of children. He prefers to pray in the chapel for a son rather than bed his lonely wife."

"Can you truly convert both so easily?"

"I have trapped more difficult prey in the past. Made them worship me. Die for me. I will visit their dreams. Shadow their sleep with images of me, their true living goddess! I will tempt them. Offer the fruit of dark salvation they can achieve only through me. It will be easy. It will be almost like play."

"A powerful ally in Thill will bring you closer to victory. What is your command for me?"

Obsydia commanded, "Give Levandius my orders. Then journey to Hadrial and show her the power of Darkness. I will visit Faustine, Morydonn's sad wife."

CHAPTER 9

Runa ran to the door, tucking Mellypip under her arm. *Grandpa is finally back! Thank heavens, I was so worried. He'll know what to do. Maybe he'll talk to Mother for me. She'll listen to him.*

I'm glad he's back too, Mellypip communicated.

The two owls briefly danced on the night air and then flew away toward the front of the house.

"I wonder if Neelam and Surya returned with him," Mellypip wondered, wiggling in her arm.

"I'm sure they did, unless they were needed in Ironia. I'm just glad he's finally home," Runa said.

Rono and Darkleaf stood sheepishly in their stalls, their heads down. "What about them? You're not mad at them, are you?"

"No, not really, but we'll need to discuss Jadon later," Runa said.

"Oh dear," Rono whimpered before bursting into tears again.

"Don't cry, Rono!" Runa begged. "I'm not mad at you."

"I'd better stay with Rono," Grimm said, looking back at the upset gryphon. "Tell Opaline I'll be in soon. Don't be too angry with Rono and Darkleaf."

Runa's face softened and she stroked the wolf's back. "I know they meant well. I'm just frustrated."

"An emotion I know all too well," Grimm said. "Go inside. I'll look after them."

Excited, Runa hurried toward the house, shaking off the damp snowflakes from her shoes before coming inside. *I'm so glad Grandpa is back. I've missed him. He'll understand about Mother and what to do.*

And maybe Belwyn will be less crabby with Cathal home again.

You do like to dream, Runa laughed.

The living room was crowded with happy sorcerers and familiars welcoming Cathal and Neelam home.

"Grandpa Cathal looks overwhelmed and Neelam just looks grumpy," Mellypip said. "I wonder what's inside the huge satchel Neelam is clutching to his chest."

"He always looks grumpy," Runa said, and gasped, seeing Riva and Buzzy slumped in a chair by the fire, exhausted. "I didn't know you were with Grandpa! We've been so scared for you both. She hugged them both. "Can I get you anything?"

"Just need a rest, then we'll get something to eat," Buzzy said slowly. "We cannot stay long, but it is good to be here."

"Are things as terrible as they say in the Ivory Kingdom?" Runa asked in a low voice.

"It's worse than you could imagine. We call it the Red Empire now," Riva replied. "But there are people resisting the evil."

"Did you see Darcus? We haven't heard from him. He was looking for his sister, Abbess Eshra."

Riva became sad. "I know. We found each other by accident when Darcus stepped into one of my sorcerous traps. Redstorm got a chuckle out of it. Yes, he found Eshra and the sisters. We have been with her since the Abbey was burned down."

"I can't believe they burned the abbey. Is she alright? Did all the sisters escape?"

"Yes, and two brave soldiers you know helped us rescue them. Pol and Korun."

"Yes, I remember them. They helped me so much. They served Darcus before they were knighted by Tarsicius."

"Well, now those boys are outlaws like the rest of us who resisted the darkness. They rebelled against Levandius and came to the sorcerer house and warned us to leave. It was in the nick of time too, because men came with torches and burned the sorcerer house down."

"It's gone too?" Runa said, stunned.

Buzzy nodded and curled up closer to Riva. "Sadly, yes. I will miss our home. Magic is outlawed. It's so odd. After the abbey burned, we all banded together. We have a camp we move around to avoid capture. Darcus tried to convince her to come with him, but Eshra refused. Darcus is not happy about it. We traveled back together by the way, but he had to stop off for little Raven, and deliver some children Eshra rescued."

"I will pray for them all, the children, the sisters, Pol and Korun." Runa said. "When you see them, give them my love."

"I will. They need it. We all do. Those sisters are as tough as any seasoned soldier," Riva said. "Never anger a nun, for those gentle women are fierce when the cause takes them. She sends her love too, Runa. Magic is much needed there now more than ever. I need to keep an eye on things for Cathal in the west. Help the sisters. I promised Darcus to help look after Eshra and the sisters. The place may have fallen to evil, but pockets of rebellion are rising everywhere. Now go see your Grandpa."

In the crowded room, Runa made her way toward Cathal, embracing his wife Yllia, and she held back, giving them a moment. She was about to run into his arms, longing for the comfort of her grandfather's solid warm embrace, when Rualla ran down the stairs and threw her arms around Cathal's neck, sobbing, "Oh Papa! Papa, I'm so glad you're home. I needed you, Papa."

Cathal held Rualla, stroking her hair gently. "It's alright, love. Papa is here. No one can hurt you now."

Runa stepped back and quietly retreated into the kitchen and sat down at the table.

"But you wanted to see Grandpa Cathal?" Mellypip said.

Opaline followed her and took her by the shoulders. "What's wrong?"

"It's all right," Runa said. "My mother needs him more than I do right now." She burst into tears, feeling foolish and selfish at the same time.

Opaline stayed with her and Mellypip, hugging Runa as she wept. No words passed between them, and none were needed.

~ * ~

Koll walked through the mirror of shadows into Levandius' private apartments. Darkly lit, the reception room's lush gold and bright velvets contrasted with Obsydia's dark beauty gracing an entire wall, the portrait framed by candles burning with scarlet light. Xabral slithered behind him through the mirror, and bowed before her glorious image.

Two warriors outfitted in black leather stood guard before the imperial bedchamber. Demon-touched by their red eyes, they bowed to Koll and opened the double doors and stood aside.

Levandius nearly jumped when Koll entered. "You should have been announced!" the new Emperor complained. "How dare you arrive in such a manner without my permission!"

"I require no such permission from you. Do not bite the hand which lifted you up so high, for it also holds the sacrificial blade." Koll's cold reply closed Levandius' mouth.

Levandius gaped openly at Koll's velvet and ebonite arm. "I see you have a new arm. It seems so real! The jewels are quite lovely. Does it hurt?"

"Pain means nothing." Koll extended it, curling the velvet fingers and feeling the dark sorcery course through his body, causing spasms of pain because of the contamination from Cathal's light. He was becoming used to its bitter mingling. Pain was devotion, and his devotion was for Obsydia, so he endured. "It can break you or give you strength." He picked up a golden cup and crushed it like paper in his grip.

Blond hair limply fell over his eyes as he lowered his head, shaking. "My allegiance lies with Obsydia, Koll. I know I wear the crown at Obsydia's discretion." Robed in purple velvet and barefoot, Levandius shivered in his sumptuous chamber like a caged mouse. He did not reek of the drugs he used to take, but looked dreadful. "Why are you here, Koll? Am I not obeying your orders? I have done everything you asked! I banned all other religions but the Dark Trinity! I've embraced Obsydia as my true goddess. I reject the pollution of drugs and alcohol for her as commanded. I've razed every religious house not aligned with our dark cause. The temples run red with sacrificial blood. Isn't that enough?"

"It's never enough," Koll replied, flexing the artificial hand which breathed with strange life. "You must be strong to serve the Dark Trinity, to worship at the feet of a living goddess. It is an honor infidels will never understand. Why are you closed away like a monk? Why does the Emperor snivel like an old woman? This is the new Red Empire; your empire. Is our sacred trust in you misplaced?"

"No, Koll! It's not misplaced. I live for Obsydia's glory. I am worthy of your trust. I swear!"

"Then rule like an emperor. Do not cower like a peasant," Koll advised.

"My guards frighten me. Their eyes are demon red and they stare at me!"

"They were chosen to protect you," Koll answered.

"I'm still afraid." Levandius crawled onto his vast bed and whimpered, holding his knees and rocking. "People hate me now. They no longer cheer when I go out in public. Rebels tried to assassinate me so often I'm afraid to leave my room, much less my palace! My food tasters keep dying because someone is always sneaking poison into my food. I've executed or sacrificed most of my council and dozens of noble families for treason. Now everyone hates me. I am alone."

"All rulers are alone," Koll tempered.

"But they've all deserted me. Me! The rightful emperor! Even members of my imperial dragon knights have forsaken me. There's rioting in the city. There are food shortages. Kingdoms once allied with us now threaten war. Ironia closed its borders to us and banished our ambassador. Thill is downright rude to me. King Caladynn not only recalled his diplomats, but cut off our trade, and refuses to acknowledge me as the rightful Emperor. He's even given my bastard sister and brother sanctuary. Their whore of a mother must have laughed. She never liked me. It's very humiliating."

"What's humiliating is your weakness. They are enemies! Heretics who must die," Xabral hissed. "You never practice diplomacy with enemies—you kill them!"

"But I fear I'm losing my kingdom!"

Koll's anger snapped. "Fool! Do not trifle with these infidels who blindly follow light and its weak ways. Soon Ironia and Thill will fall to the Dark, as will all of your enemies as long as you keep faith. Do you doubt Obsydia and her power to see our victory in the coming Obsidian War?"

Shaking, Levandius looked away. "I will never doubt Obsydia. I worship her. I wear her ring." He kissed it with quivering lips.

"Yet, you moan and throw tantrums like a brat," Koll said. "A king is friendless except for his wits and his sword. Discard your weak mantle and embrace the blood and darkness. There you will find strength. When the war comes, we will strike without hesitation or mercy. Those who are against us will die in battle or as offerings on the sacrificial altar for Obsydia's glory."

"How? When I can't even trust the servants in my own palace?"

"Stop whining to start," Xabral hissed.

Levandius wept openly, wiping his runny nose. "It's too hard. I can't do this alone.

Xabral coiled, shaking his stinger. "Koll, can I bite him?"

Koll indulgently stroked Xabral's black and red scales. Levandius' words opened an opportunity to bring up the proposed marriage he came here to discuss. "You won't have to do it alone. Queen Obsydia's not only building an army of great strength for the coming war, but she also thinks of her obedient servants. We want you to expand your imperial territory to show your power. You should take a wife."

Levandius sniffled, "A wife? Why do I need a wife? I prefer the devotion of my concubines. Whores demand little but gold from me."

"A ruler should be married, not only to ensure the imperial line, but increase his power and holdings," Koll replied.

"Who is it?"

Koll smiled. "Thema's queen."

Levandius brightened. "Queen Sarabia? She's rumored to be one of the most beautiful women of the world! Thema is a powerful southern kingdom with an impressive navy and army. Princes and kings have courted her for years."

Koll shook his head. "No, not Sarabia; her sister, Hadrial."

Levandius frowned, flopping against silken pillows. "Not Hadrial! She's rumored to be a most hideous woman. She's deformed. No one wants her."

"She will be beautiful. She will also be queen. Your queen. Sarabia will not rule for long. Obsydia will see to it. Trust in your goddess."

Levandius' voice was a whisper. "What must I do?"

"We will travel there together when the time is right, but we must prepare the way, so to speak. Start building an army for the coming holy war. Lead the Red Empire to glory for *Her*. Recruit every able-bodied man who can fight. You have legions still loyal to you, Emperor Levandius of the Red Empire."

"I rule the Red Empire," Levandius murmured like a prayer.

"Yes! And you possess a great navy," Koll said.

"Yes, power. Men, ships. And I can make them do what I want. I have great power. Armies and ships whose sole duty is to appease my desires."

"Indeed, you rule a vast kingdom," Koll whispered. "We ensured this power for you. Now use them. War is coming fast, Levandius. Why else would you even need these great legions and ships if not for war to destroy your enemies? But you must be ready. Consult with the dark priests and warlords I placed in your temple. They will guide you until my return."

Levandius grabbed his robes as he turned to leave, his eyes pleading. Are you sure she'll be beautiful?"

"Her beauty will devastate," Koll promised.

~ * ~

Runa tossed and turned, unable to sleep. Opaline snored softly in the next bed, oblivious to her wakeful turmoil. Grimm curled up on a thick blanket at the foot of her bed, sleeping fitfully. The events of the day scrambled her thoughts. Thoughts of Jadon filled her thoughts. After hours of struggle, she knew what she must do. She turned over and Mellypip's painful squeak startled her.

Sorry Melly!

You've rolled over on me twice so far, Mellypip complained, scooting deeper under the quilt.

Runa cast a spell, which tingled Mellypip's nose and he poked his head out from beneath the quilt. *What are you up to now?*

Nothing. I just cast a silence spell so as not to disturb Opaline or Grimm.

Maybe you should cast a spell to silence her snoring. It's deafening some nights.

Don't be mean. I'm just going to the stables to talk to Darkleaf and Rono.

But we're not supposed to leave the house when it's dark. Belwyn's orders!

They know where Jadon is, Melly! I've done what I can for my mother now, but she does not need me. I'm a stranger to her, and until she wants me, I can do nothing no matter how much it hurts. But I can help Jadon. He's all alone and I am done with his stubbornness!

Mellypip's large round ears folded back with suspicion. *What are you really up to?*

A rescue! Darkleaf and Rono admitted they know where he is. Rono can fly me there. Darkleaf will go with us. Jadon will need to ride home after all. And they fly so fast, no one will miss us.

But it's against curfew! We're not even allowed in the backyard and you want to go into the deep woods! It is dark and cold out there. Belwyn will chew my hide!

He'll never know we're gone. Before you know it, Jadon will be back home with us, where we can look after him. He's sick, Melly.

Let's slip away during the day.

Runa shook her head. *Too many adults watching us.*

With good reason!

She slipped on her boots and grabbed her trousers and a tunic. *You can stay here, Melly. It's alright if you don't want to come.*

I'll come, but you need to put on the ring he made for you. If you are going to extremes, wear his ring. It may help convince him you still care even though he is cursed.

Runa took the wooden ring she kept hidden away and put it on. *Happy?*

Yes, now put on your heavy cloak. It's bitter ass cold outside.

Melly, such language!

Belwyn uses such language too, Mellypip grumbled, jumping down to the floor. *And who can hear us? We're using the bonding to speak and you just cast a silence spell on the room. And if I'm going to be locked away forever for disobeying curfew, I might as well swear.*

Goodness, the cold does make you cranky.

CHAPTER 10

A cold wetness startled Opaline from her sleep. Grimm whined and nudged her, licking her face until she pushed him away and rolled over, pulling the blankets over her head. "Grimm, it's still dark, go back to sleep!"

"Wake up!" Panthara commanded, throwing off her warm layer of blankets and quilts.

The chilly blast of air and Panthara's presence stunned her. Opaline bolted upright, bleary-eyed and confused. "Damn it! What's wrong? Why are you in my room?"

Panthara pointed to Runa's empty bed. "Runa is gone."

"What? She's gone?" Opaline gasped, staggering out of bed.

"Why else would I be in your bedroom?" Panthara snapped, holding a drowsy Azmadu in her free arm.

"Where's Melly?" Opaline asked, looking around the room. Runa's bed was rumpled and empty.

"We assume Mellypip is with her," Panthara said. "Grimm woke up and found them missing. He couldn't wake you, because of a silence spell Runa obviously used to sneak out. Also, you sleep like the dead."

"When I couldn't wake you I fetched her sister," Grimm explained. "Anyone else would have raised an alarm. It would bring trouble for Runa, Mellypip, you, and even poor Rono. Panthara woke easily, though Azmadu was not happy to be disturbed from his heated rock."

"It's cold," Azmadu shivered, wrapped in a shawl.

Opaline looked at Panthara quizzically. "How did you remove her spell?"

"My sorcery once opened a mystical doorway to the Other-world, unleashed the Wraith Guardians, and summoned my father's soul. Do you think breaking such a trivial enchantment would be challenging for me?"

"No, but you are." Opaline stumbled in the dark until Panthara cast light with a wave of her hand. Grabbing a shawl from the foot of the bed, Opaline rubbed her eyes and tried to think coherently.

"How long has she been gone? What time is it anyway?"

Panthara looked at Grimm. "Is she always this slow?"

"She does not wake easily," Grimm confessed.

A combination of anger at Runa and annoyance with Panthara fueled Opaline's temper. "How could she do this? Cathal's going to be livid, I don't even want to think about Belwyn's reaction."

Grimm grabbed her boots and dropped them at her feet. "Then hurry up. Tonight Runa found out Darkleaf and Rono knew where Jadon is hiding. He's sick too. She was upset, but I assumed she would talk to them about it tomorrow." Grimm's head drooped. "Especially, since poor Rono was so distraught, it took me half an hour to calm him down."

"They knew where Jadon was?" Opaline gasped. "When did this happen?"

"Maybe you could conjure some coffee?" Grimm moaned to Panthara.

"We've no time for this," Panthara said tightly.

"All right, don't push your majesty." Opaline dressed and pulled on her boots. "Did you check the sorcery chamber? She often goes there when she's upset. So does Melly."

"Yes," Panthara replied. "Neelam was up there and he was very odd. He wouldn't let me in. Told me he was working on something important and slammed the door in my face. When I was queen of Mowad, such insolence would have condemned him to a deep and dismal dungeon."

"Did he suspect anything?" Opaline asked.

"Would you like to debate this or find Runa before the sun rises?"

"We could debate how tetchy you are," Opaline countered. "We can take Rono or Darkleaf to look for her."

"They're gone too. I suspect they are with Runa. I checked the stables when I found Runa and Mellypip missing," Grimm said.

"Hurry," Panthara demanded. "I do not care if she is punished for breaking curfew, but Koll and Obsydia would seize an opportunity to capture or kill Cathal's precious granddaughter. She's a foolish child."

"Runa's only four years younger than you," Opaline remarked.

"But I ruled a country while she still played with dolls."

"While Koll groomed you for darkness," Opaline shot back.

"How will we follow her without perytons or gryphons? I can't fly. My sorcery hasn't advanced to such levels."

"I'll conjure flying shadow mounts," Panthara offered casually, taking a spare cloak from Opaline's chest. "Mind if I borrow this?"

"I should be able to help track her by scent," Grimm offered.

"Even though she flew?" Panthara asked.

"Yes," Grimm replied.

"Are you sure Grimm can keep up?" Panthara asked, heading toward the door.

"He'll keep up," Opaline replied. "Grimm's speed is amazing when he summons it."

"At least someone is quick," Panthara, casting her own silence around them as they rushed down the stairs and out the backdoor into the cold.

"How long will it take you to conjure your magic horses?" Opaline asked, stomping her feet in the snow. "And perhaps a warmth enchantment is called for."

Panthara's sorcery spun two gorgeous blue and black steeds with smoky manes and luminous wings. Opaline gritted her teeth, jealous of her sorcerous skill, though she would never admit it.

"Let's go," Panthara called, leaping up gracefully on her mystical mount.

Opaline eagerly mounted, excited to fly on such a wonderful creation.

Two snowy wolves and four angry owls burst from the shadows, circling them. Opaline inwardly cursed. Not only Belwyn and Felisia, but her mother and grandfather. She winced when Felisia dropped on her shoulder. "Foolish girl! What do you think you are doing?"

Two of the other two owls shimmered, transforming into Cathal and Myrsalian, and Belwyn alighted gracefully on his arm. "What is going on?"

Panthara dismounted her mystic steed, which vanished at the wave of her hand. She faced Cathal without artifice or excuses. "Runa and Mellypip are missing because she thinks she knows where Jadon is. Grimm was going to track her for us."

Sirah transformed from her wolf shape and stepped into the moonlight, Arial at her side. "We already know Runa's gone. We have been searching for her. Opaline, how could you be so foolish to think you could go after her alone at night and in this weather?"

"It was my idea," Panthara confessed.

"I don't care whose idea it was," Cathal said coldly. "Go back inside. We'll find her. With Koll and Obsydia free in this world, your actions were very risky."

"Please Mother, we only wanted to—" Opaline protested until Sirah's frosty stare silenced her.

"Let me help track Runa and Melly," Grimm offered. "I can be useful."

"Very well, you may come with us," Sirah agreed. She turned to Opaline and Panthara. "You girls go inside and stay in your rooms. I will deal with both of you later."

Grimm sadly looked at Opaline and she knelt down, stroking his head. "It's alright. You go find my friend."

Cathal shapeshifted into his owl form and flew off with Belwyn. Sirah shimmered into a white wolf and ran with Arial into the night, Grimm following. Opaline watched them disappear into the night, frustrated and cold. Myrsalian and Felisia waited to escort them inside.

Panthara turned to Opaline. "I told you to hurry."

~ * ~

Obsydia studied Faustine through the scarlet haze of the mirror. She touched the glass, parting the mist to see within her thoughts. She hunted through Faustine's memories as she slumbered alone in her bed. A lonely life full of bitterness and a distant husband who ignored her. Faustine's life was quite dull, virginal even, in its solitude. She entered an arranged marriage when she was only fifteen. Prince Morydonn never wanted her but did his duty to marry her as his king and brother commanded, which is a virtue he always boasts, though his virtues are pathetically false, resenting every act of obedience. Yet, Faustine loved Morydonn. Faustine slept deeply, stirring only slightly as Obsydia probed her dreams.

"Enjoy your sleep of innocence," Obsydia whispered. "Soon it will be corrupted."

Shroud looked on, smiling hungrily. "Even I sense her soul's lonely bitterness, so concealed in pious obedience. This human will be simple to sway, Queen Obsydia."

"Yes," Obsydia whispered, "humans are fragile playthings. One must be careful not to break them too early. Her conversion is crucial to bringing Thill into the fold. This kingdom is a key strategic power for the Light. We must take care to offer Faustine the most beautiful lies. What of my claw maidens?"

"They are preparing the way in the east, killing sorcerers and followers of cursed light. It is minimal damage, but they enjoy the practice."

"Yes, they must keep sharp for the coming war."

"Would it not be easier to send them to Thill?" Shroud asked. "Your claw maidens would gladly kill your enemies most efficiently."

"I need more than a few enemies dead, but the control of the country through the puppets we choose. Things must be done with care. Have my maidens found traces of any dragons yet?"

"No," Shroud sighed. "Forgive us, but the dragons seem to have vanished."

"Oh, they are still with us, but hidden somehow. After the dragons have scattered, I could not see them in my mirrors either. Something is protecting them."

"The Winged Fey?"

"Those mutant creatures are hidden also," Obsydia said bitterly. "I cannot see them even with the power of my Father's gifts. Even Cathal and Neelam have become shadowy figures in my mirrors."

"They use foul magic," Shroud spat. "Cathal needs to die. He leads the way, and is dangerous to Ahridum's plans."

"Cathal was always a dangerous boy," Obsydia whispered. "So lovely and pure. He was immune to my charms. When I could not convert him, I tried to destroy him. Yet, he lives on all these centuries later. The Light blessed him for a reason, which is why he became the scion of light who imprisoned me. He must pay for his sins against me. Until then, we must tread carefully with certain enemies. I have special plans for Cathal, when all is lost for the Light. For now I will let him be, his focus is blinded by his family. While he is attending to family matters I am building my circle of power."

"Ahridum's love will guide you," Shroud assured her. "His dark hand will ensure this world will be yours. You are his only daughter, a living goddess born of Ahridum's touch on a mortal woman. You were chosen for this. You will rise in glory for Darkness."

"And my enemies will perish in fire and blood," Obsydia smiled. "Until then, we must plan each step. When Koll returns, send him on to Thema. Hadrial is the next key to securing our territories and blocking Thill. He can convert her easily."

"I obey, my Queen of Shadows," Shroud bowed and departed.

Obsydia enjoyed the pet names Shroud bestowed upon her. She also enjoyed the friction between Koll and Shroud. Both were proud, powerful, ruthless, and devoted to her alone. In many ways, Shroud reminded Obsydia of her first demon handmaiden, Shade, who served her when she first woke from her dark enchanted sleep of thirteen days after she was born in this strange world. Her father was an Eternal, born of chaos and shadow. Her mother, a human consumed by Ahridum when he chose her to be his dark bride. Obsydia was born with one purpose, to curse this world with darkness and destroy all light. Immortality was not enough for her. When her father truly possessed this all, she dreamed of her reward. Her moment of rapture when her father would finally strip this mortal shell from her, and raise her up, a full Eternal, and welcome her to the mysteries of his Shadow Realm at last.

Turning to the matter at hand, Obsydia closed her eyes, sending images of dark promise to Faustine. The gift of children, warm and alive in her arms. The elevation of her husband to King of Thill, and his adoration of her, wrapping her in rich furs and jewels, holding her in his arms in the night. She watched happily as Faustine wept in her sleep, tears of joy and terror. A few more nights of dreams, and she would visit Faustine. A meeting which would result in Faustine's worship of Obsydia or her death.

~ * ~

You're angry, Belwyn communicated as they flew above the dark forest against the wintry winds.

Of course I'm angry. Runa should know better! Cathal snapped.

The young never know better, Belwyn said, broad wings sweeping across the cold air. His keen eyesight tracked Grimm's sprinting across the snow through the trees, ahead of two white wolves. *Your women are upset, Cathal. Rualla cannot cope with the fact she's lost fifteen years of her life. She was denied seeing Runa grow up. She lost Striker. Her husband. She cannot face her own daughter. Just because the curse is broken does not mean the problems are fixed.*

I know! I'm at a loss. All I could do is hold her and tell her everything will be all fine, which is bull, since none of it is fine. It's all hellfire unfair and terrible. I know Runa is acting out of frustration, but it does not excuse her actions.

I remember when you acted out of youthful frustration.

Are you suggesting Runa goes unpunished? Cathal replied.

No, she needs to learn a change of command. Be strong, no matter what she says. War is coming. I'm only suggesting there are odd extenuating circumstances. Runa's been going through hell since we left our tree tower. What happened with her mother was hard for her to take, and she's confused. Rualla is confused. It's a bloody mess. I knew it was a mistake to leave our tree tower and I was right.

You love saying that.

Well, I was right, wasn't I? But if we hadn't left, we wouldn't have freed Rualla and Yllia from the tree of bones Koll trapped them in all those years ago. I'm glad we have our family back, even though we're broken.

I really hate it when you're right, too.

Am I ever wrong? Belwyn asked. *Runa suffered without understanding what was happening to her. Her nightmares tormented her. She was kidnapped by demons, offered as a sacrifice, which was topped off by losing Jadon to a weird demonic curse meant for her. Now her own mother refuses to even speak to her. It's a bit much for a fifteen-year-old to always behave rationally even in the best of times. These are not the best of times. Grimm mentioned Jadon was sick. We have no idea what hell-bitch did to him.*

You've been listening to Neelam way too much, Cathal remarked, feeling the strain of the long flight. His wings were tired, he had a headache, and longed to be on solid ground again.

They stopped, Belwyn said, diving for the earth.

Relieved, he followed Belwyn down to the snow-crusted forest floor in front of a cave. Sirah transformed into her human shape, and waited with Arial and Grimm. Darkleaf and Rono met them at the cave's mouth.

Cathal shapeshifted quickly and strode toward them. "Is Runa here?"

Solemn, Darkleaf said, "She's inside with Jadon."

Rono crouched next to Grimm.

Be strong, Belwyn told him. *She still needs to know what she did was wrong.*

I know what to do, Cathal said through the bond, marching inside the cramped, chilly cave, lit only by a small fire in the middle of the earthen floor. On the ground lay Jadon, his demon face contorted with pain and fever. Mellypip clung mutely to Runa as she knelt by his side, holding his hand.

Runa looked up at Cathal, eyes swollen and red from crying. "He's dying," she choked, shaking with grief. "I don't know what to do, Grandpa."

Be strong later, Belwyn advised.

CHAPTER II

Opaline paced around her small room, brushing her long braid with nervous fingers. "I hope Grimm is okay. I wonder if they found Runa yet. I feel so foolish."

Panthara sat in the chair, stroking Azmadu's head. He snored blissfully, oblivious to the tension in the room. "Walking in circles will not help. Do they always send you to your room like a five-year-old?"

"Mock our ways, Your Majesty, but you're also confined with me, which is in some ways a punishment itself."

"I concur," Panthara grinned. "Though you're not the only one suffering."

Opaline clenched her jaw to prevent a scathing insult from spilling out. She took a deep breath, restoring her grace as she had when she was a Princess of the Ivory Kingdoms, dealing with aggravating issues such as unwanted marriage negotiations and her spoilt half-brother, Levandius. "You're right. I'm not child anymore," Opaline said. "I should not be treated so. My mother should realize I'm a grown woman. I think I'll tell her when she returns. Right now, I desperately need some hot tea and cookies. Let's go to the kitchen." She marched to the door and flung it open. Gabriel barred her way, standing in the doorway, staff casually crooked in his hand.

"Please step aside," Opaline requested. "I wish to speak with my mother."

Gabriel smiled gruffly, and leaned on his staff, towering over Opaline. "Sorry, it's not possible, as your mother and grandfather both tasked me to insure you two mischief-makers stay in the room.

Namir poked his head in, eyes imploring. "Please, we do apologize, Opaline. Truly. But we have our orders, so we would appreciate your cooperation. I'm sure your mother will see you shortly."

"This is nonsense, I'm not a child and refuse to treaty with a hulking ruffian like you." Opaline tried to squeeze past Gabriel, but his muscular build took up most of the doorway. She tried pushing him aside, but he would not budge. "Let me pass!"

Gabriel remained steadfast. "I don't take orders from you,

Princess."

"And I don't take orders from the likes of you!" Opaline said through clenched teeth.

Panthara stood up and walked to the door. "Enough! I'm a sorceress, and can employ magic to leave this room should I choose to do so."

"Nope," Gabriel said simply.

"You dare defy me?" Panthara whispered.

Azmadu, jostled awake by the argument, growled. "You leave my Panthara alone."

"Careful, Panthara has a temper," Opaline warned. "You could end up as a cockroach or an earth worm. Once, she opened a rift to the Otherworld and hordes of wraiths flooded in, snatching souls. It was terrifying."

"Even an inexperienced sorceress like Opaline once turned an enemy into a troll," Panthara added. "She wasn't even trying."

"Yes, when Priem attacked me! I still tremble when I think about it. He was working for you too," Opaline remarked.

"I never liked him," Panthara said.

"Really? Most impressive." Gabriel remarked, "If we're keeping score ladies, I once faced down a horde of over a hundred dark priests and temple guards with only a dagger, my magic, and poor old Namir at my side." He reached down and stroked the leopard's head to his obvious delight. "I killed almost every one of the bastards and saved the lives of many innocents, mostly children they had lined up for sacrifice on their bloody altar. And I wasn't even sober. Imagine what I could do sober?"

Sirah appeared behind Gabriel, disheveled, face flushed from the cold. "It's alright, Gabriel. Thank you."

Gabriel stepped aside, but remained at his post. Sirah threw off her cloak and sat wearily on one of the beds. She looked exhausted.

"Mother, did you find Runa and Mellypip?" Opaline asked.

"We did," Sirah replied. "She found Jadon too. He's very ill. For now, I need you to behave and promise not to run off anywhere without permission." She looked at both Opaline and Panthara. "I need this promise from both of you."

Opaline bowed her head, feeling very much like a little girl who displeased her mother. "I promise, Mother."

Panthara nodded, glancing away from Sirah's stern stare. "I give you my word."

"Good," Sirah said. "Now go help Runa. She needs both of you. They're carrying Jadon up to the last bedroom. I'm going to fetch Raghnall. Thank the gods he's still here."

"I'll carry the boy," Gabriel offered. "My hulking presence should serve a purpose."

Opaline blushed at her words, but softened when he looked over his shoulder, smiling.

"Be ready, for there will be a special meeting tonight," Sirah said.

"About what?" Opaline asked.

"I cannot tell you now," Sirah answered, "but it is urgent. You will be summoned to the sorcery chamber. Words are dangerous now, and we must be frugal with what we say in public. The eyes of the enemy can reach the most unexpected places."

Opaline and Panthara ran down the hall, stopping when Gabriel met them on the landing, carrying a delirious Jadon in his arms as easily as one would carry a feather.

Opaline took Runa's hand in passing. "He will be alright. Raghnall will make him well. You'll see."

Runa nodded, but she looked horrible. Pale and eyes swollen from crying. Mellypip looked frightened, and clung to his sorceress.

Raghnall met them inside the room, medicine bag in hand. "All right folks, clear out. I need to examine my patient. You too, Runa. Get some food and sleep."

"I want to stay," Runa insisted.

"Not now," Cathal said, guiding her to her own room. "Do as Raghnall says. Panthara, Opaline, can I trust you both to look after my granddaughter?"

Opaline and Panthara both nodded. Cathal led Runa toward her room.

"We will make sure she stays inside," Panthara said. "First, we need to arrange a hot bath and some food. Then sleep."

"I'm not tired," Runa replied. "Really, I'm not."

"Don't listen to her," Mellypip warned.

"I won't," Panthara said. "And I can make you stay in your room. A sleep spell will do wonders for keeping you in line."

Runa gasped. "You wouldn't!"

"I can do a lot of things," Panthara promised. "Just be glad I'm not evil anymore."

Rualla burst into Runa's room and stood over Runa. "What's wrong with you? Are you mad? What possessed you to do such a thing? Koll is out there!"

"She's safe now," Cathal comforted her.

Rualla turned and left the room without another word. Cathal closed the door.

"Goodness, such an outburst," Opaline gasped.

Weary, filthy from hard travel, and hair a wild tangle, a glimmer of hope lit Runa's eyes. "I know. She actually spoke to me."

~ * ~

Abbess Odelia and Sister Danu walked Darcus and Raven to the abbey gates. Redstorm followed, more docile than usual in the presence of the sisters. In the distance, the children they rescued played in the courtyard.

"Thank you for taking them in," Darcus said. "My sister will be grateful they are in a safe place. I fear more will be needing shelter in the future, not only because of war, but what is happening in lands under the blood knife."

Odelia nodded, primly keeping her eyes downcast. "I will send letters to all the holy houses to ask for their assistance. We will do anything to save the innocents. Poor poppets. Bless your sister for her sacrifice and we will all pray for her and the sisters of her order."

"I will speak to my father," Danu offered. "I know he would want to help save children from such wickedness. We can arrange for shelters, food, and clothing for refugees. We will miss Raven. She's such a sweet child."

"Has she spoken at all?" Darcus asked.

"Not yet," Odelia replied. "But she smiled like the sun when we told her you returned."

Darcus shifted her in his arms and brushed back Raven's hair. "I will take her to my new home soon. But now, I want her with me. I'm not sure what is going to happen. There have been some new developments. For now, the sorcerer house is safe as any." He mounted Redstorm, securely holding Raven in front of him. "Take care sisters."

"Good day, sisters!" Redstorm said, taking a running leap, spread his wide crimson wings and took flight.

~ * ~

Koll studied Hadrial in the mirror. The princess kept to her private rooms, and did not mingle with her ladies. Even in her room, she kept her face covered when someone else was present, even her sister, Queen Sarabia.

Sarabia visited her, offering genuine affection and a sisterly kiss. Hadrial accepted the embrace, though Koll saw her body was stiff and unwilling to return Sarabia's love. Even through the mirror he sensed her bitter hatred of Sarabia.

"Dear Hadrial, we are holding a banquet tonight. Please come and sit by my side. I told them to prepare your favorite dishes."

"I have a headache," Hadrial said. "I wish to be alone and rest."

"Shall I send the physician?" Sarabia offered. "You're often unwell and I'm concerned."

"No, I will be fine, Sister. I just need to be alone." She turned away, keeping her face veiled.

"You need not hide from me," Sarabia pleaded, "Or anyone. We all love you."

"I know and I am grateful."

Such hollow words, Koll thought. After Sarabia departed, her supper was brought. Hadrial dismissed her servants. Only when they departed, did she remove her concealing scarf, exposing her face. Evidence of beauty once possible remained before childhood disease had ravaged her face and afflicted her legs with partial paralysis. Most did not survive the disease, which was brutal in its fever and quick death. Highly contagious, one of her servants infected her when she was only seven, destroying her looks and her future.

"It may have been wiser to let her die," Shroud remarked. "Such a waste to keep something so useless alive."

Koll shook his head. "Hadrial will serve our cause, giving her existence value for the moment. See now half her face looks like putty stretched down, and the other side is firm and fair. She limps when she walks and hates life. She embraces her life as a recluse and not even her sister is welcome in her private hell. She sits alone in her sumptuous chamber, devoid of mirrors, hating everyone. She might have been beautiful and queen of a great kingdom, but for the disease."

Shroud squinted her eyes. "I don't see it, but all humans look alike to me."

Xabral looked at Hadrial, bored. "She possesses neither glory nor the illustrious stamp of darkness. But I am spoiled, for I see the beauty of the shadows all around me here."

"Your snake is flirting with me," Shroud remarked, but allowed a cold smile.

"He likes the claw maidens. He misses Chimera, I think."

"She was glorious," Xabral agreed, his raspy voice sad. "She perished in glory too. Still, Cathal swung the death blow. He must pay for her death."

"Cathal will pay for his sins against us," Koll promised. "Now let's see if I can offer this princess a revenge of her own."

Eager, Xabral begged, "May I come? Please!"

"Another time," Koll said. "Hadrial may not appreciate your magnificent beauty."

Xabral shook his stinger. "But she's so homely. Her face is saggy."

"Which will serve our goals to convert her to the Dark," Koll added. "Now, watch as I offer her the temptation of a new life, replete with beauty and Thema's crown."

The eye of shadows became liquid shadow as Koll stepped through. It was easy to find a sliver of shadow in Hadrial's room, with all the drapes closed to shut out sun and life. She reclined on a silken couch, oblivious to his presence or anything else but her misery.

"Hail, Queen Hadrial," Koll spoke, striding toward her. "Your destiny awaits you."

Koll sudden intrusion shocked Hadrial. Terror stunned her into muteness for a heartbeat, her clumsy flight on unsteady feet caused her to stumble and fall. He knew what was coming next, and a flick of his fingers cast a shield around her.

"Guards! Help me!" she cried.

"No one hears you," Koll whispered, standing over her. "My power ensures we will have a private conversation."

"Who are you? What do you want with me?"

"What do you want, Princess?"

"I don't understand what you want or who you are," Hadrial shouted, tears flowing. "I am nothing. It is my sister you want. She is the queen, not me."

"But you would have been queen, if not for the disease which ruined your beauty. What if you could be beautiful? What if you could rule as is your right?"

"You are mad, though even I sense you must be a sorcerer. Not even magic can make me whole again. Nothing can."

"But you are wrong. There are powers which can transform you."

She shifted by the couch, remaining on the floor, but no longer bound by fear. Curiosity aroused her interest. "You called me Queen Hadrial. Why?"

"Because you were born to be the true ruler of Thema. Have your gods of light shown you any mercy? You were firstborn, destined to be queen, until disease took your beauty and weakened your body." Koll reached down and pulled her to her feet. "Light cheated you. Now your younger sister rules in your place, adored, beautiful, and powerful. You live like an old crone, bitter and full of bile."

"It is the law," Hadrial whispered. "The rulers of Thema must be whole in body and mind. I cannot change the law."

"You can change your fate, if you can see the Darkness."

"Who are you?" Hadrial demanded, jerking away from his grip. "I command you tell me."

"I am your salvation. I offer you the redemption of shadow. Obsydia's blessings are bountiful."

"Obsydia? The Bloodstone Queen? She is evil! The books and priests all say so."

"She is Darkness, but not evil. She is the true path."

"No, go away!" Hadrial wept.

"I will go, if you wish, but first let me show you what the Dark offers." He took her arm and pulled her toward the dressing table. Before there had been no mirror there, but now a rich mirror framed in ebonite stood. Koll shoved her before the glass. She covered her face with her hands. "Look, Queen Hadrial, if you dare to see the truth."

"No!" she cried.

"Look!" Koll commanded.

Hadrial dropped her hands as she gazed at her beautiful reflection. The mirror showed her face as whole again. A golden crown floated above her head, glittering with jewels. Voices cheered her, crying her name with adoration, "Queen Hadrial."

"See what Darkness offers," Koll whispered in her ear. Her emotions exposed on her naked face, he sensed how the temptation of beauty and power affected her very soul. Years of isolation and envy roiled inside of her, rupturing her resolve. She touched her face, her tears streaming. Finally, the resolution of her choice. Hadrial straightened and lifted her head, dropping the silk scarf she had hid behind her whole life.

"What is your price, Sorcerer?"

CHAPTER 12

A strange potent scent, ripe with magic, woke Mellypip from heavy sleep. Curled up at Runa's feet, he sniffed the peculiar magic in the house, curious and wary. Tiptoeing across the quilt, careful to not disturb Runa who still slept deeply, he jumped to the floor and scurried over to the window. It was night, but hard to say how late. The sun went away so early now, and Belwyn tried to explain it to him, but his explanation about the seasons still didn't make much sense.

The door was ajar, so he thought he would look in on Jadon and see how he was doing. The halls were empty and silent. *Where was everyone?* He peeked inside Jadon's room, looked after by Raghnall and Baldur. Jadon tossed and turned, mumbling odd words, his strange demonic face contorted with fever.

"Is he better yet?" Mellypip whispered from the doorway.

"The boy's still alive, which is a miracle in itself," Raghnall replied. "How is little Runa doing?"

"Still sleeping. I didn't want to wake her."

"Good boy," Raghnall nodded, waving his hands over Jadon, faint blue beams of magic emanating from his fingers, showering Jadon with the mystical shower. "I added a drop of sleeping potion to her warm milk. Poor girl was a wreck."

"She was worried about Jadon. Will he get well?" Mellypip asked. "If he's better will his curse go away?"

"We'll do our best," Baldur assured him. "He's suffering a nasty bout of bronchitis. First, we make him better. Then we worry about his damned curse. Belwyn said you and Runa should go upstairs to the sorcery chamber when you wake up."

Mellypip nodded. "I'll get Runa."

"Cathal and Caliste are already waking her up," Belwyn said from behind.

Mellypip nearly jumped out of his fur. "How long have you been there?"

"Long enough," Belwyn said. "Come on, up to the sorcery chamber now, Furball." The owl took wing and flew toward the stairs.

"What's going on?" Mellypip demanded, chasing after Belwyn to the top floor of the house.

In the sorcery chamber, everyone in the house had gathered in a circle, mage and familiar alike, except for Raghnall and Baldur. Even Rualla attended, Liat at her side. Mellypip noted she clung to Runa's staff. He wondered if Runa would have to create a new one. Cathal and Neelam, stood in the middle. They murmured amongst themselves, curious for the late summons. There was a large object covered with a heavy cloth. To Mellypip's surprise, King Caladynn, Queen Sorcha, and even Prince Ulric were there too. Mellypip milled through the crowded room, searching for Runa, finding her leaning against Opaline's shoulder, rubbing her eyes. He scurried quietly to her and she scooped him up, snuggling him close.

What's going on? Mellypip asked.

I've no idea, but this is strange, Runa remarked back.

How are you feeling? Mellypip asked.

I feel groggy and cranky. I think my hot milk had more than nutmeg and honey added. Have you seen Jadon? Runa asked.

Jadon is tucked into bed with lots of blankets. Raghnall and Baldur are looking after him. They're using lots of magic to heal him.

Neelam rapped his staff on the floor three times, silencing the voices but not the curiosity. "Thank you for coming. Though Cathal and I have woven multiple layers of magic to shield us from Obsydia's prying eyes, we cannot take chances, so listen carefully."

"What you are about to see must remain secret for now," Cathal added. He lifted the heavy cloth and beneath it was a large oval egg, striations of red, silver, white, and blue shimmering, nested in a circle of heated red stones.

"Oh my gods," Sirah gasped. "Is that a dragon egg?"

"Yes," Neelam confirmed. "Sandhya, the Drajina of the dragon clans, has entrusted us with the protection of her egg."

"Is this egg the next Drajina?" Runa asked.

"Which is why it is imperative we protect it," Cathal said.

"With Obsydia free and threatening the world, we must take precautions," Neelam warned. "The other clans are securing their eggs, the next generation of dragons, all around the world, but the Drajina is entrusting us with her egg. Sandhya is old now. She tells me she will die soon. This egg contains the next Drajina."

Neelam's stern tone echoed. "Until the dragon hatches, this room must remain secure. We will post guards. We will use magic. We have special dragon spells from Sandhya herself to shield not only the egg but us from Obsydia's spying. The bitch is not happy to have lost out on this, so she may even send her cursed claw maidens."

"Claw maidens?" Caladynn interrupted. "What the hell are they?"

"Demon women from Darkness itself, sent to Obsydia by Ahridum," Neelam answered. "Obsydia always had demon hand-maids from the dark realm. Even though they are semi-human in shape, they are supernatural and deadly. They do more than just wait upon hell-bitch, they are part of something more insidious to bring about the end of this world."

"I learned from Sandhya that Obsydia sent her demons after the eggs, to destroy or steal them, but they failed" Cathal said. "Obsydia is moving quickly this time, which concerns us. The dragons have broken hibernation and the clans have broken up, hiding the rest of the rookery for safekeeping. They found me in Ironia."

Neelam flashed a grim smile, leaning on his staff. "It was inter-esting to see really. The Sovereign and Queen of Ironia did not know whether to rejoice or fear for their lives when a thunder of dragons landed in their courtyard."

"Why did they go there?" Sirah asked. "Rapiveshta Island is far away from Ironia."

"They were looking for Cathal," Neelam answered.

Neelam and Cathal exchanged glances. Cathal shrugged and replied, "When I was a boy, during the Bloodstone Wars, Obsydia used a mystical poison in an attempt to kill all magical creatures and folk. The dragons were the first who fell to her dark poison and they nearly went extinct. I helped develop the antidote for it, and saved the dragons. When we gave the dragons the antidote, inadvertently, I also happened to save the next Drajina when Obsydia's demons tried to destroy the last rookery. She hatched right before me after the demon was killed, and we bonded."

"Bonded?" Myrsalian asked.

Yllia smiled broadly. "When dragons are first hatched, they are rather helpless and tend to bond with a particular dragon, or in Cathal's case, a person. It was adorable really. Fortunately, they grow fast."

Belwyn chuckled and Cathal blushed, wincing. "Well, the baby

Drajina I saved was Sandhya. They made me a dragon friend. It involves magic, a mental bonding, so they can more or else find me anywhere."

"When do you think the egg will hatch, Grandpa?" Runa asked, curious about the shimmering egg. "How do we care for it? What do we feed it?"

"She will hatch soon, from what Sandhya told me," Cathal replied. "Fortunately, we have two special guardians who will be staying with us to help us care for it."

Mellypip eagerly climbed to Runa's shoulder, longing to touch the magical egg. "Guardians? What guardians? Who are they?"

"We are they," answered a small, long, black dragon, appearing from the shadowy corner of the room. "I am Fallon."

Another black dragon joined Fallon, as if appearing from nowhere. "I am Talon. We are rookery guardians."

"And brothers," Fallon added.

"Where did they come from?" Runa gasped. "They're beautiful!"

Seeing a dragon of any clan was rare, especially this close. Mellypip was transfixed. He read a lot about dragons, but never thought to actually see a real one. The black shadow dragons were the smallest of the seven clans, and though they could fly, they were adept at tunneling, and apparently, were official egg sitters. Large luminous eyes and long like caterpillars, these two were only about four feet. Their movement was fluid with iridescent skin, not scaly at all. He knew this would make a great tale in his bard book.

"We blend into the background when needed," Fallon said. "We have many little magics."

Azmadu was beside himself, wiggling in Panthara's arms. "They're dragons, just like me."

"I think your familiar has delusions of grandeur," MacTabbish remarked.

"Hush, Azmadu," Panthara scolded. "We want to make a good impression, don't we?"

The sound of Neelam's staff rapping the floor silenced them. "Now, we have a duty. While we fight Obsydia and look for a means to destroy the bitch for good, we keep this egg safe no matter what."

Melly, real dragons! And there's going to be a baby dragon hatched right here, Runa sent to him, her sorrow and worry broken for a moment by her excitement.

And the dragon egg will need brave protectors, Mellypip thought back, wondering where his blue cape and staff were.

~ * ~

In the dimly lit hall of mirrors, Obsydia watched the mirrors in frustration, fury creasing her fair face. "I cannot see Cathal, nor his friends. It is like the dragons, they have disappeared." Black mists burst from her hands and lips, clouding her perfect beauty.

Shroud waited patiently until her mistress calmed. The mirrors where she sought Cathal and the dragons reflected only shadows now. "Remember, the dragons marked Cathal as friend, so they must have already allied. Your handmaidens are working on shattering their mystical shields. Let it be. They matter not, for they are mere fragments of what we plan, Queen Obsydia. Not all the magic in the world can change what is to come."

"We must take the next step. My Claw Maidens will be needed for some tasks."

"Will they start the ritual now?" Shroud asked.

"Not yet, but soon. We have other strategies to initiate first. Here, stay with me, Shroud until Koll returns from Thema. Let us watch this mirror. I have been waiting for this. It should be enjoyable. We may need your assistance though." Obsydia waved her hand over a different mirror, revealing Faustine. "We too have allies no one knows of. And more are to come."

~ * ~

Morydonn was furious. As he paced in his bedroom, his face a black cloud.

"What is wrong?" Faustine asked, entering with a tray.

"My brother the King is in conference with the mages again. I am not invited of course."

"You hate magic," Faustine said. "You make no secret of it, so be glad to be free of them."

"Caladynn's hiding things from me."

Faustine handed him a cup of mulled wine. "Drink this, Husband. It will soothe you."

"How can it? Dulling my senses solves nothing. Magic is bad enough, but for one of our family to marry a sorceress is intolerable. A bastard sorceress at that! It will bring shame to us all. And I know my brother is hiding something from me. Me! I am his blood."

"He never appreciated you," Faustine said. "You have sacrificed much to support your brother."

"Do you know what he told me? Ulric is going to propose to the sorceress whore, Opaline. He and Sorcha actually approve of this abomination. She's a bastard and witch. Even Tarsicius banished her from his realm when he learned she was cursed with magic."

"Sirah's daughter? Sirah, a whore and slave from the Rygon's temple, before Tarsicius brought her and made her his official whore. The old emperor rightly banished Sirah when her magic emerged. She was a common concubine. Opaline is just another bastard slut with delusions of nobility. Tarsicius was never a friend to Thill, but perhaps he should have been. We have much in common with the new emperor."

"You're unusually talkative, Wife."

Faustine stood in front of the tall oak-framed mirror, brushing her hair. "I only speak out of concern. We have been married so long, yet we hardly ever talk."

"I did my duty when I married you," Morydonn said. "As did you, for the good of your family. Marriage to a prince of the House of Rhule brought prestige to your family."

"Was your duty so distasteful? Am I hideous or misshapen?"

"No, of course not, but our marriage was part of a peace treaty with a rival house. I never claimed to love you."

"No, but I was offered as your personal reward," Faustine smiled. "I want more than resentful obedience." She put the brush down and faced him. "If anyone has a right to be bitter, it should be me."

She touched his cheek and he brushed her hand away, noticing a ring of black stone set in ebonite and circled with tiny rubies. "What's this? A new bauble to ease your loneliness?"

"It's just a ring. A bauble of obsidian stone. It's the new fashion. I think it suits me."

"Jewels are a woman's weakness."

"I am not weak. Perhaps it's because I have been silent for too long, Morydonn. I know I was not your choice for a wife. You rarely spend time with me. Court functions do not count. What about me? Do you ever think about me or my feelings? You speak of family loyalty and nobility, but I know you secretly hate Caladynn. The

House of Rhule is an ancient noble line, but its throne will not be inherited by you. Caladynn's sons are next in line since Danu took the veil. Your brother is a blessed man, but only because he was born first. He is a king of a powerful country. He has a loving wife, children, and the devotion of his realm. You are just his younger brother, the spare heir, doomed to be a footnote in history."

Morydonn kicked an elegant velvet chair over and grabbed the wine, downing it in one gulp. He set down the empty glass and refilled it. "Caladynn has everything and I have nothing but the crumbs from his table."

"You can become more than a footnote. With my help, we can achieve greatness. I am devoted to you. Now I ask you do me the same courtesy and show me a fragment of the same devotion. We could have so much more, more glory than you ever imagined," Faustine whispered, stroking his thick, muscular shoulders. "I am your wife. Let me be your wife, your helpmate. Let us work side by side to create something wonderful for us. Our own kingdom. Our own destiny. And children! I want children, Morydonn."

He turned away in disgust. "You've been drinking."

She stepped in front of him and refused to move, stubbornly lifting her chin. "No, I have not been drinking. But I did have a revelation. I hate magic, as you do. It's unfair they should have such strange powers. It must be unnatural. What if someone powerful hated magic and wanted to destroy it? Would you make an alliance with those who thought like you? Your brother is blind to the peril of sorcery and it will be his undoing."

"You speak treason!"

"I speak the truth. There is path which hates magic as much as you do. It's the path to the glory you were born to follow."

"What are you talking about?" Morydonn stumbled, blinking. "What's wrong with me? Was there something in the wine? Have you poisoned me?" His knees buckled and he clutched his head.

Faustine knelt at his side, stroking his hair. "No poison, my beloved, but a draught to make you pliable so you will listen. We're going to visit someone very powerful. She hates magic too. She wants to eradicate magic from the whole world."

"What are you talking about? Are you mad?" Morydonn cried as he fell onto his back, helpless.

Faustine stood and faced the mirror. "He is ready."

The mirror glowed, changing from silvered glass to a shaded mass as Shroud stepped through the mirror. She picked up Morydonn as though he weighed no more than a child, and carried him through the smoky mirror. Faustine followed her husband into the darkness, smiling.

CHAPTER 13

I hate this, Mellypip grumbled, dangling from the brittle thin tree branch, praying it would not break. He tried to hear what Opaline and Ulric were saying below, but was uncomfortable spying on them. Concealed from sight by being several feet above their heads and camouflaged by dead leaves stripped of their green by wintry winds and snow. The dried leaves tickled his nose. He waggled his whiskers, hoping to avoid sneezing and exposure to the censure of Opaline.

What's going on? Runa prodded. He looked across the yard to the house, where Runa safely waited in her room, peeking through the curtains.

I can't tell. I think he's kneeling.

Really? What else?

Opaline is crying. I think he's giving her something shiny.

Do you see what he gave her? What is she saying? Runa exclaimed.

I'm cold.

Opaline said that?

No, me. I said it. I'm cold! You're a sorceress. Surely you know a spell to spy on them. I do protest, since you're spying on your best friend. I feel dirty as a troll. I want to go inside and have hot drobba. Why are they freezing outside instead of being warm in front of a fiery hearth? Has love made them crazy?

They're out here because they want privacy. Now listen to what they are saying!

True, all the mages tended to stay close to home now with the dragon egg in their care. The house was crowded and often noisy now, even though Riva left a few days ago, heading west again to help Eshra and the sisters. He would miss Riva and Buzzy. Darcus returned, which made him so happy. Darcus tried to distract Runa from her worries about Jadon and her mother by engaging Runa in her fighting practice again. This time Opaline cheered from afar rather than taking up the practice again. She was prone to black eyes. He supposed even princesses were clumsy. Darcus also brought little Raven with him. She was still a silent child, but everyone doted on her. Even Rualla was drawn out of her shell and made her special treats and read to her since Darcus helped keep dragon watch. He knew this hurt Runa, but she was trying to brave about it.

When Ulric showed up today with a serious but eager face, formally asking permission from Sirah to speak with Opaline, Runa became very curious, almost giddy with excitement. Opaline quickly changed her gown and brushed out her hair, pinching her cheeks as she ran down the stairs to meet him. Runa watched them, happy for her friend, and it made Mellypip happy too. Prince Ulric was nice. Runa had been sad and frustrated for so long, he agreed to throw away his gallant ranger principles to spy on the couple in the garden when she asked him.

As it turned out, Mellypip was not alone in spying. Most of the other familiars were hidden about the snowy garden. Dabiro hid in the bushes. MacTabbish lay flat in the grass near the tree, but he thought the marmalade cat had fallen asleep. He was sure someone was snoring. Sanura was secreted a few feet away, crouched by the hawthorn tree. Pointessa watched from behind a stone birdbath. Grimm was in the open with Opaline, sitting nobly while Ulric declared love and promises. Apparently, human mating involved marking territory and mating rituals, according to Dabiro. Grimm knew he was watching, for nothing escaped the wolf. He had glanced up and saw Mellypip clinging to the tree limb, and shook his head. Grimm did not expose him because they were friends.

Felisia landed on the same branch he clung to, her delicate little talons gripping the fragile wood which made it droop further. Her golden eyes glared suspiciously. "What are you doing?"

Mellypip was about to plead, but a dangerous sneeze erupted, throwing him off balance. The reedy branch snapped. Felisia took wing, but Mellypip plummeted toward the cold earth, screaming. Right before he hit the ground, he just stopped, floating magically an inch about the snow. Opaline and Ulric, briefly entwined in a lover's kiss, burst apart.

Belwyn flew down and landed next to Mellypip. "It's a good thing I keep an eye on you, Furball."

"Mellypip! What do you think you're doing?" Opaline asked.

Ulric was laughing so hard he doubled over and Grimm howled up at the noon sky.

"Trying to satisfy a female's whim," Mellypip moaned, cradled by the invisible magic. "And failing miserably."

"We always do," Belwyn replied.

Dabiro grunted, poking is head up, not even trying to hide anymore. "Hey, what's happening? Are they going to mate or what?"

~ * ~

Koll sensed Hadrial's anxiety, but was resolved to be sympathetic with her, at least on the surface. Secretly, he wanted to slap her and force it down her throat. The promise of beauty he showed her in the mirror was an illusion to convert her. It was not a lie. To become beautiful, throwing off the shell of the deformed and ugly, she had to drink the potion and swear fealty by putting on the ring. Yet she delayed.

Does she know about the potion's price? Xabral asked.

Most of it, Koll replied,

Hadrial sat in front of the mirror, clutching the vial of red liquid. It reeked of sorceries not born of this world, but harvested from a distant darker realm. Koll did not brew this potion, the claw maidens did, circled around a cauldron of stone, chanting ancient words of power. The ring gleamed on the vanity, as yet untouched. She must put on the ring. Then Hadrial would belong to Obsydia. The potion would give her what she wanted, the beauty denied due to a crippling illness.

She is taking her sweet time, Xabral remarked, impatient. *I thought she wanted to be beautiful. Why does she dawdle? Humans are exasperating.*

Patience, my sweet snake, Koll said. *She is afraid of change more than of evil. Humans are weak, but want to be coddled even when they sin. The seed of evil within her is not yet bloomed. Hadrial will drink it. Then she will be ours forever.*

"Will Levandius come to me soon?" Hadrial asked.

"He longs for you," Koll assured her. "His love for you is beyond word or deed. He will soon be at your side. You will be queen not only of Thema, but empress of the new Red Empire. You will part of a marvelous new world."

Hadrial looked at Koll, her voice eager and desperate. "Will she suffer, as I have suffered?"

"More than you could ever imagine," Koll whispered in her ear.

Hadrial uncorked the bottled, her hands shaking. "I will be Queen."

"Yes, you will rule Thema. Your people will worship you, for your wisdom and beauty. I promise you beauty, power, and love. But in order for you to receive the bounty of Obsydia's gifts, you must drink and put on the ring. The potion gives beauty and health. The ring will be a symbol of your devotion to Obsydia. Even Levandius wears such a ring as a sign of his devotion."

"Then I will drink. Obsydia shall be my only goddess. Thema will no longer be our patron goddess." She extended her hand and Koll put the ring of obsidian stone upon her finger.

Sarabia knocked on her door, calling out, "Hadrial? Are you awake? I thought we would dine together. May I come in?"

Hadrial held the vial to her chest, clutching it. "Come in."

Koll and Xabral simply slipped behind the door to her closet when Sarabia entered.

I see why Hadrial is so jealous of her sister. She's ravishing for a human. The epitome of beauty so splendid even the gods would be jealous.

Koll agreed, peering at them from the shadows. *Her beauty is her undoing, and our benefit.*

"What's in your hand?" Sarabia asked.

Hadrial looked at the vial and then at her sister's perfect face. "Just a healing draught."

"Are you ill?" Sarabia asked, concerned. "Should I send for a doctor?"

"No!" Hadrial snapped. "Please go. I don't want your pity."

"You are distressed," Sarabia said. "I cannot help you if you will not tell me."

"Tell you what? How an illness deformed me. You stole my crown. I should have been queen, not you!"

"Hadrial! Stop this."

"You've always been the beautiful one and I'm the ugly one! Well, now you will know how I suffered. You'll be the ugly one now." Hadrial drank the potion down and threw the vial to the floor.

"What have you done?" Sarabia asked, now suspicious of her sister.

"I changed the rules," Hadrial cried, doubling over in pain.

"Is it poison!" Sarabia asked. "Oh my dear, you didn't."

"No, she did not," Koll said, stepping into the light.

Sarabia's dark eyes flashed with hatred. "Koll! What evil have you done to my sister?"

"Nothing, but she has done evil onto you."

Sarabia suddenly fell to her knees, crying in pain as well. "What is this? I feel so strange. Guards! Guards!"

"They cannot hear you," Koll said. "No one can. I made sure of it. Soon you will be like your sister, only more hideous. She will be queen."

"I will kill you," Sarabia promised as she writhed on the floor by her sister.

Koll's looked down on Sarabia, Xabral coiling at his feet, enjoying the suffering. "Many have promised but all have failed."

~ * ~

Secret meetings in the middle of the night never bode well, Belwyn thought to Cathal as they gathered around the kitchen table with Sirah, Caliste, Myrsalian, Iona, Darcus, Yllia, and their familiars.

It's more than half the house and hardly a secret, Cathal remarked. *Anyway, best to do these things when the children are asleep.*

Neelam uncorked a tall, amber-colored bottle and poured spirits into several glasses. "This whiskey should warm you all up."

"I must decline," Darcus said. "I am on guard duty in an hour. I never thought I would help protect a dragon egg."

Cathal accepted a glass from Neelam and downed it in one swallow. "Shame, Darcus. Dwarven whiskey is always the best. Fiery as a red dragon's breath."

"You would know," Belwyn said. "A fire dragon almost toasted you once."

"It was an accident," Cathal explained. "Things get confusing in battle."

"Battle is simple," Gabriel said, taking a glass of whiskey eagerly. "You split a few skulls."

Namir gazed up at Gabriel. "Just limit how much fire you drink. Your skull hasn't recovered from your last bout."

Sirah poured Darcus a mug of coffee and handed it to him. "I made a fresh pot for you, Darcus. There will also be plenty for Gabriel should he require its healing benefits."

"Are the girls sleeping?" Neelam asked.

Yllia took a whiskey for herself. "Runa and Opaline are sound asleep, finally. They talked for hours about Ulric's proposal."

"Are you sure it's a good idea to approve of their betrothal," Myrsalian asked. "Opaline is so young. Ulric is not a mage. When he is old, she will still look as she does now."

Sirah took Myrsalian's hand, squeezing it. "I know, Father. Opaline is too young but at the same time she is more mature than many girls her age. Growing up in the court of Tarsicius, she had to face more than most. But she's in love, and when a girl is in love, nothing can stop her. My daughter at least has a choice. I never had a choice, being a slave and concubine before my magic manifested. We have no idea what will happen. I want her happy."

"In case we fail and Ahridum inherits our world?" Cathal asked.

"I have faith we will win," Sirah said. "Though, even I admit I have morose thoughts about the future."

Welcome to my perch, Belwyn thought to Cathal.

You're always gloomy, Cathal replied.

I'm a realist. Especially when dealing with evil.

Yllia's sympathetic smile concurred with Sirah's words. "As a mother is it hard to protect your children in such times. Rualla is too frail for any of this. I am glad Liat and Caliste are here."

"How is Rualla?" Neelam asked.

"She is better, but she does not tell me much," Caliste said, holding Sanura in her lap.

"Does she still have Runa's staff?" Cathal asked, concerned.

Yllia nodded. "It gives her strange comfort. I wish she would talk to Runa." Yllia put her face in her hands. "So much is happening at once. I feel all turned around, though not from the whiskey. I never thought we would have to fight Obsydia again."

Sirah helped herself to shot of whiskey. "We already know what Obsydia is planning. She wants to give the world to darkness and we must destroy her."

"I love your simplicity," Neelam grinned. "But have you ever wondered exactly how Obsydia is going to make this a world of darkness for her bloody father, Ahridum? Why is it the dark lord needs followers? He's an Eternal." Neelam asked.

"I'm not sure what you mean," Darcus asked.

Neelam leaned back in the chair. "I mean, exactly how? And what does it really mean and what are the consequences if hell-bitch wins. Ambera warned us if Darkness wins, all ages will be of Darkness; if Light wins all future eras would be of Light. It won't eradicate all evil of course, not as long as there are people in the world. In the old days, Ambera talked like we were pawns in a great and terrible game the Eternals are playing."

"Sounds dreadfully unfair," Sirah said. "And rude."

Surya, perched on the back of Neelam's chair, added. "Ambera was the oracle and we all trusted her with good reason. But not even an oracle knows everything."

Neelam nodded, stroking Surya on the beak. "I think the wars themselves were nothing more than a smokescreen to the true objective. It's happened before. In the last few days alone we have had reports of assassinations, kingdoms once allied now at war, invasions by the new Red Empire. Distractions of chaos, to keep us from focusing on the real task at hand. I saw it during the Bloodstone Wars. You did too, Cathal."

"What are you saying? All the terrible wars and sacrifices cropping up all around us are nothing to worry about?" Liat asked.

"No, they are dangerous, because Obsydia's puppets are causing the wars: feeding the chaos, banning magic and killing mages, blood sacrifices, and political assassinations. It's not an accident Obsydia chooses weak and vain people to rule, because they're dumb and selfish. They do her bidding without question. But, there is a reason behind the chaos, a simple one we will not like."

"Which is?" Cathal asked sharply.

"Obsydia is secreted in some hidden fortress with her demonic maids, far from the madness and war. Because the real focus is there. The truth of what is really happening is there, wherever she is hiding, because darkness likes to hide. Those demon women have a much bigger purpose, but Obsydia is the central jewel to the ritual they are planning."

"This is all for a spell!" Sirah exclaimed.

"To put it simply, yes. Granted, it's only a theory. Darkness wants this world. The Eternals, if you believe all the Holy Scriptures and have read the Gospel of Shadows, there is a similar theme. The dominance of good or evil. The Eternals of Dark and Light have warred since time began, before our world even came into being."

"Are you saying we are fodder for which Eternal power wins this battle?" Gabriel asked.

"What I am saying is we need to think beyond the wars. They have nothing to do with what will happen. We need to find a way to destroy Obsydia before her rituals send us into darkness. Ambera was trying to warn us about this."

"Why don't the Light Eternals help?" Namir asked. "Evil cheats.

Obsydia shouldn't exist in this world, but Ahridum used a mortal priestess to bring Obsydia into our mortal realm."

"Gods are generally not helpful," Belwyn replied.

"What about the Winged Fey?" Caliste asked. "You know them. Can you contact them, Cathal?"

"I've tried," Cathal said. "We did not part well the last we met. They are hidden from me."

"When you punch someone, it rarely does," Neelam remarked.

"They were willing to sacrifice Runa," Belwyn said. "Never an option in my nest."

"We have no idea where Obsydia even is," Iona said. "And even if we did, how could we defeat her?"

"I know where she is," Jadon said from the doorway.

"Jadon, you should not even be out of bed," Cathal shouted, rushing to him before he collapsed to the floor.

Raghnall ran into the kitchen, Baldur roaring after him. "Damned boy slipped by me when I dosed off."

Jadon waved everyone away. "No wait, Listen! I've had dreams. Bad dreams. The nightmares led me to the old Elfsharan lands of our people. It's a dead and cursed country, full of demons and ghostly things. I came back because of what I saw there. A tower has risen in the heart of old Elfshara, a tower of shadows."

CHAPTER 14

Restless, Hinkleburr Crowyn tossed and turned for hours. Neither wine nor a good book helped lull him to slumber. An irksome feeling he could neither name nor shake haunted him. Everything seemed normal here at court. He was reporting back to Cathal and King Arawn using the calling crystal, with Jiana as his liaison. Queen Sarabia was fully committed to the Alliance of Light. He had a lovely visit with the lovely Lady Helga, before she returned to Thill to take up her new duties. King Arawn was pleased with his work. He even got to see dragons in Ironia when they came to find Cathal. So exciting. Cathal had some very interesting friends.

Yet, a terrible feeling of doom lingered. He threw off his blankets, and walked to the window, enjoying the beautiful view overlooking the city. The beauty of twin moons bright in the sky and bright stars gleaming above the capital did not ease his prickly feeling. Throwing on a robe, he tiptoed to the reception room, heading straight for the table where the wine and spirits were kept. Quiet as a mouse, he thumbed through the bottles. *A nice snifter of brandy*, he thought, pouring a generous glass.

The door burst open and several palace guards charged into the room. He dropped his brandy glass, finding himself hemmed in on all sides by guards with long spears, Hinkleburr made no attempt to fight back, but remained still, trying to assess the crisis and dearly wishing he had more alcohol in his blood to bolster bravery he did not possess, but must somehow summon.

"What the hell is going on?" Hinkleburr demanded

"You must come with us, Dwarf," one of the guards said, gruffly pushing him toward the door. "Search the rooms. He has two aides. Bring them along."

"I am the Ironian Ambassador. I demand to know what is going on. You're on Ironian soil when you are in my chambers. You're in violation of a sacred treaty."

"You're under arrest, Dwarf. Is that sacred enough?"

"The correct address is Your Excellency or Ambassador."

They ignored his barb, as the other brutes dragged poor Talwyn and Broda out of their room. The brothers, helpless and weaponless in their nightshirts and bare feet, struggled against their captors. The tall guards laughed as they hurled them to the floor. Broda cursed with a vengeance in their native tongue, curses so vile it was best they did not understand the language.

"Easy boys, let's not rile our guests into more violence. May we at least get dressed?" Hinkleburr inquired.

The brutal shove of a boot to his back answered his question.

~ * ~

Mellypip woke at sunrise, letting Runa sleep as he tucked the covers around her, hoping Opaline's snoring in the next bed would not wake her. He visited Rono and Darkleaf in the stable before their morning exercise, with a gift of apple slices to share. He always liked to visit his friends in the morning. The thrill of the dragons and the egg in the sorcery chamber enticed him. The house was beginning to stir. The aroma of coffee, toasting bread, and oatmeal filled the air. He scurried inside for a quick breakfast. Some of the familiars were already up. Sirah fixed him a bowl of oatmeal and walnuts, and then put down two dishes of meat mixed with leftovers from last night for Grimm and Arial. Pointessa munched on pumpkin and apple pieces, which were her favorites. Dabiro must still be sleeping; else he would definitely be in the kitchen demanding food. Myrsalian gave little Felisia toast and jam, which she ate with dainty ferocity.

Grimm looked at Felisia on the table. "I never knew owls liked toast. I thought you were predators."

"Familiars are magical. We like many things and are not like regular animals of our clans," Felisia explained between bites. "But I can be very predatory."

Myrsalian grinned indulgently, scratching her tiny head. "People who do not understand magic are often confused by what familiars are capable of or what they like."

"You would think because we can do magic, speak human tongue, and live for centuries that would be a clue," Felisia tittered. "But some folk are dense. Once, a homely old woman saw me eating sweets, and insisted I would sicken and die. What a dolt."

Mellypip licked his bowl clean and donned his blue cape. He made sure his staff was polished.

"What are you doing?" Grimm asked Mellypip. "Are you going

to play ranger-mage with Rono?"

"No, this morning I have serious ranger-mage duties. I'm going to help protect the dragon egg."

"Most impressive," Arial complimented him. "Your cape is very dashing."

"Be wary, little Melly. We know little of dragons," Grimm warned.

"Where are you going dressed up in your blue blanket, Furball?" Belwyn asked, flying into the kitchen.

"I'm going to help Talon and Fallon protect the dragon egg."

Belwyn looked at Mellypip quizzically. "Who gave you leave to act as a what?"

"Ranger-Mage," Mellypip finished. "You did yesterday."

"I did?"

"We were getting ready for bed. Opaline kept showing off her emerald betrothal ring and talking—"

Belwyn winced. "Yes, yes, human females get very chatty about such things."

"Darcus said he would be glad of my assistance as a ranger-mage."

"I thought you were a bard?" Belwyn asked.

"A good familiar must hone many talents," Mellypip said seriously.

Belwyn heaved a great sigh. "Very well, go on then. I'll tell Runa you have a hallowed duty. Do not annoy the dragons. If they tell you to go, you go."

"Thank you, Belwyn," Mellypip cried, eager to prove his worth.

Mellypip, staff gently clenched in his teeth, ran up the stairs to the sorcery chamber. Darcus was still standing duty, and the two shadow dragons were coiled nearby, seemingly asleep.

"Morning, Darcus," Mellypip whispered, entering the room. "Are the dragons awake?"

"We are quite awake," Fallon said, suddenly hovering over him. He could tell the difference because Talon's voice was slightly higher pitched than his brother's. Otherwise they were identical.

"Good morning," Mellypip mumbled, startled. "How did you do move so fast?"

Fallon seemed to chuckle, looking down on him with large golden eyes. "Dragons are swift, and shadow dragons are the swiftest of the seven clans."

Mellypip straightened his cape. "I am here to help protect the egg."

"A generous little wampu," Talon said, stretching out on the carpet. "Which is your mage, fuzzy familiar?"

"Runa is my sorceress. She's Cathal's granddaughter."

"Ah, Cathal, is a dragon friend. Our Drajina trusts him. We normally do not trust humans, or anyone else," Fallon said, coiling at the base of the heated nest of rocks. "Darcus is tolerable for a human. He is not afraid of us, which is rare for his race."

"Darcus is the bravest warrior I know," Mellypip said.

"And Mellypip is very trustworthy," Darcus said, smiling. "Have you seen Gabriel?"

Mellypip scratched his head. "Not since yesterday. Should I look for him?"

Talon sniffed him all over with intense ferocity, burrowing his nose deep into his fur. "He is small to be battle worthy, but his soul is valiant. Little fuzzy warrior smells like oats and magic. I like him."

From the corner of his eye, Mellypip saw Azmadu peeking in from the doorway.

"My friend, Azmadu, would like to meet you," Mellypip said.

Fallon nodded, and Azmadu flew in, eager and wide-eyed.

"You should be in a desert," Talon told him. "It's cold in this part of the world."

"I'm from the desert of Mowad. Iona and Panthara made me a heated stone to keep me warm."

"Wise Azmadu, crill lizard of Mowad," Fallon nodded.

Gabriel stumbled in with red eyes and an unshaven face, indicating a long bitter night. When he came closer, the pungent order of ale was overwhelming. Namir was at his side. The clouded leopard looked very sad.

"I'm here to relieve you, Darcus," Gabriel announced.

"I see," Darcus replied, looking him over intently. "I have some special orders for you from Cathal. May we speak in private?"

"Happy to oblige," Gabriel agreed, rubbing his eyes.

"He's drinking heavily again," Mellypip whispered after they left the room. "What's going on?"

"Yesterday, Gabriel was a little sad," Namir answered.

"Why?" Mellypip asked.

"Opaline," Namir confessed. "Tell no one, but he loves her. He knows he's not the right man for her, but when Ulric proposed it affected him more than I thought it would. He was maintaining until after the meeting last night. He finished off Neelam's whiskey and then went to a tavern."

"I'm sorry," Mellypip said, stroking the leopard's head.

"Thank you, Melly," Namir said. "I'm going to watch over Gabriel now. I doubt he will be able to help guard the egg today. He needs me."

Mellypip felt sorry for Namir, and for Gabriel.

Fallon took a turn sniffing him all over. "You are right, brother. Wampu smells good."

~ * ~

Taran's lab was a messy wreck. Piles of notes and spilled ink littered his desk. The worktables crowded with beakers of mysterious potions simmering. Panthara put several potion bottles and vials in a tub of soapy water. "Taran, you really do need to clean your equipment. Your scientific experiments can be quite filthy, and sticky. Not to mention the foul odor coming from the bucket under the table. I still smell the residue of scorch and ruin form your previous experiments in this room."

"My chaos is a sign of a brilliant mind. You're being unusually domestic, Your Majesty," Taran quipped, lifting a box off the shelf. He placed it on the long table and opened it up.

"I told you not to refer to me by royal epithets," Panthara said. "What are those?"

Taran grinned and held up a rusty looking stone. "Sarod stone, from which you can make sorcerer bane."

"Keep those hateful rocks away from me," Panthara shivered. "What are you doing with those anyway? Isn't playing with fire enough?"

"Relax, Highness. These stones only prohibit magic when forged with iron," Taran assured her. "Where's Azmadu?"

"He's with Mellypip and the shadow dragons in the sorcery chamber. He's beside himself with joy. Where's MacTabbish?"

"Eating a late breakfast," Taran replied, laying the smaller sarod stones and thin bars of silver on the table.

"How energetic of him," she smiled. She watched him arrange

the metal with a touch of trepidation. "Should I flee the room now, before fire consumes it?"

"You're overestimating how often my experiments blow up, Highness."

"I told you to stop teasing me" she scolded him. "Anyway, you're a Prince, aren't you?"

"Only by default, since the laws of Tiamet state any child is considered legitimate if the father acknowledged the baby as his, even without marriage. Else I would just be a bastard. It hardly mattered because Levandius frequently joyfully called me bastard to my face when my father was not in earshot."

"Did it bother you?"

"It bothered Opaline. She's protective of those she loves. She also despised Levandius. One afternoon, we were nine or ten, he called us the twin bastards at breakfast when father wasn't there. Opaline chased him with the bread knife and threatened to cut out his tongue."

"Opaline does have a temper," Panthara remarked, laughing.

"Levandius fled and we did not see him at breakfast for some time, even though he was much older and bigger than either of us." Taran put the silver and tiny sarod stone into a marble bowl, He flicked his hand and a flame burst within the bowl." Me, I was not so sensitive. It did bother me when my father told me mother was dead. When I became a sorcerer and faced exile, my life changed for the better. My life is good here. I have no royal burdens, I'm a sorcerer with a plump but devoted familiar, and I'm with my real family. They love me. Father could never love."

The sarod and silver began to liquefy in the bowl at an accelerated rate, blending together in bright colors of red and silver.

"What on earth are you doing?" she asked.

"I have others made for demonstration, but this one has a different purpose. The sarod stone has unusual properties. I discovered a while ago how it reacts to magic depends as to which metal or gem it is forged with. Forge it with iron, and you have sorcerer bane. Forge it with other materials, however, and you get different results. Some I found actually enhance magic. I've found silver and sarod is an excellent conduit for increasing magic. If my theories hold true, a sorcerer could simply wear an amulet of this new metal and it would increase their spell powers. It would also be good for more complex rituals. I've more testing to do of course. It's also rather pretty and unusual."

"This is fascinating," Panthara observed. "With what's coming, we will need all the help we can get."

"I plan to show Cathal and Neelam examples of my work."

"Just make sure there are no explosions."

"Where is Cathal? I haven't seen him or Neelam this morning."

"They're talking with Jadon."

"Is he awake? Wonderful. How is he?"

"He's sickness is better, though his face still demon-cursed. He has information about where Obsydia is holding court. Iona told me to keep Runa occupied until they are done talking. Runa is still abed."

"Runa is sleeping rather late. Unusual for her, though not for my sister."

The sarod and silver stone cooled with a flash of icy magic from Taran's hand. He molded it with sorcery, shaping it into a lovely ring of silver with delicate striations of red. "Perhaps my sister's betrothal is impulsive, but love is rare. It should be treasured, like oranges in December,"

"Very poetic."

He gently touched Panthara's cheek. "Marry me, Panthara. Let's enjoy our love before war and chaos erupt and crush every hope. I love you. I've loved you since the first day I saw you. It's a poor ring for a queen, I'm afraid."

"It's beautiful." Panthara lifted her chin and held out her hand. "Yes, I will marry you."

Taran slipped on the ring, and it fit perfectly. "Now what do we do?"

Panthara whispered, "You should tell your family."

"Even Opaline?"

Panthara laughed, holding his face in her hands. "If she chases me with a bread knife, it's on your head."

Sirah entered the room as they were locked in embraced. They jumped apart, embarrassed.

"Come downstairs now," Sirah said. "We've heard from Jiana in Thema. Something dreadful has happened."

CHAPTER 15

Asheni knelt before the silver cauldron, pouring the water, folding in her green and black wings. She squinted, hating the blinding white caverns where they took refuge after Obsydia escaped. She missed the warmth of the green lands or even the hot red deserts. She longed for the forests and mountains. *"I hate this cold and lifeless ice kingdom. Cold may not harm me, but I will never like it here,"* she thought bitterly.

Asheni stared into the swirling waters until her enchantment created brilliant shades of blue, lavender, and green. Faces and places emerged, some unknown to her, some familiar. Dragons flew across lands far from their home in Rapiveshta. She took this as a dangerous omen since they rarely left Rapiveshta Island and should be in hibernation. Kingdoms across the continents warred with terrible ferocity. The water became blood red as Obsydia's image appeared, startling Asheni from her scrying. She forced herself to watch, noting Obsydia had left the sanctuary of Ahridum's Netherworld fortress to rule from a Tower of Shadow in the old Elfsharan homeland; a country destroyed by Obsydia's dark magic during the Bloodstone Wars. A desolate land where only demons and goblins roamed. Ahridum's tower in the eastern oceans was the one place they could not see. Things have changed. She thought Obsydia would return to her old temple palace in the Wasteland. She took note of this change, thinking it may be important to the others.

The past rushed up, awakening her memories of the Sapphire Age. The Wasteland had once been a kingdom where powerful light magic reigned supreme. She wept, recalling the gleaming white towers and lakes of crystal blue before a dark star consumed it. Once a meeting place for mages of all races, it was a center of mystical power. It had another name once; one only the Winged Fey remembered. They were not so isolationist then. They walked among the people, sharing their knowledge. The Sapphire Age ended when this lost empire of the mages burned, bringing the first era of darkness. During the Bloodstone Age following this calamity, the world suffered storms and upheavals of nature, decimating whole kingdoms in its wake. Obsydia and her demon army rose from the bitter aftermath to wage war. She destroyed the Elfsharan kingdom, not only with battle—Obsydia's sinister magic cursed it too, culling light and life. It was no accident Darkness chose to obliterate these realms of light and magic. Dominions of evil rose in their place. Again, no accident, but a deliberate decree by Ahridum. It must play a part in the end game.

Asheni wiped her eyes, recalling how their tears kept Obsydia contained for a thousand years. Surely, the Winged Fey could still help. She forced herself to watch Obsydia in the present, pushing the past away. On an altar of black stone, surrounded by her Claw Maidens of Ahridum's Netherworld, Obsydia chanted powerful words of Eternal origin. She did not know the language, for it was Dark speak, unknown to those born of Light. The Tower of Shadow loomed like a beacon of doom over a violent wasteland. Each chant expanded the demon country. The image faded and Asheni gasped for breath, overwhelmed by the vision. Then a young girl with green eyes appeared in the water. Her innocence and light emanated like a beacon. She remembered her! Yes, she was one of the three maidens rescued from sacrifice Obsydia's temple palace. Runa—her name was Runa. Granddaughter of Cathal, who had been one of the Scions of Light.

"Dareem, come quickly," Asheni called.

Dareem entered her chamber, his face somber as ever, blue and black wings contrasting with the harsh white background. "What do you want?"

"To show you the terrors happening in the world. I have seen things—"

"The world is nothing to us," Dareem interrupted with a wave of disdain. "Let it be."

"It has meaning for me," Asheni answered. "We should summon the others. Darkness is growing faster than we imagined. It's not like the Bloodstone Age, when the forces of Ahridum moved slowly. Evil is rushing in with ominous force. We should at least hear what the others say.

"Tell them if you wish," Dareem snapped. "What we do has no consequence."

"Ahridum will conquer this world unless we do something. I've seen the Claw Maidens in my vision. Obsydia's power is growing. She has recovered too quickly from her bondage. I believe a long and very detailed ritual has already begun, something even our eyes have never seen. The Tower of Shadow has risen, just as the scrolls warned us. Unless we defeat her now, she will ascend to become a true goddess, and the world will be consumed as our world falls into darkness. We must research the scrolls again."

"The scrolls cannot help us," Dareem replied. "We are immortal, but neither are we Eternal. There is nothing we can do."

"Damn the scrolls. We can act," Asheni insisted, standing before him. "Cathal was right. You chose not to live in this world. But I do want to live in the world. You seek death. A release from a life you hate. Perhaps you should seek life instead."

"I kept my promise to Cathal," Dareem shrugged. "My help was rewarded by a blow."

Asheni turned away, unfurling her wings in frustration. "Did you even consider you deserved it? You were willing to sacrifice his granddaughter. Can you blame him?"

"Life must sometimes be sacrificed to defeat evil," Dareem countered.

"Those are the words of a coward." She considered telling him of Runa in her vision, but refrained.

"Are you defying me?" Dareem questioned, harsh black eyes staring into her own.

Asheni did not flinch and lifted her chin in defiance. "We have no ruler here—not even you. We are nine lonely souls who tried to serve the Light. The tragedy of our birth we must bear, but it is also not our fault. I've grown weary of this existence. Waste your own life. I refuse to live in oblivion anymore. The time has come to fight and live, Dareem. Perhaps even love."

"We were not made for love," Dareem whispered.

"Again, your choice. We knew one day Obsydia would escape her prison of Light. We knew about Koll's role in her release. We have seen the Obsidian Wars in our visions. Yet we did not warn the people who would suffer for it. We've had centuries to ponder a battle strategy, to find a way to kill Obsydia."

"She cannot die, any more than we can die."

"Death is not for us. Perhaps one day, the Eternals will release us. Hiding from the world has only made you bitter."

"We watch. It's been our role since we came into being. We must not interfere," Dareem said. "They are only mortals. We have no place in their fight. We have no place in this world."

"Obsydia is immortal," Asheni said. "Darkness has cheated many times to claim worlds. We should consider a new strategy. Who better to fight her than us? I would rather not live in a bloodstained world where Obsydia rules. I may become as miserable as you."

~ * ~

Mellypip needed neither magic nor the bonding to know Runa was upset about their friends in Thema. Opaline and Runa retreated to the backyard, despite the chill. He followed, feeling out of sorts and worried. Redstorm, Rono, and Darkleaf were in the yard, looking just as unhappy. Belwyn had broken the news to them earlier.

Do you think Hinkleburr, Broda, and Talwyn are safe from harm? Mellypip asked.

Oh Melly, I pray they will be. Sirah said Jiana had escaped capture so far, but could not send further messages. Jiana and Jasper are clever, Runa assured him.

Mellypip knew Runa's words were sincere, but they rang hollow for him. *How can you fight Koll and Obsydia?* He resisted the urge to suck on his paw.

Grimm comforted Rono, who was especially upset about Hinkleburr and his aides. "You must not distress yourself," Grimm told the gryphon. "Hinkleburr and the brothers are smart. They'll find a way to escape. Jiana and Jasper are still free. We won't abandon them. Remember when we spied on Koll and Obsydia? I know how scared you were, but you helped me. We helped each other. Now we must have courage for our friends."

Taran joined them, MacTabbish following at his heels. The marmalade cat was remarkably active, long tail swishing. "Damned bloody evil bastards," the cat grumbled.

"Aren't you cold?" Taran shivered. "Come inside you two."

"I'm too mad to be cold. What's going on in there?" Runa asked.

"It's turned into a war room. Cathal and Neelam are sending word to Caladynn. Neelam's trying to contact King Arawn in Ironia. The calling crystal is crashing again. It sparks and then fades, and half the messages are garbled. I think my grandfather is about to lose his mind."

"Will Arawn declare war?" Runa asked. "Ironia will not tolerate their diplomats taken prisoner or—"

"Don't say it!" Mellypip begged. "No bad thoughts."

"Maybe we should be realistic. Dealing with monsters does not leave room for happy images!" Opaline remarked bitterly. She walked in circles on the frosty grass, pulling her cloak tight around her. Grimm watched her go round and round, distressed.

"You're pacing is making me dizzy," Taran remarked to Opaline.

"Well, what do you expect?" Opaline snapped. "Ghastly things are happening. You can't blame dark gods for everything. People are all too happy to participate in evil if it suits their greed and desires."

"Now you sound like Belwyn," Mellypip remarked.

Taran crossed his arms and shrugged. "You always paced in circles when you were little, a fury in blonde curls going round and round for hours whenever you were angry."

"I did not," Opaline insisted.

"Opaline's nurse thought something was wrong with her," Taran explained, grinning.

Opaline smirked, "Mistress Toad Face had no room to criticize."

"You called your nurse Toad Face?" Runa asked, stifling a giggle.

"Opaline is not far off the mark, though it does sound mean, but not as mean as Toad-Face. She burned Opaline's favorite doll as punishment after she refused to curtsy to our brother."

"The dreadful woman doted on him and would do whatever he asked," Opaline said. "I refused to grovel. Toad-face told me I should be grateful I didn't have to beg for food in the slums. Levandius was born of noble blood, whereas I was descended from a lowly concubine. I told Father what she said, and he dismissed her. It surprised me. Levandius was stunned and threw a tantrum when she left. I showed them both." She stopped cold and turned to Taran, hands on her hips. "You're distracting me deliberately."

"I got you to stop," Taran grinned. "Come on, Sis, I know you're upset. We all are. But I do love your rants."

Grimm ran to Opaline's side, whining softly in his throat, rubbing his head against her hand. Her face softened and she knelt, hugging the wolf. "I'm sorry, Grimm."

"Grimm hates it when you're upset," Runa said.

"Are they talking about sending rescue to Thema?" Mellypip asked.

"We don't know yet, Melly," Runa replied, her face was pinched with worry.

"I want to do something. I hate being useless when people are suffering because of the wars and murders," Opaline said.

Belwyn flew into the yard and landed on Redstorm's antlers. "What are you children talking about?"

Redstorm shook his head, but the owl did not budge. "Do I look like a perch?"

"No, but you are convenient," Belwyn replied. "Cathal thought I should watch over the children."

"We are not children," Opaline insisted.

"What are they talking about in there? Will we try to rescue them?" Runa asked, hopeful.

"I can't say yet," Belwyn replied. "We've just received another message. It was very brief before it cut off. Stupid crystal. Jiana says Levandius is in Thema, which bodes no surprise for me. He has proclaimed Hadrial, Sarabia's sister, as the rightful queen. He insists he is liberating Thema and declaring Hadrial as his bride."

"A match made in hell," Opaline remarked dryly. "I hope they get the happiness they deserve. There'll be more refugees too. There will be more sacrifice. More wars. Why must I be related to such an evil dolt?"

Taran put his arms around Opaline, and kissed her on the head. "It's not blood, but what's in the soul and heart. Levandius' are both black as pitch. I always knew Levandius was a degenerate brat. He will pay one day for his sins against our father and for what he is doing to his people. I swear it."

"It's obvious Koll and Obsydia are guiding his moves," Belwyn commented. "He's too much of an idiot to conquer so much so soon."

Opaline took a deep breath and straightened. "Queen Sorcha told me refugees from the Red Empire have been crossing our borders, begging for help. She' been doing what she can. They're desperate and in need of shelter, food, and warm clothing. The children Darcus rescued are just a fragment of what's happening. I'll offer to help Sorcha with the refugees. I can contact the religious houses to see how many people they can shelter. Arrange for food and medicine supplies. Contrary to opinion, a true princess has more practical duties than choosing pink gowns or going to balls. I've supervised many charitable organizations in Tiamet to benefit the poor and promote education. I can be quite ruthless convincing rich merchants and nobility into donating for good causes."

Sirah had joined them in the yard, her pale face flushed with the cold. She kissed Opaline's cheek and squeezed her hand. "A marvelous idea. You're a good daughter, even if you exasperate me. Worthy of being a Princess of Thill. Now come inside. We won't let our friends perish without a fight. But we must take care. There's so much at stake now."

Runa picked Mellypip up and held him close. "Poor baby, you're shivering. Let's warm up. Hot drobba will make you feel better."

Mellypip suffered not just from cold, but the ominous feeling of danger creeping closer to their new home in Thill. He rested his head on Runa's shoulder, heavy with anxiety. When he glanced over her shoulder, a white peryton flashed before his eyes. Startled, he blinked, but when he opened his eyes the peryton was gone.

~ * ~

Neelam's cold expression chilled the blood. "The fall of Thema is not acceptable. It will provide Levandius with an advantage, with the Red Empire to the west and Thema to the east. Obsydia is moving faster than during the Bloodstone Age."

Cathal laid a map on the dining table, pinning down the edges with dots of magic. "Has Myrsalian gotten through to the Rowan and the new Drusane?"

"The crystal is still garbling messages. I think poor Myrsalian is about to have a nervous breakdown. It's no matter. The Drusane is new and young," Neelam stated flatly. "I doubt she would be capable of handling what's coming. I wish Ambera were still with us."

"I miss her too," Cathal said. "She also kept your temper in check."

"My temper's fine," Neelam replied dryly. "I just wish I had something to fight."

Cathal raised an eyebrow. "You enjoyed punching out goblins in the old days. They've risen like cockroaches in certain regions."

"Any idea what forces Levandius used for such a speedy conquer?" Darcus asked. "There have been no rumors of legions marching across the continent. Levandius has the military skill of a kundra beast. You don't just take over a kingdom so easily."

Neelam took a drink from his flask, scowling. "I agree, Darcus.

The idiot wouldn't know how to utilize war strategy. Levandius is nothing more than the symbolic face of the overthrow. This is clearly the machinations of Obsydia and Koll."

Gabriel joined them at the table, Namir at his side. "Let me help. Give me something useful to do."

Neelam glanced up at him. "Gabriel, have you sobered up yet? And don't think Darcus told me anything. I saw you come in drunk."

"I apologize," Gabriel said. "I let you down. I can serve the cause, even if I get drunk at times. Send me where I can do some good. Scouting and rescue are what I do best. And breaking heads. If Hinkleburr and his friends are alive, I'll find them. If Queen Sarabia is alive, I'll find her. If Jiana and Jasper are about, I'll find them too. I'm good at fighting. My combat and sorcery skills will make Koll's head ache."

"Then go," Neelam agreed. "Just don't get yourself killed."

~ * ~

The serious talk was too much for Mellypip. Worried about the safety of the dragon egg, he ran up to the sorcery chamber. Fallon and Talon, coiled near the dragon egg, acknowledged him. Liat was there too, with Dabiro, helping stand guard.

"What's the kid doing here?" Dabiro grunted.

"He is a powerful ranger-mage," Talon said. "We like him."

"A great and fuzzy warrior who smells sweet," Fallon laughed. "Where is your cloak and staff, mighty one?"

"My cloak is in the wash," Mellypip sighed. "I got drobba on it."

"You're still a warrior," Liat grinned. "I think your mighty staff is in the corner."

"Don't encourage him," Dabiro grumbled.

"Be nice, Dabiro," Liat warned.

Mellypip brightened and grabbed his staff, sitting erect near the egg, holding his staff.

"Very impressive, little warrior," Fallon commended.

The nest, warm with magically heated stones, was nice and toasty after being outside in the cold. In a few moments of his watch, a strange crunching sound startled him. He remained at watch until another cracking sound made him turned around. A thin fissure along the egg appeared.

"Um, I think something is happening," Mellypip whispered as

another fracture opened in the egg."

"What now?" Dabiro complained, rolling on his back.

"Shut up, Dabiro," Mellypip barked. This time a huge piece of the egg broke off. Mellypip dropped his staff and picked up the shell fragment and tried to press it back into place. Fallon and Talon swarmed around the egg, eagerly watching. The top of the dragon's head poked out and a pair of tiny eyes locked on Mellypip. "The egg is hatching!" Mellypip cried, panic rising.

"Egg is hatching too soon," Talon said, concerned.

Liat rushed over and his eyes widened. "I think I better get Cathal."

Dabiro waddled over, chuckling. "You're in trouble now, kid. You broke the egg."

CHAPTER 16

Xabral's stinger vibrated with excitement as he slid along the polished floor into the throne room. He resisted coming to Thema, but it proved to be exciting, with battle and bloodshed. Victory complete, Koll promised him a great spectacle. He sought out Koll, calling out through the bonding. *Is she here yet? Is it time? The sun has set, and she promised.*

She will come, sweet snake, Koll said, waiting by the mirror.

Hadrial wore a red gown, as instructed, for the ceremony. She fussed with the soft chiffon, uncertain of the color. "Is this truly appropriate for my marriage ceremony? Blue is the tradition for brides. I never thought I would ever be a bride." She glanced at herself in the tall shadow mirror, mesmerized by her new beauty.

Levandius complimented her, kissing her hand, redirecting her focus from the mirror to him. "You will set a new tradition, sweetheart. Your dazzling magnificence will make them all love you."

"Am I dazzling? Truly?" she asked eagerly, clutching his arm. The distant sound of battle and screams distracted her. Hadrial looked back, frowning. "There is still fighting going on? I thought it was all over. Have many died?"

"Do not fret about the deaths of lowly people who never cared for you," Levandius said. "They are nothing to us."

"Are we safe?" she asked.

"Just a few scattered skirmishes, mostly outside the palace walls," Koll assured them.

"We're safe," Levandius told her. "Soon, all our enemies will perish and we will rule supreme. The world will be ours."

"We will beget a new dynasty, beloved," she whispered, her lust evident.

Xabral turned away, bored with their base human desires. He glared at Koll. *If they start copulating in the throne room, I want them killed. We do not need them. Why are we fussing with them at all? Thema is ours now. Most of the nobles who resisted are being executed or saved for the sacrificial altar. Sarabia is captive and helpless in her new state. Our legions have triumphed.*

They will die soon enough when the world belongs to Obsydia. Then only SHE *will rule. Many loyalists to Sarabia escaped us. They must be hunted down.*

But Koll, I thought the army blocked the borders and shut down the city?

They did, but with war it's never absolute. Until then, we must maintain a façade of order to keep control, Koll assured him, maintaining his neutral expression for the couple.

Xabral coiled at his feet, resting his head on his red and black scales. *The mirrors were useful in the overthrow. The soldiers marched right through the glass Obsydia summoned for us. It just took so long with so many soldiers. But then they let in the legions hidden beyond the city walls. Then came chaos and fire. The screams and blood. It was wonderful. The warriors took the palace with swift, brutal force. The goblins got unruly and caused too much havoc in the end. We needed to save some for sacrifice and some for bargaining with enemy realms. The Thill Ambassador died, and we could have used him.*

I agree, Koll replied. *They're hard to control. We should restrict their freedoms; else they will run rampant and cause more trouble.*

We kept Hinkleburr Crowyn alive. Why isn't he dead?

Koll's black eyes reflected deep hatred as he smiled. *The Dwarf will die on the altar, and I will wield the knife myself after I carve out the hearts of his bothersome aides before his eyes.*

Ah, I understand, Xabral giggled, bobbing his head. *The virtue of vindictiveness.*

Xabral kept glancing at the mirror of shadows, towering in mystical majesty. Its ebonite frame glowed with shadowy light. Dark jewels flashed on the gleaming black metal, and runes of Otherworld origin carved deep. Xabral's anticipation was finally rewarded when the demon warriors, sensing her coming, turned to face the glowing glass, their red eyes burning. Hadrial and Levandius stepped back, still clinging to each other like pathetic worms.

A dozen dark priests swinging incense parted the shadow light singing hymns as they marched down through the chamber, lining the walls before falling mute. A silent chill passed as Shroud, scarlet braids swinging, glided in with a look of disdain for the mortal born, Koll included.

Koll glared back at the demon, refusing to cower. Only when he sensed Obsydia's coming did he bow before the great mirror, drumming his staff three times on the marble floor. "All kneel before the living goddess, Obsydia, Conqueror of the Bloodstone Age, Queen of the Obsidian Realms, beloved sister of Rygon, God of War, and the dark-blessed daughter of Ahridum, Eternal Lord of Chaos and Darkness."

Obsydia emerged from the mirror's shade as a true goddess masked in a red nimbus; her ethereal presence stunned all who witnessed her regal coming. Glorious in a black spider silk gown, her adornments were elegant. A ruby necklace gleamed on her alabaster skin and a jeweled obsidian crown sat upon her shadowy mane; silver eyes gleamed with satisfaction as her worshippers prostrated themselves.

Hadrial gaped at Obsydia, mouth open like an idiot. In a panic, Levandius pulled her down to kneel at his side.

"Welcome to Thema." Levandius cried with head bowed. "We are your humble servants. We worship you. We serve you."

"All mortal things serve me," Obsydia replied with indifference. "But this land shall no longer be known as Thema. Only Dark Eternals shall be recognized with such honors."

"Then let us call this country Obsydia," Hadrial stammered. "In your honor!"

"Charming, but not necessary, as I will rule this world soon. This kingdom once known as Thema is now *Valkorr*, named after my brother Rygon's pet mount. He's a type of bull, though it hardly describes this demigod since it is a demon roughly the size of a mountain."

Xabral inwardly giggled, sending his humor to Koll. *Hadrial just learned her kingdom went from being named after a goddess to a demon bull which sprays gaseous death fumes.*

"We have a holy task to perform this great day," Obsydia commanded. "The birth of a new nation requires a new temple to worship the Dark Eternals. Koll informs me there are no temples dedicated to the Dark here. How can it be true, Hadrial?"

Hadrial bowed her head, shaking violently. "Forgive me, Great Goddess, but none exist. They have been banned in Thema, I mean, this land, for a thousand years."

"No longer," Obsydia smiled, gently cupping her chin with her hand. Hadrial's lovely face contorted with terror at her touch and she paled, as though her life ebbed with Obsydia's touch. Obsydia smiled, as though feeding on her fear, and spoke gently in her ear. "You are so beautiful now, Hadrial. Treasure it."

Obsydia released her hold and Hadrial crumpled to the floor.

She struggled to force herself up, but remained on her knees. Her voice, barely a broken whisper, replied. "I promise, Queen Obsydia."

The priests ripped the silken drapes down from the tall, revealing the private balcony overlooking the city of Upal. Obsydia stepped into the moonlit night, a vision of pure wicked beauty. Koll and Xabral followed her. Across the palace grounds in the distance, rose the great temple of Thema. It had stood in the center of the capital for centuries as a center of devotion for Thema, their patron goddess. Obsydia raised her hands, her voice spoke words of Eternal power in the language of shadows.

I wish I knew the language, Xabral sighed, listening to her deep, musical voice.

One day, she will share all with us, her devoted, Koll said through the bonding, rapt by her powerful presence.

A great black cloud swarmed around the white temple like a cyclone. Obsydia's voice echoed through the wind, rising to a powerful boom which stunned even Koll and Xabral. The ground shuddered, forcing the spectators to their knees, except for Obsydia, who rose into the air like a beautiful phantom. The Theman Temple with the pristine white towers vanished from the world, as though its image were a misty dream easily erased. In its place, a black temple rose from the rendered earth, cascading darkness across the city like death. Koll and Xabral watched unafraid, reveling in its glory. The dark priests wept with joy. The mortals bowed in terror.

Obsydia reveled in her triumph, and whispered just loud enough for Koll and Xabral to hear. "At last, my revenge on Thema is complete. Let none ever interfere with me again."

Xabral knew she spoke of the ancient legend of Princess Upala, who fought Obsydia during the Bloodstone Age. The city was defeated and all was lost. Obsydia was victorious. Upala refused to submit to Obsydia when they brought her to die at her feet. Upala prayed for strength. Thema not only granted Upala strength to fight, but according to legend, Thema herself briefly appeared in human form and struck a mighty blow upon Obsydia. This rallied the defeated to fight back. No such hope today. Light had been extinguished here.

Obsydia floated to the floor and turned to them, spreading her arms in welcome. "Behold your new sacred house, a gift to you as part of our covenant. Now go forth and pray in the true church!

Unsheathe your sacrificial blades to offer blood to me. Be glad of it, for it will consecrate your marriage under my blessing."

~ * ~

Hinkleburr opened his eyes and rolled over, head and back aching. Groaning, he pushed himself up and looked around the cramped windowless cell; dingy with filthy straw and grimy walls. Palaces, fortresses, and towers may all differ in design and luxury, but dungeons were the same everywhere. His two aides, Broda and Talwyn slept a corner. He noticed they were badly bruised and bloodied, no doubt courtesy of their charming guards.

"Boys, wake up." Hinkleburr croaked, shaking them.

They woke startled, shaken they stood up and looked around. Broda was roughed up but seemed okay. Talwyn concerned him. The gash on his head, crusted with dried blood, looked bad.

"Will they ever let us out? How long we been here?" Broda asked, rubbing his neck.

"Not sure, boys," Hinkleburr answered. "Best take it easy. You took the brunt of the beating."

"Only 'cause the bastards outnumbered us," Talwyn sniffed, wiping his bloody face with his sleeve. He wavered on his feet and Hinkleburr gripped his arm.

"Steady now," Hinkleburr cautioned, examining the deep gash on his forehead. "This nasty cut needs stitches. Doubtful they'll provide any humane care."

"I can manage," Talwyn insisted, gritting his teeth.

For several hours, they waited in tense misery without food or water. They finally fell asleep from exhaustion, huddled together in a corner until loud voices and footfall outside their jail alerted them.

"How long we been asleep?" Broda asked, rubbing his good eye.

"Not sure boys, but keep still," Hinkleburr cautioned. "We won't get far if we aggravate these brutes. If we're going to survive, we must be smart."

The door unlocked and several guards dragged them out of their cell. Hinkleburr did not resist the rough hands of his captors but was alert to anything he could see or hear. The sounds of moans and protests coming from other cells filled his ears. They ordered them to climb the winding stairs. He glanced back once to see the brothers close behind. He wondered if they were being taken for judgment, execution, or would they just exile them to the border. He prayed for the last one. He tried not to think, but it would lead to worry and panic over the fates of friends.

Once out of the dungeon, clean, fresh air revived him a bit, until they passed through some halls with servants on their knees with buckets and rags, scrubbing away blood from the floors and walls.

"Gods, what's happened here?" Broda gasped, helping his brother Talwyn walk.

"Quiet," Hinkleburr cautioned. *We'll find out all too soon,* he thought.

After a long walk, he finally recognized where they were in the palace, close to the royal reception hall. Panic about Queen Sarabia suddenly filled him with anguish. *I could never imagine Sarabia behind these atrocities. What's happened to her? Is she even alive?*

Braziers burning with blue flames lit the enormous throne room, casting shadows on the colossal blue marble pillars. Sentinels in black armor wearing sheer crimson cloaks lined the room with mute threat, their faces concealed by dark helmets. They carried spears tipped with black obsidian blades.

The soldiers shoved them to their knees as more people were dragged in, chained, beaten, their finery torn and filthy as his own. Hinkleburr recognized fellow victims of this vile insurgency as fellow courtiers, diplomats, and royal officials. All he could do was wait and wonder the worst in silence.

A black-robed priest, not a *Theman* priest, but a worshipper of darkness with a shaved head cloaked with red ochre, stepped in front of the royal dais and rapped his staff on the floor. "All Hail Emperor Levandius and his bride, Queen Hadrial of Valkorr."

Hinkleburr clenched his teeth, fighting a flood of curses when he saw Levandius walk into the room, garbed in black velvet trimmed with gold, his oversized jeweled crown garish with rubies and black diamonds. The surprising image of Hadrial's face, unveiled, her back straight, limbs strong, strutted at his side. She wore the royal Theman crown and the queen's blue cloak with rich gold embroidery. Her beauty was devastating like a blow, but Hinkleburr knew the effects of the cruel disease she suffered as a child and how it disfigured her.

Then Koll joined them, his face streaked with ceremonial ochre, his damned snake slithering at his heels.

Hinkleburr gritted his teeth. He was sure the sorcerer noticed him, despite the crowd. He was probably eager to slit his throat. "Damn. Koll is here. I hate his snake almost as much I hate him."

"He's got two arms," Talwyn remarked. "I thought Cathal's magic destroyed one of them."

"Think dark magic," Hinkleburr whispered. "Notice how one is shimmering with gems and metal. This is bad though. Very bad."

"I'll show them bad," Broda said, his voice nearly drowned out by the moaning and protests of the other prisoners. "Xabral's hide would make a fine belt to hang Koll's evil head."

"You make me proud," Hinkleburr replied, smiling weakly. "But we must escape this wretched mess."

Levandius raised his arms with a disgusting smile, even though everyone in the room, sans the soldiers, was terrified. "People of Valkorr, we are your liberators. The false queen, Sarabia, has been overthrown by her sister, Hadrial. The Dark Trinity has brought justice at last."

No one spoke. They were too afraid.

"I am your true ruler," Hadrial said. "Do you see me as deformed or disfigured? No, because magic made me ill and damaged my looks, all because of a sister's desire to wear my crown! For years she usurped my rightful place as your queen. The true goddess, Obsydia, has freed me from my sister's curse and restored me."

That's a lie, Hinkleburr fumed inwardly.

Hadrial gestured and a woman in rags was dragged into the court. Hinkleburr recognized the lustrous mass of black hair and the voice, but Sarabia's body and face had been mutilated a hundred-fold more than what Hadrial suffered.

Hadrial smiled down on her helpless sister. "I am your Queen now. With this new reign, guided by my beloved husband Emperor Levandius, I will bring the true faith to this realm. Tonight, we will wed. Thema is no longer the patron goddess of this realm. Thema's name will be banished forever. We are part of the noble Red Empire. To honor our new alliance, we must offer sacrifice. You are enemies of the state. In my mercy, I offer you a death to honor the Dark, rather than a traitorous end."

"They're gonna bloody kill us," Broda gulped.

"She's trying to make it seem like a good thing," Talwyn said.

"What are we going to do?"

"Bitch is mad," Broda mumbled.

"Have faith! I won't let you die," Hinkleburr swore as the guards grabbed him. "I promise boys. We need to fight. Fight!"

As he fought his captors, he glimpsed Xabral's gelid eyes peering down, shaking his stinger like a demonic rattle and heard him say, "Time to polish your knife, Koll."

CHAPTER 17

Mellypip felt out of sorts with what Belwyn called, *a passel of fury and worry.* The horrid news in Thema brought anguish. Gabriel and Namir left for Thema to help their friends, so now they lived in agonizing suspense over their fate. And worst of all, he was not allowed in the sorcery chamber because of the baby dragon.

Belwyn flew over his head, nearly knocking him off the couch, and landed on his perch with a sullen stare.

"Dare I ask?" Mellypip replied. "Or is this just a continuation of yesterday's cranky?"

"Continuation," Belwyn replied. "You don't look so chipper? What's wrong? Is the world out of drobba?"

Mellypip swished his long tail and flattened his ears. "No, but I am out of patience. You have done nothing but snap at me lately."

"Only verbally," Belwyn countered. "Shouldn't you be in bed?"

"Who can sleep?"

Yllia swept into the room, her golden beauty bringing light to the moody gloom he felt. She looked at them and crossed her arms. "What's all this?"

"The world's gone to hell," Belwyn replied.

"Belwyn's leading the way," Mellypip added.

"World traumas are not uncommon," Yllia quipped. "Complaining will not deliver us from the chaos at our doorstep." She turned to Mellypip, tickling him under the chin, making him purr and easing his mood. "And what is wrong with you?"

Mellypip's glum answer followed. "I've been banished from the dragon nursery."

"Why?" Yllia asked, interested. She picked him up, stroking his furry ears. "You can tell me."

"They won't tell me. When the egg started to hatch, I tried to put the pieces back. I was guarding the egg as any good ranger-mage," Mellypip explained. "Then the baby dragon poked her head out and looked right at me. It wasn't scary. I thought even a baby dragon would be intimidating. Part of the shell was still on her head, like a funny little hat. It was cute. Then Cathal and Neelam stormed in. They sent me away. So I sit here in abject banishment. I can't even talk to Fallon and Talon now."

"Dabiro's banished too," Belwyn added.

"Good," Mellypip said. "Why?"

"Fallon and Talon got annoyed with him."

"What color is the baby dragon?" Yllia asked. "You were the first to witness her hatching, you know best."

"Red," Mellypip replied. "With a silver star mark on her head."

"Really? A true sign of a Drajina. You are lucky, Melly."

Mellypip gazed up at Yllia, basking in her warmth. "I am?"

"It is rare for anyone to see a dragon hatch, and you witnessed the birth their new queen. It is lucky indeed. My Cathal is not angry, but concerned. Do not fret."

Runa walked in, flushed from the cold, sweaty and dirty from her fighting practice with Darcus.

"My, you look a sight!" Yllia laughed. "How is my granddaughter progressing, Darcus?"

"She's getting better," Darcus nodded. "Knocked me off my feet a couple times."

"And I didn't even use magic," Runa said, dropping into a chair and wiping her face with a towel. "It was so cold I feared my hands would turn to ice! About halfway through the fight, I was sweating! I just wish I had my staff, rather than this substitute. I miss seeing Melly's handsome face on top."

Yllia put him down so he could run over to Runa. "I will talk to Rualla, dear."

Mellypip jumped on Runa's knee, enjoying a cuddle, but her strong smell was too much. He stood back, balanced on his hind legs, sniffing her critically. "You stink."

"Humans are prone to odd smells," Belwyn said. "They are the only species that require extra bathing."

"Nonsense," Darcus said. "Sweat never hurt anybody. It's the result of a hard, healthy workout."

Runa ruffled his ears and smiled. "All right, I'll take a bath."

Jadon came downstairs, weak but determined. "I saw you fighting when I looked out the window. Who won?"

Runa's smile vanished, replaced by a scowl to rival even Belwyn. "Darcus, but I nearly beat him. Raghnall ordered complete bed rest for you. Why are you out of bed?"

"Why are you angry?" Jadon asked. "Does my demonic face offend you?"

"No," Runa said. "But your rash behavior does. I told you I didn't care. We will fix the curse someday, but you couldn't wait! You ran off and almost died. Now you have a fool idea about going back to the Elfsharan Badlands to spy on Obsydia like an idiot!"

"Here comes the fight," Belwyn said. 'Brace yourselves."

"Jadon isn't really going to spy on Obsydia's shadow tower is he?" Yllia asked.

"No," Mellypip sighed, feeling sorry for Jadon. "He threatens to leave and be all brave and noble, but he's still so weak Runa just pushes him back to bed. This time he made it out of his room, so he's getting stronger."

"Come on boy," Darcus said, grabbing Jadon's arm and helping him up the stairs. "Best put you back to bed else you'll anger this tiny sorceress. We don't want to rile her up, do we?"

"I am not tiny!" Runa shouted, following them. "And I will be up there with soup soon! So you better be hungry!"

"I think she takes after you, Yllia," Belwyn observed.

Mellypip trailed after Runa, watching from the doorway as Runa and Darcus put Jadon back to bed. Runa's anger tempered as she tucked the quilt around him.

Baldur could only shake his massive head. "The boy is stubborn. He's sad and confused. So is little Runa."

"Don't tell Runa she's little," Mellypip warned. "She might get all furious. Jadon wants to help, but he can't because he's ill. Where's Raghnall?"

Baldur joined him in the hall. "Getting some much-needed rest."

Mellypip climbed on top of the grizzly and snuggled in, feeling out of sorts and, well, just a bit miffed.

"What's wrong, Little Brother?"

"I feel helpless, just like Jadon. I can't do anything right."

"Because of the dragons?"

"I didn't do anything wrong," Mellypip said. "When Cathal came into the room, he yelled at me and told me to leave. He never yelled at me before."

"What does Belwyn say?" Baldur asked.

"He's been extra cranky lately. I'm afraid to ask."

"Maybe you should go to the source," Baldur suggested.

"But I am banished," Mellypip said.

"You're not banished from the hallway," Baldur whispered. "Knock on the door and ask."

Mellypip considered Baldur's words. It was so sudden when it happened. It's not like he caused the egg to crack open. Taking a deep breath, he jumped down. "If I do not return, tell Runa I was brave."

"I will, Little Brother."

Mellypip ran up the stairs to the top floor where the sorcery chamber was. The door was closed, and the dense aroma of magic was strong, partly dragon magic. Summoning his courage, he knocked on the door. "Hello! It's Mellypip. I'm knocking because I know I'm not supposed to be in the sorcery chamber, so I am in the hallway which is not the sorcery chamber. May I ask why I was banned?" He sat on his hunches, wringing his paws with worry. *Please, don't let them yell at me,* he prayed. But nothing happened. No one came. He waited, hesitant to knock again and anger them. Angering a sorcerer was not wise. Angering a sorcerer and a wizard would be downright stupid.

Cathal opened the door and looked down. Before Mellypip could speak, Cathal swept him up in his arms and carried him to the center of sorcery chamber.

"Welcome, Melly," Fallon welcomed, coiling around a newly created mock mountain in the center of the room. It looked like stone, with little trees planted around the formation. There was a little pool to bathe in, or drink perhaps? In the far corner was a discreet sandbox made to look like moss-covered stone.

"Yes, we missed you," Talon said, peeking up over the mountain -like shelter.

"I missed you too," Mellypip said, and looked up at Cathal. "Are you still mad at me?"

Cathal gently scratched his ears. "I was never mad at you. But newborn dragons are often fragile. She was hatched a bit early, so she is very small even for a hatchling. I'm sorry I hurt your feelings."

Mellypip looked around the room. "Where is the new dragon? Is she okay?"

Cathal pointed to the large reddish stone behind the mountain, burning with warm magic. Mellypip could not tell if she was there until her long tail moved and she uncurled from the rock to change position. She was a deep crimson, but for the silvery star brand on her forehead. She looked out the window, wings drooping, silent.

"She looks so sad," Mellypip whispered.

"She is," Cathal replied softly. "This is not a normal home for little dragons. She wants her mother. Talon and Fallon are fine watchers, but dragons are usually hatched together and have each other."

"Does she have a name yet?" Mellypip asked.

"Usually the Drajina or her mate chooses a name for the next ruler of the dragon clans, but she is far from here," Talon said.

Fallon raised up on his hind legs, swishing his ebony tail. "Sometimes, the one who witnesses the birth is also blessed with the honor of choosing a name for next Drajina. You witnessed her hatching so we would be honored. Are you honored?"

"If you are agreeable to the task and great responsibility," Fallon added.

"Of naming her," Talon said, bright eyes eager.

"Just make sure name is proper," Fallon pointed out. "Must be regal."

"And pretty," Talon suggested.

"I am overwhelmed," Mellypip said, his mind racing with ideas. "But I am honored." He did not want to disappoint the dragons or Cathal. There were many heroines in the scrolls and books he was studying. It must be special. Then he recalled a story Belwyn told him when they still lived in the tree tower. It was a fairy tale about a dragon queen called Sephya, who saved the world from endless night when a wicked sorcerer stole the sun. Sephya battled the sorcerer in the night, using her bright fire breath to light the sky. She found the mountain where the sun was hidden and returned it to the sky. "I would like to suggest Sephya. She was a heroic dragon in one of my favorite tales."

Talon and Fallon tittered together, going round in circles, considering his choice. "Seph-eee-ya, Sephya!" they repeated, over and over.

Mellypip glanced at the baby dragon, who was no bigger than he was. She seemed uninterested in her naming, even with the antics of Talon and Fallon. He wiggled out of Cathal's arms. Hesitant, he moved closer to the heated stone where she lay. "Do you like it?" he asked, earnestly. "I will find another name if you don't. It's a pretty name, I think. I love dragon lore. It was my favorite thing to study."

The baby red dragon turned and looked at him.

"Do you want to play?" Mellypip asked. "I'm a wampu. I'm fuzzy and not immune to fire. Just so you know. I love jam, drobba, and games. Oh, and I am a great bard and ranger-mage." She did not reply but rested her head on the rock, staring at him intently. Mellypip sighed, feeling helpless.

After a moment the baby dragon deftly climbed down the rock, and nosed Mellypip, sniffing strongly. Mellypip stilled himself, praying she could not breathe fire yet. She sat back and looked at him with golden eyes. She burped, faintly, a touch of gaseous mist. No fire yet, but close. She burrowed her head against his furry chest, and he petted her, confused. The touch of her skin was not scaly, but soft to the touch like a combination of velvet and leather.

"Sephya," Talon confirmed.

"Yes. She is Sephya," Fallon nodded.

Belwyn flew into the chamber and perched on Cathal's shoulders."

"We think she imprinted on you," Cathal explained. "I was afraid it would cause a problem, but they grow out of it fast enough."

"Is that why everyone was so mad?" Mellypip asked.

"Not mad, but you are still so young, Melly," Cathal said. "She needs you, I'm afraid. You must help take care of her. We hoped you would not have to, but she has been closed off until you came back. We had to be sure. Now we know. We did not want you to be burdened with the responsibility."

"So I'm an official dragon guardian."

"Think babysitter," Belwyn corrected.

~ * ~

Alert and focused, Grimm watched the calling crystal for any messages. Happy to help his pack, he glanced at Myrsalian, napping in his chair, Felisia perched delicately on his shoulder, dozing. *Let them rest,* he thought. *There has been enough stress of late. They were exhausted.*

Opaline entered with a tray of refreshments. Sandwiches, hot tea, cookies, and apples. He wagged his tail when she entered. Tiptoeing, she carefully set the food on the end table so as not to wake them.

They have been sleeping for a short time, but the crystal has been silent.

Opaline knelt down and hugged him. *Thanks for watching them, Grimm. I almost wish the damn thing would stay silent. I fear the news.*

I know. I have seen the evil we must fight.

You'll never have to face such evil alone, ever, Grimm. We will always be together.

Opaline ruffled his fur, her smile full of warmth, like sunshine. Grimm loved her smile. He never knew joy or contentment until he bonded with Opaline as her familiar. His spirit father guided him to her, and he as grateful for his new home. The threats to Opaline and all his new friends worried him.

We shouldn't be so pessimistic, Opaline said. *Cathal and Neelam defeated her before. I know they will again. We must be hopeful the good in this world will win.*

How was your meeting with Queen Sorcha?

She was so happy! I am going to lead the committees to help the refugees. Mother is proud of me too. We will be working in concert with the religious houses. I'm meeting the Bishop of Rhone tomorrow. We have a long list of rich nobles to extract donations from.

Grimm looked at the food tray with longing, for he was always hungry. *I would like to extract sandwich from the tray, if there is enough.*

Opaline handed him a chicken sandwich, knowing it was a favorite. Taran and Panthara were heard in the hallway.

"I think we should marry now," Taran said. "Mother has no objections and neither does Iona."

Opaline bit her lip. *Marry! My brother and Panthara!*

Oh, dear, Grimm thought, seeing the stunned look on Opaline's face.

"We should wait," Panthara whispered. "And keep your voice down. Do you want the whole house to hear?"

Opaline stood up and stepped into the hall. Grimm jumped up to follow her. Panthara and Taran were startled by her interruption.

"You're engaged?" Opaline asked, her tone even.

"Yes," Taran announced. "We are."

Grimm did not like his tone. It was almost belligerent. Opaline's demeanor went from shocked to a cold calm.

"And you did not think to include me?" Opaline asked. "You obviously have told others, but not your sister."

"Well, I knew you wouldn't like the idea," Taran explained, his bravery reduced to embarrassment. "You and Panthara are not exactly friends."

"We were almost sacrificed together," Opaline quipped. "That creates a unique closeness, even if we do not see eye to eye."

"You two are hostile to each other all the time," Taran said. "I did not care to hear your opinion on the matter."

"You're telling it all wrong, my boy," MacTabbish warned. "You're doomed."

Azmadu just sat there watching everyone, unsure of what to do.

"We thought we would wait until after the King announced your betrothal," Panthara added.

"Do you think me so small and selfish?" Opaline asked them in a low voice, standing calm and erect.

The calling crystal beeped with rapid bell sounds. Myrsalian cursed briefly, roused from sleep. Opaline and Grimm rushed into the room. Swirling with a myriad of colors, Myrsalian activated the crystal. Instead of Jiana's voice, or even Gabriel, it was Koll.

Grimm's ears flattened and he growled at the sound of the sorcerer's voice.

"Thema has fallen," Koll's voice announced. "Tell Cathal his friends died for Obsydia's glory."

"We have more important things to worry about now," Opaline stated. "I will inform Cathal."

CHAPTER 18

The newly arisen Obsidian Temple gleamed with sinister origin, casting a shadow across the entire city. Hinkleburr looked at the colossal temple, stunned by its supernatural force. The night flared with battles still raging throughout the lost city. Hinkleburr's eyes darted back and forth, desperate for any avenue of escape. Broda and Talwyn clung close behind in the upheaval. "Stay close, boys," he shouted above the deafening noise.

Crowds still fought back with anger in the background. Hinkleburr recognized few of city guards fighting back in the chaos. Sacrifices seized by Koll's forces fought their captors, unwilling to die on a dark god's altar. The massive double doors opened. Priests in flowing black robes and faces painted with red ochre, streamed out of the temple, singing hymns to Obsydia. Goblins snarled from the stairs, feral and wild-eyed in ragged leathers, clutching spears with talismans of bones dangling from the points.

"Sir, look out!" Talwyn cried, stumbling against him when black vines sprouted from the cracked earth. "What the devil are those?"

Hinkleburr noticed the bizarre plants spreading all around with rapid growth. "More evil," he said. "Pay it no heed. We've got bigger troubles." Hinkleburr racked his brain as he scrutinized their surroundings for weak points. Dozens of guards armed with clubs and swords blocked them from escaping, forcing the victims up the stairs to certain death. Some guards were human, plain, immoral humans. Some of the guards were not fully human, but red-eyed demon men, transformed by Obsydia. Feelings of defeat swelled along with guilt, thinking of Broda and Talwyn who served him so bravely. He failed them. He failed the alliance too, not seeing this calamity coming.

Inside the temple, blue flames in large bronze braziers lit the inner sanctum with a shadowy glow. The interior was massive, beyond mortal comprehension. Paintings of Dark Eternals on the walls decorated the walls. The images seemed to move in the flickering shadows.

Koll watched from the altar, face painted with red ochre like a priest. Xabral slithered around the altar, eager for bloodshed. Levandius and Hadrial waited on the altar, deaf to the cries of innocents being herded for slaughter.

Hinkleburr looked away, sickened by the very sight of Koll and his cursed snake. Shoved closer to the altar by rough hands, he pushed back at the guard. The guard's dagger in a hip holster gleamed. Being shorter of stature than regular humans was sometimes a problem for a Dwarf, but it could also reap an advantage. Hinkleburr spun around and grabbed the man's waist. "Please, let me go," he cried. "I don't want to die! King Arawn will pay ransom."

The guard shoved him to the ground. Broda and Talwyn surrounded Hinkleburr quickly. He pretended to cower, slipping the dagger into his coat. It wasn't much, but it was something.

~ * ~

Jiana rushed through the palace halls, her ragged cloak concealing her precious Jasper, tucked away in a canvas shoulder bag. A group of Koll's soldiers marched by her. Jiana hovered near the wall in dumb reaction at their passing.

Please hurry, Jasper begged.

I am going as fast as I can.

The tiger hare's nervous suggestions interrupted her thoughts. *Hunch over more, and wave your arms. Grunt. Blend in.*

I am! This is humiliating, Jiana complained. *The halls are mostly empty, At least there are fewer people roaming the halls.*

She noted how empty the corridors were in this wing of the palace, but many had been compelled to go to the cathedral of horror Obsydia summoned. No one bothered with a goblin, which gave her some leeway. Jiana turned a corner and collided into a tall, black-armored guard with a masked helmet. *Damn, I don't need this.* She grunted and bobbed her head in supplication, drooling like a good goblin.

"Damned demons!" the guard muttered, thrusting his sword at her. "How many of you hideous things do I have to kill?"

Jiana barely evaded injury by levitating above him, cursing herself as she did so. *Wonderful. I just exposed myself. Brilliant!*

The guard lowered his sword and stared up at her. "Goblins can't levitate."

"Who are you?" Jiana demanded.

He removed his helmet. "Gabriel. Is that you, Jiana? We all feared you dead, girl. Why, I almost killed you just now!"

Jiana dropped to the floor and shape-shifted back to herself. "I'm getting used to it. Koll and his demon thugs have been hunting me." Jiana impulsively threw her arms around Gabriel, relieved to see a friendly face. He smelled of ale, magic, and sweat. She relished it. "When did you get here? Who sent you?"

"I just arrived. Took this uniform off one the guards, but he won't miss it or anything else again. Cathal and Neelam thought I could do some good here. Thema's fall came as a shock. I like your disguise. None of this lot would suspect a goblin," Gabriel laughed, sheathing his sword. "Why are you still here? Causing trouble?"

"I'm good at it," Jiana shrugged, brushing her hair back nervously. "There was no warning. No one saw it coming because the invasion was from within. Hadrial, the queen's sister, did this. She's allied with Levandius and Koll. Her price was beauty! After the overthrow, Hadrial ordered the city gates open to let in Obsydia's army. I hope the bitch rots."

"It's not your fault," Gabriel said.

"It doesn't make me feel better. I stayed to help. I managed to warn some of the court and soldiers when it started to go down. I didn't get to Hinkleburr in time. They already took him. Broda and Talwyn too. I sent messengers to warn the people in the city too. Koll himself hunted me. I was an annoyance. So far I've eluded him and the soldiers. Did Cathal get any of my messages?"

"Some of them. The messages were hard to understand, but Myrsalian blamed the calling crystal."

"Poor Myrsalian," Jiana laughed weakly. "He always has trouble with the ridiculous crystal. The sorcerer house is destroyed. Koll burned my home to the ground. I used the calling crystal in the palace until Koll finally smashed it so I couldn't send any more messages. I've been helping folks escape, when not evading capture myself. Look, they've just taken Hinkleburr and his aides for sacrifice. I feared Queen Sarabia dead, but she's still alive! Many other innocents are on their way to death! I can't just abandon them, but I can't do it all either." She hid her face with her hands, fighting the useless urge to burst into tears. She hated crying.

"You're not alone now," Gabriel told her gently. "Do you know where the queen is?"

"I just learned she's being held in Hadrial's room. People tend to talk freely when they think you're a dumb goblin. She's been put under a curse. I'll get her out somehow."

"Find your queen. I'll go to the temple," Gabriel said.

"What are you going to do?" Jiana asked.

"Raise some hell," Gabriel replied.

"Be careful. It's not a normal temple. Obsydia summoned it from the Dark Realms. I saw it rise when I was on the roof hiding from Koll. He's gone to the dark temple to oversee the slaughter."

"Good. Maybe I'll finally get to kill him too." Gabriel removed the helmet, scratching his head. "Is Jasper with you?"

"I'm here," Jasper squeaked from the bag.

"Where's Namir?" Jiana asked.

"He's cloaked in a stealth spell and almost invisible to the eye. Aren't you, love?"

"I'm here," Namir replied, appearing as though unfolding from an ethereal cloud. "We're glad you're safe, Jiana."

Jiana grinned. "Good spell."

Gabriel tossed her a yellow crystal tome. "Here, I have extras. It's handy to have. Breathe on the tome and say the words *magic cloak* three times to activate the enchantment. If I survive, I'm taking the northern path back to Aybarr. Meet me at the first way station near the river."

"I know it. It's about twenty miles outside the city."

"Good. If I'm not there by sunrise, just get the hell out and go as far as you can." Gabriel rummaged in his bag and handed her a small bag, "This might help too."

She opened the pouch of dark orange balls glowing with magic. They smelled fiery, the sensation tingled her nose and mouth. "What are these?"

"Just some explosives I concocted. My own sorcerous recipe. Just pull off the red seal, toss, and duck very fast. Don't worry. Got lots of them. Now go."

Jiana turned and ran, glancing back once, but Gabriel had already vanished.

~ * ~

Hinkleburr never thought a sacrifice could be so dull. Koll raised his hands in prayer on the holy altar. Xabral coiled nearby, but he watched the crowd closely with increasing interest. Bloodthirsty reptile. The only exit seemed to be the main one they entered. Hinkleburr did not know if he was brave enough to run willy-nilly through a temple from Darkness itself without a map. Hundreds of priests chanted prayers to Obsydia as Koll stood with head bowed in deep prayer. The devoted listened with rapt devotion. The prisoners howled in defiance and despair.

Koll summoned Hadrial and Levandius to come forward, and they knelt. Koll recited vows of marriage and devotion to the Dark Trinity. Their foreheads were anointed with blood. Hadrial visibly flinched when Koll touched her.

Good, Hinkleburr thought. *She should feel bad about something.* Once he felt sorry for the princess, but no more. He reached into his coat for the dagger. The guards were all around, but they were occupied with the ceremony. "Boys, we need to try now. Duck and try to sneak away. Then run. No matter what, keep going."

"No," Broda said. "We won't abandon you, sir."

"We stick together," Talwyn swore.

A soldier gripped Hinkleburr's shoulder hard. Panic flooded through him, and he gritted his teeth. He had to take a chance now, gripping the dagger, ready to strike.

"Don't spoil the surprise, my little friends," the soldier whispered.

~ * ~

Jiana found Sarabia guarded by only two dark priests and a guard. Before they could react to her intrusion, she quickly disabled them with a sleeping spell. Then she bound and gagged them all for good measure. She cast light in the room and knelt by Sarabia's bed. She appeared asleep. The odor on her breath indicated she had been drugged. The condition of her body was much worse than Jiana realized. The curse or whatever Koll used had twisted Sarabia's body and face.

"Sarabia," Jiana shook her, frantic. "Please wake up!"

Jasper poked his head out of the bag. "We can't wait. She's clearly drugged. You may have to do it now."

"It's a tough spell," Jiana said. "Dangerous if things go wrong. A spell on top of what's been done to her may be more than her body can handle."

"Look at what they've done to her!" Jasper pointed out. "She has nothing to lose. We'll never get another chance."

Sarabia's partially paralyzed body and twisted muscles contorted her body. It was similar to what Hadrial suffered, but this was far worse. Jiana had no idea how to undo this damage. It reeked of dark magic. "Hand me the green crystal tome."

Jasper pushed it out of the bag with his paws. Jiana held it in her hand, whispering the magical incantation to activate the spell. Jiana was glad she had one prepped in her tome collection. She just hoped it worked. The green crystal sparkled, unfolding a stream of glimmering sorcery swathing Sarabia's body, which began to shrink rapidly.

"It's working," Jasper whispered, his long ears twitching.

Sarabia's body was no more than eight inches long, like a twisted doll. She carefully tucked Sarabia in the satchel with Jasper. "Watch over her. She's very fragile."

The sounds of soldiers outside the room urged her to hurry. Jiana pulled up her hood, and ran to the tall window, pushing it open. She patted her bag gently. "Hold on, Jasper." She took Gabriel's tome, activated the cloaking, then levitated to the roof. The air stank of smoke, the smell burning her eyes and nostrils. Jiana avoided looking at the Obsidian Temple as she ran into the night.

~ * ~

"Gabriel, is that you?" Hinkleburr whispered.

"Who else would be this crazy, my friend?" Gabriel replied, reaching into his pouch. "I suggest you cover your ears, boys."

Koll completed the wedding ceremony and turned to face the crowd. Levandius and Hadrial stepped back, hand in hand. Koll's eyes locked on Hinkleburr when he raised his blade. "Bring the sacrifices to give thanks to the Dark Trinity. Bring me the Dwarves, for theirs will be the first blood to consecrate this Obsidian Temple."

Gabriel ripped off a red tag and hurled a flaming orange orb directly at Koll. Gabriel shoved them to the ground and used his own body as a shield right before it exploded. The aroma of sorcery and sulfur filled the air.

Levandius and Hadrial whimpered and fled the altar, their fine clothes burnt. Several priests sprawled dead across the altar. Koll and his snake survived the blast.

Soldiers rushed Gabriel only to be hurled across the room with a sorcerous gesture. The prisoners began to revolt with fresh hope. Gabriel's magically undid their chains, freeing them to act. Several goblins jumped Gabriel, crawling over his tall, muscular frame. Snarling, biting and clawing at him until he jerked them off, one by one, and pitched them to the floor. Namir appeared, unseen until now, to protect his sorcerer. The clouded leopard roared and pounced, claws ripping goblin flesh until black demon blood splattered the floor.

"Back now, Namir," Gabriel warned, staggering to his feet, covered with bites and scratches. Namir retreated to Gabriel's side, muzzle and fangs stained with blood. Gabriel shot sorcerous fire at the goblins, charring them as they squealed.

"Kill that sorcerer!" Koll commanded, his blood mixing with his red face paint, crawling up from the rubble of broken stone. He conjured orbs of black fire and flung them at Gabriel.

Gabriel deflected Koll's fireballs with his staff. "Why won't you bloody die?" He tossed more fireballs at the altar, his laughter fueling the madness as explosions sent more guards, priests, and goblins hurling across the temple. A guard charged and knocked his staff out of his hands. Gabriel pulled off his helmet and struck the sword out of his grasp, hitting him across the head with it. Before he could recover his stance, Gabriel rammed his fist into his face and ran him through with his sword. Gabriel summoned his staff to his grasp and waved it in a circle above his head, shooting sorcerous beams of blue all around, covering the prisoners with a blue nimbus. Confused and shaken, Hinkleburr noticed he glowed with blue light and wondered why, until a spear struck him and bounced off.

Gabriel shouted above the din. "Run! You're all shielded!" Then the sorcerer charged Koll, his staff burning with sorcery in one hand and a sword gripped in the other.

He cast a shield around all of us. Bloody mad genius! "Come on! Run as he says." Hinkleburr grabbed Broda and Talwyn, then ran for the doors.

Koll faced down Gabriel, protected by his scarlet shield, Xabral huddled at his feet. Impervious to the violent destruction of Gabriel's explosive balls, his sorcery closed the double doors of the temples, raising more panic.

"No one leaves this temple," Koll commanded. "And I'm sick of you, Gabriel. You must die."

"After you," Gabriel taunted, stalking toward him.

Koll's artificial arm radiated sorcery and unleashed a crimson torrent which tangled around Gabriel like a snake, fragmenting his protective shield. The sizzling scarlet rope dragged Gabriel across the floor and up the broken stairs to the ruined altar. Gabriel swore, his magic flashing in defiance to shatter Koll's mystical bonds.

Namir leapt to attack, but Koll trapped him in the same sorcerous web. Namir clawed with frantic desperation as Koll stood over them.

With the temple doors closed and Gabriel's defeat, Hinkleburr's resilience was succumbing to dread. People crushed around him, pounding the metal doors. The smothering mass of prisoners depleted air and rational thought. The howl of demons advancing and the terrified faces of Broda and Talwyn tore his reserves.

A long blade of obsidian glass flashed in Koll's hand. "I offer the first hearts to the Dark Trinity."

"No!" Hinkleburr shouted, his hope draining with each breath as Koll raised the dagger to carve out Gabriel's heart.

A flash of white light blinded Hinkleburr. He shielded his eyes, shaking from the intensity. Dazed and breathless, he realized he was on his knees, and the temple doors were wide open. Prisoners and guards alike were scattered across the temple, stunned but alive. His gaze followed the trail of light to the altar where a shimmering Winged Fey floated over Gabriel. She flung Koll and Xabral across the room with a sweep of her hand. Gabriel and Namir's bindings vanished. Gabriel jumped to his feet but had the sense to bow before her.

She glided to the floor, luminous green and black wings unfurled. "There will be no blood spilled in this place, unless it is yours, Koll."

CHAPTER 19

Inconsolable, Mellypip wept in Runa's arms when he learned what happened to his friends in Thema. *I can't believe it*, he sobbed to her through the bonding, sobbing so harshly he could not speak aloud. The anguish of his friends dying at Koll's hands tormented him.

I refuse to believe it, Runa affirmed as she rocked him back and forth, sitting on the floor.

Mellypip's sorrowful condition concerned Sephya, huddling close, her paws holding on to Runa's knee. "Melly sad?" Sephya asked.

"Yes, Sephya," Runa said gently, scratching the baby dragon's head. "But it's not your fault."

"Bad people," Sephya sniffed, puffing tufts of smoke from her nose.

Talon and Fallon forlorn for their little friend nodded in unison. They settled close to Runa and Mellypip, resting their heads on the floor, but keeping a watchful eye on Sephya.

"Yes, very bad people. But we must not lose all hope. Bad people also lie," Runa pointed out. "And Koll is the worst of them. If you looked up the word evil in the dictionary, Koll's face would be there."

"Koll is evil incarnate," Panthara added, standing in the doorway.

"Koll nasty," Azmadu affirmed, looking at the baby dragon with longing. "And Xabral is his evil equal. They're mean. Don't listen to everything they tell you."

"We try not to, but the truth is hard to find right now. Come in, please," Runa invited.

"Do you need anything?" Panthara asked, entering with regal grace, Azmadu padding eagerly after her into the room.

"No," Runa whispered. "But thank you. It's just so hard on all of us. Melly and Hinkleburr are especially close. Broda and Talwyn always gave him extra treats when I wasn't looking."

Panthara sat in the chair next to Runa. Talon and Fallon gingerly snuffled Panthara and Azmadu. Panthara patiently waited as they inhaled her scent. Talon's nose burrowed into Azmadu's tummy and knocked him over.

"Consider it an initiation ritual," Runa said. "Grandpa says shadow dragons always greet someone with a good whiff. Any news?"

"Sadly, there's nothing new to report. I just thought I'd check and see how you're doing. I know they mean a lot to you both. I prayed to my patron goddess Ydalia for the safe delivery of your friends."

"Thank you," Runa said. "She's the goddess of fate isn't she?"

"Yes," Panthara nodded, her hands folded in her lap, back straight. Runa noted how she still sat like a queen. "Ydalia is the daughter of Tysis and Uros, rulers of the Underworld. As a child, I had a pendant of blue stone called the eye of Ydalia. It was for luck and a traditional charm among my people. Koll took it from me. He insisted I pray only to Ahridum, Rygon, and other dark eternals. Since I've freed myself from his influence, I have found comfort in the faith of my girlhood."

"Comfort is always good," Runa agreed. "I just can't imagine them dead. Damn Koll!"

Mellypip wiped his eyes. "But what if they are truly dead?"

"Do not believe Koll's words so easily, Mellypip. You must keep faith they are still alive, because faith is what Koll destroys," Panthara warned. "Curse Koll and his wicked snake. But take heart, for your friends are clever and not prone to stupidity. Their wily actions gave me a hard time when I was doing Koll's work. I regret my alliance with Koll, but because of this I know how strong they are. There's a reason why there are so many legends about Dwarven warriors."

Mellypip wanted desperately to believe her. Runa's gentle cuddling helped calm him. He felt a little embarrassed. He was not acting like a brave warrior ranger-mage at the moment. Warriors do not blubber. They banish tears and fight on. Tears alerted Mellypip to another problem. "What about Rono? Poor Rono is so sensitive, and he really liked the Dwarves. I don't want to upset him."

"Maybe we should wait, just a little while," Runa suggested. "Until we have more news."

Panthara nodded, her expression pensive. "I was there when Koll spoke those terrible words on the calling crystal. He gloated far too much. I think he just wanted the last word before destroying the crystal on the other side. Myrsalian told me how often Jiana tried to communicate news to us. We will know soon. Gabriel went to Thema to help. He may love his ale far too much, but he is a master warrior and a fine sorcerer when sober. If anyone can rankle Koll, it's Gabriel. He will make his head ache!"

Mellypip and wiped his eyes with his blue blanket. "I think Gabriel would prefer to break Koll's head."

"We all do," Runa affirmed, laughing a little.

Panthara smiled and leaned over to pet Mellypip. Panthara was usually so reserved, it took Mellypip by surprise. Her touch was gentle and her kindness genuine. "If anyone can save your friends, Gabriel can. Don't forget about Jiana and Jasper. Jiana is just as tough a warrior, and she knows the palace in Upal as one of Sarabia's advisors. Koll's soul is black. I know because I've seen it. It still gives me nightmares. It doesn't mean Koll will win. We must believe good will win, and the looming darkness will be defeated."

"Have faith, Melly," Azmadu said, sitting close to Mellypip next to the baby dragon. "I will sit with you until you feel better. We can read about the dragons later."

"Yes, read about us," Fallon said, his head perked up.

"Little Sephya needs to learn about her heritage," Talon added. "It will be educational."

"Thank you, Azmadu. It's very sweet of you. I think it would be a good thing and help us clear our heads," Runa said. "What's going on downstairs?"

"Everyone is acting busy because they don't want to think about the worst. Cathal and Neelam are meeting with King Caladynn. Opaline is attempting to bake a cake, but she does not have her mother's talent for it. Caliste is helping her, but I think she is there to make sure there are no kitchen fires. Taran is sequestered in his laboratory."

"Something else is bothering you," Runa said, noticing the tension on her face.

Panthara sighed deeply. "I'm afraid Opaline's miffed with me, again."

"Why?" Runa asked. "I thought you two were more harmonious of late? Or at least in a state of truce."

"Taran and I are betrothed," Panthara whispered.

"Yes! We're all going to be related now," Azmadu added, flapping his wings. "Since Panthara is your sister and Taran is Opaline's brother, when they're married we will all be family."

The news stunned Runa, but she was not surprised. The two had grown so close, it was a natural evolution. "I'm happy for you. Finding love is wonderful."

Panthara stroked Azmadu's head. "Thank you. Funny how one marriage can unite so many? I'm not sure if Opaline is ready to call me sister. I'm afraid she found out by accident. It happened right before we heard the news on the calling crystal. Words were exchanged. Taran and Opaline are both stubborn. They're not speaking to each other. Opaline is not speaking to me. Taran won't discuss it with me. It's all a mess. A looming darkness threatens us all, and we still squabble like children. I don't know what to expect."

"From the looming darkness or Opaline?" Runa asked.

"Must I choose?" Panthara grinned.

"I'll talk to her," Runa offered. "She's just upset. Taran and Opaline are not just brother and sister, but twins. They're so alike, yet they fight constantly. Just don't take sides."

"I would rather face Ahridum," Panthara replied dryly.

Sephya crawled into Runa's lap and nuzzled Mellypip. *She needs her nap*, Mellypip communicated to Runa. He shared his blanket with the baby dragon as she nestled in, tucking her head beneath her wing.

Talon and Fallon coiled around Runa on either side, keeping a watchful eye on little Sephya.

~ * ~

"This news is indeed grim," King Caladynn said. "Queen Sarabia was an ally and a friend. If Thema has fallen to Obsydia's forces, we'll be blocked on the east and west. We will be forced into war with both the Red Empire and Thema."

"Yet, there has been no official declaration of war?" Morydonn added.

"They want to force our hand," Neelam said. "This must be avoided as long as possible. Protect your borders."

"What does King Arawn say?" Caladynn asked Neelam.

"He feels the pressure of war too. Our country is just as vulnerable," Neelam replied. "We have closed our borders to trade, but our King has also accepted refugees."

Cathal sat at the table, feeling too exhausted for rational thought.

His headache was like spikes in his brain.

You look terrible, Belwyn remarked, a bit too loudly in his head. *This could have waited. There is much we do not know. Gabriel has not contacted us. You need sleep and food. You cannot defeat evil on an empty stomach.*

Now you sound like Melly. Things are falling apart way too fast.

I know. I'm watching it crumble too. It's all suspicious.

"How can we guard our borders against the enemy?" Morydonn interrupted. "Refugees are crossing into our lands by the hundreds. They are useless outcasts."

Caladynn's patience waned with his brother's remarks. "They are innocent victims of war and persecution. I will not turn away women and children escaping war and the abomination of sacrifice."

"Many are able-bodied men and women willing to serve you, Caladynn," Cathal added. "They will gladly fight for you in gratitude for the sanctuary you provided them."

"They are a threat," Morydonn swore. "A drain on our resources. If we aid these refugees, it will incur animosity from our enemy. We should stay neutral as long as possible. The Red Empire is powerful. And some refugees could actually be their spies."

Neelam's patience dissolved and his eyes narrowed when he addressed Morydonn. "I'm fed up with Levandius and his Red Empire. I refuse to acknowledge the name. It's a pretense of over-blown ego to promote fear. I'm sure Levandius had nothing to do with this new moniker. He's a puppet and a weak one at that. Koll's sycophants began spreading the name, Red Empire, to instill terror. The name took because people are afraid. Facts are being manipulated and shaped by the enemy. Truth is in the dustbin along with honor. People can also be stupid and believe whatever they're told. I refuse to run in fear or swallow their bloody cant of darkness. Levandius and Koll want to frighten other nations into thinking they are more deadly."

"Aren't they?" Morydonn asked.

"Levandius is suffering more troubles than he's admitting too. Koll's power can only hold so much influence. The country is split with civil war they are not advertising," Neelam replied. "Many are fighting back and the enemy wants to conceal the nasty truth."

"There are so many lies and truths, but which is which?" Morydonn asked simply.

Surya looked down at Neelam, "My Wizard speaks truth,

though his words are hot-blooded."

"Do not forget, we have been through this before," Belwyn added. "You have not, Prince Morydonn. We understand your doubts, but never forget we fight for the Light."

"Am I to be lectured by a pair of birds?" Morydonn exploded, standing up.

"No Morydonn, not just birds," Cathal countered in a resolute voice. "But familiars, intelligent and magical. They witnessed the Bloodstone Wars. I too was witness and speak the same, will you accept the lecture from a human?"

"Can a sorcerer truly be human?" Morydonn asked.

Prince Ulric took Morydonn's arm, his voice calm as he guided him back to his seat. "The important point is we fight on the same side. We must have compassion, Uncle. Mother and Opaline organized aid for the refugees, tapping donations of food and money from wealthy nobles and merchants. They are organizing the religious houses to distribute food and offer shelter. Our people are not suffering yet. But we can aid those who are."

Did you see the sour look on Morydonn's face when Ulric mentioned Opaline? Belwyn asked. *It could have curdled fresh cream.*

Cathal's neutral expression revealed nothing. *Morydonn's distrust of mages is well known, but he has always been loyal to his brother despite their differences. His attendance at this meeting was unexpected. He usually avoids being in the same room with us.*

I don't trust him, Belwyn said. *And something else is bugging me. I sense something, a mystical scent I cannot detect.*

I smell it too, Cathal nodded, studying Morydonn.

"Wars have broken out everywhere," Neelam said, "All across the continent Koll and Obsydia instigated conflicts not for conquest, but distraction. Neither Obsydia nor Koll really pay any heed about official declarations. They're causing chaos to keep their true agendas out of sight."

"What is their agenda?" Morydonn asked.

Neelam leaned back in his chair and smoothly answered. "We cannot say yet, but I assure you we will reveal any information to our trusted allies, once we have definitive proof."

Belwyn's talons gripped the back of the chair, digging into the wood. *If Neelam is right, all this war and muck is just a diversion. It means Obsydia's schema may already be in place.*

I know. The problem is what can we do to stop her.

~ * ~

Faustine paced around the bedchamber. Uneasiness with their new task made her pace in circles When Morydonn entered the room, she rushed to him, enjoying the warmth of his arms around her. She felt safe in this dusky room lit only with a few fading candles, with Morydonn at her side again. "I was so worried. The meeting lasted for so long. What did they say?"

"Nothing, my love," Morydonn replied.

The mirror glowed brightly and Obsydia's face appeared. The dark goddess's presence unnerved her to the core, but she bowed her head. "Great Queen, we await your command."

Obsydia's shadow hair floated, framing her bone-pale face and silver eyes. She smiled slightly, curling her crimson lips. "Tell me what you have found."

Morydonn stood before the mirror. His face paled and his eyes turned red. "My Queen, they know nothing. They are fools chasing the darkness. They suspect you have a reason for starting wars, but have no answers. They are afraid."

"Then I have a mission for you, Prince Morydonn. Thill must fall, and you will be the hand to bring its fate. Kill the king, your brother, and all of his family. Then you will rise to take the crown to build your own empire."

"I will obey," Morydonn responded with a deep bow. "I worship you, Queen Obsydia, my Living Goddess. When do you wish to strike?"

"Soon. Very soon, my dark warrior. I will tell you when."

~ * ~

The mirror darkened on the other side. Obsydia's satisfied look extracted a grin from Shroud.

"The fool is very obedient," Shroud remarked. "You have discovered a new technique to conceal your converts from the enemy?"

Obsydia's eyes bright were with humor. "Yes, a new idea I had been playing with. I cast enchantments to conceal his true face. The Hooded Guardians wanted to make me a special gift, and conjured this dark magic for me. Morydonn was my test subject. The red eyes will no longer be the mark of my warriors. They can walk among men undetected."

"What about Faustine? Can you trust her to remain true? Perhaps you should do the same to her?"

"Faustine is simple. Easily ruled by her emotions. She believes he loves her now. So sad. As long as I control her husband, she will be obedient. Morydonn was quite opposed to me. He hated magic and me. There was no pleasing this mortal, so I chose for him. He was not as pliable as Faustine. I could not turn him with my words of wisdom, so I took his soul."

"How was it?" Shroud asked, licking her lips.

"Delicious. But you are not here for pleasant repast, Shroud. Something has happened."

"Yes. Koll failed you."

Obsydia's face hardened. "How?"

"In Upal, the sacrifices escaped. There was an intruder, an insane sorcerer who fought and tried to free the offerings in the great temple Ahridum gifted you. Koll managed to subdue him until—"

"What happened?" Obsydia demanded.

"A Winged Fey entered the temple."

Obsydia flamed with bright shadows as she paced the floor, her crimson train sweeping the black floor. "Winged Fey dare to trespass on my holy ground? A being of Light? Desecrating me in my house!"

"Koll failed you," Shroud insisted. "He must be punished."

CHAPTER 20

Belwyn perched on the bedpost, digging his talons in while he waited. *I hope Sirah does not inspect for claw marks. Maybe Cathal can magically buff them over.* The day had been stressful enough. Worst of all, there has been no word from Gabriel or Jiana, which led to highly emotional people. It frayed Belwyn's nerves. He wanted to find a tree with a deep hole somewhere in the forest and hide from the world. It did not help that the bloody calling crystal was broken again. Perhaps it was hexed?

Rualla entered the room, shaking off her snow-dusted shawl. She started when she saw Belwyn. "Goodness, Belwyn! You scared me. Where's Papa?"

"He's busy, but we haven't had time to chat with all the world ending doom going on. I wanted to be sure you are fully recovered."

Rualla smiled. Belwyn's heart ached realizing how much Runa took after her mother. A little more mature, of course, but they could pass more like sisters than mother and daughter.

"I'm much better," Rualla said, putting Runa's staff on the bed. "Liat took me for a walk. He's so dear, you know."

"Liat cares a great deal for you," Belwyn said. "We all do."

"I care about him too," Rualla said. "I care about all of you."

Belwyn's golden eyes leveled at her. "Why won't you talk to your daughter?"

Rualla chewed her lip in the same manner as Runa when she was frustrated. She sat on the bed and held Runa's staff. "I have talked to my daughter."

"You banished her from your sight, and since then you've had monosyllabic encounters. Stop it!"

"What can I say to her? I failed her? She grew up without her mother, and it's my fault."

"Runa grew up loved, treasuring your memory. Runa loves you. She's tormented and confused. She has troubles too. She needs her mother. Dealing with teenage girls is not in my tome. Cathal and I have enough muck going on without dissension within our family." After a moment of tense silence, Belwyn gently added, "I know it's been hard for you."

"Do you?" she challenged.

"Yes, I do. I helped bring you up, Rualla. I know you. I know how much you loved Ashur, despite all your differences. He was a good man with a tragic end; even more tragic his good name was blackened thanks to Koll's lies."

"I know! What happened to Ashur was horrific. War and death, all because of Koll! But at the time I despised my husband until Mother and I were bound to the tree, and I realized a demon lived in Ashur's body. My husband was dead, and I never mourned him."

"None of us knew. We all thought Ashur had gone mad," Rualla said. "When mother and I were captured, only then did I learn Ashur was dead, and his poor body possessed by a demon. He died alone, because of Koll; Runa grew up alone, without me."

"Runa was never alone. She was surrounded by love. Downright spoiled, really. Runa was saved from Koll, thanks to Striker's sacrifice. The loss of a familiar is just as bitter. You lost Ashur and Striker, and then underwent a demonic curse meant to kill you. I praise the gods it didn't. Thanks to Runa's dream seer ability, we found you and Yllia. You suffered a great deal, more than any of us, but it's time to let go of the past. Embrace the love of all of your family."

"You make it sound so easy," Rualla said, looking away.

"It should be. She's out of diapers and can talk."

Rualla laughed a little, wiping a tear from her cheek. "I know. I just don't know where to start. I didn't mean to send her away. I had no idea so much time had passed. I was living a nightmare. When I last saw Runa, she was just a baby. Then the darkness entombed me."

"It hurts you," Belwyn added.

"Yes," Rualla nodded. "Mama and Papa have been gentle since I woke. Indulgent even. Everyone has. Liat dotes on me. Even Dabiro is gentle."

"It's odd seeing Dabiro so demure. I should taunt him about it."

"There's no answer for my pain but time, I know."

Rualla moved closer to him, and Belwyn brushed his wing against her cheek. "We love you, but you need to show Runa you love her too."

"I will," Rualla said. "I promise."

"And give back her staff," Belwyn added.

"It holds Striker's soul. I feel it."

"I know. It hurts me too."

~ * ~

Opaline sat on the stone bench in the backyard for over an hour despite the chill. The white afternoon sky snowed lightly. Not a trace of cloud or sunshine dispelled the winter cast. "I know it's odd, but I like the snow. We never had snow in Tiamet. It's pretty. I just wish it wasn't so darn chilly. It's grown even colder since morning." Grimm sat nearby, watching the snowflakes fall. "You don't have to wait outside with me."

"I like the snow," Grimm said, "I can handle the cold."

"It's the cold inside I can't handle," Opaline said, wrapping her wool cloak tighter around her.

"I don't like it when my pack fights," Grimm said. "Taran is always hotheaded."

"I tried to bake his favorite cake. It was a miserable failure."

"I liked it," Grimm said, nuzzling his nose in her hand.

"You are sweet," Opaline whispered, patting his head. "It was burnt."

"It was crunchy and sweet," Grimm told her. "And you did nothing wrong. He assumed you would criticize his betrothal to Panthara."

"Oh, Grimm, I hate fighting, yet all we do lately is squabble."

"I can bite him for you." Grimm offered.

Opaline laughed and hugged him. "Why Grimm, are you developing a sense of humor?"

"Mellypip told me it is an imperative skill, especially when dealing with cranky owls."

"Belwyn is something of a crabby beak," Opaline laughed.

Neelam marched into the backyard, Surya on his arm. The white eagle launched into the air, her high-pitched cry filling the air. Opaline was hesitant to speak, as the Mage-Chieftain was usually a private fellow. But it would be rude to ignore him.

"Afternoon Neelam," Opaline called bravely. "Is Surya going on an adventure?"

"My girl needs some exercise," Neelam said, rubbing his hands together.

"I take Grimm for a long walk each morning, though he does like to race ahead of me."

"Wolves are magnificent creatures," Neelam said. "Be they familiar or one of nature's animals. They're intelligent and devoted, with a complex social structure. They mate for life."

"My Grimm is truly intelligent and devoted," Opaline agreed with genuine affection, patting his back. Grimm wagged his tail happily. "Any word from Thema yet?"

"Not yet," Neelam replied. "Gabriel and Namir made it there. That's all I know."

"Gabriel is reckless," Opaline remarked. "He'll get himself killed if he's not careful."

"He'll manage, despite his shortcomings. He's a skilled warrior and sorcerer, when he's not drinking. I meant to congratulate you on your betrothal to Prince Ulric. He's a fine young man."

"Thank you, Neelam," Opaline replied. "It's all right. I know you're busy fighting the dark immortal queens and the end of the world. His family approves, which is a blessing."

"They're lucky to have you," Neelam replied, scrutinizing her face. "But something is bothering you."

"I am so obvious?" Opaline looked up at the sky. "Ulric is a wonderful man. Mother says I'm too young, but she won't stand in my way. He has every good quality a prince should possess. Marriage is something I never thought about until I met Ulric. I do love him so, but after the initial joy of his proposal, I must admit I'm a little bit—"

"Afraid? Terrified?"

Opaline blushed at his astute observation. "Yes. It's not just because it's a lifetime together. There are factors unique to our situation which worry me. A sorceress can live a long life. My lifetime is not the same as a *normal* princess. I will not age the same as Ulric. When he's sixty, I will not look much different. I'm also concerned about children. Can I give him children? What will happen if they are sorcerers? Will it trigger turmoil with the royal succession?" Her secret torment, which she kept to herself except for Grimm, bubbled to the surface. "I'm not sure I want to go give up my freedom. It's not just marriage, but I know the price of a royal life. I would not be free as the wife of the Crown Prince of Thill. I love him, I do. But I don't know what to do. I drive myself mad with what ifs. How do I know if I am making the right choice?"

"I understand your concern. Your personal experiences in

Tiamet are not the best foundation. Your father's imperial family are a pack of high-born cutthroats. No offense."

"None taken."

"Thill's royal family is different. The history of the house of Rhule is one of honor, on the whole. You know that. They are loving and care about each other. Your fears are more personal."

Opaline looked down at her hands, pink from the bitter chill. She should have worn gloves. She rubbed them together, fighting the irrational urge to cry. "Yes. I'm afraid."

"No shame, my dear. It's normal. Despite your sumptuous taste in dresses, you're not the imperial princess anymore. You've found a different path and fear Ulric's love will not be enough for you to return to the cloister of royal life. Your worry your love will not be enough because of your differences. Not politics, but the true things in life. You've tasted adventure and find it hard to give up. You wonder about your children's fate, or if you will have any. I know. I was married to a woman who was not mageborn."

"I never knew you were married!"

Neelam's voice became somber as he sat down next to Opaline, but a wisp of a smile lit his face. "Marriage was the happiest time of my life. Her name was Alethea. She wasn't a mage nor of my race, but I loved her from the first moment I saw her." Neelam opened his hand, and the scent of magic permeated the air. A beautiful woman appeared in his palm, a miniature image of a voluptuous woman in a red dress with long black hair, dark blue eyes, and deeply tanned skin.

"She's beautiful!" Opaline gasped at the lifelike image, the nimbus of magic flickering around the form.

"We were married for forty-seven years. It was a long time ago of course. We met toward the end of the Bloodstone Age, so luckily most of our married years were during the Topaz Age which followed. What's even stranger, it was because of hell-bitch Obsydia I met Alethea."

"Oh, please tell me," Opaline begged.

"My niece, Magda, had been abducted, along with many other women across the continent. She was only sixteen and had not come into her magic yet. Like you, she was only half mage. Her father was a wizard, bur her mother wasn't mage caste. They loved each other too and made a leap of faith. When Magda was taken they were devastated. She was their only child and they treasured her, as did I. So I went hunting in the east and her father searched in the west. As I searched, I heard rumors of women being held prisoner in the demon city of Ralnazarr. It was in the Wasteland, not far from Obsydia's temple palace."

Opaline shivered, remembering Obsydia's gruesome temple palace when Chimera abducted her for sacrifice. It still gave her nightmares. A demon city in Obsydia's realm was not surprising.

"Goblins and trolls lived there, along with those demon men enslaved by Obsydia," Neelam continued. "Ralnazarr was a small fortress city surrounded by a fence of human bones. Goblins in ragged leather stalked the night with trolls on chains. Strange creatures of impish origins scurried across the desert sands. Human soldiers also lived there, why they chose to serve Obsydia I never understood. I gathered a force of men from the desert tribes to rescue them. They suffered from demon raids too. Not just fighting demons but when they stole their daughters and wives, they were quite willing to join forces together. All the petty tribal feuds vanished when their women and children were threatened. What I found when I infiltrated the prison enraged me. Diabolistic magic was conjured to breed human women with demons. Not goblins or trolls or any earthly born monster, but *true demons* summoned from Darkness. Neither victims nor offspring survived. They were still trying to create a demon-human hybrid. What they did to those poor girls was an abomination."

"How horrible!" Opaline gasped, the romance suddenly turned to terror.

"I'm sorry," Neelam apologized. "Bloodstone tales always have a dark origin. I found their prison and my niece Magda was still alive. There were many women held captive in the company of demons and dark sorcerers. Alethea was in the same prison as Magda. She was brave and full of fire. She protected Magda and had no fear of those scum. I had infiltrated the prison."

"A dangerous act in such a vile place. How did you manage it?" Opaline asked, rapt with the tale.

"I shapeshifted into a desert rat. It's good to have magic. Inside the prison a mix of humans and goblins guarded the women. The sight of it made me sick. All those young women, crammed into cages. I remember the terror in their eyes. But when I first saw

Alethea, she was fighting off a human guard. She had just hurled a bucket of waste at him when they tried to take her and Magda. She pounced like a panther, clawing at the guard until he bawled like a baby. Goblins tried to peel her away and she kicked at them too. She was magnificent. I shapeshifted back into myself and finished off the goblins and guards with my sword. Surya flew in, fighting at my side. When the battle ceased, for some reason which still stuns me to this day, I told Alethea she was a comely wench. We were in the midst of hell, surrounded by blood and demons. Alethea just looked me up and down, hands on hips and chin lifted with pride. She told me, "Don't let these rags and stink fool you. I'm worth at least a hundred horses for a bridal price."

"Don't stop!" Opaline begged. "What happened next?"

"Did you kill the goblins?" Grimm asked eagerly. He hated goblins.

"Chaos and blood. Surya and I killed them all, goblin and human guards both. The human scum deserved it for siding with evil. We unlocked the cages. But it wasn't over."

"Obsydia stopped you," Grimm remarked, the memory of observing her in the Wasteland still haunted him.

"Yes, my first confrontation with Obsydia. I had only heard the usual horror about her until then. I wasn't expecting her there. She usually resided in her vast temple-palace, but was attending to supervise another ritual. Hell-bitch trapped me and Surya in a mystical ball of dark energy. She deliberately chose Magda and Alethea as the next victims in her evil conjuration and ordered them bound to a stake. She knew they would die. She did it to spite me and made sure I had a full view of the ceremony. Obsydia's demon handmaidens appeared and circled Magda and Alethea and began to summon the Dark. The words were demon gibberish. All I remember was red-hot rage. Fortunately, little Magda's magic suddenly burst. Her wizardry scattered all around, striking Obsydia's demon handmaidens with chaotic energy, blackening their foul skin and sending them scuttling back to Obsydia. The enemy was stopped in their tracks as streams of magic tossed them about. Poor little Magda. She had no control, which was actually helpful."

"I think I can relate to Magda," Opaline said, rapt with the story.

"Magda freed herself and Alethea. I shattered the shadowy prison Obsydia cast on me. How I still don't know. I magically opened the gate of bones and summoned the army. Fighting exploded. I put Magda on a war pony and sent her off with the gift of magical speed. I remember Alethea's war cries as she jumped astride a war-horse, her rags barely covering her sweaty thighs as she rode out, swinging a scimitar dripping demon blood. She cut off a few goblin heads too before she escaped into the starless night. The look on Obsydia's face was most satisfying. We rescued all the women. I shapeshifted into a white eagle and flew off with Surya. I earned Obsydia's rancor and the respect of the tribal alliance the same day. I returned Magda to her parents. Not long after, I brought Alethea a hundred horses and asked her to marry me."

Opaline felt breathless after the tale. "That is the most violent and wonderful love story I ever heard."

"Please tell Mellypip," Grimm begged. "He would love to include the story in his bard book."

"Alethea sounds like an amazing woman," Opaline said. "It was so long ago. You have been all alone since she passed?"

"I need no one else," Neelam said softly. "I have our memories." He closed his hand and Alethea's image vanished.

His words struck at her heart and filled her with even more doubt. Was her love for Ulric as strong? Would she treasure their years together, as Neelam did with his Alethea? "Did you have children?"

"No," Neelam replied. "Our one regret. I know she wanted a child. It is not always easy since we live so long and mortal humans do not."

Opaline desperately wanted to give Ulric children, but if she couldn't? Would he regret marrying her too? Would she regret giving up her life? Her own mother gently spoke of this concern. Why was the heart so complicated? She recalled Ulric's tender proposal. How could she say no to such a man? But could she walk away from what she had become?

Grimm sensed her shift, putting his head in her lap. *You are sad now. What is it?*

Oh Grimm. I don't know what to do.

Your love for him may endure. You cannot know the future.

You sound so optimistic. It's very unlike you.

It's your fault. I am happy. That's very odd for me too.

Neelam jumped up, gazing into the sky. "What the hell?"

Opaline stood, shading her eyes against the glare of white sky and snow. "What's wrong?" She saw it and gasped.

"Find Cathal," Neelam commanded. "Now."

A Winged Fey with green and black wings descended toward them.

~ * ~

The Shadow Tower vibrated as the Claw Maidens sang hymns to Obsydia, dancing before the altar embellished with magical runes burning with demon origin. Obsydia's image glittered in stained glass over fifty feet high, resplendent in red robes and a crown of black stars above her shadow hair. On her right was her Eternal Father, Ahridum, an ominous figure shrouded in flame and shadow, swathed in robes woven of night.

Obsydia entered the temple, barefoot, wearing only a plain black shift, her face covered with a sheer red veil. The Hooded Guardians followed her, the mysterious demons of the Otherworld who presided over her birth when her mortal mother, Lilith, succumbed to Ahridum's touch. These spectral figures carried chalices of blood and they too sang in ghostly voices.

Shroud stopped her dance when Obsydia reached the altar. She went to Obsydia, bony hands crossed over her chest, singing softly with her sister demons. Obsydia bowed her head as Guardians circled her, a ring of darkness as Shroud stripped away her veil.

"Behold, the rise of Darkness," Shroud cried out.

"Behold," the Claw Maidens resonated, dropping to their knees before Obsydia.

"Rejoice, for Darkness rises," Shroud chanted.

"Rejoice," the demon maidens sang.

"I am Darkness born," Obsydia said, raising her arms to the sky. "Daughter of Ahridum, I claim this world in your name. I claim this world for Darkness. Only our kind shall walk this world."

Then each hooded specter took a turn and anointed Obsydia with blood, each mark swirled in a runic design the same as those carved into the altar. With each touch, the red blood glimmered, and then vanished into Obsydia's skin. The Claw Maidens rose and formed a circle on the altar. In the center of their ring, a deep hollow of blue and red flame lit the chamber. They chanted in demon tongue.

"How long is the ritual?" Obsydia whispered. "How long before

I ascend?"

"Thirteen days," Shroud replied. "This is the true reason why your handmaidens were summoned from the Netherworld of Shadow and Fire. They cannot be mortal born for this holy ceremony. I must join the incantation now. When the thirteenth day sets, you will take your place on the sacred altar and offer yourself to Ahridum. The Hooded Ones will guide you in your last rites before you cast off your mortal shell. If enough blood has been sacrificed and Darkness blesses us all, the world will belong to us. Demons and shadows will dance forever beneath the night and day will burn with a red sun and black sky."

"Shroud, when this ritual is done, I shall truly ascend and become Eternal."

"Pray it be so," Shroud whispered, brushing Obsydia's pale cheek with her hand. "If you fail Ahridum again, your fate will be cruel."

CHAPTER 21

What in the blazes is going on? Belwyn asked.

When I figure it out, I'll let you know, Cathal replied. *Asheni says she is here to help.*

Belwyn perched on the wooden dining chair, eat tufts folded back. *This is either really good or really bad. Winged Fey are notorious for avoiding folk. They're secretive and not exactly helpful when you need them. Downright rude if you ask me. Now one just shows up on our doorstep. I doubt she's here for tea.*

The mages gathered, wordless and trying not to stare at Asheni. She stood in the dining room, her luminous pale skin shimmered in the candlelight, and her green and black gossamer wings were folded in. Jiana joined them and thankfully broke the silence.

"Sarabia is resting. Raghnall gave her a sleeping draught." Tired but bright-eyed, Jasper in her arms, she sat down wearily between Hinkleburr and Gabriel. "Talwyn has a nasty concussion. Broda is looking after him." Jiana glanced at Gabriel and Hinkleburr, sharing a flagon of ale, clothes bloodstained, bruised and covered with lacerations. "Are you sure you two are up to this? You should get those cuts and bruises treated."

"My sorcerer is stubborn," Namir answered, curled at Gabriel's feet.

"I suggest a hot bath," Opaline pointed out, wrinkling her nose. "Goblin blood has an unpleasant sour odor."

"Forgive my shortcomings, Princess," Gabriel apologized, grinning. "Fighting demons has its drawbacks."

"I wouldn't miss this for the world," Hinkleburr insisted, taking a swig of ale and passing it back it to Gabriel.

Jiana plucked the flagon out of Gabriel's hand and took a long drink. "If Asheni had not arrived, I'm not sure we would have made it out of Thema alive. Hadrial betrayed her own sister. She forged an alliance with Koll and Levandius. Asheni used her magic to carry us all back here. I got Sarabia out, but it was risky. Her condition is critical."

"What did you do?" Runa asked Asheni with eager curiosity.

"Yes, please tell us," Mellypip begged.

"It's hard to explain," Asheni answered softly.

"I can't describe it." Jiana rubbed her temples. "Some of it is like a dream."

"You made the right choice bringing Sarabia even with the risk," Sirah said. "At least she has a chance now."

"What happened to her?" Cathal asked. "Her symptoms reek of diabolistic magic."

"Koll happened, what else? Sarabia cursed with some extreme form of Hadrial's paralytic condition now. I know he did." Jiana snapped, taking another drink. "Obsydia was there."

"What? Unusual for her to make a public appearance," Cathal remarked. "Obsydia usually stays in her temple palaces and sends her filthy minions to do her dirty work."

"Obsydia's appearance was personal, from what Hinkleburr told me. Also, along with the city under the control of Obsydia and Koll, the ancient Theman temple is gone."

"Destroyed?" Neelam asked.

Jiana held Jasper close, her eyes haunted. "No, it just vanished. Obsydia's temple emerged in its place like a wicked curse. I didn't see it coming." Jiana hunched over, angrily wiping tears away.

"None of us did, my dear," Hinkleburr assured her. "You saved the queen. No one could have done more."

"Obsydia's interest in Thema was personal," Asheni said. "She suffered her first defeat there during the Bloodstone Age."

"Just like the legends!" Mellypip exclaimed.

Jiana shook her head. "It must be some mystical trade off. Hadrial's paralysis and deformities are gone. She rules Thema now. Hadrial is beautiful, cold and barren of soul, but beautiful. She married Levandius."

Opaline shivered with disgust, shaking her head. "I suddenly feel sick."

Taran, prodded by a firm push by Panthara, went to his sister and put his arm around her. "We share the same burden of blood. Maybe you should have turned Levandius into a troll when you had the chance."

"At least you're not evil. Just stubborn," Opaline laughed. They exchanged a brief smile, mending their rift.

Jiana took another drink, her voice bitter. "I hope Hadrial

suffers."

Asheni looked at Jiana. "Indeed she will, though Hadrial does not know the true price. She will pay, whether the light or darkness wins."

"A rather ambiguous remark," Cathal said.

Gabriel saluted Asheni. "Well despite all, this lovely butterfly saved our asses when Koll was about to offer our hearts to Obsydia on a platter. She tossed Koll across the temple like a ragdoll. It was beautiful. If I had not been bleeding from goblin bites and claw marks, I would have kissed her."

"It's a problem. People think we are sacred. We are not gods. We were put here with a duty."

"But were your fathers really gods?" Mellypip asked boldly.

"Melly!" Runa scolded, shifting the chubby wampu in her arms.

"No little wampu, not a god. My sire was of eternal origin, but one of their messengers. My mother was Elfsharan. And yes, she died giving birth to me, as did all the other women who bore our kind."

"Your answer is cold," Sirah remarked.

"My heart is not for you to judge, Sorceress. The legends about us are not the whole truth, but only a thread, as is my warning to you now about what is to come and what it means."

"Thank you for saving our friends," Mellypip said earnestly. "I will write a heroic tale about it."

"I am sure it will be a wonderful read," Asheni replied, flashing an unexpected smile.

"Why are you here?" Neelam asked. "You're not known for volunteering your help, even in the darkest times. Do your fellow Winged Fey know you are mingling with lower beings?"

Asheni was not angered by Neelam's bluntness. "I understand your frustration, Neelam. You suspect what is at stake more than the younger mages among you. You've seen Obsydia's rule in the past. Cathal and Yllia also know the danger having survived the Blood-stone Age too. You were chosen to be the scions of light. You did your duty. But your calling is now for a danger far greater."

"You've watched the ages pass," Surya said, the snow eagles bold gaze fearless. "We fought the wars. We lost kindred in the bloodshed. What we need is your help. You and your kind need to stop watching and do! Fighting a god, even a half-god, requires powers even mages do not have. You're immortals. Half-eternal with powers we do not possess. Use them."

She took the words out of my beak, Belwyn remarked to Cathal.

Asheni nodded, her manner almost apologetic. "You are right. There can be no more watching. The time of hiding has ended for us. Our solitude no longer serves the world. The other Winged Fey do not see yet."

"They are divided," Cathal remarked.

"Yes, I could not wait for them to follow. I've seen what will come to pass if Obsydia's ritual succeeds."

"What ritual?" Neelam asked, leaning in suspiciously.

"You suspect the truth more than the others do, Wizard," Asheni replied. "The violent surge of sacrifice and war, the rise of her shadow tower in the ruined Elfsharan homeland, the coming of her claw maidens."

"Designed to keep us occupied from the real truth," Neelam said. "What is the truth?"

Cathal remembered Ambera's final words on her deathbed. They haunted him since that day. "Ambera's last words were if Obsydia wins, it would be a world of darkness forever. Light would be vanquished."

"What exactly did her vision mean?" Belwyn asked. "Because I have a nasty feeling the consequences are going to be disastrous."

"I will explain, for you deserve an answer. I must begin with the genesis of this shadow. In the great Sapphire Age, a great seer, a Drusane of the Elfsharans, suffered an ominous vision. He saw Obsydia's coming."

"But I was taught the Winged Fey were born in the Emerald Age," Runa interrupted.

"Runa!" Belwyn scolded.

"It's all right. I know our legends are often rife with misinformation," Asheni said. "The Light Eternals Rhone and Araema sent the Drusane a warning about the coming of Obsydia. A darkness was coming, wielded by Ahridum. Rhone and Araema sent their messengers, the seraphim to our world. They would bless nine maidens and from their touch, nine children would be born. The Winged Fey. Immortals born with powerful magic to watch over the world and rise to help in the final battle against evil. Nine Drusai priestesses volunteered to make this sacrifice. Common folklore among most of the races says they visited these women because of their beauty and fell in love. That's the poetic version. In truth, we were created to give hope to the world and stop the darkness from taking over the world. We were born only a handful days before Ahridum hurled the dark star upon this world, which brought destruction to whole nations and created a dark age of chaos."

"Which led to Obsydia's birth," Cathal nodded.

"And more hell," Neelam remarked.

"But that means the Winged Fey and Obsydia were birthed almost at the same time!" Runa exclaimed.

"Yes, to a point," Asheni nodded patiently. "The seer saw Obsydia's coming, but her actual arrival was some decades later. From the rubble of destruction, people struggled to live. So much was lost. Forgotten."

"And you just watched?" Cathal remarked.

Asheni looked at Cathal. "No, Cathal. We also had times of compassion. Your life would have been dust if we had not carried you away after Obsydia's demons killed your parents."

Cathal stopped in his tracks. "I never knew how my real parents died. Borel never spoke of it."

"Obsydia's chief handmaiden Shade was a seer. She saw you as a threat, Cathal. Obsydia ordered your village razed to make sure you died. You were no more than a toddler. We managed to rescue you, but were not in time to save your parents. We took you to the Raven-Wing. They brought you to Borel the Sorcerer in the north. We were not just idly watching all the time. In the age you were born, darkness reigned. Ahridum's temples rose to power as people despaired. Then we saw Lilith in our visions. A mortal priestess Ahridum chose to become his bride. We saw this in a vision and tried to stop it. We flew to the grim land where Lilith lived. We even brought an army with us. It was Ahridum's country, where blood sacrifice and terror reigned. We had to stop her, even kill her if need be before she was taken, but—" Asheni stopped and looked away.

"You failed," Cathal said. "We know what happened if the legends are not misleading."

Asheni sat down, her brow furrowed. "We were created to stop her. We had her in our grasp, and she was transported away before our eyes. I sensed Ahridum's hand, and the force of his evil was a like a blow. We could neither see nor feel where Lilith was taken. We only knew we had lost her."

"Evil never plays fair," Neelam said.

"You were created to stop Obsydia from being born," Cathal said.

"Yes," Asheni said. "We failed. Lilith didn't know being chosen meant not only the death of her body, but her soul as well. Ahridum's touch brought forth his dark daughter within moments as Lilith withered. Obsydia slept for thirteen days after her birth, and then she woke fully adult and ripe for evil. Obsydia's coming is only part of the threat."

"And what of your poor mothers," Opaline asked shyly. "What became of them? They sound like they were sacrifices. How could our gods, gods of light, do this?"

"I know. They gave birth to us within hours of the touch of the seraphim. We swiftly became adults within a short span of days as our mothers faded. The touch of an Eternal is powerful and deadly, even one of Light. Their bodies became pure light when they died. We watched them rise to the heavens to be welcomed in the Other-world. Even the Light requires sacrifice sometimes. I am not proud of this."

"We're digressing," Cathal interjected. "Why have you come to us?"

"Obsydia has begun a ritual. For thirteen days her claw maidens will sing incantations to Ahridum. The Hooded Guardians, creatures of the Dark Realm are with her, summoning all dark powers. If this ritual is successful, in thirteen days this world will belong to Ahridum."

"How can such a thing happen?" Sirah cried. "They cannot just claim our world."

"Apparently we have no say in our fate," Panthara remarked. "We should remind them they will fail."

Jadon spoke up, pushing back his hood, for once unafraid to show his face. "If we lose and Obsydia wins this battle, it does not mean we will give up. As you see, I am cursed to look like a demon, but I am still Raven-Wing and Drusai. We will never give up. We will fight until we win."

"Bold words," Asheni cautioned. "But Darkness never relents. If Obsydia's ritual is completed, she will ascend to become a true Dark Eternal."

"If hell-bitch is gone from this world, I can live with that,"

Neelam remarked.

"You don't understand," Asheni snapped. "In the Bloodstone Age, Obsydia was already on this path. Her blood sacrifices were part of the ritual, as were her demon handmaidens. We did not know how to kill her, so we helped you imprisoned her."

"You never told us," Neelam accused.

"You did not need to know. We trapped Obsydia in a prison of living light. We knew it would not hold forever."

"Then why did we even do it?" Cathal demanded.

"Because it kept the world from ending!" Asheni shouted. "She was close to performing it then. The blood sacrifice from both ages count, because the Claw Maidens sing their incantations even now. If Obsydia completes this ritual and ascends as a true eternal, the world will belong to Ahridum. Light will lose its hold forever."

"What the hell does it mean?" Belwyn demanded.

"We must stop her," Runa said, her face bright with fury and determination.

"You're so young," Belwyn moaned.

"It's a valid question. How do we do it?" Runa asked. "Do we imprison her again? Is there a way to kill her? What must we do?"

"What will happen if Obsydia completes her damned ritual?" Cathal asked, grey eyes unflinching.

Asheni's voice was strong, fear shaded her words. "You will not live in a world of darkness because everything, all life, animals, oceans, mountains, and forests—everything will be destroyed to make way for a dark realm where demons walk. Ahridum will vanquish all in the blink of an eye. If we do not stop Obsydia; in thirteen days the world belongs to Ahridum."

Belwyn swiveled his head around to Cathal, glaring at him with golden eyes. *I knew this would be bad news. I told you so!*

~ * ~

Rono paced, awash with concern for his friends who had just returned. Runa and Mellypip promised to see him with the news about everyone. He did not want to go outside. He did not like the cold. The snow was pretty, but it was still cold.

"You look upset," Grimm said, running into the stable.

"Oh, Grimm! I have been all alone. Darcus and Redstorm are flying patrol. Darkleaf is with them. I've been afraid. So much evil.

But don't tell them I'm scared. Please."

"Don't worry I'm here now," Grimm assured him. "Opaline and Runa thought it would be nice if I kept you company until they can give you more updates on Hinkleburr and the brothers. They are fine so far. Just some minor injuries, but nothing fatal."

"Thank you," Rono exclaimed with relief. "Everything is so scary now."

"I know," Grimm said, sitting close to the gryphon. "I'll stay with you until the others return."

A flash of bright white caught Rono's eye from the open door. It was not snow because it had a shape. Another glimpse of snowy vision and Rono caught his breath. A white peryton stood before the door, looking right at him, wings open.

"Grimm, do you see a white peryton outside?"

Grimm nodded, ears flattened with suspicion. "Yes."

"Then it's not a ghost," Rono sighed nervously.

"Nope, not even close," Grimm agreed.

CHAPTER 22

Grimm waited with Opaline in front of the cathedral. "Sirah told us to return before sunset. It's not safe you know."

"How can I even tell what time it is," Opaline replied, looking at the grey sky. "Nothing is safe anywhere now. Not even our world."

"She worries about you," Grimm added. "I worry."

"I know, but I must see him now."

While I have the courage.

Ulric rode up on his horse, cloak whipping with the wind. He reined in his horse and dismounted with practiced speed. "Opaline!" He rushed toward her and picked her up in his strong arms.

The wintry chill Opaline felt vanished with Ulric's warm embrace. The anxiety and terror of a dark goddess rising in thirteen days fell away for a heartbeat. "I missed you."

"I miss you whenever you're away." Ulric brushed a lock of her hair from her face and kissed her. "What's wrong? You're so nervous, darling. And you're shivering."

"It's just cold."

"We can go inside the church," he suggested.

Opaline knew she needed the bite of cold to keep her honest. *Oh Grimm, I long to tell him the truth about what Obsydia is doing.*

Cathal and Neelam insist it's best to keep this secret among the mages. Cathal is speaking with King Caladynn now about their plans for battling Obsydia and Koll.

Except for everything ending in thirteen days. If we had a real plan, my stomach would not be in knots.

"Opaline?"

She glanced up at him, shaking her head. "Sorry. I was distracted for a moment."

"You and your wolf must have some interesting talks," Ulric laughed.

"I didn't mean for my thoughts to stray. So much is happening now."

"It doesn't matter," Ulric said lightly. "When all this is over, you will have nothing to worry about. Father is certain, with the help of the mages and our army, we will defeat Obsydia and Koll. Then you need only be my princess and have lots of children."

Opaline's shoulders tensed as he noticed her shift. She looked away. The prick of fear irritated her. Was it stemming from her childhood as an imperial princess? Why was she so afraid? "I can be more just a princess. I'm a sorceress. I can help make the world a better place. And what if I can't give you children?" she whispered.

"Opaline, we've been over this," he replied, a little frustrated. "I believe we will have children."

"The fertility of mages is strange. We can go centuries without having children. Perhaps it is nature's key to balancing everything since we live so long."

"Your mother had you when she was only fifteen," Ulric replied.

"My mother wasn't a mage when she became pregnant with Taran and me. Her magic manifested years later. We could have a child or we could not. We'll never truly know."

"No one can know the future," Ulric whispered. "There is hope. We are both young."

"I'm only sixteen," Opaline agreed, looking away, her thoughts a tangle. "But it's more than my youth or fears of the future." *And I may not live to see seventeen. If the world is done in a handful of days, this will not matter. Why am I torturing myself?*

Grimm's dry response broke her jumbled thoughts. *Your moral compass is driving you. It's causing you suffering because you don't want to leave this world with doubts or falsehoods.*

How can I tell him what I feel without hurting him? Should I marry him now and enjoy our love before darkness obliterates us? Opaline asked.

It would be less traumatic, until we all die by Ahridum's dark hand.

Why am I so concerned about this now? What's wrong with me? With Ulric, I will be safe and loved. I'll have security. Why am I afraid of giving up my independence? Why must he be so patient and kind? It would be easier if it were Gabriel. I can always speak the truth to him.

Why are you thinking about Gabriel? Grimm asked.

Opaline froze in a panic. *No! No, I could not love such an oaf. He's drunk half the time and infuriates me the other half. Why am I even thinking of him? Grimm, why aren't you answering me?*

Grimm hung his head, avoiding her gaze. *I have no opinion.*

"Opaline, what's wrong?" Ulric asked.

"What? Oh, I'm fine," Opaline said quickly. "It's just so hard to explain."

You are confused, Grimm thought back.

What's wrong with me? But Ulric is wonderful, Opaline disputed. *I love Ulric. Why am I even thinking about Gabriel?*

The truth of doubt unfolded. Gabriel vexed her the moment they met, when he beat up half the king's guard on the lawn and told her she was the prettiest girl he ever saw. Gabriel did whatever she asked of him, no matter how rude she was. She insulted him, yet always made sure he had coffee and a hot meal when he was feeling the pain of too much ale. Ulric was strong, brave, loyal, and honorable. The perfect prince. She recalled Neelam's story about his wife, Alethea. Their love endured even a thousand years after her death. Would her love be as strong? Or would she be the one to regret marrying Ulric? The world as they know it could end in days, yet she could not cling to him as her husband. She cursed her honest heart.

Opaline clung to Ulric, crying. Grimm hung his head, feeling her pain. Patient and silent, Ulric held her close until her sobs finally quieted.

"Ulric, I don't think I can marry you," Opaline confessed. She despised herself when she saw the pain hit his face.

"You know, don't you?" Ulric asked. "I'm sorry. I had a moment's weakness. Frankly, marriage scares me too."

"Weakness?" Opaline asked.

"I have been seeing my mistress. She's a lady of the court, but we have been discreet. I know you wanted to remain chaste. And my parents have been happy, but I know it is not always so for others. I see my uncle Morydonn and his wife Faustine and pity them both. I feel there is more to your feelings. What is it?"

"My freedom matters too," Opaline replied, recalling her talk with Neelam. "And chastity is not why you strayed. I'm not sure I can return to the cloistered life of a royal, even for love. And you do not love me enough to be faithful."

"You were born a princess, but I noticed you love the liberty. Your stubborn independence has worried me on more than one occasion. I admit I've wondered if you could give it up. I know you hated royal life. You regaled me with enough bleak stories about your life in Tiamet. I feel the same. The weight of royal duty. It didn't mean anything. We can put this behind us."

Opaline took a deep breath. "Men always say this, but while you were with your mistress, I was less than nothing." She felt no bitterness. Just disappointment and relief. "If this happened now, while our love is fresh, what future do I have with you? Yes, I was born an imperial princess. The jewel of the Ivory Kingdoms. A prize for the marriage block wrapped in silk. When I met Runa, I not only found the sister I never had, I also discovered the courage to live the life I wanted. I accepted I am a sorceress. When your life is turned upside-down, you learn about who your true friends are and who your family really is. I was exiled by my father even though I saved his life, all because I was a sorceress. His hatred of magic extended to his own daughter. Freed of my imperial chains, I traveled to Ilyrra, fought battles, burned meals on the campfire, and got dirty. I was never allowed to get dirty before. I turned an evil man into a troll, bathed in streams, and was kidnapped by demons. I witnessed the wraith guardians of the Otherworld summoned to our mortal realm by high magic. It's chaotic and wild. I love it. You are not ready for marriage. And neither am I. I would have to give up my life when I just found it. It may sound strange, but I'm not the same princess I was. My path in life is different now."

"I know," Ulric whispered. "I'm so sorry. I love you dearly. I envy your freedom. I will not take it from you."

Opaline wiped her tear-streaked face and runny nose with her sleeve, wishing desperately for a handkerchief. She was about to take off the emerald ring he gave her when he proposed, but his hand gently closed over hers.

"Keep the ring, dear Opaline. Keep it as a token of love. I accept the blame. I only hope you will forgive me one day." He kissed her on the forehead. "Now, it's bloody freezing. Let me give you a lift back to the sorcerer house."

They rode back to the sorcerer house in silence, Grimm running alongside. When she entered the house, everyone was busy. Thankfully, she could retreat to her room without notice; without explaining anything to anyone. The apocalypse was very consuming.

Gabriel passed her on the stairs. "Sirah's looking for you. Where've you been, Princess?"

Without missing a beat, Opaline slapped his face and marched upstairs, Grimm at her heels.

~ * ~

Runa and Jadon sat side by side on the bench. The stable's warmth and privacy drew them away from the house. Rono and Darkleaf were outside getting some air, so Runa relished this rare moment. "I always thought the world being taken over by darkness was more of a metaphor. Who knew our fate would be so literal. I wish I knew what to do."

Jadon shrugged. "There's a houseful of mages inside saying the same thing. If Asheni is correct, we will need more than magic to stop this. We need a god's intervention."

"I thought I would be more hysterical, you know, with the coming of doom," Runa laughed. She took Jadon's hand and squeezed it close to her heart. "Or at the very least lie in a hot bath eating nothing but drobba. Rather, I feel invigorated. I've lost my shyness around you. It's silly to be so flustered about romance and boys when the world might end in thirteen days."

"I've lost my nervous stammer too," Jadon laughed. "But I think you lost your shy demeanor when you threatened to punch me whenever I attempted to escape the sickroom."

"You had it coming. Don't you ever run away again! I forbid it. But it's good to hear you laugh again," Runa remarked, nuzzling into Jadon's shoulder.

"Why does it take a crisis to make us see things?" Jadon asked, putting his arm around her.

"We are all a little stupid, I think."

"Do you think we'll find a way to stop Obsydia?"

"We don't have a choice. We must find a weapon, magic, or anything to stop her. This is the domain of mages, employing magic to protect world and life when mortal laws and weapons no longer serves to defend it. My grandpa taught me this when I was little. Magic is in this world to serve a purpose."

"I wish I could look as I was before, for you, Runa," Jadon said. "I would kiss you now."

"Then kiss me." She tenderly touched his demon-cursed face. "This is just a false mask."

"I'm hideous," Jadon said, unable to make eye contact.

"No, I see you. When I look in your eyes I see you, Jadon. I love you." Jadon looked into her eyes and leaned in so close.

"Step away from the sorceress," Belwyn snapped.

They jumped apart, surprised by the owl's presence. Belwyn

glared at them. "Just because there's a possible apocalypse, doesn't mean we lose all moral sensibilities."

"Have you been eavesdropping, Belwyn?" Runa demanded. "How long have you been spying on us?"

"Long enough to know when to ruffle some feathers."

"I'm not a child," Runa fumed.

"You're fifteen. In my scroll, you're a baby barely out of diapers. I'm your guardian when Cathal is not present, Missy. The gift of silent flight is one of the boons of being an owl."

"We're having a private conversation," Runa cried. "We were just kissing."

"Don't mind me. As long as you don't start mating I won't stop you."

"Belwyn, you're being very rude!" Runa shouted, her face flushed beet red.

"Oh, the children are just fine," Pointessa chirped, waddling out from a pile of straw.

"Pointessa! How long have you been hiding in here?" Runa cried.

Pointessa was covered with bits of straw as she sat down between them. "Not hiding. Napping. At least I was until this owl barged in clapping his beak."

"Aren't you worried about the end of the world?" Belwyn asked.

"Of course, but tormenting myself with worry and terror will not help."

"The wisdom of porcupines," Jadon laughed.

"Where's Furball?" Belwyn asked. "He's your familiar. Why isn't he guarding your virtue?"

"My virtue is just fine!" Runa shouted. "And Melly's in the sorcery chamber with Sephya."

"I think I better go inside," Jadon said. "I can help Raghnall in the sickroom."

"Good idea," Belwyn approved. "Go see how they're doing. You might want to bring Furball some snacks too. And then go see Opaline. She's upset."

"What's happened?" Runa asked. "Is she alright?"

"Some female emotional things I've already had enough of—"

Rono's cries outside ended any arguments. The gryphon cried out over and over, "Evil. Evil is coming."

They fled the stables for the backyard. Runa gasped when she saw the black vines bursting through the ground, rending up chunks of frozen earth.

"What is happening?" Runa cried, trying to calm poor Rono.

The black vines snaked along the snow-crusted grass and up alongside the trees and the house. Red thorns sprang from the dark creepers.

"Darkness is coming," Belwyn repeated grimly. "Obsydia's ritual is already vanquishing the world."

CHAPTER 23

Koll noticed the strange silence when he stepped through the mirror. His disastrous venture in Thema was besieged with conflicts and chaos. The capital city was plagued by uprisings, and many sacrifices eluded capture. The infuriating clashes with Gabriel the Sorcerer and that damned Winged Fey bitch induced unrequited fury, for they escaped along with the sacrifices. Even Koll knew fighting one of the ancient fey would be futile. Levandius and Hadrial were useless, so he dealt with the aftermath of the collapsed city. When he received Obsydia's cryptic summons to return to the tower, he forced Levandius to take control, since Hadrial was besotted with her own reflection. Koll gladly left the pasty-faced emperor and his incessant questions behind. Levandius may relish darkness, but he was nothing more than a gleeful bystander in fate who resented getting his hands bloody. Even with the unknown consequence of what Obsydia would do to him after what happened with the failed sacrifice in her temple, he welcomed the escape.

Where is everyone? Xabral asked silently, looking around, tongue flicking in and out nervously. *Why isn't Obsydia here to greet us?*

They traveled through the empty halls. The essence of gloom touched everything here, which Koll found comforting. But a distinct shift left him uncertain, sensing a powerful surge crackling through the air.

"The Shadow Tower feels different now," Xabral hissed. "Something has changed." Xabral's forked tongue tasted the air. "An essence of darkness I never touched."

Koll knelt and stroked Xabral's head. "I feel it, my sweet snake. I'm relieved Shroud is not here. Demon or not, I will make her pay for her barbed tongue one day."

"It agitates me Shroud doesn't like you," Xabral commented sadly. "She should love you, as I do. She dotes on me though which I don't understand, except I am beautiful. Obsydia chose you after all. The Dark chose you."

"Perhaps the reason for her vile bitterness is common jealousy," Koll shrugged. "No matter. She is only one of Obsydia's she-demons, a mere servant called from the abyss to work. A handmaiden to serve our Queen."

"As you serve me, Koll."

Koll turned around, stunned by Obsydia's ethereal splendor. Glorious in flowing crimson chiffon, her shadow hair floating down her back. There was a marked change in her which Koll could not name. "You are…different."

"Yes," she whispered, walking toward him. "The hands of eternity have touched me. The blood of this world is inside me. The night fills my soul."

"You're are transforming into a full god," Koll gasped, falling to his knees.

Obsydia touched his face, brushing his hair, ever so gently. "The ritual of thirteen days began while you were away. My claw maidens dance and sing the words secret to mortals. When it is done, I shall rise a full eternal and sit by my father in the netherworld. This world will belong to Darkness, and I shall reign over it in Ahridum's name."

"Shall I be allowed to see your glorious ascension?" Koll asked.

"Yes, Koll. It will be my last gift to you before I become a goddess."

And me too?" Xabral begged eagerly.

"Yes, sweet snake."

"You are not angry about Valkorr?" Koll asked, sensing her beneficial mood would be a ripe time to confess his troubles in Valkorr.

"It no longer matters," Obsydia replied evenly. "All my enemies shall perish soon. The world will go through a new genesis when Darkness takes it."

"Which we long to see, but we sensed an astonishing power here," Koll said. "I feel it when I breathe. I feel it on my skin. An essence of the ethereal and the shadow, mingling."

"Yes, something beyond magic. Follow me and see what no mortal being has witnessed."

I wonder what she wants to show us. I do love surprises. What dark mystical goodie awaits us? I'm so excited, Xabral tittered in his mind.

I am intrigued, Koll agreed, *but I sense something strange*, following Obsydia up the winding stairs to the great temple at the top of the tower.

Within the sacred space, Koll felt chills of timeless power as he had in Obsydia's black tower in the great sea. Her places of power were created by the hand of Ahridum himself, and the mystical energy alone made him feel insignificant in the presence of such glory. The open dome which spiraled into mystical imagery from battles between dark and light eternals, portraits of the dark trinity, but the ritual scene which greeted him in mortal form seemed so simple at first glance. The Claw Maiden's dance around the altar's fire and the chanting in their dark tongue was in no way simple. The complexities of this ritual required precision; each step, word, and nuance performed must be flawless to appease a god. The Hooded Guardians stood upon the altar making symbols on the air which flared bright red in strange runes before vanishing. The maidens danced as they sang. Even Shroud was too involved in her solemn song to cast insults at him. Good.

"It's a conjuration," Koll whispered.

"Yet beyond the simple magic summoned by mere mortals," Obsydia declared and turned her face to him, her silver eyes bright as moons. "My Claw Maidens and the Hooded Guardians will perform this ritual without pause for thirteen days. This is the conclusion of blood sacrifice begun over a thousand years ago. This is why each temple has purged hearts and offered innocent blood to me. It is only part of the sacramental prayer to the Dark, but for one purpose. Me. Everything we have done has been to make me a goddess and make this world one for Dark Eternals. When my shadow world is born, demons will dance beneath a red sun burning in a black sky. I shall look upon my world of blood and fire in blessing as I sit at Ahridum's side."

"I will help deliver this dream," Koll cried.

Obsydia touched his face, her face softened for a brief moment. "We could not wait for you to see the initiation as we had to start when the Guardians decreed. This is a ritual no mortal has ever witnessed and the first time it has been performed on this world. A synchronized ceremony to summon Ahridum and all the dark powers to both destroy and create. When my maidens are finished, I shall take my place upon my father's altar and the ritual of ascension shall begin, for which a final sacrifice is needed. It is a token, but an important symbol. I will need an innocent, preferably a child. If the Dark Eternal's powers converge, I will slough this mortal skin and become a full goddess. Light will finally lose its hold on this world, and it will be transformed."

"This will mark the world as one of Dark rule," Koll whispered in awe. "And I shall witness your ascension to Eternal power. A goddess birthed before my humble eyes." Koll bowed his head and knelt at her feet.

Xabral weaved dreamily, "It is a dream come true."

"You will be permitted to watch this sacred rite," Obsydia conceded, "It will be my final gift to you."

"I am grateful, Queen Obsydia," Koll decreed said. "When you rise to become a god my eyes shall behold your glory. When you bestow your promise of immortality upon me, I shall offer daily sacrifices to your glory."

Obsydia turned away from Koll and Xabral. "You shall be properly rewarded for your devotion, but I have some final tasks for you. Nothing must interfere in what is happening. I know there are threats, many I am blind to. I cannot see the dragons, for their magic has hidden them from my mirrors as is the sorcerer house in Aybarr. I know Cathal and Neelam are plotting. Cathal's friends and family vex me, especially his granddaughter. These sorcerers have been a bane of my existence. I also know dragon magic shields them from my gaze. There must be a reason. Nothing must disrupt this sacred ritual."

"What do you want me to do?" Koll asked.

"We will do anything," Xabral cried, shaking his stinger.

"We need to shake their sanctuary, so to speak. If they die, I will be content. Go to Aybarr and blow up their sorcerer house. Use magic or mortal explosives, I do not care. They have been hidden from me too long. I fear what they might do. The Winged Fey must also be plotting. Nothing must stop my ascension. Nothing. Take my demon-warriors and goblins. Find Morydonn and Faustine first. They serve me now, so they will help you."

Koll kissed her hand and rose. "As you command."

Her smile faded as her flawless brow was creased with a frown. She backed away, and turning in circles, hands clutching her head. "No!"

"What is it?" Koll cried. "What do you see?"

"Trouble!" Obsydia replied hotly. "The threat's true form is hidden from me, but it is coming. My ancient enemies, Cathal and Neelam, must surely have a hand in it! Especially the meddling Dwarf!"

"Then I shall kill them," Koll swore.

"Kill, kill," Xabral hissed. "I will enjoy killing them for you, Obsydia."

"They have been my ancient enemies from the beginning. The conspiracies of mages and Winged Fey imprisoned me in tortuous light for a thousand years. My father's bidding prevented my personal revenge until now, but now I want it. My rising must not be impeded by sorcerous meddling. Go. I demand it. Go. Waste no time. Destroy them and the whole house! Destroy my enemies."

Obsydia's final words penetrated his soul like a dagger. "Do not fail me, Koll, for I will not forgive twice."

~ * ~

Runa held Jiana's hand as Raghnall examined Queen Sarabia. The moments passed as Raghnall performed both physical and magical examinations.

Jiana looks mad, Mellypip remarked.

They are good friends, Runa replied, keeping an eye on Jiana. *Jasper looks just as angry too.*

Mellypip looked at Jasper, tucked in Jiana's arm, his long tiger-striped ears folded back. *He is pretty hot-tempered, almost as much as Dabiro.*

Sarabia was too frail to do anything drastic at first, so they waited upon Raghnall's advice.

Can we help her? Mellypip asked, sad to see the woman suffering.

I don't know. If Koll was involved, he had to use diabolistic magic. It may be difficult to undo.

Well, of course it was Koll. But we have powerful magic too. We undid the tree of bones curse, didn't we? And Grandpa Cathal and Neelam were the scions of light or something. Light has power, and Belwyn once told me to never forget it.

Baldur sat on the other side of the bed where she lay twisted, moaning a little. His paws rested on her gnarled hands, easing her anxiety with his empathic healing magic.

Jiana's fuming tension finally erupted. "I'm going to kill Hadrial for this."

"Of course you are," Runa agreed.

You're just placating her, aren't you?

Just play along, Melly.

"Not unless I kill her first," Sarabia declared weakly, struggling to rise.

"Rest now, Your Majesty," Raghnall said. "Let me finish before you go off on any quests."

"Who is this annoying little man?" Sarabia asked, her feeble smile heartbreaking.

"Raghnall is a great healer," Jiana said. "Just rest and let him work."

"He did wonders curing Caliste when she was affected by dark magic," Runa offered, eager to give Sarabia some hope.

Interesting," Raghnall remarked. "Not exactly expected, but interesting." He crossed his arms, deep in concentration.

"What!" Jiana finally snapped.

"Calm down," Runa whispered.

"Maybe Baldur can share his empathy with Jiana for a minute," Mellypip suggested.

Runa was put off when Asheni entered the room. *This uncomfortable feeling around the Winged Fey hasn't gone away since we met.*

This one's different from the others, Mellypip said, looking at Asheni. *She cares. The one Grandpa Cathal hit wasn't nice though. He was mean.*

How is she? Asheni asked.

Raghnall covered Sarabia with a blanket and began to rummage through his medical bag. "This is nasty spell work, but something is odd about it."

"How diabolical it is?" Jasper asked, his long wars twitching with impatience. "Come on, Wizard. What's so odd?"

Raghnall tossed out empty potion bottles, paper, and bags of herbs onto the blanket. "How simple it really is!"

Runa's brow furrowed. "I don't understand."

"Neither do I?" Jiana said.

Asheni walked over to Sarabia. Baldur moved his great bulk to the far side of the room. "Thank you," she nodded to the grizzly. She held her hands over the body and nodded. "The wizard-mage is right. This spell's effects are brutal, but it can be done quite easily with the right spell and potion. This was never meant to be permanent."

"Why would Koll go to all the trouble to do this?" Jiana asked.

Asheni's smile brightened the dim room. "Simple really. We have less than thirteen days now, remember? If you only need to achieve certain things in a short span of time, do you need to go to the trouble to do everything to perfection? The goal was to take Thema, which was a personal vendetta of Obsydia. If the world will be Dark in less than a fortnight, there would be no need to do so, as Hadrial, Levandius, and the rest of us will not even exist if she's successful. So why bother? But this works in our favor now. We can not only undo this, but reverse it back on Hadrial."

"Really?" Jiana asked.

"I will help you, Raghnall," Asheni offered and then looked sharply at Runa and Jiana. "The rest of you may watch, but do not interfere. I must focus and teach your wizard what to do."

Jiana and Runa obeyed and watched intently, afraid to move, holding their familiars close. Asheni helped Raghnall mix a potion. Her movements were precise, and her magic brightened the room even more.

What's she doing? Mellypip asked, his little nose busy sniffing the ingredients added to the mystical brew.

I can't see what she's putting in the potion. This is so exciting. Maybe we should fetch Grandpa?

No, you mustn't, Mellypip warned. *Asheni told us not to move.*

Raghnall took a moment here and there to scribble notes. Finally, Asheni mixed the ingredients with honey and water until it foamed with golden promise in a glass goblet.

"Help her drink, quickly," Asheni ordered, handing him the potion.

Jiana put Jasper on the bed and lifted Sarabia's head up so she could sip. Patiently they helped her drink the whole glass, and then they laid her back down.

"How long before it takes affect?" Runa asked.

Sarabia's body glowed with yellow light and she thrashed back and forth as she cried out. Raghnall and Runa held Jiana back as they watched Sarabia's face and body return to normal in a matter of seconds. Her beauty and health restored, Sarabia literally leapt out of bed, amazed at her transformation.

"Thank you," Sarabia cried. She was shaky, but she refused to lay back down or even sit. She walked on wobbly legs as though she were a toddler learning to stand on legs, but each step grew stronger. She threw her head back, lustrous black hair falling down her back. "I am restored to my true self, thanks to your diligence and kindness.

I thank you all. Tell Cathal we need to meet. My kingdom has been lost to evil, which I will not stand for." She bowed with reverence to Asheni. "I am honored for your aid, Asheni of the Winged Fey."

"What can I bring you, You Majesty?" Jiana laughed. "Food, wine?"

Queen Sarabia flexed her arms and then stretched backwards. "A sword. I feel a little out of practice."

"It's a miracle," Jiana cried and turned to Asheni. "Didn't you say the spell would be reversed on Hadrial?"

Asheni nodded and smiled. "Yes, and I wish I was there to see it."

"I'll get Cathal for you," Runa offered and ran out of the room. She almost collided with her mother in the hallway. Runa stood unsure before her.

Rualla handed Runa her staff, and then embraced her. Tears streamed down Runa's face as she wordlessly held her mother close, who was lost to her for so long. Mellypip, squished between them, did not fuss when something even more precious was restored.

~ * ~

Levandius rolled over in bed, kicking off the sweaty silk sheets and stretching out his body. He propped himself up on his elbows, feeling tired after such a hot night of sex. It must be late, but he also gave orders for no one to disturb him. It must be past noon now, but he didn't care and he refused to do anything today. Koll can go rot.

He quietly got out of bed and walked to the side table. He poured a forbidden cup of wine. Koll was not here to chastise him and he was a bridegroom with good cause to celebrate. He plucked a grape from the silver platter, enjoying a respite from the blood and gore for Obsydia.

Levandius decided he liked being married. Hadrial was as beautiful as promised and most submissive. She agreed with him on everything. He found her a bit clingy, but he liked the way she adored him. He loved her flawless beauty. They made love three times last night and she was still ready for more. He looked at her, wrapped in the soft sheets like a baby, her blonde hair spilling over her face. Eager again, he downed his wine and returned to bed. He smoothed the hair from her face as he leaned in to kiss her until he saw her ugliness. He jumped back, and nearly fell off the bed.

Hadrial opened her eyes, her smile distorted by the partial paralysis of her face. She extended her arms in welcome. "Come to me, beloved. What's wrong?"

"Your face!" Levandius accused. "You're hideous. Koll lied to me!"

Her eyes filled with panic and she struggled to reach for a mirror. When she held it up to her face, she screamed. "My face! It's worse than before the potion. What happened? Oh, gods. I want my beauty back. Koll promised me." She doubled over, sobbing.

"Stop wailing!" Levandius shouted.

Hadrial dropped the looking glass, and crawled toward him, for her twisted body would not stand. She reached toward Levandius, who pushed her away. The looking glass fell to the floor. Levandius jumped off the bed, his foot crushing the mirror's glass when he stepped on it.

"Damn it!" He cradled his bleeding foot. She touched his arms, which he shrugged off. "Stop it. Stay away. You're a monster."

"You're my husband," Hadrial cried, clawing at his arm. She fell out of bed and crawled toward him. "You must help me. Koll did this." She wailed like a fishwife, crawling after him no matter how much he backed away.

"No!" Levandius shouted. "And stop crying. Stop it!" Grabbing jeweled dagger from the table, his face lost all emotion as he stabbed Hadrial over and over until she no longer made any sound at all, but lay in a pool of her own blood.

"Guards!" Levandius shouted. "Guards!"

One of Koll's red-eyed demon warriors entered, and did not even look surprised at the dead woman on the floor.

Levandius pointed to Hadrial's body. "Get rid of this. Burn it. Feed it to the dogs. I don't care. And fetch me a doctor. My foot is hurt."

"As you command," the warrior replied and removed the corpse.

Levandius took the bottle of wine and began to drink.

CHAPTER 24

Belwyn's talons gripped the back of the chair where Cathal sat. The meeting was frustrating because they could not speak openly with Morydonn. Full of suspicion, Belwyn kept his eyes on Morydonn. His behavior on the surface was not unduly different, but he smelled...wrong.

You're brooding again, Cathal said though the bonding.

I don't like this. I don't care what Asheni says. Morydonn's very presence is dangerous. It's like inviting a scorpion to tea. They sting and you die before you even get to the cookies.

If what Iona and Asheni told us is true, all we can do is take precautions.

We can thank luck for Iona answering the door, Belwyn said.

What about the gods? Cathal inquired.

The gods are useless. Why would they let the Dark claim this world? Light has some explaining to do.

Morydonn clearly is here to find something out, which is why we are keeping Asheni and the dragons out of sight. We are not discussing anything new. We don't know when it happened and just because his eyes aren't red doesn't mean he hasn't been demonized. They just found a way to conceal it. We have no idea who else is infected unless we have a necromancer or Winged Fey present.

How's Caladynn taking it? He knows there's no hope, right? Morydonn lost his soul.

I know, but that is not our decision, Cathal replied, keeping a neutral expression as he watched Morydonn at the table.

He's lucky Neelam hasn't just sliced his head off.

"Cathal, what about *the gate of souls* ritual?" Queen Sarabia suggested. "It may be dark magic, but it worked before from what you told me. Since Obsydia is still half-mortal, couldn't we summon the Wraith Guardians to take her before she ascends?"

"We could also trap her in another light prison," Neelam suggested, not taking his eyes of Morydonn. "The light crystal worked before. It won't solve all our problems, but if hell-bitch cannot complete the ritual, the world will be safe for now. Then we find a way to kill her for good."

"Those dark vines aren't just evil looking, they feel evil!" Yllia remarked, looking at the vines growing up the window.

"Darkness never plays by the rules," Neelam replied coolly, "and we should not either."

~ * ~

Runa laughed as Mellypip and Sephya playing a heated game of tag under the watchful eyes of Talon and Fallon. Opaline hesitantly stepped into the chamber, Grimm at her side.

"Is it safe?" Opaline smiled, watching Mellypip and Sephya go round and round the room.

Runa encouraged Opaline to come inside. "Join us. The dragons won't bite."

"I'm not so sure," Grimm remarked, warily walking past the shadow dragons.

"Come on, Grimm, play with us! We're having fun!" Mellypip panted.

"I think I shall observe," Grimm answered.

'What's happening downstairs?" Runa asked. "Any solutions to our impending doom?"

"We have a roomful of frustrated mages and mortals trying to save the world. They've gone from drinking coffee to ale. That should tell you something. Even Morydonn is here."

"That's a shock," Runa said. "Not the ale part, but Morydonn."

"I know," Opaline said. "I was going to join the meeting with Taran, but suddenly mother insisted I check on you. I would like to think the end of the world coaxed out Morydonn's good side, but I don't trust him."

"I doubt Morydonn has changed his heart," Grimm said suspiciously. "I don't think this human is capable of change. I smell something dark on him."

"Not surprising," Runa said. "We seem to be surrounded by evil all the time."

Mellypip scampered all over the room with Sephya. *You're not supposed to fret. This is recess. Cathal and Belwyn sent us up here for a reason.*

Not even my grandpa can protect me from the dark apocalypse.

He's a powerful sorcerer. He will think of something.

Opaline stroked Grimm's head, looking away. "Time is going by so fast. We don't even have thirteen days anymore. We have seven days left if Obsydia's clock of doom is accurate." Opaline sat cross-legged on the floor next to Runa, Grimm's head in her lap. Opaline watched the baby red dragon run circles around Mellypip as they tagged each under the watchful eyes of the two shadow dragons, Talon and Fallon. "She's getting so big so fast!"

"She eats loads," Mellypip panted as he chased her through the sorcery chamber. "Mostly meat, though she does eat a little fruit."

"Explains why our meat larder is so full," Opaline remarked, looking at the platter of chopped burnt meat on the floor. "Most of us do not eat meat, though many of our familiars do."

"Dragons needs meat. Lots of hearty well-cooked meat, but diced into tiny bits for her," Talon explained. "Her teeth and claws are still developing."

Mellypip scampered along the floor, Sephya in fast pursuit. "Can't catch me!"

Sephya squealed with delight, her little legs pumping and small wings beating hard.

Grimm's head perked up, watching Mellypip with concern. "Poor Melly is wearing down. Should we save him?"

"A brave warrior-mage's fate must be to be chased by an over-excited baby dragon," Runa laughed.

Sephya's wings suddenly lifted her into the air for a brief moment. She squealed with delight until no longer able to stay aloft, she dropped on top of Mellypip. The two rolled over, panting and exhausted. Sephya breathed little smoky tufts, not real fire yet but enough to spark the rug, which Fallon quickly extinguished.

Sephya crawled on top of Mellypip and chirped, "I'm hungry, Melly. Feed me."

Talon nudged the platter of chopped meat toward Sephya. "Dragons hungry all the time at this stage."

Sephya chewed her charred meat with gusto. Exhausted, Mellypip relaxed with a bowl of drobba pudding. Sephya finished her plate of meat and noticed how Mellypip savored his pudding. She padded over to him and sniffed. "Want," Sephya begged, pawing at the bowl.

Mellypip looked at Runa. "Maybe a little? It's not on her list of foods Talon and Fallon prescribed."

"No, Sephya," Runa laughed. "Drobba is not good for little dragons. It will make you sick."

"Want pudding like Melly," Sephya piped, little tufts of flame spurting from her nostrils, her wings beating with irritation.

Mellypip sighed heavily, putting his bowl down. "Suddenly I feel a strange empathy with Belwyn."

"You must be tired," Grimm remarked, looking at the half-full bowl of drobba pudding. "You did not even lick the bowl."

Grimm stood and stretched, and butted his head against Opaline's shoulder, indicating delicately he needed to go outside.

"Come on, Grimm," Opaline said, rising to her feet. "I'll be brave and face the demonic weeds. We should see how Rono is doing. I know poor Darkleaf and Redstorm have been occupied with keeping the poor gryphon calm since this horror started."

Panthara entered, her face flushed as she blocked Opaline from going downstairs. "Don't go downstairs."

"What's wrong?" Opaline asked, seeing her concern.

"It's about Morydonn," Panthara whispered. "He has no soul. He is demon-touched."

"I knew it!" Grimm growled.

Fallon and Talon gathered Sephya close to them, though she wiggled against their protective hold.

"He may be demon fodder, but he will not know about us unless he sees us or someone tells him," Talon whispered.

"Dragon shield prevents anyone from seeing us or hearing us," Fallon added.

"What are they going to do to Morydonn?" Runa asked, holding Mellypip close.

"I think they want to learn what he knows first, but Asheni is staying out of sight," Panthara said.

"I still need to go outside," Grimm moaned.

"We'll both take you," Panthara offered. "But we should all stay together." She turned to Runa. "Cathal wants you and Melly to stay here with the dragons." She picked Azmadu up, who fussed.

"But it's cold outside."

"It will be for only a moment," Panthara assured him, stroking his head tenderly. "I don't want you out of my sight with the danger everywhere."

Panthara and Opaline rushed down the stairs with their familiars and walked past the circle of somber faces, heading toward the kitchen's back door.

"Any brilliant ideas for salvation yet?" Opaline asked lightly as she walked by the tense group around the table.

"Where are you going, Opaline?" Prince Ulric asked.

"Grimm just needs to go outside," Opaline answered quickly, not looking at Ulric.

"Be careful," Sirah said, her voice calm but her eyes wary. "Evil is everywhere."

~ * ~

Outside, the brisk air was reviving despite its chill. Opaline tip-toed on the frosty grass to avoid the black vines growing everywhere.

"Stay where I can see you, Grimm," Opaline warned, looking around with disgust. "Damn these vines are creepy."

"The steep price of evil is the loss of privacy," Grimm groaned, sniffing around the nearby bushes. With deliberate spite, Grimm targeted a patch of tangled black vines and urinated on them.

Azmadu shivered in Panthara's arms. She held him close, wrapping a fold of her cloak around him. "Be patient. Better cold than to be near such evil," Panthara remarked, looking back at the house.

"I wonder what he knows," Opaline whispered. "I wonder when it happened."

"Impossible to know, but if Koll has breached the palace who knows who may be turned into spies," Panthara whispered. "If they wanted to be merciful, they should just kill him now."

Darkleaf and Redstorm coaxed Rono out of the stable. Rono was uneasy but happy to see Grimm. They were all concerned as Rono was very agitated.

"They would come," Rono whimpered, prancing nervously near the house, unfurling his wings.

"Who?" Grimm asked.

"They promised me," Rono muttered. "Evil is coming. Too late."

"What's he talking about?" Opaline asked. "Has Rono been this anxious all day? It's not just the creepy vines and thorns sprouting from hell."

"Nervous yes, but not this bad," Redstorm replied, pawing the ground with disgust at the creeping dark plants.

Darkleaf shook his antlers with dismay. "He's been pacing all day, talking about strange things. He keeps talking about the white spirit."

Opaline stroked Rono's head, trying to soothe the panic-stricken gryphon. "Don't worry, Rono. We won't let anything hurt you."

"The white spirit?" Grimm asked, silver eyes confused. "I remember the—" Grimm stopped and growled, moving protectively toward Opaline. "We must go inside immediately."

Opaline looked up and sucked in her breath, taking Panthara's arm. A red mist formed above them, swirling into a maelstrom above them, reeking of sinister magic so potent it made Opaline dizzy, and she gripped Panthara's shoulder for support. The crimson cloud cloaked the sorcerer house like a frenzied bloodstained cloud. The crystal alarms reverberated, the shrill noise causing Grimm to howl.

"What the hell is that?" Redstorm shouted, pawing the frozen ground.

Panthara's voice echoed through the air. "It's Koll. He's trapped us here."

~ * ~

Koll relished the image of the violent scarlet cloud forming over the sorcerer house. He touched the mirror, eager to feel his enemies so close to their doom now. He longed to be the one to end their lives personally, but wisdom restrained him. Morydonn was a better choice. If he failed, his death would not matter. Koll mattered. He turned to the pack of goblins awaiting orders. "Go. Surround the sorcerer house. Make sure no one escapes."

They did not answer, but grunted and nodded at Koll's words. The band of fifty goblins and men walked through the mirror one by one.

Faustine nervously watched them leave, wringing her hands. "Are you sure no one knows? My bed chamber has become a war zone, Koll, filled with repulsive goblins."

"They are gone now, but it was necessary. No one knows we are here. So release your fears, Faustine. I've cast enough spells around your chamber to keep you safe."

"They're so feral and dangerous looking," Faustine remarked with a shiver.

"They are goblins. That's how they are made."

My husband will be safe? He will not die. They don't suspect, do they?"

"Morydonn will return," Koll assured her.

"Are you sure no one suspects you're here, Koll? The palace has been on high alert. The city is in a panic. The whole city is covered with those black vines and thorns. And then you bring goblins into my private chambers."

Your own husband is a demon now, you stupid wench. How could you be so blind to your ambitions and not realize Morydonn died when Obsydia bestowed her blood kiss?

"Caladynn will die," Koll said. "Your wishes will come true. Morydonn will be king, and you will rule Thill together."

There won't even be a Thill! Xabral tittered.

Koll restrained a rare laugh. "After Caladynn's death, we'll assassinate the Queen and his remaining heirs to remove any hindrance. You will begin in a new age under the hand of Obsydia's glory. You will reign as a great queen."

I love how beautifully you lie to her, Koll, Xabral spoke in his mind. *Her dreams are banal and human. Her only purpose now is on the altar.*

Faustine will die. Not even an altar to offer glory to the Dark is destined for her or Morydonn. They are fodder for the coming glory of Obsydia. They will perish in the coming genesis. She will be swept away like dust when Obsydia rises to become a full Eternal.

Except for us, Xabral giggled. *Obsydia will make us immortal. We will serve our goddess and rule the new dark world. I almost wish Cathal and his stupid friends could see her rising.*

"Is all this necessary?" Faustine whined. "You tell me Obsydia will become a god. What threat is that passel of sorcerers to a god?"

Koll desired to snap her neck, which would only require a flick of his finger. "Cathal and all his friends and family must die. We must ensure Obsydia's safe ascension."

"Koll, look!" Xabral hissed, slithering closer to the mirror.

The red storm cloaking the house was complete. Faustine finally silenced her tongue and watched as the house within exploded. The red mist locked the debris and flames within the space of the property.

"Morydonn, where is he?" Faustine cried. "Koll, you promised me he would leave!"

The red crystal on the table shimmered and Koll picked it up. "See your husband and be calm, Madam."

She snatched the crystal from his hand and saw Morydonn's face in its dusky glow.

"They are dead, Lord Koll," Morydonn stated, his eyes flaring red. "All of them are dead."

"Excellent," Koll replied coolly, though his heart leapt with joy. "Return to the palace and take your place as king."

CHAPTER 25

"Runa, where are we?" Mellypip asked in a hushed voice, clinging to her shoulder. They were alone, but he could not figure out where. The air was not normal, reeking of mystical energy. A mass of fog cloaked the air, and the spark of feral energy made his fur bristle. "It's strange here. The last thing I remember was playing tug of war with Sephya."

"Using my staff," Runa remarked, confused in the strange limbo. "I'm scared, Melly."

"Me too. It's all misty and weird here. What happened? Where is everyone?"

"I don't know," Runa whispered. A sound, distant yet familiar drew her on. "There's a voice calling me."

"I hear it too," Mellypip murmured. "I hear your name, but it's so distant."

Runa walked blindly through the grey fog, desperate to find the voice summoning her. The heavens above burst with bright stars and nebulas in the vast sea of eternity, but her heart chilled with panic when she saw the Wraith Guardians soaring through starlight above the mist.

The voice called again, and she ran toward its familiar sound, seeking refuge in the unknown terror. Mellypip clung to her, bouncing as she rushed through dark vapors. A vision of light appeared, and it walked toward her through the mist, shaping into a man with dark hair and deep blue eyes. Runa paused when she recognized her father, Ashur, and for a heartbeat wondered if she and Melly perished? A flash of blinding light was the last thing she remembered. Did Darkness conquer sooner than they expected? "The Wraiths are here," Runa gasped. "Are we dead? What's happening?"

An eagle's cry distracted her and she looked up. Ashur's beloved black eagle, Urvuz, flew overhead and looked kindly down on them. She remembered the lonely blind eagle, pining for his sorcerer, Ashur, and never forgot how Koll brutally killed Urvuz in the cave when her father's soul was summoned by dark magic. She took comfort knowing Ashur and Urvuz reunited in the Otherworld.

Ashur stood close now, his eyes kind as he took her hand. She was surprised how warm and alive he felt. He whispered in her ear, and she strained to hear the words, but they were so strange. The Wraith Guardians shrieks above startled Runa.

"Father, what's happening?" Runa cried, clinging to both Ashur and Mellypip. The heavens above exploded with fire, opening the Gate of Souls.

Wraiths swooped down from the tumult of heaven, ripping Ashur away from her. She grasped his hands desperately until the forces of eternity divided them in the void.

"Father wait!" Runa cried out before she spiraled down to the mortal ground.

~ * ~

Runa's eyes snapped opened and she bolted upright, looking around in fear.

"She's awake," her mother cried, holding her so tight she could not breathe.

"Thank the gods," Yllia cried. "Is she injured?"

Raghnall sat back on his heels and rummaged through his bag, "See, she was just stunned." He pulled out a brass tube with a crystal at the end. He shined it in her eyes. "No concussive symptoms. Runa's just fine."

Rualla loosened her grip, brushing back Runa's hair. "Are you sure?"

Runa rubbed her eyes and looked around. "I'm fine, really." Everyone around her was filthy, their faces and clothes smudged with ash. Mellypip, curled in her lap, blinked and sniffed, wrinkling his nose at the dense odor of smoke and ash. They were outside in the cold, but she was not chilly. She sensed magic and realized they were cloaked by a shimmering shield in the middle of a forest.

"You okay, Furball?" Belwyn asked.

"Hungry," Mellypip mumbled and curled in Runa's lap.

"He's fine," Belwyn nodded.

"Where are we?" Runa asked, looking around. There was a peculiar feel she could sense, even with the glowing shield around them.

"We are in the forest north of Aybarr," Cathal explained gently. "These were the cursed woods."

"Where we found mother and grandmother," Runa nodded.

"It's alright, Papa," Rualla said. "I'm not so fragile to be upset by this now. We have more pressing problems than the past."

"I'm just grateful you're conscious," Opaline exclaimed, relieved. She helped Runa to her feet. "We've been trying to rouse you."

Runa nodded as Opaline spoke, but the vision of her father loomed vibrant in her mind. There was something he told her, but it was lost to her now. "We're fine, I think. How long was I out?"

"Almost an hour," Cathal said. "We thought you were injured in the explosion."

"I remember a flare of light. Then nothing," Runa murmured, scanning the worried faces around her. "Did everyone make it out safely?"

"Everyone except for Morydonn," Caladynn said. "He died in the blast. The only blessing in this horror is I did not have to execute my own brother."

"We're all very sorry," Cathal told him. "But he wasn't your brother anymore."

"His soul was gone," Iona added gently. "What was left was a shell only."

Runa, you know we had a dream, or maybe it was more, Mellypip thought to her. *We saw your father and the scary wraiths.*

I know, but I cannot speak of it. Not now. I don't know why.

Panthara's cool gaze locked on Runa. "Runa, are you sure you're not hurt?"

Runa looked down, "I'm just jumbled by it all. It's just left me with a headache. Why?"

"Just concerned," Panthara said. "I've got a headache too."

"Me too," Azmadu grumbled, clinging to Panthara. "Head hurt."

"It probably just the shock of what's happened," Opaline shrugged, rubbing her temples.

Grimm laid down but kept a close eye on Opaline. "We all suffered a shock. But it is better than being blown to bits by a demon's bomb."

"Bomb?" Mellypip asked. Sephya pawed at Mellypip, and the wampu bravely cuddled her. Fallon and Talon huddled close by, keeping a protective eye on the baby dragon.

"Apparently, Morydonn planted a single but powerful explosive crystal right on our front door. We almost found out too late."

"Just one?" Mellypip asked.

"It was enough," Grimm replied. "A small jewel of some demon concoction of Koll's, and when Asheni detected it, she managed to slow the bomb until we could be saved."

"We're all very grateful you saved our lives," Sirah told the Winged Fey. "I just wish I had not lost my staff in the chaos. But I have my family and my Arial. Nothing else matters." Arial hovered close to Sirah, her beautiful white fur smudged with ash.

"Most of us lost our staffs, but we can forge new ones," Myrsalian nodded, wiping soot from his face. "But I grieve most for my books in the sorcery chamber."

"Runa's lucky she saved her staff," Rualla pointed out. "I am glad. It's special."

"Runa was holding it when we rescued her and her wampu," Asheni said.

Runa reached down and took her staff, carved from the willow oak where Striker was buried, and his eyes stamped on the wood beneath Mellypip's face. It was clean of damage, except for Sephya's tooth marks. "How did you manage to save us all?" Runa asked.

"We barely have enough time to open a portal and carry everyone out," Asheni answered. "Dareem and the others were already here in hiding. Without them, not all of you could have been saved."

Dareem, his blue and black wings striking against the wintry backdrop, looked at Asheni with sad eyes. "Asheni summoned us days ago, but I was hesitant. My pride was strong as the centuries of disappointment made me bitter."

"I prayed you would come," Asheni whispered. "But you were here all along. I sensed it but was not sure."

Dareem took her hand, his coldness gone. "I realized she was right. Darkness will win if we do not work together. I had to find the hope and when Asheni was bold enough to confront Koll in Thema, I felt ashamed. We've been watching the house for some time. Asheni is not the only seer in our circle. We saw the danger for you but had to remain concealed to deflect Obsydia from discovering us. I went to some of the familiars and the gryphon to tell them I was watching and ask questions."

"They pretended to be white perytons," Rono added eagerly.

"Yes, we did," Dareem said. "I cast a spell to keep them from remembering, for their protection."

"I remembered," Rono said proudly.

"You are special," Asheni smiled. "Rono's ability to sense evil is a magical talent few possess. He also senses good just as strongly. It's like when a necromancer can sense if someone has a soul."

One of the female fey looked up, her orange and black wings unfolding. "Obsydia and Koll will wonder about Morydonn." She looked at Caladynn. "You need to get back to the palace. There are some evil roots of your own you must weed out."

"I will root them out," Caladynn replied grimly. "I must return to the palace and make sure my family is safe."

"We will, but we must do it covertly," Cathal warned. "Thankfully, after Iona detected his lack of soul, Asheni found out what he was planning. Obsydia's Demon-Warriors are obedient but have little defense against high magic, and even less against the power of the Winged Fey. We'll use our knowledge, but we do not know who is infected at the palace."

"Are you certain Koll is not suspicious?" Yllia asked. "You pretended to be Morydonn when you contacted him, but he may have detected the ruse. Your shapeshifting talents are good, but who knows what he suspects or what powers he's acquired."

"I think he believed it was Morydonn leaving the burning house. He thinks we are all dead. We should be safe for the moment. And Koll seemed too damned happy," Cathal said. "But we'll not taunt fate. This crystal Morydonn used to contact Koll can lead us to other things if we are careful." Cathal held up a small hand-sized crimson crystal, studying it.

Belwyn winced when he looked at the red crystal. "The thing is demon conjured. It stinks of dark magic. Put it away."

"Your familiar is correct," Dareem said. "The stone is forged from dark sorcery. Koll has access to magics unknown to the mortal realm because of Obsydia."

"How long was my brother under Obsydia's control?" Caladynn asked.

"We don't know," Cathal replied honestly. "We must talk to his wife, Faustine. She may also be part of this. It's hard to say how many may be turned by Koll. Before their red eyes were an easy symptom to watch for, but we'll have to be more careful."

"Panthara and I will examine everyone possible at the palace," Iona offered.

"Thank you, Lady," Caladynn said. "Can this be done quietly? I don't want to arouse suspicion."

"Start with your guards," Gabriel suggested.

"That's a good idea," Opaline agreed.

"Are you agreeing with me, Princess?" Gabriel grinned.

"Don't get accustomed to it," Opaline snapped.

"We need only touch or get close to the person," Panthara said. "Iona's power is strong, so she needs to be only within a few feet. I am still learning, but no one will suspect."

"I know this is hard," Cathal gripped Caladynn's shoulder. "Morydonn was your brother. He was never evil and did not deserve this wretched fate. I know family is everything to you. I am sorry."

The devastated faces of Caladynn and Ulric broke Opaline's hesitation. "Cathal is right. Morydonn had many faults, but he was never evil." Swallowing pride and fear, she rushed to Ulric and embraced him.

"Was my brother aware? Was there any part of him left we could have saved?" Morydonn asked.

"Morydonn died when the demon took his body. It's Obsydia's blood kiss," Neelam pointed out. "I know its poison as it took people I cared about. You need not fret about what happened, but think about revenge on those responsible."

"I am not sure when this happened, but we need to find out who else is suspect in your house," Cathal advised. "Morydonn was never a traitor, but a victim. Remember that."

Runa tried to listen to their plans, standing in the cold forest, holding Mellypip close.

Something is missing, Runa. I know it's important. I can feel it.

Mellypip looked at Panthara and Opaline, who gazed up at the dim stars as though making a wish. He sensed a mystical imprint. It was inside him too, but he could not shake it loose, but it was there.

Runa also looked up at the sky, seeking the heavens above. *Father, what have I forgotten?*

~ * ~

Faustine paced in her room, the train of her gown swishing with each nervous turn. "Are you sure they're all dead? They are mages too. They may have found a way to escape. Cathal and the others are not stupid. They may have sensed something about my poor husband." She nervously fingered her obsidian ring.

Bored with her whining, Koll's solace was her imminent destruction in a few days. "As long as Morydonn did not arouse suspicion, I doubt it. The current crisis has them all huddled together afraid of dark like children. The crystal weapon I chose was rare. It was of Bloodstone origin. I treasured it as part of my collection for years.

Its potent magic devastated the house and all inside."

"Except for Morydonn," Faustine murmured. "Your magic protected him. You told me it would."

"As I promised he was shielded. The crystal he used to communicate with me would shield him from all danger. I created it special just for this occasion. No one could have survived the explosion unless they knew to cast a shield before, which they did not. The crimson barricade I cast upon the sorcerer house prevented their escape. The explosion burned the house and all inside. Fragments and ash smolder within the red shell still burning the ruins of their precious sorcerer house."

"But he is safe?"

She's annoying me, Koll, Xabral complained. *Let me sting her and be done with it. At least she would serve some purpose.*

Don't tempt me. Her whining is taxing my patience.

Who cares about who rules Thill now? The world will be changed! When Obsydia ascends, we will rule with her over demons and other lovely creatures of darkness.

"All will be well," Koll calmly soothe Faustine. "Our enemies are dead. Your husband will be rewarded for his heroism. He will take the throne and you will be queen."

"Not all of our enemies are dead." She tugged the ring, but it refused to move from her slim finger. "Will they suspect me?"

"There is no reason to, so you are quite safe," Koll replied. "Morydonn will be heartbroken. They will blame me for the deaths as planned. Morydonn will be a brave survivor."

"What about Prince Turas?" Faustine asked. "He is the next heir."

Koll walked toward the mirror and looked back at her. "Neither Queen Sorcha nor Prince Turas will survive long enough for this to be an issue. Now stop plaguing me about such meaningless troubles. You know what to do. Or do you prefer me to hold your hand each step?"

"Don't mock me, Sorcerer. I understand. I'm not an idiot. I've lived in the shadows of everyone else for so long, I could not accept failure now. When Morydonn returns with the sad news of Caladynn and Ulric's deaths. I will console Queen Sorcha for the terrible loss of her husband and eldest son. She will not mourn for long. I will kill her and Turas. Then I will be queen. It will be easy to blame you and your minions."

Like your husband? Koll thought dryly. *I wonder how she would feel knowing she's been bedding a demon who would snap her neck at my command?*

"Blame will not matter in a few days," Koll remarked as he disappeared into the mirror. *Because you will cease to exist when Ahridum takes this world.*

CHAPTER 26

Sandhya watched the dragons soar across the sky, guarding this small island where they took shelter. They patrolled this obscure place with care, for the dragon rookery had been secreted here. Now the baby dragons finally hatched and were under the care of their clans. *Would they have a future?* Sandhya wondered if this were the last time she would see all of her seven clans together. *This isolated rock in the middle of the southern seas is a haven for us. It allowed our dragon eggs to hatch. Our magic shielded them from dark eyes, but my own egg, my heir, is lost to me. She is surrounded by strangers. Will she hatch in safety? Will I see my offspring before we perish in Ahridum's darkness? She must have hatched by now. I wonder what they named her.* She hoped Fallon and Talon did not choose a silly name.

"You're deep in thought," Akash remarked, folding in his vast red wings and sitting next to her. "You look chilled. Shall I heat a rock for you with my fire breath?"

"No, but thank you. It's just even this tropical island is cold," Sandhya said. "This weather is unnatural."

"It's Obsydia's sinister influence. Still, we've been safe here," Akash replied. "Not all is lost. The clans celebrated when the eggs hatched. Even you were happy, but I know how worried you are about our egg."

"She is alone. She is without me," Sandhya sighed, hanging her head.

"She is not alone. You will see her soon. Cathal and his mages will protect her. Fallon and Talon are there to care for her too. We entrusted our precious egg to the sorcerer because we trust him. Cathal is a dragon friend. He will not fail us."

"You are very optimistic, my mate," Sandhya said, resting her head against his until a shimmer of sorcery unexpectedly cloaked their thoughts, and the familiar tang of human magic scented the air.

Cathal's image appeared before them on the beach. His familiar face was welcome, even as a vaporous projected image. He spoke in urgent tones. "Greetings friends, I've wanted to send you a message about your egg. As your dreams told you, she is the next Drajina, we named her Sephya. We hope you approve."

"How is she?" Sandhya asked, eager for news of her hatchling.

"She's thriving and growing very fast. As you suspected, she's a red fire dragon, just like her father."

Relief and joy swept over Sandhya. "Thank you, Cathal. Sephya is a noble name for the next Drajina. Did you choose the name for her?"

Cathal shook his head, grinning. "No, but her little guardian, a wampu named Mellypip chose it. He's the familiar to my grand-daughter, Runa. They have fun together under Talon and Fallon's care." Cathal then conjured images of Sephya and Mellypip, playing together. The warmth of hope touched Sandhya and she closed her eyes, committing the vision to memory.

"Thank you, Cathal," Akash said. "We long to see Sephya."

Cathal dispelled the vision. "Has the rest of the rookery hatched?"

"Yes," Sandya replied. "They are under the care of their guardians."

"Wonderful," Cathal replied.

"Now we hunger to fight Obsydia, the mutual cause of our fury," Sandhya cried. "I long to battle for our world and our kind. Amid this hope of our next generation, shadowy visions haunt my dreams. Obsydia is a disease. She must be destroyed once and for all. The days grow shorter now as Obsydia's ritual progresses. Bitter weather and black weeds erupting from the cold earth to strangle the light, wars and blood sacrifice poison men of all castes to do evil. Unless she is stopped before the thirteenth day, this world will die and become a realm of demons."

"There's always hope," Cathal insisted. "The Winged Fey have joined us. We work in secret to find a way. We exposed one of Obsydia's spies and learned much. There is another we will question shortly. We know where Obsydia is now. We go to do battle very soon. Even if we cannot kill Obsydia, we can still stop her as we did before. We need your help."

Sandhya nodded, knowing it was time to be the Drajina now more than ever. "I will summon the rest of the clans to battle. I have seen Obsydia within a shadowed tower in a tangled cursed wood, but she is not in the Wastelands or Ahridum's black tower in the sea."

"A Tower of Shadow has risen in the old Elfsharan country. We suspect it had to be in lands cursed by evil, and one of our people, Jadon, found it first. We've since learned Obsydia and her thirteen claw maidens have begun a ritual which endangers the world."

"To transform our world with Darkness," Sandhya said. "Ahridum's desires to claim our realm was always his plan. His only reason for seeding a mortal woman with an immortal child was to this end. She is the sacrament of shadows he will use to claim our world."

"What strengths does Obsydia have around her?" Akash asked.

"We know the Hooded Guardians followed Obsydia there, and her Claw Maidens."

"The Hooded Guardians never leave their black tower in the wild sea," Sandhya gasped. "Not a good sign. Be careful, for these hooded creatures are the spawn of Ahridum from the demon realm."

"We know their endgame," Cathal pointed out. "The Claw Maidens have already begun part of the ceremony, so they are occupied. According to our source, they cannot stop the ritual, so we aim to force them to stop before Obsydia ascends. We assume Obsydia has armies and demons lurking about on the ground, but they are a minor problem compared to the rest."

"My dragons can destroy her meager legion of demons and men. We will fly to the north, Cathal. We will meet on the last battlefield between light and darkness."

"May the light win," Cathal affirmed.

"I saw a new omen in my dreams last night," Sandhya said. "I saw a light, infinitesimal but dazzling as the Eternals."

"There is true hope then," Cathal exclaimed.

"There is a price for this gift," Sandhya replied.

"I will pay it," Cathal offered. "Whatever the cost, if it will save our world."

"You are not the one chosen," Sandhya whispered.

~ * ~

Curious about his new surroundings Mellypip sniffed around the suite of rooms, scurrying along sofas, tables, chair, walls and ever so intriguing corners. The palace was old and a treasure of strange scents. Sephya imitated him as he adapted to the smells. He detected an old mouse hole tucked in an odd corner, which Sephya focused on, nosing into the tiny mouse house. Mellypip sniffed an old mouse nest inside the hole, but the inhabitants had long departed.

"Meat," Sephya grumbled, clawing at the hole. "Hunt prey." Crouching down she breathed until a tiny spurt of flame ignited the velvet drapes.

"No!" Mellypip cried. "Bad dragon. Bad!" *Runa, help! Sephya's torchy breath is burning the curtains.* Mellypip clutched his head with his paws in exasperation.

Sephya sat up on her hind legs and unfolded her wings, confused. "Fire good! Fire strong. I make big flames with my breath!"

"Excellent," Fallon told Sephya. "Your mother will be proud."

"Now we must practice stealth," Talon said. "Quiet and steely."

"No!" Sephya puffed.

Runa rushed over, fingers flashing an icy stream of sorcery to snuff out the flame, leaving a trail of smoky odor. *We're supposed to be hiding here in secret! Doesn't she need her nap?*

You try controlling a baby red dragon!

Fallon and Talon tried to lure Sephya away, but she dashed away into the next room. Mellypip rushed after her and saw Cathal shimmering with magic in the room's center. Belwyn's sharp gaze froze him in his tracks, and he grabbed Sephya's tail before she slid into the sorcerer.

"You two be quiet," Belwyn ordered. "We're not supposed to be noticed yet."

Mellypip and Sephya huddled together in ominous silence until the light around Cathal dimmed and it was safe to speak. "The palace is huge, and we snuck in cloaked with invisibility. Nobody knows we're even here."

Belwyn's scowl deflected his reasoning with a single glance. "Be that as it may, enemies are lurking everywhere now. Morydonn is not the only spy at the palace."

Mellypip moaned and Sephya sat next to him, imitating his exasperation. "How many days until the world pops?"

"An interesting perspective," Cathal grinned. "His vocabulary is making interesting turns."

"Pop!" Sephya puffed, bobbing up and down, smoke issuing from her nostrils.

Belwyn blinked and shook his head, his tone tinged with exasperation. "Amusing but inaccurate words for a future bard. The world is not popping. We won't let Darkness rule. I forbid it."

"Do you have a plan to defeat Koll and Obsydia?" Mcllypip asked eagerly, eyes wide and tail swishing, which captured Sephya's attention. "Will there be a great battle? Will blood pour from her wicked tower? "How come the Light Eternals aren't helping? Will Obsydia finally be destroyed after eons and eons of her dark rule—"

"Stop!" Belwyn swiveled his head around to Cathal. "I'm done. Your turn." He swiveled back to Mellypip. "The dragon has your fluffy tail in her mouth."

Mellypip looked back, and Sephya gripped his tail in her jaws. He took a deep breath, hoping she would not bite down with her sharp teeth. He took a deep breath and spoke in soft tones. "Sephya, please let go of my tail. Don't exhale, no puffy smoke or flame. It would burn me. Fur burns. Burns hurt Melly."

"Be careful," Belwyn warned. "Baby red dragons are not adept at controlling their fire breath yet."

Sephya gazed at Mellypip with wide innocent eyes and hiccupped, releasing spurts of flame, singeing the tip of Melly's tale.

"Ouch, ouch, ouch," Mellypip cried out, whipping his tail back, caressing it and blowing on it.

Sephya, confused, howled when she saw Mellypip was hurt. "Sorry," she sniffled between gusts of smoke.

"Runa, we need you!" Cathal called, rubbing his eyes with one hand.

"Sorry, Grandpa," Runa cried apologetically as she ran into the room. She examined his burnt fur. "Melly, it's not too bad. It's just a teensy bit singed." She scooped Mellypip up with one hand and Sephya with the other. "Calm down, Sephya. Melly is not mad at you. Come on you two. Back to the living room."

Yllia stepped into the room. "It's time, Cathal. Faustine is waiting in the throne room."

~ * ~

Cathal observed Faustine as he entered the throne room. When she threw her arms around his neck, he braced himself. He endured her kisses of unrestrained passion.

"Is it done?" Faustine whispered in his ear. "Are our enemies dead?"

"Dead," Cathal replied in Morydonn's voice. "They burned."

"Yes! And it was glorious. I saw it through the mirror with Koll.

Now our dreams will come true, Husband. You will be king!"

Queen Sorcha rushed into the chamber, brow creased with worry. "Morydonn, is it true? Is my husband dead? My son, Ulric?"

"Yes, Sorcha. Caladynn and Prince Ulric died in the explosion," Cathal spoke. He felt strangely dirty wearing a dead man's image. "I escaped."

"How is it you escaped?" Sorcha asked, suspicious.

"It does not matter, for I am now King of Thill."

"What? No!" Sorcha cried, "My youngest son is the heir now. I was chosen as regent. It is in my husband's official will."

"Caladynn's final testament means nothing," Faustine needled. "He's dead! Morydonn is the new ruler. You need not be concerned about your son's inheritance, Sorcha. He will be dead before morning. In fact, both of you will both die this night. A new age is coming. Guards!" Several dark armored soldiers entered the chamber, swords drawn. "They serve us, Sorcha. Now you will bow to me. Obsydia rewards those who serve her well, and we will offer Obsydia your hearts as an offering of our good intentions."

A guard forced Sorcha to her knees, and her blue eyes flashed with anger. "You would murder my son on that bitch's altar? You would commit high treason and betray your family?"

Faustine's eyes shone with passion, almost making her usual pinched face beautiful. "I would hold the knife myself."

"There is no longer any doubt," Sorcha whispered, one guard holding her hand as she rose to her feet. The guards backed away and put away their weapons. "Now a traitor's death awaits you, Faustine. Any mercy I would have shown vanished when you spoke of killing my child."

"You're the one who will die!" Faustine spat. "Your mercy is nothing! Hold her down. Obey me! Why aren't you taking her prisoner?"

"They will not obey you," Cathal replied and shapeshifted from Morydonn's form to his own. He was relieved. Even wearing his shape made him feel dirty.

All around Faustine, people appeared around her as the invisibility enchantment lifted. The sorcerers and familiars she thought burned. King Caladynn and Prince Ulric removed their helmets first. As the others removed their helmets, Faustine realized her failure. Genuine, loyal palace guards were there, but the others in armor were Gabriel, Myrsalian, Prince Ulric, Liat, Jadon, and even Queen Sarabia joined the mix as part of the ruse.

Sirah entered the chamber carrying young Turas, and handed him to Sorcha.

"Your acting talents are superb, Sorcha," Sirah commended her.

"A queen needs many skills," Sorcha said, holding her son close.

The doors burst open and Neelam marched in, carrying two blood-spattered burlap sacks. Panthara and Iona followed him in. Neelam hurled the sacks at Faustine's feet. A few heads rolled out onto the marble floor. Faustine fell to her knees, the heads rolling around her. "Here's your protection," Neelam taunted.

Mellypip squeaked and burrowed his head in Runa's arms. She stroked his fur, but paled. Rualla and Liat flanked her protectively.

"Runa is too young to see this horror," Rualla protested.

"I'm fine, Mother. I've seen bad things before. I just never get accustomed to it."

"I pray you never do," Rualla whispered.

Neelam pointed to the heads. "These were members of the palace guard turned demon. Iona and Panthara pointed out the ones without a soul, and I dispatched them." Neelam unsheathed his sword and raised it. Faustine yelped when she saw its bloodstained gleam. "Is she soulless?"

"She has her soul," Iona confirmed, approaching Faustine. "But I can see how dark it is now."

"Where is Morydonn?" Faustine demanded, her eyes darting nervously.

"Dead, Faustine. He is dead," Caladynn replied.

"You killed my husband!' Faustine shrieked, her body shaking.

"No, you killed him," Caladynn declared bluntly.

Cathal looked down at Faustine, feeling no pity. "When Obsydia bestowed her blood kiss, he died and became a demon. His soul left him at that moment. Morydonn was already dead, lady."

"No!" she cried. "It's not true. She promised me a crown and children. A loving husband. We would rule in a new world. I would be queen."

"Evil lies," Cathal told her bluntly. "Obsydia is the queen of lies. She always makes promises she never intends to keep. If she rises to become a full eternal, your only reward would be death."

"You cannot touch me," Faustine cried. "She has chosen me. I have her protection."

"Her ring is not bloodstone, but obsidian," Yllia observed. "Obsidian is her new image. She has a tradition of bestowing rings to her followers. I'd wager Koll or Obsydia will contact her through the ring. It is dangerous. Those rings do not come off either."

"I can remove it," Gabriel offered, taking out his dagger.

"No need to be violent or stoop to their level," Cathal cautioned him.

"As you wish," Gabriel shrugged, sheathing it.

"We could use her if necessary," Cathal remarked quietly to Caladynn. "Koll or Obsydia will check on her sooner or later. Use it to our advantage."

"She will still lose her head," Caladynn proclaimed before all. "She has brought shame to her House. Her crimes are beyond clemency. I cannot even pray for her soul."

"No!" Faustine screamed, hunching over and crying hysterically. "Don't kill me. You don't understand. It's not my fault! I was seduced by her promises. She put a spell on me. I could not resist her lure."

Caladynn's deep voice boomed in a rare outburst. "Take responsibility for your sins, Faustine. I'm barren of sympathy for you. My brother had faults, but he was no traitor. You not only committed high treason but embraced the dark enemy. Morydonn is dead because of your machinations."

"She must pay for her crimes," Sorcha said. "But I ask Faustine to understand the consequences. If we fail in our battle against Obsydia, she'll die a terrible death when Ahridum takes power. If we win, as I believe we will, she must endure the shame of public execution. If she had shown mercy, I would have given it."

"As you wish, Sorcha," Caladynn said, and kissed his wife's hand. "We have more important things to do. Now we must lock her up and keep a heavy guard on her." Caladynn summoned the palace guards who dragged Faustine away.

Cathal sensed they were still in jeopardy. "She must be watched carefully."

"I'll do it," Gabriel offered. "We should all take turns, and at least two of us mages at a time. She may have failed now, but Koll may still try and use her."

"That's what I'm afraid of," Cathal said.

"He's right," Darcus agreed. "We'll need more than just regular guards on this one. Still, I'll take watch."

"Then so be it," Caladynn agreed. "Watch her."

Faustine wails echoed through the halls as guards dragged her away.

"We'll take care of Raven," Rualla said to Darcus.

"Thank you, lady," Darcus replied. "I want her safe."

"Come, my dear," Sorcha gestured to Rualla. "We can put Turas and Raven in the same room together."

"I almost feel sorry for Faustine," Runa whispered.

"I don't," Opaline replied. "I lived at a ruthless court where treason and betrayal are common. The reasons are always power and greed."

"I do not pity her either," Panthara said, joining them. "There are times when mercy must stay its hand, especially when treason involves the crown."

"If she loved her husband, I just don't understand why she let Koll and Obsydia hurt him," Mellypip said in confusion.

"I don't think she loved her husband," Opaline pointed out. "Sorcha told me it was an arranged marriage, and neither were happy, but it's no excuse for her actions or choosing Obsydia. She made a choice. Faustine guided Morydonn to his doom."

"Sometimes a soul is already tainted," Panthara added. "She refused to repent or show mercy even to a child. Remember this when you pray for her soul."

"Do you think Faustine would show us mercy?" Opaline asked simply.

"It's so strange when you two agree," Runa whispered, confused.

Cathal turned to Runa, his voice gentle but firm. "It's harsh, but we are at war. She chose to follow darkness. Let the Eternals judge her. Don't let the corrupt sway your sympathy or cause confusion in your heart, dear. What is coming will demand all of our strength."

CHAPTER 27

Fighting since dawn at Tiamet's city gates, the rebel army's morale weakened after hours of brutal battle. Eshra stared across the violent field of war, ruined by blood and mutilated bodies from both sides. Smoke singed her nostrils, and her ears ached from the clamor of battle. Her brother Darcus fought wars for years as a soldier, but she never understood what he endured until now. They fought not only legions of human soldiers trained in combat but goblins and trolls. Her fellow sisters fought side by side with the soldiers. The gentle nuns who prayed with soft voices were no more. Innocence lost forever. Angry, she wiped tears from her weathered wind-burnt face.

A black-armored warrior attacked, disrupting Eshra from her foolish reflections. Her reflexes took over, honed by years of instruction from her brother. Her sword deflected the strike of an enemy soldier and knocked it from his hand. The glint of red eyes through the black helmet made it easier when she ran him through. He fell off his warhorse, a poor wild-eyed creature who fled the field, happy to be rid of its demon rider. She could not blame the poor animal, as her own horse was nervous and not even a trained warhorse. She stroked her horse's mane. "Easy, boy. Easy." She winced when she looked down at the black weedy vines strangling the earth. They even shrouded the city's stone wall. Another sign of evil she could not cast aside with a prayer.

Lord Rhudon slashed his way to her side, killing enemy soldiers with swift speed for a man of his years. 'Damn it, Abbess! You'll be the death of me yet! I told you to keep a safe distance. Stay back behind the battle lines. Help the wounded."

"My sisters fight. I don't want special treatment," Eshra protested. "And he's dead. I'm no longer Abbess of Araema, but only Eshra, a poor rebel in your army of light." She smiled bitterly. "My old life is gone. Let me do some good."

"Then stay behind enemy lines and stop punishing yourself," Rhudon told her gently. "War is cruel, but this is not just any war between men. Demons and gods have marked us, and I for one will not tolerate it. Stay close for I would feel better for it, in case I need someone to pray for me. After all, I've too many sins to manage on my own."

Her weary heart lightened by his bold irreverence, she obeyed and followed him back to Pol and Korun who worked the massive war machine. The great vehicle was constructed by Riva and his friend Ulan, who joined them a few days ago. The catapult was made of wood but shimmered with magic. They even hauled it across the fields by magical wheels conjured by the sorcerer, sparing the men the staggering efforts of transporting it across the country.

Sorcery's heat seared the air as Riva created another massive fire stone, concentrating deeply as it hovered in the air, swirling with magic flame. He guided the blazing payload into the bucket and stepped back. "Fire!"

Korun grinned broadly and pulled the lever. The ball of fire grew as it hurled into the air, growing in diameter until it was ten times its size. It crashed into the city wall like lightning, destroying a good chunk of the wall.

"A devastating hit!" Pol shouted.

"I think we've destroyed enough wall for a good march into the city," Riva said. "The enemy's numbers are down." Buzzy the sloth, cozy in a special harness on Riva's back, lifted his head and grinned until they looked across the field.

"We have more trouble coming," Buzzy warned.

The city gates opened. More soldiers rushed the battlefield, but worse hundreds of goblins and trolls stampeding toward the weary and blood-soaked army. The balance shifted in a single moment, stunning the now outnumbered rebels in a moment of despair.

"What the hell!" Riva cried. "Now what?"

"Time for more fireballs," Ulan suggested to Riva. He carefully cradled Rosepetal in his hands and handed her to Riva. "Take little Rosepetal and watch her while I go back into the fray. I think sorcery might sting the demons and slow them down." Riva tucked Rosepetal in his pocket and the little hedgehog chirped and hiccupped as Ulan flew into the mayhem.

"You should fall back," Eshra pleaded.

Korun unsheathed his sword. "No rest for us now. Sir, there be goblins and trolls headed our way! What are your orders?"

"Kill them all!" Rhudon ordered. "Damn it! How many demons

live in that city?"

"Maybe only demons are left," Pol remarked bleakly. "But I will slay as many as I can."

"We can't take much more," Eshra cried. "The soldiers are spent. We've lost so many already. We must retreat, Rhudon."

"We can't pull back now. We're too close to taking the city. It's now or never!" Rhudon shouted, closing the visor of his helmet and charging his horse into battle. "

"Go after him," Eshra shouted to Korun and Pol. "Watch his back."

"Yes, Abbess," they cried, mounting their horses and riding after Rhudon.

Eshra saw Rhudon take on the rampaging horde of demons his men fought. She spurred her horse to chase after him, sword in hand.

A massive shaggy troll leapt through the air and charged at her, its hideous horns and curved yellow tusks bloodstained and dragging a stone club with its huge paw. Her body shuddered from the troll's strident howl. Her screaming horse reared up as it backed away in terror, throwing Eshra from the saddle to the hard ground, knocking the breath out of her. She moaned, her bones throbbing with pain as she struggled to crawl away. The troll loomed over her, so close she could she smell its foul breath. She braced for death.

A roar split the heavens above, deafening her. She screamed in shock as a green dragon dove so close she could almost touch it, seizing the troll with its talons. She felt the heat of its wings sweep over her body as it soared high into the air with the troll shrieking in its grip. She gazed up at the sky, mesmerized by the thunder of dragons flying overhead.

~ * ~

Koll strode through the corridors toward his chambers in the tower, the double doors flying open with a wave of his hand. Hanging lamps burning with blue-red flame offered soft light. The events of the last several days welled in his mind, shaded by a ragged-edge of frustration and exhaustion.

Coiled on the broad bed's center, Xabral lifted his head when he entered. His scales almost blended in with the black spider silk cover, embroidered with scarlet rune symbols. "Levandius has been screaming into the mirror for you every hour. It's irritating. Do something."

"The imbecile has his orders," Koll said. "Is it the rebellion in Upala again?"

"No, he's not there anymore. When I tried to contact him again, one of our priests informed me Queen Hadrial is dead, murdered by her husband. The city is also in rebellion. Apparently, Hadrial's enchantment of beauty faded overnight."

"How can it be? I prepared the potion from an ancient blood-stone text," Koll replied. "No, there are more things at play here."

"After Levandius killed her more chaos erupted, and most of his army fled or joined the rebels. The natives are angry and fighting back. There are rampant rumors Sarabia is alive, but I find it hard to believe. Obsydia will not be pleased. He must be punished."

"Where is Levandius now?"

"The pasty addlepate crawled back to Tiamet."

"What?" Koll raged.

"I suspect something is fighting us. Cathal and his friends were not our only enemies. The dragons are in hiding. Perhaps the Winged Fey," Xabral asked, "they would be a threat. They are immortal with powerful light magic."

"Obsydia's father is not just a dark eternal, but Ahridum, God of Darkness and Chaos. No one knows who sired these half-breeds. They would know what is happening. They watch the world."

"But we cannot watch them," Xabral hissed.

The mirror glowed while hysterical crying burned Koll's ears.

"It's him again," Xabral sighed.

Koll's black eyes flashed with anger as he went to the tall mirror framed in jeweled ebonite. Emanating dark mystical power, Koll touched the frame. Levandius face appeared, blubbering like a baby as he pounded on the glass. "Koll! Please help me."

"Can we kill him now?" Xabral slithered off the bed toward Koll.

"We cannot take any chances. Her ascension is in three days. Nothing must threaten her. I should see what is happening."

"Obsydia's been cloistered in her chambers since the ceremony began. I miss her glorious presence," Xabral sighed.

Koll paced the room, his black robes whipping the floor. "At least Shroud is preoccupied with the ritual. She cannot step from the altar else it will break the spell. I detest these last-minute problems. I will handle this." A shrill cry penetrated Koll's ears like needles.

"I told you," Xabral said. "Whiny."

Koll activated the mirror and the misty glass changed to liquid shadow. He walked through its shadow. "Stay here, Xabral. I will see to this insipid Emperor."

~ * ~

Koll found Levandius huddled near the mirror, stinking of wine and dream herbs. When he looked up at Koll with a puffy face and bloodshot eyes, Koll wanted to smite him right there, but he had to learn what was happening. Even from the safety of the palace, he could hear war raging outside.

"You have failed your god," Koll began. "You swore to be pure and sound of body and mind to serve the Dark Trinity."

"It all went bad," Levandius cried. "She changed. She turned into a hideous hag. So I killed her. You promised she would be beautiful. You lied."

"Did you consider our enemies were behind this?" Koll pointed out. "Did you seek me out? Obsydia granted your dreams and you have pissed on them with your weakness."

"They rebelled against their lawful emperor. I barely escaped with my life. Your demons and priests were useless, Koll. The alliance of rebels is not just confined to a kingdom, but they are everywhere now. I came back home, but they followed me. I cannot escape them. I ordered more sacrifices to make amends. They have come for me today." Levandius wept, clutching at his robes. "They are too strong. All the demons and men you sent were not enough for this?"

"Fight what?" Koll demanded.

The strange cries Koll heard outside were neither demon nor man and he knew. Koll went to the balcony overlooking the city from the palace and saw what defeated the city.

Dragons.

They were everywhere. Smaller shadow dragons stalking through the city alleys. Golden sun dragons landed on rooftops. A silver fire dragon's breath froze the legions of goblins in their tracks. Red fire dragons burned the sacred dark temples, sending the priests fleeing into the street, only to fall asleep with the dream breath of the blue mist dragons. Dragons of every clan fought alongside the traitors which stormed the gates of the city to the cheers of its people. Koll was mortified but mesmerized by the dragons in action.

Trolls and goblins fled the dragon hunt. A green earth dragon pursuing a pack of trolls landed, its impact sending vibrations along the streets, cracking the stones. The dragon's green body glowed translucent as it inhaled deeply, its chest expanding until it looked to burst. The dragon extended its long neck and exhaled, spraying the fleeing trolls with a green mist that quickly solidified into a thick, leafy cocoon that trapped the monsters within. The hardened green shell muffled their howls and not even the troll's incredible strength could puncture its thick casing.

Among the dragon clans in flight, he saw a glimpse of a white moon dragon, the Drajina. She landed on the ruined temple of Rhone and seemed to stare right at him. He longed to destroy the dragons, but had not the power to defeat this onslaught. The dragons were out of hiding, which spelled trouble for Koll's plans and threatened Obsydia.

Lord Rhudon, flanked by sweaty blood-stained soldiers, burst into the bedchamber. Koll glared at them with disdain. Levandius hunched over, terrified. Koll wanted to kick him.

"That's Koll the Sorcerer!" Riva shouted, pointing at him.

"Koll! An unexpected prize. Kill the sorcerer!" Rhudon ordered. "But take Levandius prisoner."

Koll cast a scarlet shield across the chamber. The sorcerous net prevented Rhudon and his men from touching him. Ulan and Riva moved to the front, shooting bolts of sorcery to burn through his shield. Koll simply turned and stepped into the mirror.

"Don't leave me!" Levandius shrieked grabbing onto Koll's robes, and was dragged through the bewitched mirror's shadows.

~ * ~

Koll returned with Levandius still clinging to his robes like a mewling baby. He jerked his robes from his grip.

"What's happened?" Xabral cried.

"We've lost the Red Empire," Koll replied dully. He looked down at Levandius with disgust. His artificial arm blazed as he flexed the velvet fingers. He flicked his fingers and hurled Levandius against the wall. "My new arm has been getting stronger. I expect to exercise the magical strength I possess as we discuss your failure to keep order."

FIRES OF RAPIVESHTA

"Don't hurt me, Koll. You don't understand. It's not my fault."

"Common excuses for weak people," Koll seethed. "I do not want to understand your reasons. Do you think I care whose fault it is?"

"You didn't assassinate your father," Xabral snapped. "A demon, a lovely demon I cared about, simply did the act for you as you watched and cheered. We did everything for you. We made you an emperor. We gave you power. Now you are nothing."

"I could not have anticipated the dragons," Levandius wept. "They never interfere. Frankly, I was not sure they even existed."

"They interfered a thousand years ago when they helped our enemies imprison Obsydia in a crystal of light," Koll pointed out harshly.

"They all hated me," Levandius blubbered. "I tried, I tried, but there was resistance from the day my father died. No one loved me. They hated me. I should have been loved. I was their emperor."

"Hate is an emotion," Koll instructed. "A true ruler can deflect hate. You are nothing now. You must learn there is a price for failure. I will not kill you yet. There is one more purpose for you to fulfill, but punishment is required."

Levandius crawled toward the door, but Koll's sorcery picked him up and pinned him against the wall. His mystical arm of ebonite and velvet burned brightly ion the shadowy room. "Darkness does not forgive."

Xabral watched with glee, shaking his stinger as Levandius screamed in agony.

CHAPTER 28

Mellypip loved the royal park. All the trees were very old and tall, and he itched to climb a few. Even in this wintery landscape, they were still pretty. He nibbled nuts from a little bag, sitting on Runa's shoulder. "King Caladynn has lots of trees. I wish they still had their leaves, but the ones still clinging to the branches are pretty colors."

"It reminds me of home and our tree tower," Runa said fondly, "at least until I look down at those horrible demonic vines." Runa sidestepped a patch of black weeds growing feral everywhere.

"I just don't look at the ground anymore," Mellypip told her, munching another nut. "I feel creepy when I do. Belwyn says I'm just in denial, but I told him I'm just preserving my cheery nature."

Runa stepped over a dark vine, wrinkling her nose. "Until Obsydia is defeated, we must deal with the vile things."

"Like the end of the world?" Mellypip whispered.

"The world won't end," Runa insisted. "We've faced evil before. Grandpa will fix this. He always does."

"We haven't faced a god before," Mellypip muttered, chewing his nuts with frantic passion. "If Obsydia becomes a goddess we won't exist anymore. Dark gods are mean. I was reading all about them in the library. They don't like anything good." Mellypip held up a sweet walnut, studying it in the light. "What if this is the last walnut I will ever enjoy? What if this is our last walk together?"

"Stop it, please! Don't begin a 'what if' scenario," Runa begged. "I don't have the energy."

"I do, because I'm eating my nuts, plus we had pancakes for breakfast. You didn't even touch yours, and Queen Sorcha ordered them just for you."

"I wasn't hungry," Runa replied sharply.

"Which is why you are cranky," Mellypip countered and offered her the bag. "I'll share my walnuts with you."

"No, Melly, you enjoy them. I'll eat later. I promise."

"I hope so: otherwise you will become crankier. Are all evil gods cranky? What they want makes no sense to me. If Obsydia rises to become full eternal and the world becomes a demon place, it means no more sunshine, no trees, no hot tea, no drobba, mashed potatoes, apple tarts with cream, walnuts, or anything nice."

"You would chalk up the world with your stomach," Belwyn remarked, perched on a branch above their heads. "Or perhaps the dark powers should have eaten their pancakes."

Mellypip looked up, flattening his large furry ears. "Hey! You're spying on us!"

"I'm taking care of my charges, as I always do."

"Where's Grandpa and Grandmother?" Runa asked.

"They're busy now."

"What are they doing?" Mellypip asked.

"Just never you mind," Belwyn replied bluntly.

That was snippy, Mellypip commented.

Best not to pursue it, Runa thought back.

"What are you doing out here anyway?" Belwyn remarked. "Your staff was spared."

"I'm helping the others. Moral support. We all need it I think."

"Did Grandpa Cathal find a way to save us from the world going boom?" Mellypip asked eagerly.

"I told you, it won't happened," Runa snapped and then took a deep breath, stroking his large furry ears. "That's why the others are creating new staffs for the fight. We must have hope, or we will all go raving mad."

"The Winged Fey and the others are preparing another ritual to trap Obsydia in a crystal prison again before she succeeds in her bloody rising. At least it will help stop the chaos."

"It worked before, and it took a thousand years to breach it," Runa said, holding her staff close. "Everything is so…uncertain."

"Life is uncertain," Belwyn said. "But we also have experience fighting it. And we're all safe here. The Fey have shielded us from any prying busybodies trying to spy on us."

Mellypip looked down at Runa's staff. The eerie imprint of Striker's eyes in the wood was actually comforting now, as though they had a personal guardian spirit in all the uncertainty. "I'm glad you still have your staff with my face carved on top and Striker's eyes. Is Striker's soul still inside?"

Runa touched the eyes on her staff, shaking her head. "I'm not sure. I'm afraid to ask. He' been so quiet lately. I'm thankful I didn't lose it. How we made it is special. The willow oak which grew over Striker's grave in Moonthorne seemed to be just for this. I felt like a true sorceress when I fashioned it with my magic."

"Iona would know if Striker's spirit is still there. Maybe even Panthara, since her necromancy is improving, according to Amun."

"Iona's familiar is very shy I think, as she is," Runa said. "I'm glad she has Panthara in her life."

"Amun's so quiet most of the time, I'm amazed when he does speak," Mellypip remarked. "Belwyn always talks. He never stops."

"Really?" Belwyn snapped.

Belwyn is extra crabby today, Mellypip told her.

Tell me something I don't know and don't poke the owl! Runa sent back.

"Runa! Come see," Opaline shouted from over the hill. "I think I've found the perfect tree to create my staff! I feel it!"

Belwyn's ear tufts perked up in a panic and looked down. "Oh, blast. Opaline is making a staff? So soon? She's still a bit green to advance to her making her own staff."

Runa laughed and ran toward Opaline, Mellypip bouncing on her shoulder. "Opaline's been diligently practicing her magic, with the help of Grimm and her family. We are all needed to fight Obsydia and Koll. She has come a long way."

Belwyn flew after her. "At turning people into trolls, instigating forest fires, growing your hair about a hundred feet long."

"Stop bickering, Belwyn!" Runa shouted. "We need all the magic we can muster for what's coming! Have a little faith."

"I have faith she could turn me into a toad with wings," Belwyn quipped. "I think I'll stay out of her firing range."

"Yes, oh crabby feathers," Runa muttered, walking away.

"I heard that, Missy!"

~ * ~

The quiet morning was a rare blessing. Cathal and Yllia held each other until late morning. The palace suite Caladynn gave them was opulent. Cathal almost felt guilty for such a rich room, but the large soft feather bed and lavender-scented linen sheets were bliss after all the hardship and anxiety. Being alone with Yllia without the constant interruption and cares gave Cathal a moment of relief from his responsibilities. They reveled in their solitude, feeling a little guilty, but only a little.

"Do you think Belwyn minded that we sent him away?" Yllia asked, stretching out her body in the large bed.

Cathal's smiled, resting his head on his arm, looking at her. "He didn't mind. We haven't had time to be alone since we freed you from the curse." He brushed a strand of blonde hair from her green eyes. "I cannot believe the gods would let it end like this, not when we have finally been reunited. I don't understand Eternals. Never did."

Yllia touched his cheek and snuggled closer. "No talk of gods, destiny, or fighting the darkness. I forbid it."

Cathal kissed her, gently at first, and then with passion. "Your wish is my command."

~ * ~

"What do you think?" Opaline asked, looking at the cherry tree. "I sense strong energy when I touch it. What do you think of the tree, Grimm?"

"It's wood," Grimm remarked dryly.

Impatient, Opaline put her hands on her hips. "Please be a little enthusiastic."

Dabiro waddled by, following Liat who already had his new staff made. "Maybe the wolf could piss on the tree. That's what wolves do. They pee on trees." Dabiro chuckled to himself, amused at his own humor.

"Manners," Liat warned his badger.

Grimm flattened his ears and glared at Dabiro. "I know what I could urinate on."

"Grimm, be nice," Opaline whispered.

"He started it," Grimm protested.

"Let's not do any of that," Runa said.

This could get interesting, Mellypip told Runa through the bonding.

"Where's Mother?" Runa asked. "Isn't she making a new staff?"

Liat shook his head sadly. "She told me she's not ready yet."

"I wish I could help her," Runa said.

Liat kissed her on the head. "You've done all you can do, Runa. She is better, but it takes time. She's sitting with Pointessa this morning. They've grown very close."

"I'm glad. They've both lost so much. You really love my mother, don't you?" Runa whispered.

"I do," Liat replied in a low voice. "She is getting stronger each day."

Panthara and Iona joined them, walking arm in arm. Panthara looked quite happy, holding a new staff of silver birch wood with Azmadu's face carved at the top.

"I see you have found what you're looking for," Runa remarked.

"She did a beautiful job," Iona complimented her, stroking her hair. "Taran helped her choose. He's off now to find something suitable for him."

"His familiar MacTabbish picked out a tree and fell asleep," Amun noted, perched on Iona's shoulder.

Mellypip brushed his paws together to shake the salt dust from his paws. "I often think MacTabbish is under a bizarre sleeping curse, but Sanura just says he's just lazy. I'd think a cat who could sprout wings and fly would have more energy."

Panthara laughed, touching the top of her new staff where she carved the likeness of Azmadu. "MacTabbish claims to be conserving for a special occasion. He longs to mate with Sanura, but she disdains him so far. I think she likes him and is playing hard to get."

"You don't regret losing your old staff?" Runa asked, admiring the artistry she used. You did lovely work though. I love the smell of fresh sorcery on wood. It's invigorating."

"It is, isn't it? I've no grief over my old staff burning," Panthara proclaimed. "In fact, I rejoice in its destruction. Koll helped me forge my staff when I was his apprentice. He taught me evil was good and my faith was the Dark Trinity. My mother was mad, obsessed with revenge. She did not love me. I accept that now and feel only pity for her. They chose my path for their own selfish desires. I was alone, a pawn for my mother's insane ambitions and Koll's fanatical hunt for Obsydia. After what happened in Mowad, the touch of the Wraith Guardian freed me somehow. It was a blessing, for when I woke I rejected Koll and his teachings without regret. My old staff was a reminder of those bleak days. I still felt like I carried around my old sins and his cursed memory. This new staff is silver birch and carved by me alone. It reflects my new life."

"A Koll free life is a good thing," Azmadu rapidly nodded. "A Xabral free life is even better."

"I think we can all agree on that," Opaline smiled. She looked at

Runa quizzically.

"You're staring at me," Runa said.

Panthara bit her lip but did not take her eyes off Runa. "Ever since the attack, I feel like something happened to me, but I can't remember. I feel touched by a spirit, but it is elusive. I sense the same thing about you and Opaline."

"Me?" Opaline laughed.

Panthara touched Runa's forehead and closed her eyes. "I sense something."

"Your hands are cold," Runa replied dryly.

"We've all been touched by spirits," Grimm remarked.

"I know, but we had a dream," Mellypip whispered. "But it goes away when I think about it."

Panthara touched Opaline's forehead, concentrating. "I sense a soul touched us, but it is too distant."

"My head hurts whenever I think about it, like right now. Stop!" Opaline winced, stepping away and massaging her temples.

Panthara dropped her hand and sighed. "I apologize, but I sense something. Iona touched my mind, but it is locked even from her. I cannot explain it."

"What happened rattled all of us," Runa said.

Taran joined them. Taran's big grin on his face as he carried a new staff of hawthorn wood. "I've returned victorious. Behold my new staff of power!"

Panthara kissed him with passion and beamed with pride. "It's marvelous. You cut a dashing figure with your new mage staff, even with the drowsy cat draped across your shoulders."

"I heard that," MacTabbish muttered, swishing his tail.

"I suggest we take a brief recess from this excursion," Opaline suggested. "Queen Sorcha is asking for us in the chapel. She wished us to have a brief prayer mass before tea."

"People are praying a lot," Iona remarked. "Though the people are unaware of what is really happening, they know something is wrong."

"Our burden is the truth," Amun added.

Mellypip looked up at the sky, wondering where the Eternals were hiding in the heavens. A tiny burst of light pierced the charcoal-colored clouds. It startled him. He longed to follow its path. "We have to go now, Runa."

Runa plucked Mellypip from her shoulders and firmly tucked him in her arms. "I'm going for a walk."

Opaline and Panthara followed Runa trancelike, their familiars at their sides.

"Hey, where are you ladies going?" Taran called after them. "Hey! Stop! Why aren't you answering me? Panthara! Runa! Damn, Opaline, I'm not playing games."

"The lassies are ignoring you," MacTabbish remarked, lifting his head from Taran's shoulder.

"This reeks of mystical meddling," Belwyn commented and took wing after the three sorceresses and their familiars.

"For good or evil?" Taran asked.

Iona gripped Taran's arm, "Something is happening. Perhaps it's what Panthara spoke of. Come, we must follow them." She ran, Amon flying overhead and Taran running to keep up. Even MacTabbish sprouted wings and flew. Turning back to Liat she cried, "Go! Get Cathal and Neelam. Get everyone. Now."

CHAPTER 29

Koll tossed his bloodstained robes to the floor, revitalized by the exhaustive sorcery he summoned to punish Levandius who crawled to a corner whimpering. Koll noticed his reflection in the mirror. Looks never concerned him, but the velvet arm glistening with ebonite and gems enchanted him. Not even the black metal hooks in his shoulder marred its beauty. He scarcely felt its pain and could move it naturally now as though he was born with it. He sensed the mystical energy which sprang from the Dark Netherworld of the Hooded Guardians who fashioned his mystical arm. He frowned, touching the silvery scars of Cathal's sorcery which spread across his naked shoulder and chest like a spider's web. They had purged the remnants of Cathal's light sorcery from his body, yet the scars remained. He would never undervalue Cathal's power and considered this a lesson to remember.

"I suppose the punishment you inflicted on Levandius will suffice for the moment," Xabral suggested, drawing Koll's attention away from the looking glass. "We don't want to break him completely, where's the fun in that? He slid off the bed and crawled toward Levandius, lifting his head, bobbing back and forth. Levandius did not flinch or look. He just curled into a fetal position and rocked. "Maybe we did break him?"

"He will recover," Koll remarked, choosing a fresh robe.

"I hope so. I have been so bored since Obsydia went into seclusion. I long for her wicked presence. I even miss our time with her in the Wastelands. The ruined temple-palace was our haven. She was ours then. I could sit for hours and gaze at her beauty and talk, even with the curses light of her crystal prison."

As though providence heard the scorpion snake's wish, a voice of melodic perfection born of Eternal origin, filled the room. "Come to me, my servants."

Obsydia's voice summoned Koll and Xabral. They followed her call through the mystical halls of her shadow tower, eager for her blessed image. This tower was still a mystery to them and they followed Obsydia's mystical call to a new place unknown, not her private chamber or the temple, but something new. The double-doors of red carved with strange symbols, most likely demon script. Koll paused, for this was not Obsydia's private chamber.

"Where are we?" Xabral asked, staring up at the vast doors rising over a hundred feet high.

"We are where Obsydia has summoned us to be," Koll replied.

As though sensing their presence, the doors opened into an immense shadowy chamber. Light did not profane this sacred ground. In the center of the chamber, Obsydia stood beneath a dark glass dome basking in rays of crimson shadow. Koll breathed in the essence and nearly stumbled for its power.

Eternal origin, Koll gasped. *It is almost too much to endure.*

I smell its darkness and power, Xabral cried, waving back and forth.

Obsydia twirled in the beams like a nymph beneath a waterfall, bathing in its power. She wore only a sheer back shift which barely covered her body. The mystical symbols the Hooded-Guardians painted on her in blood during the ceremony reemerged and flickered in the darkness.

I smell the essence of Eternal power, Koll communicated to Xabral. *It's darkness without stain. I am blessed by the powers of Darkness.*

Xabral merely gazed in adoration, speechless before her radiance.

"I am still immortal trapped a shell of mortal skin," Obsydia said, "but my body is changing. As my hour of glory approaches, my flesh is shifting and burning hot within. My godhood desires to spring into being. My father's rays are preparing me for the metamorphosis into a pure goddess."

Koll looked at her, raising his arms in worship. "Goddess Obsydia, you have been in seclusion since they started the ritual. We have been bereft with you."

"Enjoy my splendor for soon I shall take my rightful place by my father's side in the Dark Netherworld. My true family, my circle of Eternals, wait for me. I long to join them after these lonely centuries of duty for the Darkness." Obsydia stepped from the scarlet rays, her very essence was ethereal darkness incarnate. Her shadow hair flashed with night's spirit and floated behind her as she moved gracefully toward him. Her silver eyes glittered in the shadows as red flames whirling beneath her alabaster flesh scorched the ground around her.

Koll dropped to his knees in awe of the eternal power weakening his constitution. Obsydia extended her hand in benediction and stopping suddenly, frozen. Koll watched unaware of time until her face contorted and she hurled back her head howling, her rage quaking the chamber with its force. Koll collapsed from the impact of her scream, covering his ears. The fiery essence beneath her skin sparked, shooting streams of red flame from her fingertips and eyes.

"Fiends! Tricksters!" Obsydia shouted. "No! They will not deny me."

"What's wrong?" Koll begged. "Tell me. I want to help." Xabral coiled at Koll's side, mute with terror.

"War," Obsydia said. "War raging far from your pathetic mortal eyes. The battleground of this world is just one of many between our eternal kind. You could never understand. A danger falls from the nemesis of darkness, casting their challenge upon this finite shore to threaten me!"

"What threat?" Koll asked, standing.

Obsydia's hot gaze terrified Koll. "We've been deceived. Thill still cradles our enemies. All our enemies live! The sorcerers deceived us somehow."

"I watched them die. I saw the house burn."

"You were wrong," she spat, striking him with wrath, hurling his body across the room. She walked toward the glass dome, and it metamorphosed into a vast balcony of grey glass overlooking the cursed wood of Elfshara. "I will not punish you now, for we have work. We must summon armies. Call up my demon-warriors, Koll. Send the goblin hordes with their blades and spears and unleash the trolls. I will summon creatures of shade so vicious it will stop their hearts with terror."

"What will you do?" Koll asked. "What creatures? I have seen only shadows here."

Obsydia's cool stare cautioned silence, but then she smiled bitterly. "You have not looked deep enough, Koll. This land was cursed for a reason." She extended her arms, gazing at the vast gloomy forests beneath the tower and the grim mountains in the distance above the river. "If I had not been imprisoned for millennia I would have created more kingdoms like this one. Darkness had plans for this world."

Why?" Koll asked. "Why this world? Is it special? I ask only to learn."

"Darkness seeks dominance over all things," Obsydia whispered. "The ancient Wasteland where my first temple palace rose was once the center of strong light magic. Rivers of deep blue flowed beneath shiny white towers. Rich forests and mountains dotted their tranquil haven of peace. In this enchanted realm of light, the three mage races created volumes of mystic tomes and conjured powerful magics during the Sapphire Age. This light threatened our dominance. The Conflicts of the Eternal Realms are beyond even your comprehension, Koll. Ahridum destroyed their sanctuary of magic simply by casting a dark star upon the land, small yet devastating enough to ruin this world for generations. He did it to prepare for my coming. Elfshara, the lost ancestral home of the Ilyrran race, was also a stronghold of powerful light magic. When I curse the lands with my dark magic, I created battlegrounds with my powers as I have created my demon men. For a thousand years, they waited for me. Devils, imps, shades, wraiths, monsters and demons of mortal breeds slept deep in the caves, clinging to the dead trees, hiding in the tangled forests awaiting my call. Watch!"

Koll and Xabral followed her to the open balcony. Obsydia spread her arms and chanted in demon tongue. The dim light in the sky clouded over with black clouds bursting with lightning and thunder. Winds gusted with violence. Strange cries emitted from the shrouded lands. Growls and shrieks echoed in the unknown shadows. Terrifying sounds bloomed in the rising storm.

"They will follow you, Koll. Take my demons into battle. Go to Thill. Kill my enemies. Find it and destroy it."

"Find what?" Koll pleaded, prostrating himself before her.

Obsydia's tone sent terror through Koll's veins. "The light."

~ * ~

Runa woke as from a dream standing in the mass of colorful blossoms bursting in the middle of the wintry wood. The cold, bitter vale of winter surrounded them, but this circle of flowers bloomed untouched by frost. Mellypip snuggled in her arms, drowsy.

"What am I doing here?" Runa asked.

"I don't know, but it's nice." Mellypip sniffed the air. "It smells so heavenly here."

"Where are we?" Opaline mumbled, rubbing her eyes. "There

was a light in the sky."

"What light?" Iona asked.

Opaline shook her head and looked away. "I don't know."

"It's okay," Taran shouted, standing outside the circle of blooming flowers.

"I'm confused not deaf," Opaline snapped and then closed her eyes, breathing in the calming fragrance of the flowers bursting around her. "I feel the warmth of sunshine and smell the blossoms, yet the sky is grey and cold."

"These plants are only in this spot yet all around us it's hideous. We're still in the same woods. Look around," Panthara pointed out. "All the trees are stripped by bitter winter, and the ground cursed with demon vines, but this spot where we stand is pure. See! These black weeds are actually retreating from the spreading flowers. I still dislike not knowing what I'm doing."

"I'd protect you," Taran offered.

"I can protect myself," Panthara replied.

"How long did we walk?" Runa asked.

"Not long," Iona replied, kneeling by the flowers. "We have been following you for almost half an hour. We sent for the others. You have been guided here for a reason. We hope it's a key from the Eternals to help us."

Mellypip loved the fragrance of wildflowers growing around them. The colors were as vibrant as summer. He felt so good he leapt out of Runa's arms into the wild garden and rolled in warm petals.

"Melly, be careful!" Runa cried.

"It's like he's drunks on pollen," Grimm remarked and sniffed the rim of the flowers, warily stepping back as they advanced. "I will not chance stepping in anything otherworldly unless I know more. Maybe we're not supposed to touch them."

"Grimm is very cautious," Opaline smiled, scratching his head.

"Caution has kept me alive," Grimm said. "Please follow my example, Opaline. I do not want to lose my sorceress."

"The flowers are soft yet they do not break or become crushed when I lay in them," Mellypip swooned with contentment. "Join me, Runa!" He wiggled in the flowers, inhaling the sweet nectar and pollen of the magical blossoms, his little feet kicking in the air.

Azmadu and MacTabbish flopped into the flowers with blissful expressions.

"I think Mellypip is right," MacTabbish purred before curling up to nap. "Very pleasant. Warms my tired bones."

"Don't you dare fall asleep, MacTabbish," Taran warned.

Azmadu smelled the flowers and munched on some petals. "Tastes like sunshine too, but sweet."

"Come out of there now," Panthara insisted and took the crill lizard into her arms. He wiggled and protested, but she was firm. "It may not be a good idea to eat something so…unknown."

"I agree. Someone pull MacTabbish and Melly out of the weird flower patch," Opaline said, "they may be damaging whatever brought us here."

Taran shook his head and crouched down in front of his familiar. "Panthara and Opaline are right, MacTabbish. Come out of there. This is not normal you know."

"For you," the marmalade cat replied, snuggling deeper in the blossoms.

"That's it!" Taran dragged MacTabbish out of the widening flower circle and hefted him with both hands, stepping back. "Blast it all, MacTabbish! You're getting too chunky."

"You're just now noticing?" Opaline laughed. "You know he begs for treats from everyone when he's not sleeping. He's as bad as Dabiro, just more gracious about it."

"They find me charming," MacTabbish added. "And I'm not chunky. I have the robust build of a powerful lion beneath this fluffy fur."

"*Come in and join me, Runa!* Mellypip coaxed her from the flowers. *Be serious, this is an important key to what can help us.*

Snuggling into the bed of blossoms, something tiny but hard poked against Mellypip's back. *Runa, I think I found something.* He rolled over and began kicking up the flowers to find it. Runa joined Mellypip and searched with her hands, guided by the feel of magic drawing her in.

"Runa, what are you doing?" Panthara demanded.

"Stop them! They're ripping up the magic blossoms," Azmadu wailed.

"Should they be doing that?" Grimm remarked.

"Melly found something," Runa shouted. "It may be important."

Mellypip glimpsed a sparkle deep among the thick green leaves and flowers blooming. He spread the plants apart to reveal a tiny ball of light, the size of a small pearl but bright as a star. Mesmerized, he gazed on its pure light. "Runa? Do you see this?"

Runa gently cupped the tiny ball of light in the palm of her hand and took Mellypip in her other arm. The others gathered around her in wordless admiration as light's incandescence captivated them.

"What the hell is going on here?" Cathal shouted in his owl form, flying down to earth and shapeshifting back into himself.

Belwyn settled on Cathal's shoulder, peering the small pearl of light in Runa's palm. "It radiates the essence of mystical. Put it down."

"This is dangerous. You shouldn't have touched it, Runa," Cathal chastised her. "I don't want you hurt."

"It hardly looks like a weapon," Dabiro grunted, though he edged in closer to be near it.

"It's a jewel," Yllia gasped.

"A perfect jewel from the heavens," Panthara said. "We must keep it safe."

Darcus stepped closer to Runa, Raven in his arms. The little girl smiled at the tiny light and reached out to touch it.

"No, Raven," Darcus cautioned, pulling her hand back. "We must take care."

"But it's so pretty," Raven said, basking in its glow.

"She speaks!" Runa cried. "Raven hasn't spoken since her father died."

Darcus kissed Raven on the cheek and held her close, a tear escaping his scarred eye.

"The power of this jewel is pure," Jadon added. "And its mystery is yet to unfold."

Runa looked at Jadon, wishing she could help Jadon be as he was before the demon cursed his face. A beam of light extended from Runa's palm and shadowed Jadon with a brief glow. He cried out once, but when it faded his demonic visage was gone. He was Jadon again, the youthful Ilyrran with blue eyes. They embraced, squishing Mellypip between them.

"Dear gods," Opaline mumbled. "He's cured."

"We don't have time for romantic trivialities," Belwyn snapped.

"I'd hardly call having this demonic curse on my face cured trivial," Jadon remarked dryly. He touched his face in amazement and smiled. "I'm really me again?"

"Yes!" Runa grinned. "Who knows what this jewel can do?"

"Runa, give me the jewel," Cathal said.

"Sorry, Grandpa," she said, extending her hand.

A blinding red light burst above the trees, its force stunning everyone in the bright circle of hope, throwing everyone across the frozen forest loam. Tossed by the unexpected force, Runa landed in a tangle of black vines, the light jewel slipping from her fingers as she rolled. A horde of goblins, trolls, and other strange monsters emerged from a portal of shadow lead by Koll riding a hideous black beast with leathery wings and a long beak.

Mute with terror, she realized Mellypip was gone. *Melly?, where are you Melly? Oh dear, the jewel! I lost it!* Runa called through the bonding, scrambling to the ground desperately. *Where is it? Oh no! No, no, no!* Runa glimpsed Mellypip lying on the ground near an old oak, several yards away. His head was bleeding!

All around her mages and familiars combatted Koll's creatures as they poured into the meadow. The howls of goblins and trolls pierced her ears as she crawled along the ground. In the madness she realized her staff was gone too. Runa summoned a shield around her and cast one over Mellypip in the distance. Everything mushroomed into chaos and blood. Sorcery charred the icy air. In the lunacy of it all, the little grove of flowers was untouched.

Melly? Melly, wake up! Wake up! Oh, please don't be hurt, Runa cried into his mind, but he lay unresponsive and immobile on the ground. Terrified for him, she jumped up to run as Koll's winged-demon landed hard behind her, talons raking up soil and plants with the impact, knocking Runa off her feet. She fell on her face to the frozen ground hard, the black vines in her mouth tasted acidic. She spat and crawled away, desperate to reach Mellypip, glancing back once at the winged creature. Its eyes glowed red when its gaze locked on her and blocked her path by extending its serpentine neck and shrieked, its foul breath reeking of brimstone. The beast had a crow-like head with a long narrow beak. Choking on its putrid fumes, she stood and summoned her magic and shot blue-white sorcery at the monster's head. The monster wailed and spread its black leathery wings, rearing up in pain. Koll extended his staff and fired red sorcerous ropes which enveloped her, wrapping her body with burning sorcery, shattering her shields. Screaming in agony Koll yanked her to the ground. Thrashing against Koll's sorcerous bonds, her panic swelled as Koll dismounted the creature and strode toward her, black cloak rising on the cold wind and staff fiery with sorcery.

"Hand over the light jewel," Koll demanded, pressing his staff against her neck.

CHAPTER 30

Trapped beneath Koll, Runa looked into his cold eyes, her terror rising. "I don't have it!"

"Liar!" Koll raged. "Obsydia guided me here by her own hand."

"I don't know! Your dramatic entrance knocked it out of my hand," Runa wept. "Find it yourself, if you dare touch it!"

The sorcerous ropes binding her body contracted and flamed, cutting into her skin. Weeping, she closed her eyes, summoning magic as she cried out. Her body burst with light, dissolving Koll's bindings into smoking ashes.

Koll's rage erupted, and his black velvet hand burned red. Rolling on the frozen ground to evade him, she saw a tiny patch of black vines retreating from a glow a few feet away. She lunged for its vivid center, grabbing the jewel. The jewel's warmth in her hand soothed her pain. Koll jerked her to her feet with one hand by her long braid. Her free hand sprayed magic which merely evaporated on Koll's body. Koll seized her closed hand to pry it from her, but Runa refused to let it go of the precious stone, casting a spell to keep her hand closed from his prying fingers. Furious he could not seize his prize he snapped her arm. Screaming she dropped the jewel. Holding her with his human hand, Koll summoned the bright gem to his velvet hand.

"Choke on it," Runa cried, reeling from the pain.

~ * ~

Dazed from the red glare, Grimm found himself in the middle of the chaos. The mages were fighting off dozens of goblins and trolls. Panic overcame him when he did not see Opaline. He fought off goblins and demons, his mind calling out. *Opaline! Where are you!*

I'm over here, Opaline shouted through the bonding, running toward him, her body glowing with a soft lavender shield. Sorcery sizzling at her fingertips, she pushed the demons away from Grimm and sent them flying through the bedlam on waves of lavender-colored magic.

Be careful, Grimm called back. *Your magical combat skills are not honed.*

I'm protected and so are you, Opaline cried, running to his side.

Grimm realized he glowed with a pale lavender shield too. In the chaos, he spotted Mellypip lying several yards away. Worried for his little friend, he raced to his side. A vicious troll loomed toward the helpless wampu, but Opaline's lavender fire bolt struck its face, blinding it. Wailing in pain and confusion, the troll fled. Opaline and Grimm rushed to Mellypip's side.

Opaline felt his body and examined his head. She ripped off a strip of petticoat and bound his wound. *We need to get poor Melly to safety. He's still alive, but his breathing is shallow.*

~ * ~

Triumphant, Koll held the jewel in the palm of his artificial hand. Fiery pain shot through his arm as the gem flared with white flames. His face contorting with agony as a flash the pure light incinerated his velvet and ebonite arm. Howling out his agony, clutching his shoulder as the jewel fell from his captive hand.

The jewel dropped to Runa's feet. She dove to the ground and snatched up the jewel with her good hand, pushing away from Koll. The winged demon leered at her and goblins began to circle around her. Koll turned towards her, his sorcery flaring wildly, wailing in pain and stumbling from the searing pain of light. Bolts of green magic struck Koll, knocking him to the ground.

Shaking with pain and raw burns, Runa turned over to see her mother rushing toward Koll, her voice raging as sorcery poured from her hands like lightning. Running at her side, Pointessa shot her quills at the creature.

"Get away from my daughter!" Rualla screamed, throwing green bolts of sorcery at him in a torrent of grief and fury. "You hurt my baby! Fiend! I'll kill you, Koll!" Rualla's sorcery pummeled Koll as he vibrated from the magical assault. Caliste joined Rualla's side, combining their sorcery to push Koll down. Sanura leapt into the air shapeshifting into her panther form to attack Koll.

"You...cannot...touch me," Koll taunted as he raised a new shield, dropping to his knees. Sanura and Pointessa clawed at his shield relentlessly.

Brilliant colored lights exploded as the Winged Fey emerged on the field. Koll's winged demon shrieked when Dareem slew the creature with a single blow of magic, vanquishing it to dust. The Fey circled Runa holding spears of golden light. Koll's pain shifted to fear. Damaged from the jewel's assault and surrounded by enemies, Koll turned to face his enemies. A flare of dark magic bloomed in his one good hand, and he fell into the darkness and vanished. All around the demons quickly retreated or perished at the hands of the Fey and the mages.

"Mother!" Runa gasped for breath, struggling to stand, holding the jewel close.

The Fey parted for Rualla. "You're hurt! Your arm is broken," she cried, carefully touching her cheek. "I want to hold you, but I think I might break you."

Her arm throbbed but her first concern was for her familiar. "Where's Melly? I lost him in the battle."

Opaline rushed to her side. "He's with Grimm. He's hurt. We needed to get him away from all this. Dear gods, your arm is broken, you're covered with burns. That monster!"

Dareem stood before Runa, folding in his wings, his expression sad and strangely sympathetic. "I'm sorry," Dareem said.

Runa suspected it was not because of her broken arm.

~ * ~

Koll collapsed through the mirror of shadows. Crawling across the floor, he moaned as Xabral glided to his side, leaving the babbling Levandius to drool in the corner.

"Koll! What happened to you?" Koll's ashen face frightened Xabral and huddled next to Koll's shaking body. "What did they to do you? Your beautiful arm is gone."

"Light destroyed me. The Fey were there. They were all there as Obsydia said. We were deceived. They did not die. I rode the winged beast with an army of demons to destroy them, but I was destroyed." He moaned in pain as he rose, struggling to stand.

"I'm afraid, Koll. You have never given in to pain. You endure hunger, thirst, and torture with stoic strength. You never cried out before. This injury of light to your body must be beyond comprehension. Did Cathal do this to you? Or Gabriel? What is this weapon? Is it a spear or blade? What threatens our happiness?"

"A jewel," Koll choked, face twisting in agony. "A fragment of light the size of a pebble. Obsydia told me where to go, and I obeyed. Ahridum himself guided her hand. She entrusted me, and I failed her."

"It's not your fault," Xabral told him. "We are soldiers in a war of great powers beyond even our own magic."

"I was fueled by faith. I went to defeat the enemy for her, to take my prize and lay it at her feet. My greatest enemy was a mere girl who defied and defeated me."

"It was Runa, wasn't it? Cathal's seed will be the death of us yet."

"Runa defied me, holding the terrible light in her hand as though it were nothing. She glowed with its power. I took it from her, snapping her arm. I reveled in her pain. But the light's power took swift vengeance as it burned away my mystical arm. This...pain is beyond anything I ever suffered, beyond even what Cathal did to me when his sorcery annihilated my flesh. It is Runa, not Cathal or the others, who is the core of all my misery. Her innocent hands have destroyed my plans too often. She is the reason I lost my arm. I should have slit her throat when I had the chance. It would have made this loss bearable. I have suffered enough of her purity. It still burns me. It still torments every fiber of my being."

"Runa! The girl's purity galls me. This threat, this light is the only thing Obsydia fears," Xabral whispered.

"If the light eternals interfere, we could lose our dreams. If I confess to Obsydia, we will lose our lives and our dreams of a paradise where Darkness rules."

"What do we do, Koll? I feel lost for the first time."

Koll staggered to his feet, clutching his shoulder as he faced the mirror. He pulled open his robe to see the infection of light pulsating through his body. Veins throbbed beneath his skin, glowing with silver light. "I must purge this foul essence from my body before I go to Obsydia."

~ * ~

Mellypip slowly opened his eyes surrounded by familiar but worried faces: Runa, Raghnall, Opaline, Grimm, Baldur, MacTabbish, Sephya, and Belwyn. They looked down at him with mute concern. His head ached terribly and he realized was not in the forest anymore but on a thick pillow.

Runa? What's happened?

I'm here, Melly. We are back at the palace, Runa soothed in his mind, stroking his back. He looked up, vision blurred and blinked until his vision came into focus.

Belwyn watched him from the back of the chair, looking down at him. "Furball, you had us all worried. How's your head?"

"Are you better now, Melly?" Sephya asked with wide eyes.

"I'm better, just confused." Mellypip sat up and tenderly touched the bandage on his head. "How long was I out?

"A couple hours. You suffered a nasty blow to the head when you hit a tree," Belwyn said.

"Did we get the light?" Mellypip asked.

"Yes," Runa said. "Koll tried to take it from me, but the fey stopped him."

"Grimm got you to safety," Belwyn said. "Too many nasty goblins and trolls about to leave you there."

"Thank you," Mellypip said. He noticed Runa's bruised and swollen arm. "Your arm's hurt! What happened?"

"I wish I could say I wrestled a troll into submission but in truth, Koll broke it."

"Koll has a lot to pay for," Belwyn added bitterly. "Cathal and I were surrounded by so many demons we could not see a thing until it was too late. The fey actually showed up and laid waste to the demons on the field. Sadly, Koll escaped."

Raghnall bent down and checked his eyes with a funny light crystal. "Now my little friend, do you see double of anything? Have nausea?"

"I think I'm seeing triple," Mellypip replied. "My tummy is sick."

"Normal for your injury. Nothing permanent. Just rest for a while. I whipped up a potion to help the swelling and pain. Make sure you eat something mild like porridge or bread with it."

"How about pancakes?" Mellypip asked.

"Looks like Furball is on the path to make a full recovery," Belwyn remarked dryly.

"What happened to the light jewel?" Mellypip asked, stroking Sephya's head who huddled close. "Maybe it can make Runa's arm better."

"The Fey have it now, despite Koll's not so best efforts. Right now everyone is enclosed in a war council making plans," Belwyn said.

"Now let's look at your arm, young lady," Raghnall said. "We've waited long enough. We need to set it and it's going to hurt, dear. I may have to reset the bone too."

"Is all this necessary? I think my arm has been twisted enough," Runa begged, chewing her lip. "Can't you magically mend it?"

"Magical healing works to a point, but it only goes so far," Raghnall replied patiently. "I'll make a sleeping draught to ease your pain when I reset the bone. You can hold on to Baldur as I do the rest."

Reset the bone? Mellypip shivered. *It sounds horrible!*

I'm not jumping for joy about this either, Runa sent back through the bonding.

The Winged Fey entered. Mellypip noted people and animals always fell silent when they appeared.

Asheni went to Runa. "You will come with us now to the meeting."

"But her arm is broken and needs to be set," Raghnall protested.

"She has no choice," Dareem said.

Tira, a shy fey with golden and white wings went to her and touched her arm, flooding Runa's body with cool soothing light. After a moment, Runa felt her arm completely healed.

"It's amazing,' Runa said.

"I'm pea green with envy, Tira," Raghnall exclaimed. "You wouldn't want to give me your mystical recipe for this would you?"

"Can you heal Mellypip head?" Sephya asked.

Mellypip was not sure why, maybe because Sephya was a dragon and they were revered, but Tira touched his head. After a few seconds, he felt all better.

"How do you feel, Furball?' Belwyn asked.

"Better, but I still want pancakes," Mellypip replied.

CHAPTER 31

The guards opened the doors to the council chambers and bowed their heads in fear when the Winged Fey passed them. Runa hurried behind the Winged Fey to keep up since she was much shorter, unable to match their long strides. *They're scared of them,* Mellypip told Runa, observing their terrified expressions.

We all are scared now, Runa replied through their bond. *But I find Dareem and the other fey more intimidating than scary. What frightens me is Obsydia.*

And Koll, Mellypip added. *He's a malevolent bastard and should be sucked into a pit of hellfire with demons poking him with pitchforks. Belwyn told me that.*

I recognize his colorful vernacular, but you shouldn't swear, Melly.

You do all the time, even when you don't say it out loud, I can hear you quite plainly when I go into your thoughts.

The room fell silent when Runa entered the council chamber. She glimpsed Cathal's tense face across the large room when Belwyn flew towards his waiting arm. King Caladynn sat at the head of the long wooden table, looking exhausted. He gestured for her to come closer. The tension in the room was so thick she felt suffocated by it. She barely stepped across the threshold before her mother threw her arms around her.

"I'm so relieved you're alright," Rualla cried, holding her close for a moment. "They told me they healed your arm and little Melly's injuries too."

"I'm all better, Mother," Runa assured her, enjoying the freely given hug. "And grateful I do not have to wear a cast for weeks. Why was everyone yelling?"

Yllia embraced Runa and kissed her on the head. "Oh my dear, you were brave but far too foolish out there. You must take better care of yourself when facing down an evil shit like Koll."

Runa gasped and blushed beet red.

See, Granna Yllia swears too! Mellypip piped in her head.

Pointessa chuckled to Rualla, her quills shaking. "Children are always amazed when the adults curse. Like only the young can be naughty."

"Liat and Dabiro found your staff," Rualla told her, handing it to her. "We brought it here for you." She brushed her cheek. "Are you sure you're alright?"

"I'm fine," Runa lied. *Actually Melly, Dareem's words still haunts me. Why would he be sorry? It bothers me.*

I don't know, but it bugs me too.

"Welcome Runa," Caladynn called out, gesturing her to come closer. "We're happy you escaped Koll's clutches and are safe. This new find gives us hope. You found this light jewel in the forest."

Iona told us you, along with Panthara and Opaline, were drawn there in a trance when it fell from the sky. Can you tell us anything else to help us? Have you had any dreams? Cathal tells me you're a dream seer and sometimes have prophetic dreams."

"No dreams about the jewel." *Technically I am telling the truth. I just wish I knew what I was keeping from everyone.*

Mellypip's voice piped into her head. *Your father came to us in a dream remember? When Koll blew up the house, and the Winged Fey saved us.*

We cannot speak it, Melly.

Why?

I don't know, Melly. I don't even remember what he whispered to me.

I think we're enchanted, Mellypip hinted.

"Did you have any impressions when you touched the jewel?" Neelam asked.

"I wish I could help," Runa replied. "I don't remember anything. I'm sorry. I sensed only its magic and the light was beautiful."

"It even smelled pretty," Mellypip chirped eagerly. "Like sunshine and flowers." He frowned and his ear drooped. *That's wasn't helpful, was it?*

Of course it was, Melly. Belwyn always told us everything is important, even the most insignificant details. It's important.

I just wish I knew why, Mellypip replied.

Cathal's grey eyes were penetrating when he looked at her, but he did not press too deeply. "It's all right, Runa. Panthara and Opaline don't remember either."

Runa glanced at Opaline and Panthara, noting their neutral faces. "I'm sorry, Your Majesty. There is nothing I can tell you. Maybe our only purpose was to find the light jewel."

"It's no matter. Surely we will figure out a plan with all of us working together," Caladynn declared. "Damn, but I need some ale. Send for some!" he motioned to one of the guards lining the room. "I can't be expected to fight gods and demons without alcohol."

"We would be doomed if we did," Neelam agreed heartily.

"Stay sober," Surya cautioned. "I won't have you weaving with intoxication on the battlefield like a dunderhead."

"It has been suggested some of you should not go into this battle," Caladynn announced. "That includes you, Runa. Cathal agrees and I agree some of you should stay behind."

"But I want to go," Runa insisted fervently. "We all must go. I'm fifteen not five."

Prince Ulric nodded sympathetically. "We understand everyone wants to fight. I am opposed to Opaline going."

"As am I," Gabriel added.

The fact these two very different men who challenged Opaline's affections were in agreement stunned her, but she remained resolute. "Try and stop me and I'll turn you both into slobbering trolls," Opaline replied dryly.

"She has the magical skill to do it too…on purpose," Grimm warned.

"If we do not win before the thirteenth day, there won't be a world," Opaline reasoned. "We will simply be exterminated by the hand of Ahridum. I would rather die fighting than twiddling my thumbs waiting."

"I have faced tough battles before, Grandpa," Runa challenged.

"Of course Runa will go. I must go as well," Panthara added, lifting her chin. "I long to strike a final blow against Koll."

"I'm going too," Taran said to Panthara. "If only to keep you safe."

Panthara's smile was gentle, but her tone resolute. "Taran, I love you, but none of us are safe now. We are dealing with an arrogant dark god's usurping our whole existence. I will not accept this fate. I will fight it. I do not need protection, but I do need your support."

"Surely this mystical jewel has the power to destroy Obsydia," Sirah said.

"How do we get close enough?" Cathal asked.

"I agree its power is immense and deadly to those touched by darkness," Asheni said. "We will be the ones to confront Obsydia and her demons with the light jewel."

Neelam laughed, his voice tinged with sarcasm. "You mean, unlike last time when we faced hell-bitch alone with a crystal, an incantation, and some vague hope? We could have used your help in the fight then, Fey. What's changed?"

Surya pecked him on the shoulder. "My Wizard is feeling querulous Forgive him."

"Realty," Dareem answered. "Isolation has not helped this world. We may be immortal, but we have mortal faults." He glanced at Asheni and smiled, ever so faintly. "It has been pointed out we must have faith in others."

A Winged Fey named Adair, an imposing figure with orange and black wings and glossy black hair, stood up. "We saw it burn away Koll's mystical arm. The Hooded-Ones, Obsydia's personal guardians from the Netherworld, created it for him at her request. The jewel disintegrated it in a flash. It is clearly what we all have prayed for, but there something is missing. A key which I cannot see."

Dareem shook his head and cast an image in the center of the table, shimmering and detailed in design. "One of our fey, Grania, channeled images of Obsydia's Shadow Tower and its surroundings. It will give us a base from how we will assault her defenses."

Mellypip noticed how Grania seemed to be the shyest. Her amber and blue wings were demurely folded in, and her amber hair fell over her eyes as she stood behind the others. Dareem was the most broody of course. Asheni, he liked. Bran was the most imposing with black and red wings. Tinashe's green and black wings were bold, but Star's silver wings with black tips were beautiful. He observed how their intricately patterned wings were each stamped with different designs. He wondered if the Winged Fey would retreat into hiding if they won the war against Obsydia. He was eager to write their descriptions into his little bard book, but he remembered it burned up with the sorcerer house and the loss saddened him.

Melly, are you listening? Runa poked into his mind.

Mellypip dispelled his musings as Dareem continued to explain Obsydia's tower. "It recently arose and the stones are summoned from living shadow. It is similar to Ahridum's black tower in the Isini Sea and like the place of her birth was created by Ahridum, an immortal haven of shadow intruding on a mortal world. It stands in the middle of an overgrown cursed wood rampant with demon creatures of all kinds. Obsydia defeated the ancestors of the Ilyrrans there a thousand years ago, and her diabolism made the country a place of darkness and demons. Like the ancient Wasteland, we believe now it was a testing ground for the future war against light on this world. Goblins, demon men, and trolls guard the area. We need warriors to fight them and keep Obsydia and Koll occupied while we assault them directly in the tower."

Mellypip gulped, clinging to Runa. *The Shadow Tower looks scary. I thought it was just a name, but it looks like it's made of shadow.*

Dareem spread his hand, widening the image of the surrounding countryside. Dead trees rose like crumbling stones and bore the fruit of blood red thorns. Strange creatures roamed the land, prowling in darkness with red eyes. Mellypip knew he would have more nightmares tonight. "This is a now demon realm. Monsters have hidden there, growing in darkness for centuries, awaiting Obsydia's summons. These are the demons Koll brought to the fight in the forest spawned there for centuries. They are stronger than most earthly-based demons. We will need all the magic you can summon to battle them. I am sure what is in the tower and what circles it will be deadly."

"My son's developed something to help us," Sirah announced proudly.

Taran stood and passed out small squares of shiny metal. "I've created a new metal. Even though our home was destroyed, this metal was not damaged. Fortunately, I forged several small pieces in my laboratory before it all went up in flames. I had these samples locked in a box and sealed with magical layers of protection. I invented it recently, but I shared it with Neelam and Cathal and they are impressed with its potential to increase our magic. It's a blend of silver and sarod metal. Before you all balk, this increases magic instead of blocking it like sorcerer bane. I will infuse all of our new staves with this metal to increase the spell power we store in them. I even made Panthara's betrothal ring from it."

"Which I wear proudly," Panthara beamed at him.

"Your son is a genius, Lady Sirah," Neelam complimented her.

"Thank you," Sirah nodded. "I just wish his genius was less destructive at times. I think it even makes up for the times he blew up his lab."

"And disturbed my rest," MacTabbish said.

Caliste's own expression was inquisitive. "Do you truly know what to do with the jewel?"

"I sense a fragment of doubt. Haven't the eternals sent you an instruction guide through your visions?" Sanura asked, swishing her tail.

Dareem confessed. "We had no visions. We must take that on faith." He looked directly at Runa with sympathy. "Fate has chosen. Time is running out. The thirteenth day is close, so we must get to work."

Neelam poured a glass of water and leaned back in his chair. "If it gives anyone hope, we've even had good news today. Riva contacted us an hour ago. Myrsalian was manning the new calling crystal Caladynn installed here at the palace."

"For which I am grateful," Myrsalian added happily. "This one actually works."

"It has not sparked once…or exploded," Felisia said.

"The Ivory Kingdoms have been liberated," Neelam proclaimed to the stunned audience. He nodded to Darcus. "Your sister Eshra sends greetings and many prayers by the way. Lord Rhudon has won. He is now the uncrowned Emperor of a mess, but he is on the right side. Apparently, the dragons even showed up to help."

"What about Levandius?" Opaline asked urgently. "Was he killed or did he have the grace to commit suicide?"

Neelam shook his head, pouring a glass of water. "Sadly the worm eluded the justice of man. Koll was there with Levandius when Rhudon stormed the palace. They attacked, but his sorcery shielded him. Levandius just cowered being the weakling he is, after Koll escaped through a mirror Levandius followed behind him. Rhudon smashed the mirror."

"And what of my traitorous sister?" Queen Sarabia inquired. "Was she with him?"

Neelam inclined his head. "Hadrial is dead. Levandius killed her and fled Thema. I am sorry."

"Do not be sorry," Sarabia replied stoically. "My love was not enough to save her from darkness. Her hatred of me was stronger. Hadrial must pay for her sins on the Otherside."

Cathal's eyes brightened. "If the dragons showed up in Tiamet it means they are on their way to the Shadow Tower. They can help with the battle outside the tower."

"We will have the strength of the dragon clans to help us when we fight," Yllia said.

A guard rushed in and bowed. "Forgive me, Your Majesty, but Princess, I mean, Sister Danu and Abbess Odelia are here asking for you."

Caladynn's broad smile lit his face, and he jumped up to greet them with amazing agility for a man of his thick girth. Sister Danu and Abbess Odelia entered the chamber. The Abbess hesitated at first, seeing everyone, including the Winged Fey, gathered together.

Danu gently took her arm and guided her forward. "It's all right, Abbess." Her accusing stare focused on Dareem. "You may be immortal and possess ancient magic, but it does not give you leave to be rude, especially to those who are defenseless against your harsh words."

Dareem bowed his head. His voice was kind as he addressed the shy Odelia directly. "Forgive me, Abbess Odelia, for I spoke harshly when we met before. Danu is right. I was unforgivably rude. I ask your pardon."

Abbess Odelia blushed and bowed her head. "Thank you. Of course, you are forgiven."

Caladynn picked up his daughter and hugged her tightly. "My dear, it lifts my heart to see you in this troubled time. Why are you in Aybarr?"

"We've come to offer hope," Danu replied. "We know there is a terrible evil rising. It is literally taking over the world. Father, I know you and the others are going to face this force of darkness to save us. We come to help. Some of our sisters stayed behind at the Abbey to look after the orphans and refugees, but the rest have come to bring light and hope to the people. They are terrified. The people need guidance and strength. My Father and King, I know your shoulders are already burdened. We will sing and pray for you, for the world, while you fight for our deliverance from Obsydia."

Odelia lifted her head, her voice soft but her emotions fervent. "We are singing in the streets and beckoning the people from the temple steps. We may only be able to fight with faith and prayer. We will give comfort to whoever asks. We offer what we can while you go forth to fight. I refuse to believe the Light Eternals have abandoned us to fall into Ahridum's hands."

"I thank you," Caladynn said with genuine gratitude. "Your prayers and song are most welcome."

"Good," Danu smiled, "I will see Mother and little Turas before I go, but I know I will see you again…in this world."

After they departed the chamber, Asheni calmly turned to the others. "We have prepared a summoning to the Gate of Souls once we are within the tower. It is a powerful new version of the ritual which will be fast to invoke with our help. When the Wraith Guardians are summoned, they will take everyone in the tower only, not outside, so do not fear. Our hope is they will take Koll and even Obsydia if the jewel is not successful."

"How will we protect ourselves when they come?" Opaline asked. "The last time the Gate of Souls was beached by magic, we all almost died but for Runa's quick thinking. And her light! Its magic is a mix of sorcery and Drusai. It held them back."

"And once again, I apologize," Panthara remarked.

"It's not an indictment against your wicked origins," Opaline said. "It's just a fact, and we need to know how to handle this before we open up a bottle of worms."

"We will all be protected by our shields when it happens," Asheni said. "Within its protection, the wraiths will not be able to touch you."

When everyone began to gather over the battle plans, Asheni went to Runa and whispered in her ear. "We have seen visions, Runa. During the final battle, I have seen the Wraith Guardians take you through the Gate of Souls. I am sorry."

Asheni walked away. Runa found a chair near the wall and sat in it quietly, Mellypip in her lap. Panthara, Azmadu, Opaline, and Grimm joined her. Their familiars sharing the silence they as they looked at one another.

CHAPTER 32

Runa bundled up a few flowers with strips of green satin and tied the bow. "Are you sure Queen Sorcha doesn't mind that we pilfered these from the palace hallway? Maybe we should have asked her."

Mellypip tried to occupy Sephya's attention from the dangling ribbon. Attracted by the shiny ribbon, she breathed little spurts of smoke trying to reach it. *Stop acting so casual, Runa. Asheni's words scared me. We must tell someone.*

It wouldn't help to say anything. And Grandpa would just get angry with them. Remember when he punched Dareem after we were rescued from Koll and Obsydia.

But what about the Wraiths, Runa? She said they would take us.

Runa flinched and fluffed the bow out of Sephya's reach.

See, it bothers you! It bothers me. We're going to be taken by the Wraith Guardians somehow when they open the Gate of Souls again. Asheni is Fey. They prophesize. It's what they do.

Belwyn once told me prophecies are fragile promises. And she did not specify they would take you, Melly. You may be safe.

I don't want to be safe, I want to be with you. And the Wraiths are anything but fragile. I still have nightmares about them.

Opaline slipped into a fresh gown. "What are you two talking about?"

"Nothing," Runa replied quickly.

Opaline turned to Runa, hands on her hips. "I know better, but I also know the bonding is a sacred trust, but come on. You're both bothered by something."

See, Opaline knows, Melly communicated smugly.

Grimm sat next to Mellypip. "This is no time for secrets, Melly. Secrets can keep one safe, but also leads to doom and despair."

Mellypip looked up at the wolf. "You are really gloomy today, Grimm."

"I think we're all carrying something inside us we cannot speak of," Runa said, looking down at the ribbon.

"I know. It disturbs me too," Opaline replied uneasily. "I feel something inside me burning to get out. I also know Asheni said something to you. The Winged Fey don't whisper in one's ear unless there's something important to be said. I doubt it was about sunshine and fluffy bunnies."

"The world is mutating into a demon realm and killing us all is bothersome," Mellypip replied. "And Runa is acting stubborn."

"My words, you're becoming quite the fuzzy little Belwyn," Opaline laughed. "Of course Runa's stubborn. We both are, which is why we have so much in common."

Sephya fluttered her wing, rising a few inches off the floor, her meager flight a struggle as she chased the ribbon. The shadow dragons circled her, encouraging the baby dragon to take chances.

"Yes, beat the wings faster," Talon encouraged.

"You will grow stronger," Fallon promised as Sephya struggled to rise higher.

"I think we need more flowers," Opaline observed, looking at the skimpy bouquet.

"I don't want to," Runa protested.

"Send Dabiro then," Opaline shrugged. "He loves to steal things. Make him useful. He stole many jars of jam from mother's pantry without so much as an apology. I doubt anyone will fuss about some flowers when the end of the world is imminent." She studied her reflection in the mirror, tugging at the bodice. "The queen was so kind to loan us some dresses. All of our clothes are nothing but ashes now. This is lovely, but it's a little tight around the bosom."

"At least you have a bosom," Runa remarked dryly. "I'm still waiting for mine. Maybe you could magically alter it to fit?"

"I'm honing my magic for the staff I am about to create." She smiled and hugged Grimm. "And it will have your noble face on it."

"It is a custom I will honor," Grimm vowed, embarrassed but happy with the attention.

Opaline brushed back her hair and braided it in a single thick plait. "The royal greenhouse has lots of flowers, but outside nothing wholesome is growing out of the earth, so we had to do something. We're too short on time to fuss with trivialities. Hurry up. The Abbess is waiting in the chapel."

"Goodness, but you're bossy today," Runa remarked, glancing her reflection in the mirror, she gasped and grabbed a brush. "My hair's a mess. Why didn't you say something?"

Opaline snatched the brush out of her hand. "Too late now. Your hair is fine. Let's go."

"Are you coming, Melly?" Runa asked.

"Can Sephya come too?" Mellypip asked. "And Talon and Fallon of course."

"Just don't' set anything on fire," Runa warned. "And behave."

"We always behave with dignity," Fallon told her.

"We will observe the rituals of somber behavior," Talon promised.

Sephya dropped to the carpet and burped little tufts of smoke out from her nostrils as she chewed some ribbon. Mellypip tugged the leftover ribbon away from Sephya.

"Hurry!" Opaline shouted.

"By goodness, but she is bossy," Mellypip muttered.

They rushed to the royal chapel, a small private sanctuary for the Thill royal family. Inside, Abbess Odelia stood on the altar with a prayer book in hand.

"Do they even know?" Runa whispered as they went to greet her.

Everyone began to gather. All the mages of course, Hinkleburr and his aids, and the royal family. Mellypip wondered about Prince Ulric since he and Opaline broke their betrothal. But there was no anger on Ulric's face when he saw him look at Opaline. Just love and a little sadness. Gabriel was oddly sober and clear of eye. When Panthara and Taran entered, they were stunned by the gathering. Opaline swiftly led them before Abbess Odelia.

"I thought this was a mass before battle. What's going on?" Taran asked, shifting MacTabbish in his arms.

"A wedding," Opaline replied smoothly. She took the bouquet from Runa and gave it to Taran. "You two want to marry. Well, best do it now. If we win, we can consider it a good luck ceremony. If we all perish, you'll know you kept your promise to each other. Now put MacTabbish down. He can wake up long enough for the wedding rite. Now give her the flowers as a token of your troth and bow as is the Thill wedding tradition."

Taran set MacTabbish on the floor. The marmalade cat yawned but sat regally by his sorcerer. "You did all this?"

"Yes," Opaline replied. "Abbess Odelia has agreed to officiate the marriage ceremony. I excel at planning events. Princess training can be useful."

Panthara burst into tears when Sirah called her daughter. A lot of emotions filled the chapel. Runa glanced at her grandparents holding hands. Liat and Rualla stood close, her head against his shoulder. Even Neelam's wistful expression was unexpected. She looked across the chapel to Jadon, his face restored and smiling at her. She did not look away, frozen by her shyness as before. She looked at Jadon, twisting the beautiful wooden ring around her finger. He made it for her with love and nearly lost that love because of darkness, but he had been restored by light's grace.

"Hurry boy," Neelam urged. "We have a world to save."

Taran turned to Panthara and gave her the flowers. She accepted them with grace and smiled at Opaline. "Thank you."

Abbess Odelia began the marriage ceremony as Panthara and Taran held hands and faced each other. Opaline, Sirah, and Myrsalian stood behind Taran with their familiars as Taran's closest family. Azmadu grunted happily at Panthara's feet. Iona stood with Panthara as her adoptive mother. She wiped a tear from her eye, Amun regal on her shoulder.

Runa leaned against Opaline and whispered. "You realize this makes Panthara your sister too."

"Damn it," Opaline whispered back, patting Grimm's head. "But it also makes me your true sister."

"You already were," Runa nudged her.

~ * ~

Koll passed through the Eye of Shadows deep within the Thill dungeon. He may be magically blocked from seeing what is happening because of dragon or fey magic protecting the palace, but he could still walk its halls. Relying on the mirror was an indulgence, especially when potent mystical powers could block its vision. He knew this dungeon all too well. His connection to this place was enhanced by something his enemies did not count on; the ring Faustine wore. She was still alive. He knew it the moment he arrived. The sensed the ring he gave her was still active. As he followed the ring's dark magic to her, he shapeshifted into a guard and followed the hallways down deep.

It was easy to locate Faustine's jail, for she was heavily guarded.

Looking through the slots in the door to her prison, he counted ten guards, with Darcus and the sorceress Jiana among her watchers. Taking them down would be no impediment for Koll, but killing them all right now would be time-consuming and would attract attention. Weakened by the light of the strange jewel he failed to retrieve for Obsydia, his body throbbed with pain. Occupied with her coming divinity gave Koll time to act to save him from her anger.

He vanished, reappearing in Faustine's cell amid a cloud of dark mist. She jumped up in terror when she saw him, but then he shapeshifted back into his own form and put a finger to his lips. She remained silent as spoke.

"I cast a silence spell around us, so no one will hear. Do you wish to see your husband?"

Tears welled in her eyes, her hands flew to her face. "They told me he was dead!"

"They lied," Koll answered smoothly. "You may come with me. Obsydia will grant you sanctuary, but you need to do something for your goddess to earn it."

"But where is Morydonn?"

"Safe in Obsydia's Shadow Tower and waiting for your return. I found him among the rubble. They deceived you, Faustine. He was injured, but Obsydia's grace healed him. He waits for you."

"Thank you," Faustine wept. "What must I do?"

"I will take you out of this prison, but you must obey me. I need you to retrieve the jewel they found in the forest."

"I don't know where it is," Faustine cried. "They will tell me nothing."

"I will make you into an image they trust. It will be an illusion, but just long enough to protect you from harm. This jewel will destroy your hope and dreams."

"Who will I be?" Faustine asked.

"One of the fey," Koll replied.

"They will surely know!" Faustine cried.

"It is only a ruse to get you back into the palace. I know they are here. Find them, and you will find the jewel. Once you find the Winged Fey, you need only be patient long enough for an opportunity to take it. I know what it looks like." Koll reached into his robes and extracted a glowing pearl-like gem. "I conjured a replica to replace with the true gem. You need only switch the jewels and bring me the true one. If you do not find it and replace it, we will lose this war. You will die a traitor's death. They will cut off your head and bury you in an unmarked grave with no prayer or shroud even. You will never become queen. I know the sorcerers are all gathered in the palace. They have nowhere else to go. The Winged Fey are helping the mages bring us to ruin. Do this one deed, and I will personally carry you to Morydonn."

Faustine stared at the gem and snatched it, holding it tight as though it were her salvation. "How will I find you?" she asked, shaking.

"Summon me through the ring and I will hear you." He wrapped his arm around her, and they vanished from the cell.

~ * ~

"What's wrong?" Jadon asked Runa when everyone was busy congratulating Taran and Panthara.

"Nothing," Runa replied, "but something will be wrong if I don't get a piece of cake."

You should tell him, Runa, Mellypip piped in her head.

Hush. There's nothing I can tell anyway.

Our dream? And Asheni's warning we will be sucked into the nasty Gate of Souls.

"You're stalling," Jadon challenged. "I and know when you two are having at it. I know you."

"Then you know I love cake." She squeezed his hand. "Jadon, I can't tell you anything, because I don't know."

Darcus marched into the chapel. His angry expression was not a good sign as he strode toward Cathal and spoke in a low voice so they could not hear.

Mellypip perched on Runa's shoulder, his long tail swishing. "Something is wrong."

Sephya growled, which was neither fierce nor intimidating, but it did snag Runa's attention. Talon and Fallon immediately put themselves between the baby dragon and whatever upset her.

Runa, something is upsetting Sephya.

"Evil eyes watching," Sephya puffed. "Evil!"

"We sense it too," Fallon said suspiciously.

"Something wicked is near," Talon confirmed.

From the corner of her eye, Runa caught a flash of Asheni near the door.

"What is it?" Jadon asked Runa, taking her arm.

"I just saw Asheni in the doorway. Then she vanished."

"The Winged Fey have a habit of doing that," Jadon replied dryly.

"No Asheni just ran off, she didn't disappear," Runa corrected.

"You should specify more when talking about mages and mystical beings," Mellypip suggested.

Runa shook her head. "Look, the point is I know Asheni isn't here in the palace. She's guarding the jewel with the others. They took it yesterday to a hiding place." She tucked Mellypip under her arm and rushed into the hallway. "Tell Grandpa what's going on."

"Don't you dare," Jadon shouted after her.

But she was already out the door.

Runa saw the winged figure running down the hall and into the outside stone corridors. Runa did not sense the mystical aura she knew as fey, but something else darker and malicious. The Winged Fey she pursued glanced back in a panic as she raced out into the courtyard through the archway.

Is she were fey, she'd vanish into a portal or just fly away. She's not fey.

Fey or not, we are going to be in trouble…the kind where they lock you up in the tower without supper.

"Stop Runa!" Cathal's booming voice froze her in her tracks… literally. Unable to move, she watched Asheni's image change before her eyes into Faustine!

"But it's Faustine!" Runa shouted. "She's escaping."

Black mist swirled, revealing a dark-robed man with one arm. Koll. He opened his arm for Faustine, and she ran to his embrace as the black vines coiled around their bodies, streaming high like waves of shadows, cocooning them. Runa saw the gleaming gem in her hand, just like the light jewel! She saw it, but she knew it was not the true gem she found in the forest.

"It's Koll!" Runa screamed, struggling to move. "They're getting away."

"I have your weapon, Cathal," Koll taunted coolly. "Come for it if you dare."

Cathal and the others circled Koll and Faustine as they vanished before their eyes in a cloud of mist.

"Will you let me go now, Grandpa?" Runa begged. Cathal

dispelled Runa and she ran to see. "They escaped!" Runa cried.

"No," Dareem said, appearing with them in the circle. "We suspected they would do this. They have left us a direct trail, however. Both Koll and Obsydia will be placated by the replica so we may act according to our plans."

"Faustine's escaped," Opaline said. "Is that wise?"

"Faustine and Koll think they duped us," Caladynn told her. "We knew Koll would seek out the jewel of light the Eternals gifted us."

"You let her find a fake jewel?" Runa asked. "To sway them for a time. Risky trick."

"But in truth, we tricked them," Cathal said. "We left a replica of the jewel with some magical enhancements added by the fey knowing this might happen. Koll will not risk touching it again, but he needed a patsy to get what he needed. We knew Obsydia would demand it from our possession. Remember, when Koll tried to take the light jewel from you Runa, just touching it incinerated his mystical arm. He will not touch it, and neither will Obsydia."

"You bought time," Jadon nodded.

"It was dangerous to lure Koll here," Runa said.

"Like you chasing after dangerous enemies!" Cathal reprimanded her and then took her in his arms and held her. "Don't do that. I swear one day you'll drive me mad with worry."

"Bad sorceress," Belwyn said and swiveled his head around to Rualla. "See what we've had to put up with for fifteen years?"

"Sorry, Grandpa," Runa apologized, feeling penitent when she saw the pain on his face.

"Faustine made her choice, but it saves us the pain of executing her," Sorcha said. "For I know we will win. She will receive her just fate, Runa."

"Faustine's fate by Obsydia's hand will be far worse than anything you would have done," Belwyn told Sorcha.

CHAPTER 33

Anxious as the hour approached, Rualla kept busy, brushing her hair, changing into a fresh tunic and trousers, and polishing her boots. She tried not to think about what was about to happen, but it haunted her every moment. "They're leaving soon. I feel like I've just reclaimed my life and it could all end if we do not defeat the Darkness." She sat on the bed, looking at her hands.

"You should have made yourself a new staff, dear," Pointessa told her. "You need a new beginning."

"I know," Rualla sighed. "I couldn't bring myself to do it. I'm not going with them. Mother is going, but they wanted me to stay and help with the children. Darcus is worried about little Raven. He did not want her to be alone all if the end does come. So I offered to stay with her. Anyway, a staff is more symbolic than anything else."

Pointessa crawled into Rualla's lap. "And a handy storage device for the more complex sorceries."

When Liat and Dabiro entered the room, Rualla rushed into Liat's arms.

"Hey, what about me?" Dabiro asked.

"Wait your turn," Pointessa warned.

"Be safe," Rualla begged him, the barriers of her heart melting. "Come back to me."

"I promise," Liat swore and kissed her. "And we will start a new life…together if you will have me."

Rualla nodded. After they departed she sat on the bed and stroked the porcupine's back, no longer needing special gloves since she cast a permanent enchantment on her hands to protect them from her quills. *I pray he will be safe and it is not too late for us. Oh, I do love him.*

Oh dear, of course you love him. His crabby badger is the problem.

"I heard your voice in my head," Rualla burst out in disbelief.

"I heard you too," Pointessa said in awe. "I never knew I could bond with another after my poor Eberr died. I never even knew this could happen. It's never happened before."

Rualla burst into happy tears. *Oh Pointessa, we're bonded now.*

Yes, we are truly bonded together, Pointessa replied, nestling in her arms, feeling content and no longer alone.

~ * ~

Cathal and Belwyn entered the chapel to find Dareem and Asheni together. "You two managed to fool Koll. We know these little tricks are only temporal solutions."

"Koll will not dare touch the jewel after what happened to him. I doubt Obsydia will even want to get close to it. It will distract them from interfering with us. It's a simple ruse."

"A dangerous one. You should have told me what you were doing," Cathal told them sharply. "Runa went chasing after Faustine and could have been hurt."

"Your granddaughter is attracted to trouble," Dareem remarked. "It must be a family trait."

They're holding something back, Belwyn told him.

I know!

Don't snap at me, Belwyn replied hotly.

Cathal looked at Asheni. "You whispered something to Runa. What was it?"

"She looked confused and a little frightened," Asheni replied, though she did not look him in the eye. "I told her not to worry. She is just a girl, for all her bravery."

She's lying, Cathal remarked.

"Have you found a way to use the jewel? Or are you just going to toss it at Obsydia and pray a lot?"

"Your owl is facetious," Dareem said tightly.

"Not yet," Asheni answered, putting her hand on Dareem's shoulder. "We are all tense now. No, we do not know, so we have attached it to the tip of a silver spear." She picked up a slim spear of shimmering silver, the light jewel glowing at its tip.

"Is it enough?" Cathal asked, her brow creased with uncertainty.

"Surely the effect it had on Koll's arm was enough proof?" Dareem said. "His arm was clearly fashioned by the Dark Netherworld. Your frantic sorcery which burned Koll's original arm into mist served a purpose."

"And an enchanted arm is not a vicious immortal woman," Belwyn pointed out.

"We will confront Obsydia if you deal with her demon handmaids and the hooded ones," Asheni told him.

"And Koll," Belwyn added. "Whether we win or not, Koll and his slimy snake Xabral need to be put down."

"I recall the last time we were thrown together against Koll and Obsydia. You were willing to let my granddaughter die that day," Cathal reminded Dareem. "Don't make that mistake again. I don't want to hear about the greater good. It's an excuse to let someone die. This is also not a time for secrets. Secrets and sorcery do not always mix well; secrets and immortals never do."

"We only seek to rid this world of a dark immortal," Dareem replied tersely. "Are you ready to go?"

"Yes," Cathal replied. "Where are the other fey?"

"They are about to bring the armies to the arranged rendezvous. Are the rituals prepared?"

"Yes," Cathal replied. "Everyone's in the courtyard waiting."

"I will bring you and the others," Asheni offered. "Dareem will carry Caladynn's army to the meeting place."

"Have you heard from the dragons?" Dareem asked. "They talk to you more than me."

"The Drajina Sandhya sent me a message," Cathal confirmed. "They will meet us there."

Cathal turned to leave, walking at a fast pace and gripping his newly made staff. *I don't trust their words. I know there is something missing, the way I miss my original staff. This one feels different. I don't like it.*

Give it time. Does Runa know what is about to happen? Belwyn asked.

No, and she won't until it's too late. Rualla is taking care of it.

~ * ~

Koll led Faustine to Obsydia's temple at the top of the tower. Dark mystical energy permeated the air, and the chanting of strange tongues frightened her. Faustine followed meekly through the strange shifting corridors of shadow, clutching the light jewel in her hand, head jerking back and forth with each strange whisper or shift of the corridors. The Eternal essence of this tower was unsettling to the uninitiated.

"There is no need for fear," Koll promised her, "you are welcome here, Faustine. This tower is your sanctuary now. You've been here before."

"When I brought my husband to Obsydia, she swore to me she

convinced Morydonn of her just cause. Caladynn told me he was already dead, a soulless demon."

"Lies," Koll said. "The false words of enemies who hate you."

"When will I see Morydonn?" she asked, bright notes of hope lighting her eyes.

"Soon," Koll replied casually. "But you have other important things to do first before you are reunited."

She held out her hand to Koll, exposing the jewel and its terrible light. "Perhaps you should give it to Obsydia."

Koll's icy smile made her pause. Pain still vibrated through his whole being from the light's assault. He would not touch it. "You should have the honor. You will be rewarded for your loyalty and bravery. You will get what you deserve." He conjured a cloth of black silk and laid it over the jewel. "We want it to be a surprise."

When they entered Obsydia's temple the Claw Maidens howled in song, dancing around the Altar's flames. The Hooded-Guardians swung incense so strong it made even Koll dizzy. They chanted in demon-tongue as the ritual reached its zenith.

"What's happening?' Faustine asked, shaking in the presence of the primal scene.

"A miracle is happening," Koll cried out in reverence, "promised to this world long ago by Ahridum. Rejoice and kneel before Obsydia, your new God."

Faustine obeyed, falling to her knees, though she stared at the dancing demons in horror. "What are they doing?"

Savoring the mystical power of the darkness, Koll ignored her as he observed the spectacle of shadow. "A prayer. A single prayer to Ahridum to claim this world. They offer a queen born of a priestess and Ahridum to the Ethers of Shadow. For thirteen days and nights, they prayed for her to rise and shed her mortal shell. Their song pleads with Ahridum for her to ascend to the mystical throne, to discard the ravages of flesh."

"Why?" Faustine asked, her voice trembling. "How?"

"You know the history?" Koll whispered. "The star Ahridum cast upon this world bringing chaos and darkness?"

"It was not just a myth?"

"Myths are truths long forgotten. It was key to Ahridum's grand design to claim this world. It had to be an era of darkness. So, during the Bloodstone Age he chose a bride, one of his own priestesses named Lilith. He brought her to the safety of his black tower in the Isini Sea, and his essence merely touched her, like a breath upon a fragile leaf which burned with its heat. Lilith gave birth to Obsydia within moments. She perished into dust, but the first stage was complete. A true immortal whose sire is a god. Years of worship and sacrifice are required before this ceremony could take place. Even the Darkness has its rules. The birth of Obsydia was part of Ahridum's great plan to wrest this world from Light. See how sweetly they sing so Obsydia may be crowned a goddess and take her place in the great Dark Netherworld, for if a dark god can rise from this world, only then Darkness can claim it. Can you feel it? Breathe it in and feel its force spread throughout your mortal flesh."

Xabral slithered in, Levandius shuffling after him, head bowed and drooling. *That's our story.*

I know, but it is one all should share.

I have ached with worry, Xabral chastised Koll. *Going to Thill was perilous, and I longed to be with you in a fight. You know you could not touch the jewel.*

They could do nothing. Faustine took the jewel. I took Faustine. Nothing can stop us now.

Obsydia walked into the chamber, her very essence devastating. A sheer black robe draped her body. Her pale skin pulsated with the blood red runes, and her eyes gleamed dark silver now. Obsydia stood over Koll as he prostrated himself on the floor. "What gifts have you brought me?"

Koll rose, her image so potent he had to shield his eyes. "I bring you the dreaded light jewel. The Light Eternals cannot trick us now. We have their weapon. They cannot win now. You will rise to become an Eternal now."

"Show me," Obsydia demanded.

Faustine approached her, cupping the jewel with shaking hands she extended them to show her.

Obsydia hissed when she saw its pure glow. Her potent anger so frightened Faustine she crouched in terror, clutching the gem close.

"You did well, Koll," Obsydia whispered. "They can do nothing to us now. The Light will fail." She touched his cheek, the currents of energy in her body sparking on his skin. "You sacrificed your beautiful new arm to bring this wretched weapon to my keeping. It was a hidden blessing to warn us thus, for things of darkness cannot touch it." She gestured, and one of the Hooded Guardians approached with a box of black ebonite. "Put the jewel in the box and close it, for it offends my sight."

Faustine obeyed quickly, dropping the jewel into the black velvet lining the shimmering box. The Hooded-Guardian closed the lid, snuffing out its brightness. The shadowy being stepped away.

"We must prepare for my rising," Obsydia whispered. "For thirteen days and nights, the Claw Maidens danced and sang the ancient prayers of my Father. Now they will stop their prayer dance to continue the ritual. It is time for the next phase of the ceremony. Shroud, come forward."

The swirling demon women paused around the altar fire. Shroud, her Chief Handmaiden, stepped from the altar and went to Obsydia. She knelt and bowed her head, kissing the hem of her diaphanous gown and rose.

"What is happening?" Faustine whimpered.

"More than you deserve to see," Obsydia snapped. She looked at Shroud. "You have successfully completed the ritual, and all my handmaidens must be weary…and hungry."

Shroud's ghoulish face expanded into a hideous grin. "We hunger."

"Then feed," Obsydia told her, pointing to Levandius crouched in the background. "Fresh meat to restore your vitality."

Levandius yelped like a whipped dog. He had barely been aware since Koll's punishment. Now his eyes reflected his terror as the thirteen demons surrounded him, their feral eyes hungry.

Oh, I do want to watch this, Xabral thought to Koll.

"What is happening?" Faustine screamed, stumbling away. "Are they really going to eat him?"

"Not all at once," Xabral remarked, shaking his stinger.

"Silence," Koll commanded.

Faustine crawled along the floor to Koll and grasped his robes, sobbing. "What is going to happen to me? Where is Morydonn? You told me he lived and wanted me. You promised me if I brought you the jewel I would be rewarded."

"And so you shall be," Koll told her, touching her cheek with tenderness. "I could not touch the jewel. But you could, and for that we will show you mercy and honor."

"Mercy and honor?" Faustine choked. "I will live?"

"You are chosen to offer your heart to me," Obsydia replied as the Hooded-Guardians approached.

"Sacrifice? No, I will not do it!" she screamed, scrambling away, but was blocked by the Hooded-Guardians.

"Sacrifices do not command," Obsydia shouted, her voice echoing like thunder throughout the temple. "They offer their hearts to me. I need one more to complete this ritual. You should kiss my feet in gratitude, for it is an honor. We own your body and soul. You lost possession when you swore allegiance to me. Be glad, Faustine, for you will join your husband in the next world. He awaits you in Hell."

Faustine's hysteria rose as she ripped at her gown and hair, wailing for mercy. The Hooded-Guardians dragged her to the altar and strapped her on a stone of black marble. An obsidian blade gleamed in the red shadow light. Levandius howled in agony as the Claw Maidens fell upon him in a hungry rage.

In a moment, their screams stopped.

In the following silence, Obsydia walked barefoot across the bloodstained floor toward the altar of Ahridum and gazed up at his stained-glass portrait; its mysterious image of a crowned faceless god, concealed in black and red fire, seemed to gaze back at Obsydia. The Claw Maidens followed, wiping the blood from their faces, sated by the feeding.

"The thirteenth day is here," Obsydia proclaimed, kneeling before the image of Ahridum above her. "Prepare me for my rising my handmaidens, for I shall soon become an Eternal."

The chamber shuddered as though battering rams pounded the mystical barriers of the tower. The roar of dragons pierced the shadowed walls. Obsydia's face jerked up and her eyes burned. Koll and Xabral clung together with each violent crash against their sacred refuge.

Obsydia walked to the Eye of Shadows and passed her hand over the gleaming glass. The mirror glowed bright, revealing the land outside the tower. Dozens of dragons bombarded the tower as well as the demons and soldiers who held ground below. Mist dragons sprayed the onslaught of soldiers with their dream breath and they fell to the ground, bound in a dream state. Red fire dragons burned the cursed woods with fire, setting miles of land blaze. Green earth dragons pursued fleeing goblins and trolls with vengeful glee, spraying their green mist until it solidified into a green leafy shell, leaving the captives alive for later feeding. Shadow dragons burrowed through the black weeds unseen, emerging to grab unsuspecting demons and pulling them into the darkness. Silver frost dragons froze their assailants with their icey breath as sun dragons glowed with such brightness they brought light to this cursed kingdom for the first time in a millennia.

Koll's black eye narrowed when he saw the Drajina herself flying over the Shadow Tower. The white moon dragon swept over the tower, and the impact of her passing was felt.

I saw her in Tiamet, Koll told Xabral.

Ugly white worm with wings, Xabral remarked.

Dragons," Obsydia hissed. "I hoped they would come out of hiding before my father destroyed them. I want to watch them become nothing as my darkness continues to creep through the world." Obsydia turned to Koll. "Deal with these vermin, Sorcerer. I have better things to do. Make sure they pose no threat."

Koll bowed deeply, "Yes Goddess Obsydia. For to me you have always been a goddess. I long to watch you ascend and hope to be at your side when you grant me and Xabral the immortality you promised to us when we found you imprisoned. We will help rule this world for you. I sacrificed all for you. We freed you to take your place in this world to rule and to become what Ahridum decreed long ago…a goddess."

Obsydia's touched Koll's cheek briefly, her expression impassive and mysterious. "You will be rewarded, Koll. You will witness what no mortal man has ever witnessed-the birth of a god. Go and make sure the dragons do not enter my temple. It would be a desecration for them to touch this hallowed ground of darkness. This is my father's house."

A rare twinge of confusion haunted Koll as she turned her face away to return to the altar and the ministrations of her handmaidens. Shroud, feral black eye glinting in the shadowed light, smirked as she walked by him, muttering under her breath. "Did you think you would actually become immortal, Koll? Did you think you deserved it, *mortal?* You are nothing but worms walking this world. You will not even be a memory when Ahridum comes to take this world." Her guttural laugh infuriated him as she turned, her tight red braids whipping across her bony shoulders.

The Hooded-Guardians, faceless shadows in flowing robes,

circled Obsydia on the altar, their incense choking the air, the barrage of dragons shaking the tower.

Xabral coiled around Koll. *We are not going to be immortal? How can Obsydia let us die with the others? They were unworthy! We saved her. She promised.*

Promises die, Koll replied. *We will not die so easily.*

CHAPTER 34

Lost in a strange abyss, Runa struggled to find her way out. Mellypip clung to her in the shadows, bravely refusing to leave her. A bright light appeared through grey vapors, drawing her closer, stepping into a void before the Gate of Souls. The intense mystical fire of the gate terrified her, and the Wraith Guardians buzzed like hungry flies within its spectral orb. They sensed her and turned, flying toward her with menace. Holding Mellypip, she fled through the grey mist but had nowhere to run. The Wraiths screamed as they closed in. Then Runa heard her name on the ether and looked around, desperate, calling her over and over. She finally looked up, and Ashur appeared in the distant starlight. He was calling to her. Runa could not touch him, for she was too far away. She was so lost and scared in the mist, and the Wraiths were coming for her.

"Wake up, Runa! Wake up!" he cried to her. The sharp cry of his black eagle familiar Urvuz flying overhead startled her.

"Father, what is happening?" Runa cried as he drifted further away, into the abyss. "Help me!"

"Wake up, Runa!" Ashur shouted.

Runa opened her eyes, gasping for air as she bolted straight up. Ashur's dream image remained stamped in her mind, driving her to rise. "Melly! Opaline!" she called as she stumbled out of bed, feeling sick to her stomach. Her limbs felt numb, and she had a headache. "What's happened?"

Mellypip rubbed his eyes. "I think we fell asleep."

"On the eve of a dark apocalypse? No, I sense something else here," Runa said, pushing the hair out of her eyes. "I smell Grandpa's hand in this."

Mellypip fought the urge to suck his paw in fear. "I dreamed about the Gate of Souls. And I saw Ashur. He was trying to tell us something."

"I know," Runa said, her voice shaky. "My mouth feels like cotton."

Grimm woke and stood on wobbly legs. "I feel odd."

Mellypip ran to Runa and scratched his head trying to remember. "We all had a cup of tea and some drobba chip cookies. They even brought Grimm a treat of chopped meat. Damn it! Belwyn was pretty insistent we drink the tea and eat the cookies."

"You never need to be encouraged to eat," Runa said.

"An insidious plan," Mellypip agreed.

"I ate the meat," Grimm added, hanging his head.

"What's wrong?" Sephya asked, rousing from her little bed. She went to Mellypip. "Is nap time over? Why are you all sad?"

"It's okay Sephya," Mellypip gently told the baby dragon. "We just have to be somewhere."

Opaline snored in her bed, oblivious to everything. Runa shook her by the shoulders until Opaline reluctantly opened her eyes.

"What's wrong?" Opaline moaned, rolling over.

Runa pulled her out of bed. "Our families drugged us. They left without us."

"Why? I thought we all were going with them. They needed every hand and spell at their disposal. I still haven't even made my staff."

"Damn it!" Runa cried. She began spewing a series of nasty swear words in several languages. Even Opaline blushed at her choice of words.

Opaline winced as Runa rattled on. "I'm quite a linguist too. Those are pretty foul phrases for so early in the morning. Is it morning? Damn, I need some coffee."

"This is trouble,' Runa said. "You know why."

Opaline paused and looked at Runa. "I know. It's time." Grimm whined in his throat and put his head in Opaline's lap.

Mellypip knew it was time too, but not sure exactly what. "I know it's something to do with Runa's dream seer magic, but it is all so hazy now. Why would Ashur whisper something, Runa? It bugs me. Mysteries are fine for storytelling, but in real life it makes me twitchy."

Panthara stormed into the room, her black hair wild and blue eyes angry. "Where are they?"

"And there's my wake-up call," Opaline sighed.

Runa sat on the edge of the bed, rubbing her temples. "They left without us."

"My new husband lied to me," Panthara said. "Taran gave me a cup of honey wine. It was the last thing I remember before waking up in an empty bed."

Azmadu darted into the room, his eye-patch crooked. He pawed at Panthara, but she angrily shouted. "Do not try to make up to me, Azmadu. You participated in Taran's plot to prevent me facing my enemies in battle! How dare he do this! You are my familiar, not his!"

"Don't be angry. We wanted to save my Panthara from harm," Azmadu pleaded.

"Traitor!" Panthara accused. "How could Taran do this? Our wedding night became a bed of lies instead of promises." She turned on Opaline. "Your brother tricked me."

"Welcome to the family," Opaline muttered. "We were all drugged by good intentions, but I think what I need now is a pot of strong black coffee with a heavy dose of sugar."

"It's the thirteenth day," Grimm said to Opaline. "We do not have time for coffee."

The shadow dragons meekly hovered near Sephya, not looking at anyone. In fact, they looked guilty. Runa narrowed her eyes at Talon and Fallon. "You knew what they planned?"

"Not just them," Rualla said, stepping into the room, Pointessa at her side.

"Mother! Not you too?" Runa asked.

"Yes, dear. We all agreed," Rualla replied. "The Winged Fey and the all the other mages went to the Shadow Tower to fight Obsydia."

"It's for the best," Pointessa said gently. "Cathal and Yllia need to confront Obsydia without worrying about you three. You're young and impetuous sorceresses. You need someone to be watching over you, so you don't do something stupid and die!"

"I make my own choices," Panthara swore. "Taran is Opaline's age, and yet he was permitted to go. They are twins! How are we are denied the right to fight for this world?"

"Cathal decided," Pointessa said. "And they needed Taran for his new metal invention which boosts magic."

Rualla tenderly touched Runa's cheek. "Sweetheart, Cathal is my father and your grandfather, but he is also the Archon of Sorcerers, as Neelam is the Mage Chieftain of the Wizards. They made a hard decision. Prince Ulric remained to protect the realm. Even Hinkleburr and the little brothers who serve him stayed."

"Broda and Talwyn," Mellypip told her. "They're our friends."

"And they obeyed Cathal. I wanted to go too, but chose to stay with little Raven for Darcus, as I chose to be with my daughter."

"We must go there," Runa begged. "We must go now. You don't

know, Mother."

We are not staying here, Melly, Runa thought to him.

I know, Melly responded. *We must go now.*

"How long ago did they leave?" Panthara asked.

"About an hour ago," Rualla said.

The three young sorceresses and their familiars wordlessly looked at each other. Bound by whatever enchantment linked them in this cause, they moved as one with a single purpose. Opaline and Grimm left first. Runa and Panthara took their staves and left the room. Rualla followed after them, confused. Little Sephya chased after Mellypip, much to the dismay of Talon and Fallon.

"Where are you going?" Rualla demanded. "You can't get there in time. Elfshara is days away even by peryton or gryphon."

They did not answer. With resolute determination, they walked out into the courtyard to the spot where Faustine and Koll vanished in a surge of dark magic. Sorceress and familiar formed a circle in the black vines which polluted the land. Runa glanced down and extending her hand, streams of blue-light magic which combined her sorcery and Drusai abilities, burned the offensive dark things to ashes and they retreated from them, as though the demon vines sensed her power.

"Runa, what are you doing?" Rualla shouted at them. "Answer me!"

Runa embraced her mother tightly. "I know you meant well, but you cannot stop this. I love you."

Runa stepped back, and the three women linked hands, and their familiars huddled close. Runa lifted her staff and spoke an incantation in a strange language. Her staff glowed blue-white and the brightness exploded, covering them like a cloak of stars.

Panic seized Rualla and Pointessa as they leapt into the circle of light to be with them. Sephya cried out for Mellypip and flew into the shimmering light to be with them. Terrified for their charge, Talon and Fallon pursued her into the bright whirl.

A burst of light carried the sisters and their companions into the unknown.

~ * ~

Cathal witnessed the first truly unified alliance of nations since the end of the Bloodstone Wars. King Arawn and Queen Dagmar of

Ironia, Lord Rhudon, the liberator of the Ivory Kingdoms, the Oak and Rowan of Ilyrra, Niall and Talaith, Queen Sarabia of Thema, and King Caladynn of Thill. Other leaders gathered here from the reaches of the continent—rulers of small kingdoms banded together from Ithuli, Narunia, Ucara, Mowad, and others. They gathered on the borders of ancient Elfshara. Obsydia's Shadow Tower rose like a black beacon from hell beneath a turbulent sky. Amid cursed kingdom and storm clouds, dragons flew overhead. The gathering of rulers and their warriors were momentarily stunned by this rare vision of these magical creatures.

"I never thought to see this again," Cathal said.

"Do you mean the dragons or fighting hell-bitch?" Neelam asked.

"Both, I think," Cathal laughed. "The last time I was just a boy."

"Your network of alliances roused more than we ever imagined," Neelam told him.

"They can only distract Obsydia and her forces," Cathal said wearily. "We must do the harder work."

Ryen led the Raven's Wing, commanding several hundred rangers and their perytons. Among the Ilyrrans gathered, Darcus' scarred human face stood out. Jadon, his curse lifted and face restored, joined his father in the lead.

"At least we aren't sweating buckets in the desert of the Wasteland like last time," Neelam said.

"Then let's make a good show," Cathal said, plucking a flask out of his cloak pocket. He uncorked it and passed it to Neelam. "This land has been cursed since the Bloodstone Wars. Tangled and dead with nests of demons spawning like roaches. The trees are dead, petrified into stone. Ambera lost everything, as did Yllia in those dark days. She brought us all together. She guided us and even convinced the Winged Fey to help us."

"Then let's drink to Ambera," Neelam grinned. "Damn, I wish she was with us now. At least she is in paradise." Neelam raised the flask to heaven. "For old battles and friends. For our families. And for Ambera, may she be in happy in paradise and free of this bloody worry." He took a long drink and passed it back to Cathal.

"Amen," Cathal nodded and took a swig.

Yllia rode towards them on Rono, her green eyes sharp. "Spare me a little, Cathal. Facing great evil makes me thirsty too."

"How are you, Rono?" Cathal asked the gryphon with concern.

"I know this evil frightens you. You don't have to do this."

"I will be brave," Rono promised. "Ryen of the Raven Wing made me an honorary member. I will fight with Redstorm. He said to stay close to him."

Yllia patted the gryphon's head and dismounted him. "We underestimate this gryphon. His sense of evil is special, from what Redstorm and Darkleaf told me. He wants to be part of this." Yllia looked at the gathering of Raven Wing. "Jadon loves Runa very much you know. I think they are a good match."

"I've enough troubles today," Cathal replied dryly.

Yllia's smile was like the sun. "We weren't much older when we found each other."

"You haven't minded a wild sorceress for fifteen years," Belwyn said.

"You're late," Arawn laughed, riding up to Neelam on a shaggy war pony. "The dragons have nearly done all of our work for us. Won't be much fun now."

"There's plenty of demons to kill, don't fret," Neelam replied tersely.

Surya perched on his shoulder, glaring at her wizard. "Just don't get drunk before the battle."

Yllia took the flask from Cathal and drank. She looked at the cursed country with bitterness. "This was once my home. Now it is a nest of demons and darkness. Once it was green and beautiful."

"We will avenge what Obsydia has done to this world," Arawn promised.

Queen Sarabia joined them, her long black hair flying behind her as she rode up to them. "I brought what was left of my Theman army. Obsydia's forces ravaged us, but those who followed me here are brave and will fight to the last man. Each Theman warrior is worth a hundred men and I will lead them into victory. The Winged Fey carried us here through a portal of colored lights. It was most dizzying but invigorating," shouting to be heard above the chaotic din of warfare around them. "Those dragons are a wonder but loud," Sarabia shouted.

"So are the demons they're killing," Arawn laughed. Very enjoyable to hear them snapping on the burnt bones of our enemies."

"Why don't we send in more soldiers to help the dragons? Sarabia asked. "Finish off her filthy demons so we can bring down

Obsydia. We have the strength of all the free nations at our backs, wizards, and sorcerers."

Dareem appeared through a ring of bright light. He folded in his wings and marched to Cathal, ignoring the others. "Be patient, Queen Sarabia, and let the dragons finish their work. Nothing can bring down the demons with such efficiency as a dragon."

"Except for a Winged Fey," Yllia added.

"And it is best to stay out of their way," Dareem replied. "Allowing the dragons to attack the enemy forces without fear of harming an ally in their fervor is best. We will journey within first with the mages. The purpose of the forces gathered here is to keep the evil contained."

Caladynn looked up and pointed to the sky. "The moons are turning red, and the sun is darkening."

"Take us inside," Cathal commanded. "Before it's too late."

Cathal summoned the mages and familiars of the three castes, Sorcerer, Wizard, and Drusai, to venture into the darkness of Obsydia's lair. He watched his friends form a circle in unity. Neelam and Surya, wild Jiana and her Jasper, Ulan and his delicate familiar, Rosepetal. Gabriel and clouded leopard, Namir, volatile but devoted, Riva and Buzzy the sloth, clever and shy. He fought back tears when his adopted daughter Caliste and her Sanura stepped in. He had loved and raised her as his own from the time she was twelve. Taran and his cat MacTabbish, Raghnall and Baldur, though a great wizard healer he walked as a warrior today. With that massive bear at his side, no one would doubt it. Gentle Liat and grumpy Dabiro. Liat had loved Rualla for years and now had hope of a life with her. Iona and her Amun, mysterious in her veils and sad blue eyes. Her heart was so full of love she helped redeem Panthara. Myrsalian and his little owl, Felisia on his wrist. He never sought anything but protection for the family he fought so hard for. Proud Sirah and her white wolf Arial stood next to her father, Myrsalian.

Yllia squeezed his hand, his beloved wife since he was seventeen. They had faced this evil before when they were little more than children.

Yllia whispered to him. "Do you think Runa will be very angry with us?"

"She will be furious," Cathal nodded. "Rualla agreed to stay with her and the girls. We wanted them safe to the end. Opaline and

Panthara are her sisters now too. If we fail, they will have each other to cling to. I know we will win. I have faith."

"You better, old man," Belwyn retorted. "I'm not doing this for my amusement."

The maelstrom exploded above them, unleashing fire rain and lightning on the battleground, but something else was emerging from the crimson hazes above. Red demons with leathery wings similar to the ones they fought in the forest, but much larger and more vicious looking. Their breath spewed flame. The dragons turned their assault from the ground battle to the sky, clashing with the demons in the sky.

"Oh hell has come for us now," Neelam shouted, raising his staff for battle. He turned around to Arawn. "You wanted demons to fight? Well, you got your wish."

"We can't abandon them to this new madness!" Cathal cried.

"No, you all go! Go!' Darcus shouted, spurring Redstorm into the sky. "We'll handle this."

"We will fight here," Ryen cried, following Darcus. "Your battle is in the tower."

Cathal struggle to stay or leave them to this unknown evil bore no argument. The nine Winged Fey gathered around them, unfurling their broad wings as their light emanated from their bodies, covering the mages in brilliance as they vanished from sight.

CHAPTER 35

Koll watched men and demons battling below from the tower's terrace. High above the ground from the carnage of dead bodies, the reek of burning flesh still filled his nostrils. The dragons devoured legions of goblins and trolls during the fight, but the human men they did not touch, only killed, as though they knew they were demon-kissed and soulless. He saw his enemy gathering in the distance. The vast armies of men and mages gathering at the borders of this dark hell would have amused him, but he had more pressing concerns.

Xabral glided onto the balcony. "How many of Obsydia's blood warriors have fallen?"

"All I think, but it is no matter. Ten thousand bodies are willing to sacrifice for her."

"The dragons are destroying our forces!"

"Darkness watches. See, Xabral, Ahridum has sent winged demons to smite the infidels."

"What are they?" Xabral asked, gazing in wonder at the flying demons emerging from the turbulent sky, sweeping across the battlefield as they roared with hunger. Demons and dragons clashed in flight, ripping with talons. The Ilyrran warriors rode their perytons across the sky and on the ground soldiers stampeded the blood-soaked terrain.

"Behold, the gifts from the Dark Netherworld," Koll cried. "Even I sense the veils shifting between the realms of mortal and eternal, breaking down for the metamorphoses of this planet." Koll pointed to the ground. "None of them matter they are fodder to serve a higher cause. Death was their destiny, but our fate is bound to Obsydia. We are chosen. Shroud's jealous barbs will not change Obsydia's promise to us."

"Shroud hates you," Xabral agreed. "She was jealous of your influence over Obsydia and the power you had. I miss Chimera. She truly understood us."

"The world is changing before our eyes. The old is being swept away," Koll said. "Soon the sun will turn black and light will be just a memory to frighten demons and monsters."

"Some demons are trouble," Xabral remarked slyly.

"Yes. Obsydia promised us a place in this new world, but she is not our problem."

"Shroud," Xabral hissed. "She is our enemy."

Koll picked up the Scythe of Rygon, holding it in his hand. "No common demon slave shall influence Obsydia against me."

~ * ~

The Winged Fey transported them to the heart of the tower's temple, the massive chamber of shifting dark walls and red light. Incense choked the air, and blue fires raged all around. Shaking from the journey, Cathal cringed as the howls of demon handmaidens pierced his ears. They surrounded them on all sides, but he soon realized the Winged Fey's glowing dome shielded them from the rabid she-demons. Disoriented from the transference, the mages and familiars clung to each other in this wicked place.

"Get your bearings fast," Cathal warned, eyeing the she-demons circling the dome. Obsydia remained on the altar, her body shuddering as black mist tangled around her like a snake.

"I hoped you would come," Obsydia said, her voice echoing through the temple. "Cathal, do you think you can stop me now? You could not even stop Koll, a mere sorcerer like yourself. I am a god."

"Ignore her," Belwyn cautioned.

"You're not a god yet," Cathal shot back, eyes scanning the temple for other dangers besides the feral demon handmaids. He saw Faustine's body on the sacrificial stone. Levandius, or what remained of him, was scattered across the temple floor. Only because the head was more or less untouched could he identify him.

She's changing, Belwyn shouted in his head, snapping his attention back to the altar. *Hurry, start, the incantation. We need to contain her before it all becomes a dark hell.*

"Begin the ritual," Cathal commanded. "Speak the conjuration prayer!"

Obsydia glared at Cathal, her voice a thunderous assault. "You have lost. I am becoming a goddess before your eyes. You will be consumed by Ahridum's fire."

"Don't count on it, hell-bitch," Neelam shouted, slapping Cathal on the back of the head. "Don't look at her. Focus, boy!"

The Claw Maidens continued to beat against the mystical barrier, black obsidian knives in their hands, fangs bared as they screeched at them.

Obsydia, writhing in agony on the high altar, commanded his focus now. Her pale skin burned, shadows flared around her skin, and red runic symbols formed in a language Cathal could not decipher flickered on her body. Her eyes changed from silver to crimson and her shadow hair was a black storm rising on the tide of darkest magic. She became bestial as Darkness consumed her mortal essence.

Cathal began reciting the incantation as the others joined him, speaking the same words he recited a thousand years ago to trap Obsydia. Dareem removed a brilliant diamond from his tunic the size of his hand. It shimmered like a star, pulsating with light. The Winged Fey circled the sorcerers and wizards, chanting the incantation with them. Cathal remembered the words he chanted so long ago. This diamond was not just a jewel, but contained the essence of the Winged Feys blood and tears which they offered in its making. Fey and mage chanted together in this dark church, repeating the prayer over and over.

Ancient Eternals, show compassion for our plight. Fuse our magic with this blood of light. Bind this wicked queen with your grace. Forever banish her to endless night.

The diamond radiating pure light. The Claw Maidens wailed before its brilliance but defended Obsydia, putting themselves between Obsydia and the offensive light. Obsydia did not cower, laughing as the streams of light shot from its center and spread throughout the temple. Bursting into a thousand tiny stars the light struck down the Claw Maidens first. They shrieked in agony. The starry essence ripping and burning their demon flesh into ashes. In the end, they were ashes scattering on the mystical wind whipping the air.

So far so good, Belwyn twittered.

The Hooded-Guardians arose, faceless shadow monks from the Netherworld Cathal read about. He often wondered if they were myth. In flowing robes of shade they formed a defensive boundary before Obsydia. The mystical light of hope they conjured with their prayers struck the Hooded-Guardians with great force, but its bright spark evaporated along with hope.

"What the bloody hell?" Gabriel shouted.

"Keeping chanting!" Cathal shouted when the others began to falter.

The Hooded-Guardians swayed back and forth, their deep voices calling out in a demon tongue until a shadow dome appeared around Obsydia

"We failed!" Dareem cried, his stoic façade crumbling into despair.

The Fey are afraid, Belwyn observed. *Not a good sign.*

Obsydia's laughed as her body continued convulsing, dark energy sparking off her body as he wailed with her own birth into godhood. Her black energy struck their shield with thunderous force, the dark streams ricocheting struck the ceiling of stained glass. Glass fragments rained in the temple, exposing the darkening sun through the exposed temple ceiling. Outside the rage of demons and dragons continued. The cries of men and women fighting and dying chilled the blood. The Hood-Guardians remained untouched by the light and remained a barricade around Obsydia.

A Claw-Maiden entered the chamber, her corpse-like face grinning and blood-red braids falling across her skeletal body. "We were prepared for infidels."

Did she really say that? Belwyn remarked. *Do all demons talk in bad clichés?*

Cathal turned to Dareem. "Open the Gate of Souls."

"That won't work, but do try. You're Cathal the Sorcerer," the Demoness laughed. "I am Shroud. I serve Obsydia. My sisters fell out of devotion to their charge. Another sacrifice for *Her* glory."

"Wonderful," Neelam muttered, "another hell-bitch."

Shroud looked Cathal up and down. "You're the one whose sorcery vanquished Koll's arm. I commend you, mortal."

Interesting. Even the demons hate Koll, Cathal commented.

Where is the bastard? Belwyn asked, looking around. *Keep Shroud occupied while the fey finish summoning. Evil loves to gloat.*

Shroud boldly approached their shining dome of light without fear, her crimson gown sweeping the floor, her grey bony hands holding a dagger of obsidian glass. "Obsydia's mortal shell is burning away, releasing her Eternal essence…her godhood. The Hooded-Guardians are sacred immortals of the Dark Netherworld. Even we demons tremble and bow before their sacred powers. They are beyond your hand, Sorcerer. Did you think your puny flame would snuff them out? Do you think you could even touch her now? When she ascends, this world will belong to Darkness."

"Where is Koll?" Cathal commanded. "I would have thought he would be with Obsydia in her triumph. I would also like to kill him."

"Stand in line," Gabriel mumbled.

Shroud's black eyes glinted, looking at Cathal with contempt. "I do not answer to you. I am not his keeper. It does not matter anyway because Koll and his snake will die like everything else in this world."

A cloud of black smoke appeared behind Shroud. Her eyes flashing suspicion but before she had the chance to turn, Koll cut off Shroud's head in a single stroke with Rygon's scythe. The impact of the blow tossed her head hard against the light dome. It hit the floor with a thud and rolled to her twitching corpse before both demon parts crumbled into black ash. Koll clutched Rygon's Scythe in his only hand, Xabral coiled near his feet hissing and shaking his stinger. "I warned you not to prick my temper too far, Demoness. I promised you a death to compliment your corpselike beauty."

"Drop the shields," Cathal commanded.

Are you mad? Belwyn shouted in his mind.

Yes, I am. Facing his frightened companions, Cathal's strong voice commanded them with hope. "We fight with magic and blade now. The dome won't help us now. Let's find out if Taran's science experiments are any good. Fey, open those damned gates. Mages, keep a shield around yourself when the wraiths come through."

The Fey banded closer and continued their summoning as the dome of light which protected the mages vanished.

Cathal confronted Koll, his new staff blazing with sorcery.

~ * ~

Runa opened her eyes, gasping for air. She felt the very air sucked out of her body when the light carried them here. Shaking but feeling oddly energized, she looked at the others. "Is everyone alright?"

Melly, are you okay?

Still clinging to her shoulder, he squeaked. *Are we there yet?*

Opaline and Panthara actually held onto each to keep from falling. Azmadu lost his eye patch somehow. Grimm looked dazed but remained steady on his feet.

Runa looked around. *I know we must be here, but I don't know why or even how.*

I'm afraid, Mellypip said. *I want to be brave, but I'm afraid.*

They were in a long hallway of shifting walls and shadows. The massive doors before them bore frightening images of demons carved into the ebonite. Ancient runes of darkness covered the ebonite, and an image of Obsydia's face was set in the center.

"Where are we?" Opaline asked, eyes darting around. "We were in our room. What happened to us?"

"This is bad," Grimm said, looking around with suspicion. "How did we even get here?"

"Is anyone hurt?" Runa asked, pulling Rualla to her feet. "You should not have come, Mother."

"Try and stop me, I'm fine," Rualla insisted. "I've been through worse. Pointessa? Are you hurt?"

The porcupine shook her body, trying to regain equilibrium. "I'm fine dear, just shaken a bit."

The baby dragon, sensing the evil of this place, spurted flames from her nose and mouth as Talon and Fallon tried to calm her. "Wicked. This place is wicked."

Where are we?" Rualla demanded.

"We are in the Shadow Tower," Runa answered.

"This is where Obsydia's ritual is taking place," Panthara whispered. "You do not need to possess magic to smell the stench of an evil ritual. How are we here?"

"Don't ask," Azmadu grumbled. "My head aches. When we went through this portal, it was like when we came to rescue you, Panthara. Mellypip let me ride with him. But this was different. I cannot explain it."

Panthara picked up Azmadu and held him close. "I know, dear one. I know."

Runa looked at the ominous doors, fear knotting her gut. "We had to be here. The ritual to trap Obsydia is failing. Ahridum's hand is close now, so close for us all to die."

"Stop it," Opaline begged.

"I hate it when mysticism taunts and still hides the answers," Grimm growled.

Rualla took Runa by the shoulders. "You're not yourself." She gasped when she looked into her eyes, stepping back when she saw their faces. "Your eyes, all of you, they are like silver stars now. What's happening to you?"

"Forces beyond us," Pointessa cried. "There is a strange power over our girls. One we cannot sway I fear."

Runa shook her head. "Mother, I'm sorry. Ashur is sorry. He's doing this for us."

"What?" Rualla cried, tears flowing down her face.

"Stay with Pointessa and the dragons," Runa told her. "When the time is right, run."

Sephya clung to Mellypip with trusting eyes. "No, don't go away."

"Talon and Fallon will watch over you," Mellypip whispered. "Stay out of sight. Do you promise?" Sephya nodded and held Melly, wrapping her crimson wings around his furry body, and then letting go.

"Obsydia is rising," Panthara warned in a strange voice.

"We must go now," Opaline whispered, trancelike as they all moved as one.

Their familiars remained close to them, locked in their mystical path with their sorceresses. They stood side by side before the grand doors to Obsydia's temple. Their bodies' radiant blue-white light lit the whole corridor. Runa held out her staff, sending waves of fiery brightness blasting the temple doors open.

They walked into the dark temple together.

CHAPTER 36

Depleted of spears and crossbow bolts Darcus fought on with what he had…a sword and an angry peryton. He tightened his body against impact as Redstorm rammed a flying demon head on. He felt at least one of his ribs crack in the collision. His sword arm throbbing with exertion he struck at the beast when it swerved against them, the air currents pushing against his body. Redstorm rammed the demon back.

"Redstorm, go left," he commanded. "Let's drive this beast back to hell!"

"How many of these damned things are there?" Redstorm bellowed.

"Hell is fertile with demons," Darcus shouted.

Forcing the creature out of their path, Darcus' sword strike cut deep into the demon's neck. Darcus turned Redstorm around for a second pass. The demon's screech pierced Darcus' ears like needles. The creature spun around, broad leathery wings beating the stormy air. Redstorm roared back, crimson wings pushing against the air and his rack and feathers spattered with black demon blood. The beast raged, twisting its body in flight, sweeping toward them with open jaws, exposing dozens of razored teeth.

Jadon flew between them, his Drusai light burst from his hand, showering the flying creature with pure blue light. Wailing in agony the demon flew backward in retreat.

"Now!" Jadon shouted.

Shaking his head with fury, Redstorm flew at the demon, his massive rack ramming into the creature's skull crushing bone and tearing out one of its eyes. The sulfurous stink of demon blood sickened Darcus. Striking the demon hard with another pass, he cut deeper into its gaping wound. The flying demon screamed as it struggled to beat its wings before plummeting to the earth. Shaking his antlers free of blood and gore, Redstorm' victorious roar rang in his ears.

Darcus and Redstorm swept across the tower. Even from this high, they saw the tower shudder violently, and the ceiling exploded like a colorful volcano.

"What's happening down there?" Jadon cried, guiding Darkleaf toward Darcus.

"Demon coming!" Darkleaf warned, charging into the beast with his rack.

A grey-skinned demon turned in flight and swept toward Darcus. Darcus veered Redstorm around to confront the beast and raised his sword to strike. A white dragon struck the monster from the side so fast Darcus did not even see her coming.

"It's the Drajina!" Redstorm cried, sweeping wings beating backward.

Rono joined them, talons gripping the winged demon's tails. Spinning in aerial combat Rono and the demon snapped and clawed. Sandhya assaulted the demon from the side, ripping out the demon's throat. She let go and watched the demon plummet, blood gushing from its neck.

Darcus looked down. Some of the dragons were already attacking the Shadow Tower. Like bees in a hive, the dragons covered the massive fortress, striking and breathing their dragon magic on the defenses. The sky's haze around them turning red and the sun darkening into a black star.

The Drajina's broad luminous wings sweeping the air, she circled around, looking directly at Darcus and Rono. "I have commands for you."

~ * ~

Runa led her sisters and their familiars toward the Hooded Guardians. Inside she was quaking with fear. *What are those scary things, Runa?* Mellypip asked.

Darkness, Runa answered. *They are powerful and from the Dark Netherworld of Ahridum, though I do not know how I know this.*

Mellypip bravely remained with Runa, though he was very scared. The forces driving them forward were a mystery to him. Runa smiled at Mellypip with pride and love, her green eyes luminous. Runa continued to walk through the madness, her staff a dazzling beacon in her hands, and the imprint of Striker's eyes glowing brightest. The battle of light and dark magic charred the air, but not even the Winged Fey's magic could breach the dome of shadow protecting Obsydia, not even with the light jewel.

Then it all just stopped.

Runa's eyes darted around the room…everyone stopped moving. *Why aren't they moving?* Mellypip asked.

Koll and Cathal were still locked in their moment of combat, Rygon's scythe in Koll's hands. Runa glanced back to see Rualla and Pointessa frozen at the entrance of the temple, watching her with pained eyes.

"All of our family and friends are still as statues, as though time stopped."

"How come they could not freeze the evil ones?" Mellypip grumbled.

As Runa and the other approached, the Hooded Guardians howled and grew to gargantuan height as they expanded their shadows around Obsydia.

Obsydia's harsh laughter chilled Mellypip to the core. Writhing on the altar in agony, the Bloodstone Queen was transforming. Her ethereal beauty was being burned away as her god powers within her emerged. "You are too late," she mocked.

"You have not risen yet," Panthara replied coolly.

"You stopped the wrong side," Opaline accused.

Dareem flew down between Runa and the Guardians. "We have no power over them. We could not let the others interfere. They are awake, they just cannot move. The amount of cursing they are shouting internally is even amusing. You are all confused. Not my doing, by the way."

"Why?" Runa asked. "Why are we here?"

"Because you're the unfortunate ones to be chosen…all three of you. You are the Scions of Light. The Eternals chose you, so don't blame me. We only watch," Dareem replied sharply, then added in a sympathetic tone, "I am sorry." Dareem's gaze shifted to Cathal and Belwyn. "Did you think you would still be one of the scions? I did not choose them, Cathal. So stop cursing at me in your head."

"You are opening the Gate of Souls," Panthara said, fearful.

"Which is why you must hurry! Our shield will protect your loved ones, and sadly even Koll and his snake. We must make sure Obsydia is eradicated from this world even if it means your deaths. If this does not work, we must pray the Wraiths take Obsydia."

"I…am…ascending," Obsydia wailed in a burst of darkened glory, raising her arms to the sky. "Ahridum, lift me to the Dark

Netherworld. Consume this world as my gift to you."

The Hooded Guardians attacked them with a cloak of shade, inky clouds of malignant magic streamed from their hands as they swayed before the altar. Their mystical death evaporating around the shield protecting Runa and the others.

"Stop them!" Obsydia screamed. "Kill them all!"

Runa and the others suddenly fully woke to what they must do. The secret imprisoned in their minds opened, and her father's words became clear. They were all given a secret on that fateful night the sorcerer house exploded and the Winged Fey rescued them. In a heartbeat when they lost consciousness, Ashur visited her as a conduit for the Light Eternals. She remembered what he whispered in her ear.

Runa, the Light Eternals have not abandoned you. They will send a jewel of pure light, a piece of their power to you and your sisters. You, Panthara, and Opaline will wield the true weapon. The jewel is just one part of the weapon. You need a word of power, one sacred Eternal Word to destroy Obsydia. To speak it whole would burn you to cinders. It must be spoken in parts and inscribed on your staff, protected by Striker's soul. This has been planned for a long time, Runa. The Eternals would have let me rest in Paradise, but I wanted to be the one to help you and guide you to your destiny. The jewel will embed itself within the staff, and once it is complete, you must be the one to strike.

I will face Obsydia? I'm afraid, Father.

I know, Ashur whispered to her gently. *Forgive me.*

Standing between Runa and Panthara, Opaline took their hands and smiled bravely. "Come sisters, as Neelam says, we have a hell-bitch to kill."

Panthara lifted her chin with pride and grinned. "Yes, we do."

"Then slay the dark queen," Grimm agreed. "Before she does ascend."

Their familiars stayed with their sorceresses because of the love they shared as a family. Azmadu, the flying crill lizard, stayed with Panthara, their bond stronger than ever. Grimm Darkrunner, loving and loyal to his Opaline, would remain at her side whether it meant death or life. Mellypip puffed bravely upon Runa's shoulder. He would never leave Runa, no matter the cost.

Bolstered by the love of her companions, Runa raised her staff suspended it in the air above her hands. Each of them spoke part of the mystical word of power. Opaline, Grimm, Panthara, Azmadu,

Mellypip, and finally Runa whispered the single final syllable in the Eternal language. Runa felt the tingling heat on her tongue as she spoke. Each fragment spoken formed into a golden runic symbol of shimmering light as it attached itself to Runa's staff. The imprint of Striker's eyes burned brightly on the wood. Asheni took the light jewel from the spear and held it out for Runa who summoned it to her hand. The jewels' warmth was comforting amid the terror. Pressing the jewel against the wood, it melted within.

"Sorceress, you think you can stop me!" Obsydia challenged, a glint of fear in her eyes as the golden images formed on Runa's staff into the Eternal word of power. "A girl with weak mortal magic. I will watch you perish in the darkness. I was sired by a god! Eternal blood is in my veins. You are dust!"

Runa knew they would have to drop the shield around them to strike. *Melly, it's time.*

I know, Mellypip answered.

The protective light around Runa and the others fell away, but Runa's blazing staff touched the shadowy barrier of the Hooded Guardians. It burned away. The brilliant light blinding as the sun, the Hooded Guardians shrank from its power.

"Do you think you can touch me?" Obsydia cried, trapped in her own metamorphoses. "I am a goddess rising."

Runa did not answer or banter. The staff transformed in blue-white light, the Eternal word blazing golden and the light jewel a blaze above Striker's eye imprint. Sure of what she must do, she grasped the staff and hurled it into the dome of shadow, past the Hooded Guardians. The staff struck Obsydia, and she wailed in pain. The howl of the Hooded Guardians deafening.

"You got her!" Mellypip cried.

"We're not done yet," Runa shouted.

Obsydia convulsed as the light consumed her. The tower shook violently, throwing them across the room. Flames sparked all around them. Mellypip hung on to Runa, his fur singed and smoking. They rolled across the bloodstained floor, buffeted by the tremors. As the mysterious word of the Light Eternals consumed Obsydia, the Hooded Guardians were swept into a cascade of destruction; the fiery fury consumed these shadow beings within seconds. The power of the Eternal Word incinerating Obsydia like a moth in a flame. Obsydia howled as glaring rays of light burst forth from her skin.

"Obsydia is dying," Runa cried out, holding on to a pillar as she tried to stand. "Don't open the Gate of Souls."

Obsydia's final scream was deafening as they shut their eyes in pain, covering their ears because not even the mute spell Runa feebly raised helped. The light razed the darkness which walked this world for so long. Obsydia became a pillar of molten ashes as a powerful circle of light spiraled around her remains and then exploded in an intense boom, sending massive shockwaves across the chamber. Obsydia was finally and utterly destroyed as her mortal mother had been centuries ago, abolished by Eternal powers until nothing was left.

"She's gone," Asheni cried with joy and shock. "Obsydia is finally dead. We can close the gate!"

"Too late," Dareem replied. "They are coming."

Asheni's words haunted her briefly. *We have seen visions, Runa. During the final battle, I have seen the Wraith Guardians take you through the Gate of Souls. I am sorry.*

"What!" Mellypip cried. "Well, stop it! You did this!"

"Fix it," Opaline demanded, holding onto Grimm, shaking violently.

The Gate of Souls opened.

"We can shield you from the wraiths," Asheni promised, casting a glowing light around in the chamber.

Runa's staff was still vibrating across the temple floor with the power of the Eternal's inside. Intense light burst and flowed across the chamber, enveloping the Winged Fey around them. The mortal shell they had endured fell away, revealing their own eternal origins. They rose like giant colorful butterflies, iridescent and beautiful beyond words. The Winged Fey were free of their immortality in a world meant for mortals. They rose into the air shining beacons of colorful light and flew into the Gate of Souls.

"They left us," Grimm howled in disbelief.

Everyone in the temple was free to move again, but the powerful protection of the Winged Fey vanished.

The Wraith Guardians came through the portal, darting through the air as they hunted for souls.

CHAPTER 37

Darcus ran through the hallways, Redstorm following closely behind. Tremors shook throughout the tower, making each step a dangerous gamble as floors heaved and cracked.

"I don't like this," Redstorm complained. "The place is falling around my antlers. It stinks of evil and goblins. Did I mention the evil?" Another jolt shook the walls. "What the hell was that?"

"Your guess is as good as mine, friend. The Drajina said to come this way." Darcus said, stepping over a fallen pillar. "The dragons rammed a lot of holes into the sides of this cursed tower to give us safe passage."

"Is Sandhya sure they are really here?"

"She's a moon dragon. They have visions and see the future. What do you think? Do you want to argue with a dragon?" Another boom quaked the whole tower, throwing Darcus across the corridor. The impact rattled him more than he wanted to admit. His broken ribs made it hard to breathe, and every inch of his body throbbed with pain.

"Are you all right?"

"Wonderful," Darcus groaned, holding on to Redstorm as he jumped onto his feet.

"You're hurt and being quite stubborn about it," Redstorm snorted, lowering his massive head and shaking his rack. "What the hells was that? I don't think it was the dragons."

"Something either very good or very bad," Darcus replied, exhaustion sapping the last of his energy. "Let's keep going."

Redstorm followed, "It's a good thing I trust you, Darcus. Try to stay alive. I don't want to break in a new ranger."

"I'll try not to disappoint."

Redstorm looked over Darcus' head. "I see them!"

Two dragons racing down the dark halls, two shadow dragons and a baby fire dragon riding atop of one of them.

"Ranger Darcus, we are so glad it's you," Fallon cried, screeching to a halt, Sephya clinging to his neck.

"We are so lost," Talon said. "There is no place to burrow in this wicked tower. Mellypip told us to keep Sephya safe. The temple doors slammed shut during the battle."

"Mellypip is in trouble," Sephya cried.

Darcus picked Sephya up with one hand and tucked her under his arm. "You were supposed to stay safe, little dragon. The Drajina sent me to find you."

"My mother is here?" Sephya asked excitedly, fluttering her wings.

"Yes," Darcus replied, mounting Redstorm and turning him around. He glanced back at Fallon and Talon. "Follow me. The dragons have been breaking through the walls, so I know a way out."

"What about Mellypip and the others?" Sephya cried in protest, wriggling in his arm.

"They are being watched over," Darcus answered.

"How do you know little wampu is safe?" Talon asked, flying alongside as Darcus reached a broad opening in the wall.

"Melly is too small to face such evil alone," Fallon agreed.

"The Drajina told me," Darcus replied. "Now be quiet while I finish rescuing you."

~ * ~

"Everyone out," Cathal shouted, "before the temple falls around our ears."

The floor quaked, and the pillars cracked and crumbled around them. Everyone was scattered in the chaos. Runa heard Cathal's desperate voice called out to her. Runa stumbled, Mellypip tucked in her arm. Her staff, still vibrating with mystical power rolled toward her.

"My staff! It's still intact," Runa cried, crawling toward it. "I thought it would have been destroyed with Obsydia."

"Don't touch it, Runa," Mellypip warned.

"Something else is happening," Runa gasped, pausing as she watched. Cathal and Rualla reached her, lifting her by both arms but she resisted. "Wait!"

"The staff," Rualla cried, gripping Cathal's arm. "Father…look at the staff."

"The wraiths are coming," Belwyn shouted as he flew over their heads.

"We don't have time," Cathal said, and then he glanced at Runa's burning staff.

Runa's staff rattled as the light of the Eternals consumed it. The wood was a rod of pure light radiating, but something was emerging from her staff. Striker burst from the staff but...he was not spirit. The red panther sprang hot with magic. Translucent and hot with magic, Striker convulsed on the floor and then lay still as he breathed with new life. The remains of Runa's staff then burned into white ash that blew away.

"What is happening to him?" Rualla cried.

"He's not a spirit," Grimm said. "He is changing."

"Help him," Pointessa cried. "Quickly before we are taken by the wraiths."

Striker was no longer spirit as life was restored to him. He lay on the floor, debilitated by the travails of his resurrection.

Tears of joy flowed down Rualla's face as she hugged Pointessa. Liat and Dabiro rushed to Rualla's side. Liat flung Striker over his shoulder, taking Runa and Rualla by each arm as Dabiro and Pointessa followed.

The Wraith Guardians buzzed around the room, attacking the light from their staves pushing them back with ease, the power of the magic was intensified a hundred-fold using Taran's mystical metal. Opaline had no staff, but Panthara and Taran sheltered her and Grimm, using their staves to fight off the angry wraiths.

Runa picked up Mellypip and ran, her own light magic, a combination of sorcery and Drusai, kept the wraiths at bay. The hideous beings swept across the room. A mystery gnawed at Mellypip thoughts as he held onto Runa. *I think we forgot something.*

Runa stopped, her heart pounding and breathless. *Koll...he's free.*

Koll! He stalked toward them cloaked in a black shield, Xabral following him, shaking his stinger with venomous intent, freed of the Winged Fey's shield which imprisoned them, they did not flee but hunted...for her. He held Rygon's scythe in his hand.

"Koll's free!" Runa cried, turning to run the other way.

Gabriel and Cathal stopped in their tracks first and turned to charge Koll, Namir and Belwyn in hot pursuit, leading the others to follow.

"The Wraiths come," Koll said. "I want to watch you all die before Darkness calls me to judgment. But you Runa, I want to kill personally."

"Stay away from her!" Cathal warned, sorcery streaming from

---

his staff.

"You can do nothing to me now," Koll said calmly. "Death is my destiny. I will pay the Darkness for failing Obsydia after I make Runa suffer."

"Wrong choice of words, Koll! Cathal replied sharply as he turned his staff on Koll, as did the others, firing an energy of pure light energy amplified by Taran's metal. The Wraith Guardians gathered around Koll and Xabral, snapping at the light, eager to take Koll's soul.

The powerful light disrupted the dark shield Koll summoned. It scorched and wavered as it weakened. The wraiths buzzed around Koll and Xabral with malicious torment until the shield was shattered by their combined light, striking Koll and Xabral with such intensity it lifted them into the air as Koll and Xabral cried out in pain. A wraith snatched the scythe from Koll's trembling hand and flew into the burning portal with the ancient weapon. They seized Xabral from Koll's hold. Xabral's screams of terror ceased when the wraith disappeared into the Gate of Souls with him.

Furious his revenge was ruined, and his familiar lost to him, Koll cast his black eyes on Runa as the wraiths pulled him toward the gate. Runa rushed toward Cathal, Mellypip bouncing in her arms. Koll conjured a black mystical rope from his hand, its dark mist coiling around Runa's waist just as the wraiths carried Koll's body and soul through the portal. The cries of family and friends filled Runa's ears as she was pulled inside the gate at such speed she thought her soul would wrench free from its force.

Within the Gate of Souls, a solid presence caught Runa, holding her and Mellypip close as Koll's sorcerous rope evaporated in the mystical realm. Runa turned and saw Ashur was holding her safe in the strange abyss.

"Father, what's happening," she asked.

"You are safe," Ashur comforted her. "Koll and Xabral are not. They are about to face judgment in Eternity. The Darkness is not forgiving of those who fail." Ashur's sharp gaze watched the wraiths drag Koll and Xabral deeper into the abyss as they shrieked with agony beyond the mortal, their bodies falling away to expose their black souls before they vanished on the horizon. "The suffering they face is beyond mortal comprehension."

"Try me," Mellypip quipped.

Wraiths buzzed around them, still eager to take her and Mellypip. Golden light in the shape of butterflies formed a protective ring around them, their powerful light forcing back the wraiths. She knew it was the Winged Fey. She saw Urvuz flying in the eternity with them, the black eagle protecting her and Mellypip from the Wraith Guardians. Finally, the wraiths followed their companions into the gates beyond.

She looked at the mysteries as they hovered in the heavens. A dark night with thousands of stars surrounded them. Clouds of vibrant colors streamed across the shade of eternity. The beauty here is astounding. "Is this Paradise?"

"It is a gateway to Eternity, which is vast and holds mysteries I cannot reveal."

"What will happen now?" Runa asked, embracing him.

"You are going back, but we must hurry. The Gate of Souls cannot stay open long. The Light Eternals permitted me to be your guardian beyond the gate so you could have safe passage back to the world. Tell Panthara and Rualla I will always love them. I'm glad they have found happiness."

"How will we go back?" Runa asked.

"You have help coming," Ashur assured her as Rono the gryphon burst through the portal on black wings.

"Come Runa and Melly," Rono cried, flapping his wings.

Incredulous, Runa asked, "But how?"

"Koll trapped you here, not the wraiths. If the wraiths did not take you, then they cannot keep you." Ashur looked at the gryphon and smiled. "Rono is braver than you think. The dragons did the rest."

Tears in her eyes, Runa looked at her father and hugged him for the first time before she leapt to the gryphon's back, holding Mellypip tightly as she flew Rono back to their mortal realm.

~ * ~

The Gate of Souls closed and vanished just as Runa flew into the chamber on Rono. No one abandoned her but had remained anxiously at the gate for her.

Runa laughed, exhilarated and frightened at the same time. "It's all right. Ashur saved me, as did Rono! Too much to tell you now. We need to leave!"

"Welcome back, Runa. Finally, some common sense. "We've some help coming," Neelam shouted, shapeshifting into a snow eagle and following Surya out the opening in the wall. "For those of us who can't fly."

The dragons broke down more of the walls and hovered in the air for the others. The whole tower was falling now as they jumped on the strong backs of the dragons. Jadon flew alongside Runa as they flew out into the open blue sky beneath a yellow sun. They glided along the wood which was slowly turning green again, Obsydia's ancient curse dissolving with her death.

Yllia rode by them on a great red dragon. "This is Akash. Riding a dragon is most exhilarating," she laughed.

They flew far beyond the tower and landed with the armies who bravely came and fought the darkness. Runa landed Rono and dismounted. She hugged the gryphon. "You are the bravest gryphon in the world."

"Of course Rono is brave," Grimm agreed. "I witnessed his bravery many times when we were in the desert together."

Mellypip hopped on top of the gryphon, holding him tight. "I'll write a tale just for you. You will be the hero."

Rono beamed with the affection, his voice trilling with contentment. "The dragons told me what to do. They did magic on me so I could return you to our world with Runa. The Drajina told us about her vision. I could not let you or my best friend Melly die because of evil."

Everyone gathered together, exhausted and shaking. Cathal wept as he held Runa so hard she thought her bones would break, but she welcomed it. The hugs of her family and friends were warm and wonderful, but she clung to the memory of her father in the stars holding her. She wept, committing it to her memory to treasure. Jadon kissed her boldly on the lips and Belwyn did not even threaten him.

"The Shadow Tower is vanishing," Neelam shouted. "Hell-bitch is truly dead, the gods curse her memory."

"Can we go home now," Surya asked. "I've had enough adventure."

In the distance, Ahridum's Shadow Tower did not just crumble into ruin, but a wave of shadow erased it from the world, as it did the fallen demons and monsters on the battlefield. Only the dead men and women who fought remained for them to gather and mourn.

"It is a new age," Caladynn cried. "Darkness has been defeated."

"Not just contained," Cathal added. "Now we can go home in peace."

"Except for the brave souls who died on the field today," Ryen said. "We will honor them all as heroes."

Runa took Mellypip in her arms and sat on the grass with Jadon. The Drajina approached with her mate, Akash. Sephya was sitting atop of Akash's head. The baby dragon flew over to Mellypip, and they embraced in a shared moment of silence.

"My mother says we are going home," Sephya told him sadly. "I will miss you, Mellypip."

"I'll miss you too," Mellypip said, brushing a tear off his fuzzy cheek.

"The fires of Rapiveshta will burn once more with dragons," Sandhya told them. "We are grateful you helped us when Obsydia threatened us. You are welcome to visit us, Mellypip and Runa. You are dragon friends now." Sandhya lifted Sephya atop her head. Sandhya flew away so fast with Sephya, Mellypip thought his heart would break. He heard the baby dragon call goodbye a final time before vanishing in the horizon. The dragon clans followed Sandhya and Akash, majestic as they took to the sky for home.

Runa picked him up and held him close as he wept. "I'll miss Sephya."

"I will too, Melly," Runa whispered.

Please don't cry, Furball," Belwyn begged. "We just saved the world."

"Even heroes need to cry sometimes," Runa told him.

CHAPTER 38

The Shadow Tower did not just fall, it vanished from the world in a wave of mysterious shadows. The cursed land of Elfshara was green as life was restored to the ancient kingdom. All remnants of Obsydia's rule gone like a bad dream when you wake. Mellypip paused writing, scratching his head with his pencil. The flow of words must excite the reader as he detailed the events of that fateful day. He pondered, then scribbled. *The heroes rejoiced when the tower vanished. The sky was blue and the sun golden again.*

"Mellypip hurry! It's time," Runa called, scooping him up from his journal.

He dropped his pencil in the tussle. "I'm writing the critical chapter about our great battle with darkness," Mellypip protested. "The muse was speaking through me."

"We're late, your muse can wait a little while," Runa scolded as she laughed. "I promise you can finish your epic later."

"There better be drobba," Mellypip pouted. "My bardic skills need drobba to hone the words."

"Yes, great ranger-mage," Runa said.

"And bard," Mellypip corrected.

"But most of all, you're my familiar," she said. "And you can carry the new staff Jadon carved for you."

Mellypip nodded eagerly as she handed him the tiny staff, the top carved with Runa's face. Her own new staff was shiny, and though his face gleamed on top, he missed Striker's eyes which had been part of the old staff.

"You look pretty Runa," Mellypip told her. "The green dress matches your eyes."

They joined the gathering outside in the lush royal gardens on the palace grounds. All their sorcerer friends were here. Riva and Buzzy discussed the new drawings for the house with Taran and Myrsalian. Ulan visited with Sirah and Panthara as their familiars enjoyed the sunshine. Jiana and Jasper eagerly sampled the delicacies. Iona sat quietly in the shade with Amun sipping tea. Neelam and Raghnall arrived from Ironia this morning, just in time. Mellypip enjoyed seeing Baldur and Surya again.

King Caladynn and Queen Sorcha generously hosted this wedding as a token of their appreciation for everything the mages sacrificed during the threat of Obsydia and Koll. Yllia planned a lovely wedding for the couple. All their family and friends joined in to celebrate the happy day…and there would be a great big, iced cake.

Prince Ulric greeted Opaline fondly when she greeted Sorcha. There was no tension between the two, but even so, Mellypip saw a little sadness in the Prince's eye when Opaline walked away.

"When will our new sorcerer house be ready?" Mellypip asked.

"Not long," Runa said, smoothing the folds of her leaf-green dress. "Riva and Taran are designing it. It better be soon because I'm getting spoiled by all the royal pampering."

Opaline greeted her with a kiss on the cheek. "There are worse things. After what we endured, a little luxury is due." She straightened the floral wreath Runa wore on her head and smiled. "Now you're ready, Maid of Honor."

Runa took a deep breath, walking down the archway alongside Caliste. Even the path was strewn with blossoms. Mellypip and Sanura endured the silliness of wearing a wreath of blossoms around their necks, but Mellypip planned to eat his later. Behind them, Cathal and Yllia walked Rualla down the aisle, their familiar's following. A nervous Liat and an unusually well-behaved Dabiro waited next to Abbess Odelia beneath the arch. Pointessa and Striker walked side by side in friendship. The miracle of his resurrection was a gift, Mellypip believed. The day was warm and sunny, though a true winter would be coming soon. Mellypip did not like winter, but Belwyn assured him real winters were not as wicked. Runa cried with happiness as Rualla and Liat kissed passionately for the first time as husband and wife before the cheering crowd who showered them with flower petals.

Hinkleburr and Helga stood arm in arm, newly betrothed themselves and very happy. They were the first to throw the petals at the new bride and groom. Broda and Talwyn stood next to them, blowing their noses and wiping tears away.

Opaline hugged the newly married couple, wiping her eyes with a silk handkerchief. "It was a beautiful ceremony. I'm so happy for you both."

"Thank you," Rualla told Opaline, beaming at her new husband. "You must visit us."

"I heard you are going back to Cathal's tree tower in the west," Opaline said.

"Yes, we leave in a few days," Liat grinned. "Cathal and Yllia generously agreed to give us their tower as a wedding gift. Rualla grew up there, so it is home." He kissed Runa on the cheek. "And it is your home, always."

"We especially expect frequent visits from our daughter," Rualla said and embraced Runa as they both began to cry with happiness.

"No tears!" Dabiro grunted with rare emotion, butting his head against Liat's leg.

"We wish to use our new home for good," Rualla nodded, kneeling between her two familiars. "I have been doubly blessed with Pointessa and Striker. Many suffer terrible losses when they lose their familiars, as familiars experience the grief of losing their mages. Liat and I are starting a sanctuary for familiars. We want to give them hope and a loving home with us. Mages who have lost their familiars can visit and perhaps discover they can bond with another again."

"Your cause is noble," Grimm said. "There is dire need for this. My own sire lost his sorcerer and returned to the wild in grief, but never found a real home or happiness. Even his mate died before he was killed. If you can offer hope to them, it is good. "I'm just glad Striker is not a ghost anymore and is reunited with his sorceress."

Striker's ears perked up. "Thank you, Grimm. I'm happy to be home again, and to enjoy food and sunshine." He paused and rubbed his head against Rualla's leg affectionately. "And to be with my family again."

The bride and groom were swept away by well-wishers and to share cake and wine.

Abbess Eshra and Darcus, carrying Raven in his arms, were among the guests.

Raven smiled brightly, "Hello."

"Hello, Raven," Opaline smiled. "Goodness, you look very pretty today in that yellow dress."

Runa embraced Eshra, tears in her eyes, remembering how she saved her when she was injured. "I am so glad you came. I hear Emperor Rhudon has appointed you to his council."

"I have seen too much to return to the veil," Eshra nodded sadly. "Perhaps someday, but now I can do some good helping to rebuild the churches and abbeys. To aid the displaced people who have suffered so much."

Runa kissed her on the cheek and looked into her sad eyes. "Peace will come, dear Eshra."

Eshra squeezed her hand, but with a genuine smile took Raven into her arms. "Let's go get cake."

Eshra and Raven disappeared into the crowd. Darcus put his arm around Runa, and she rested her against his shoulder. "I hope she finds her light again. She is the most generous soul."

"Her faith is still intact, but her own code of conduct torments her," Darcus said. "My sister is strong. She adores Raven. I'm glad we're going back to Moonthorne so she can grow up with her own people."

"We can visit all the time since we'll be living there too," Mellypip exclaimed.

"It will be good to have friends," Darcus grinned, "and a chubby wampu for her to play with. Emperor Rhudon promised me he would look after my sister. I think the old widower loves her. Either way, we will all make sure she comes through this. War is not something you recover from soon. It changes you forever." He hugged both Runa and Opaline. "I better fetch some treats for Redstorm, or I'll never hear the end of it."

"I hope Eshra heals," Opaline told him. "I cannot imagine her not being an abbess."

After Darcus left, Opaline turned around and collided with Gabriel. The gruff-looking sorcerer towered over her. He shyly greeted Opaline and Grimm, looking unusually clean-shaven and clear-eyed in a deep blue tunic that looked new.

"You both look well," Opaline smiled timidly and ruffled Namir's head. "I heard you are leaving Thill. Is that true?"

Gabriel shrugged and leaned on his staff. "Well, many kingdoms need help after all the damage Obsydia and Koll did. They may be gone but they left a hellish mess in their wake. I thought it would be a good thing to help folks."

Opaline looked down at her shoes, twisting her handkerchief. "I will miss you."

"I will wait for you," Gabriel whispered to Opaline.

Mellypip, I think we should walk away, Runa told him, politely backing away.

No, no stay! Mellypip begged, tugging at her hair.

Opaline's head shot up, her eyes wide. "What?"

"I will wait for you," Gabriel repeated. "You're just learning your magic. You're a young girl, though you're a princess and heroine, you're too young for the likes of me now. But I will make myself worthy of you if you want me. I do not drink ale anymore. Namir has been nagging me to stop anyway. I know you need time to become the woman you are meant to be. When you are ready, if you want me, I'll be waiting."

Gabriel walked away, Namir following alongside him as he said. "I apologize if my sorcerer is too blunt Opaline, but he is sincere in his affections. Good day."

Opaline was left speechless.

Runa whispered to her. "I think you need to sit down and have some cake while you ponder all that."

Opaline nodded and joined the others at the long banquet table. Runa smiled when Jadon joined them.

"It's a happy day," Jadon said. "Darcus says you are going to come to Moonthorne to stay."

Runa nodded, excited at the prospect of a new adventure. "We won't be separated by long distances or curses anymore. The combination of my Drusai and sorcerous abilities still need training. Granna Yllia is going to teach me herself. I guess even saving the world does not mean I'm finished with my education."

"I'm glad you'll be close…to me," Jadon murmured and kissed her again.

A loud harrumph broke them apart. Cathal and Belwyn suddenly stood between the two young lovers.

"I'm going to bring you some punch," Jadon grinned.

After he had left, Runa's eyes narrowed at her grandfather and his owl. "Which of you two interrupted?"

"We both did," Cathal confessed.

"I have a long history of guarding the virtue of this family," Belwyn said proudly.

"My virtue is fine," Runa remarked dryly, scratching Belwyn's beak.

Cathal sighed and looked at everyone gathered. "I never thought I would feel as happy as I do now. My family has been restored, my daughter found love again, the Eternals gave Striker back, which is the happiest of mysteries."

"The gods usually have the last word in all of this. The trouble is which gods have the power over you…light or dark," Belwyn pondered.

"I'm not in the mood to be philosophical," Cathal replied.

"The light jewel came from the Light Eternals," Runa said thoughtfully. "I believe the gem held the grace of creation within it. Remember the flowers which bloomed where it landed. It may even have been accidental or planned, but who knows."

"Sometimes a mystery is good," Mellypip said. "Let's not poke at the gods or their gifts."

"I will drink to that," Belwyn said.

"Indeed," Cathal hugged Runa close to him. "Our family is growing, isn't it? Your mother and grandmother restored, you have two sisters now and a brother, though it is through marriage, and a stepfather who loves you."

"And Dabiro," Mellypip sighed with resignation.

"It's a magical family," Runa whispered, "And Rono will be coming to live with us."

"I'm glad," Mellypip nodded. "I can help take care of him. Rono likes to listen to my stories."

"They're wonderful stories," Runa smiled.

The sun was setting in the sky, and they could just glimpse the twin moons rising. Cozy in her arms, Mellypip thought about his adventures since Cathal brought him to his tree tower for Runa. They suffered tragic losses, made great friends, and faced terrible enemies. The dark immortal queen, Obsydia, and her sorcerer, Koll, were defeated. They confronted the wondrous mysteries of the universe, but most importantly, they built a family which was the best magic of all. Mellypip would record these exciting journeys in his book, but this tale was done.

Do you think Ashur is watching us? Mellypip asked, gazing at the sky.

Ashur is looking after us, Runa whispered. *He is family. Like the magic we carry, they are always with us.*

Other Books in the Familiars' Tale Trilogy

Gate of Souls – Book One: A Familiar's Tale

Familiars.

Magical animal companions of sorcerers.

Keepers of spells and secrets.

Most important, devoted friends for life.

When one such familiar, Mellypip, bonds with the young sorceress Runa, he shares in the wonders of magic. Together, Mellypip and Runa train under the tutelage of Runa's grandfather, Cathal, and his cantankerous mountain owl familiar, Belwyn. But secrets and spells do not make for good sorcery. Old friends begin to vanish even as enemies from Cathal's past return, threatening to reveal the truth of Runa's parents; a truth from which Cathal must protect his granddaughter at any cost. When Cathal is kidnapped, Runa and Mellypip rush against time to save their family and friends from dark sorcery that will not only destroy them, but shatter the Gate of Souls and release demonic creatures of The Otherworld into the mortal realms.

Tree of Bones – Book Two: A Familiar's Tale

Two Curses

A curse of Darkness... Deep within the Thill forest, stands a tree made of human bones, crowned in black leaves and red thorns.

A curse of Light... Beneath the Wastelands of Skarros, a crystal imprisons a dark, immortal queen.

The Sorceress, Runa, is tormented by horrific images of this tree of bones in a distant, lifeless forest. Even as the visions debilitate her, Mellypip, her beloved familiar, also experiences these sinister dreams, bound by the same dream seer magic as his mistress. The tree of bones summons Runa, and she must risk madness and death as obsession drives her on. What she finds reveals a devastating truth.

Koll the Sorcerer awaits trial for his crimes. His familiar, Xabral, searches for allies to free him. Driven by his own dreams of dark prophecy, Koll seeks to free Obsydia, the Bloodstone Queen, from her prison. Determined to let nothing stop him, Koll will commit any evil to achieve his goal.

Runa and Mellypip's newest journey reveals truths behind ancient secrets, as Koll's obsessive hunt for a fallen queen threatens to doom the world forever. Runa and Koll, bound by opposing magical destinies of Light and Dark, will ultimately face frightening revelations and unimagined consequences.

About the Author

Verna McKinnon is the author of *War Poet*, *The Bardess of Rhulon*, *The Bastard Sorceress*, and The Familiar's Tale series, *Gate of Souls, book 1 & Tree of Bones, book 2. Fires of Rapiveshta, book 2.* Avid lover of fantasy and science fiction, Verna believes in the power of heroines. With a list of planned fantasy novels to create, she writes obsessively and drinks lots of coffee. Check out her published short stories and news updates at her website, *vernamckinnon.com* & follow her on Instagram and Facebook.

More Books from
WolfSinger Publications

The Dark See – M.R. Williamson

As Helen Durkin's journey to find out about herself continues, she finally realizes she needs the help of someone with more knowledge than dwarves, elves, or even dragons. But, just how do you approach the old Wizard Andsell Phagan?

As she tries to solve that problem, yet another dangerous situation presents itself. This mysterious person is no friend of the Phagan family. And, Helen quickly finds herself on a collision course with a halfling who most refer to as Scar—one who dabbles in the dark side of magic.

With this added pressure, the effort to approach and perhaps train under Andsell Phagan intensifies. As time progresses, an old friend comes to her aid and presents the young girl's plight to Andsell. Now, the race is on and the old Dragon Pragamore takes the lead in Helen's plight.

Will Helen finally find out why the Faes are calling her Bright Helen?

What of Pragamore? Will his years keep him from helping?

And who is Scar really after—Helen, the old wizard, or Pragamore?

The Steel Fist – Rob Jackson

The survivors of Recon 9 are needed in the Ozarks where some home-grown autocrats have taken over parts of Arkansas and Missouri. They've looted National Guard armories and hoarded weapons, ammunition, and vital supplies, just waiting for the opportunity to take over the area. While most of their transport, armor, and aircraft are obsolete, they face people with no protection against such deadly equipment. And they're trying to get the local natural resources to gain control of weapons even the military have no defense against.

Recon 9 has gained four new members and formed an alliance with locals, many of them veterans, against a common enemy. The locals have some grasp of tactics, an excellent knowledge of the hilly, forested countryside and a burning desire to be rid of the terrorists, who call themselves: THE STEEL FIST

Crisis in Big-G City – S.D. Matley

Olympus, Inc., is locked in battle with climate change!

Athena's Secret Ops program steps in when bad boy and technological genius Hermes can't come up with a carbon-curbing solution. Undercover agents Cleo Petra and Pan are deployed in the mortal world to vanquish the notorious East brothers, chthonic fossil fuel magnates who pass as human and eat humans, too…

Two-month-old Pablo, the one-quarter chthonic infant son of two fathers formerly known as P.B., employs his extraordinary abilities of adult speech and intellect in pursuit of climate justice!

Meanwhile, David Bernstein, whose hot romance with Cleo Petra meets a rocky end, recovers the memory of his century-old love affair with a beautiful Spanish nurse. He time travels to 1918 to find her and encounters love, loss, and the City of Mount Olympus —a dark and sinister place where every inhabitant lives in fear of volatile and destructive Zeus!

David's birth father and Hera's former fling, Saul Crispin, is outed as a mortal made immortal. Will Hera's high crime of granting Saul eternal life land her before a jury of her peers for judgment?

And what of baby-crazy Queen of the Underworld, Persephone, pregnant at last but not by Hades?

Intrigue, espionage, crimes of passion, secret babies and looming existential threats—everywhere you look there's a Crisis in Big-G City!

The Seven Exalted Orders – Deby Fredericks

Arkanost has Seven Exalted Orders. No more, no less. When a magus goes renegade in a far-off province, the Mage Lords demand something be done.

Ryamon is bitter and frustrated. He longs to be a Fire magus; as a Stone magus, he's miserable. If he can bring the rogue back, he has a chance—his last chance—to fulfill his dream.

It's a great plan—until he actually meets Valdira.

Tails from the Front Lines 2: The Thin Blue Line

– edited by Carol Hightshoe

Come meet some of the four-legged members of Law Enforcement who also serve and protect.

Here our authors will introduce you to the brave K9 officers who serve alongside their human partners. They are their eyes, ears, noses and sometimes, when necessary, they are their shield, protecting others.

Proceeds from this anthology will be donated to the El Paso County (Colorado) Sheriff's Office K9 program in memory of K9 Jinx who was killed in the line of duty on April 11, 2022.

Ring of Fire – edited by Dana Bell

Enter the Ring of Fire, as unpredictable as the land masses shaking a city and volcanoes erupting covering the landscape. Could there be other reasons for these events? Or could these rings be more than a geological location.

They may be dragons playing tricks
or magic portals opened to mysterious realms
or sacrificing the best work of a lifetime.
Perhaps a rescue during a forest fire
or an attempt to raise the dead
or even while attending a high school reunion.

Journeys are taken to far off lands, another world, and through caves, each with their own unique twist.

Each tale presents a new idea on what the Ring of Fire could be. It is more than what many have been led to believe. Pull up a chair and warm yourself by our fires—just don't let yourself get burned.

Coyote – Charles Combee

While camping in a remote canyon in Utah Jim accidently sees an ancient rite taking place with a coyote like creature presiding over it. Now this creature wants Jim dead.

Audrey and her family go hiking in Utah and are attacked by this creature. Audrey is the only survivor, but she is pulled into a strange world of darkness and glass. She is 'rescued' by Jim, but is still linked to the creature, whose hold on her will end in her death unless Jim can find a way to break that link.

In his dreams, or are they ancient memories, Jim begins to learn more about Coyote as well as the magics that previously bound him. But those dreams end without teaching him the full magics. Can he find a way to free Audrey and stop Coyote from once again terrorizing humankind?

Believing is Seeing – Joanna Michal Hoyt

What we believe shapes what we see. Sometimes the stories we tell free us. Sometimes they trap us.

Some people see things their neighbors can't or won't see. Are they inspired? Delusional? Who decides?

As the faithful people of her village cry out for their god's help in disaster, a young peasant woman faces the terrifying possibility that she may be that god.

A time-traveling Jewish refugee visits 21st-century churches and confronts almost unrecognizable versions of himself.

Three troubled people make the dangerous visit to The Library where the maddening stories lodged inside them can be removed—on certain demanding conditions.

Having been warned away from the vacant lot which is said to house a portal to Hell, the new girl in town naturally goes to investigate.

Early in the grid collapse—or apocalypse?—a Christian lesbian farm couple paint "WELCOME" on their barn and await visitors.

An old man in the Terran diaspora enlists in a crusade to save humanity and belatedly wonders if he's on the wrong side.

Step inside these stories and see what you believe—but don't believe everything you see.

Out of the Darkness – edited by Carol Hightshoe

Mental Health issues have long been stigmatized, with those facing them pushed into the shadows, often unable to deal with the darkness they find themselves trapped in.

In this collection, stories explore many types of darkness— Suicidal Ideation, Death from Suicide, Survivor's Guilt, PTSD, Chronic Pain, Chronic Illness, Depression, Death of a Loved One, Secrets, Bullying, and other forms of darkness are explored. Some related to mental health issues and some not, but all of them offer very human perspectives. As in real life, some stories have happy endings and sadly others don't.

We offer these stories without judgement, but with hope and compassion. Some roads should never have to be traveled —but we understand that for many they are being traveled alone.

Proceeds from sales of Out of the Darkness will be donated to the American Foundation for Suicide Prevention—for more information on AFSP please visit their website at: afsp.org.

Never Cheat a Witch – edited by Carol Hightshoe

Magical curses. Arcane revenge. Being transformed into a frog. Things evil witches do to mere mortals who cross their path. But, what if there is more to the story...

Deals made with a witch are magically binding and can bring dire consequences to those who even think about breaking them.

Whether they are seeking revenge for wrongs done to them, helping others or simply trying to live their lives—it is NEVER wise to try and cheat a witch.

Open your spell book and join our authors as they relate tales of witches and mortals. From classic fantasy witches to modern day witches and even the legendary Baba Yaga. Good and Evil as well as every shade of gray in between.

And, yes—there is a prince who is turned into a frog.

And more – check out our books at

www.wolfsingerpubs.com